In a move more ins
and bring her int
the viewfinder as s
beautiful girl in I

passionately than my supposed life partner has in over three years; she smiles, this beautiful outsider who has promptly incorporated herself into all my near-future wet-dreams; she smiles, as if happily posing for the picture I'm about to take.

She smiles.

My sweaty finger presses the button.

Click.

MISSED CONNECTION

AN EROTIC THRILLER

MICHAEL LAIMO

ISBN 978-1-63789-012-7
Macabre Ink is an imprint of Crossroad Press Publishing

For information address Crossroad Press at 141 Brayden Dr., Hertford, NC 27944
www.crossroadpress.com

First Edition - 2024

What good is faithful if faithful doesn't do any good?

—Peter Delmonico

PROLOGUE

The pain.

It's extraordinary: head pounding from skull to jaw, wrists and ankles burning beneath layers of duct tape, bare nipples chafed under loops of once-white-now-pink fishing rope. The threadbare necktie knotted around my head holds the dress sock in my mouth, making it nearly impossible to breathe.

Somewhere, just beyond the closed door, the people I love the most are silent. *Where…are…they…?*

No answer from the devil or the angel.

The room is a suburban battlefield. Computer in pieces. Clothing strewn. Standing lamp a fallen comrade in the center of it all. Early-morning wall-shadows threaten to suffocate me, boding a traumatic end to my life.

The door bursts open. The man who put me here limps in, slams it, *crack!*, a towering heaving behemoth in need of an answer. Gripped in his tattooed fist, an eight-inch kitchen knife, steel blade slick and red.

He demands, "Where is it?"

I squirm, buck, grunt, a man with no answer.

He yanks the necktie down, pulls the sock from my mouth, grabs a fistful of my hair and presses the knife against my throat. The bloody hilt creeps into focus, the hand gripping it, the cursive snake tattoo slithering across his knuckles, revering *Lola*. "Last chance. Where's the fucking money?"

My words are beaten down, every syllable a life of agony: "Where…is…my… daughter…?"

He backhands me across the face and I drown in a wash of pain *(…you're six-seven-eight years old hiding in the closet dusty shoes mothballs the BELT comes down your mother screams she flees she can't stop it she can't help you…)*.

He clenches and grinds. "If you don't tell me now, *I will kill her…*"

My tearful silence is torture to us both.

He circles and growls, a caged beast, then exits the room, slamming the door in his wake, *crack!* Moments or hours later he returns with my crying daughter in one arm, angel face hidden beneath hills of tattooed muscle, golden curls wet with sweat and tears.

He presses the bloody knife to her neck. *"WHERE'S THE FUCKING MONEY!"*

No-no-no-no-no-no-no! My body seizes, my muscles scream, a chain reaction consuming me: adrenaline flowing, nerves igniting, speeding heart rate, labored breathing…*synapses bursting, amygdala shutting down.*

I face my attacker.

I must act now.

If I don't, my daughter will die.

And to think, all of this happened because I chose to take some photos in the park.

I lie. "I'll show you where the money is…"

ONE WEEK EARLIER

CHAPTER 1

Point.

Click.

The August sun casts its golden beams across 5th Avenue.

A perfect day for shooting.

I pluck a dust cloth from my attaché and gently clean the new Nikon lens on my camera. It'd cost a bundle but was worth it. Never in the past have my pictures come out so detailed. So crisp and clear. So lifelike.

As far back as I remember, I've always loved photography. At age nine *(...you struggle to forget ages six-seven-eight, you REPRESS...)*, I graduated from a Polaroid Instamatic to a Canon digital and have ever since developed a love for purchasing supplies I don't really need. You should see my little darkroom, jam-packed with enough equipment to fill the shelves at B&H Photo. Buying all these things serves as a diversion from all the wrong in my life. Some people set their sights on Dunkin' Donuts. I turn to telephoto lenses and developing tanks.

Jolie, my wife, focuses on working out, putting in two hours a day at the Central Park Sports Club. Once upon a time (prior to her three-year affair with the gym), she supported my love of photography. That was a happier time, when I liked her, and she liked me. Then she got pregnant, and anger and depression and irrationality became her most enduring (not endearing) qualities. Once Rachel came into our lives, she pushed me away even further, both mentally and physically, forcing me to spend more time pointing and clicking at strangers, and less time regarding her in the flesh.

Whatever I like, Jolie hates. I'm Soundgarden and steaks, she's Britney and beets. I've often wondered if this is how relationships actually work between married couples: living lives at opposite poles, marching to different beats, harboring anger, resentment, hostility.

I look at my gold wedding band and ponder the choice I made six weeks before my thirtieth birthday: *It was a good day. Forty of our closest friends and relatives. My dad, your mom the cunt, remember how we joked about fixing them up? You were showing a bit but it didn't matter because you looked like a queen with your dirty-blonde hair and Audrey Meadows eyes and spray-on tan. You were the most beautiful woman in the world to me that day. And making love to you in the hotel was the height of our most memorable night together, because ever since then…*

I peer ahead, seeking a distraction from my problems.

There. Between 41st Street and 42nd Street. The columns of the NY Public Library, towering like monolithic sentries. The angle of the sun's rays striking the coarse detail of their grooves makes me wonder how they might develop at this time of day; how the multicultural cast of people on the expansive steps would just *pop* with three-dimensional clarity.

Point.

Click.

If only Jolie could see the beauty (and humor) I see in my photos. If only she could feel the thrill of capturing the perfect shot, then maybe she'd understand my love for the craft. Then maybe she'd be more agreeable to my hours spent away from home. Then maybe we'd get along. *Maybe*. See? I really do want things to work out between us, if only for the sake of our daughter.

Missed Connection

I glance at my cell. Just after 6:00. Late again. Five unread texts from Jolie corroborates this. I snap the lens cover on and pace up 42nd Street toward the N-line subway entrance.

On my left: the open lawn of Bryant Park. Lots of activity. Hundreds of people enjoying a beautiful day. So many sights and colors, so many potential moments to capture on film. I think of Jolie and glimpse the subway entrance. She's at home, brimming to rip me a(nother) new one for being late again. To remind me just how fucking miserable my marriage is.

Only a few more pictures.

I head off into the park.

CHAPTER 2

Like Jolie, Bryant Park is brimming. With picnickers. People of all denominations soaking in the faultless summer climate, more than likely pleased their workdays have come to an end.

Ahead, near the 6th Avenue entrance, a seven-piece jazz band performs upon a fold-away stage. The music is bright and cheerful, speaking the tongues of nearly everyone present. Sometimes after a tour of duty in the darkroom, I can easily evoke the sounds of the events I capture, as though a soundtrack has been recorded in my head to accompany the developed photo. It's a talent inventive photographers possess, and I've got it. The jazz band and the assembly of people facing the stage would make for a wonderful picture, one worth making a detour for. My heartbeat ramps up a few notches, validating my choice with this prospective shot.

I march along the gravel path, passing the reading room and the well-read books shoved into portable shelving units. Behind me, the chatter of happy hour attendees at the outdoor bar and grill—businessmen who've loosened their ties and women who've let down their hair—succumbs to the buoyant sounds of cymbals crashing and horns blaring at the opposite end of the park.

I love people-browsing. It's an integral part of the process as I search for the ideal candid. I've built a shameless habit of taking pictures of strangers *(...neighbor...)* and have a portfolio that satirizes those happy-people portraits that come with the purchase of a new frame. A portion of my work is made up of photos like these—photos poking fun of someone.

I also have a lookbook that takes my inner caricaturist to the next level. This one is filled with more colorful types, body-modified weirdos and the like that have no trouble turning heads, even in Greenwich Village. Aptly titled Freaks & Geeks, it focuses more on my morbid curiosity of those choosing to take paths less-traveled. They don't know I'm taking their photos and I don't show them to anyone other than myself, but the practice makes me laugh and exhibits my talent as a photographer, all in a single click.

This moment in the park is a people-browser's dream. Late-afternoon sun shining. Everyone coming and going, mindful of their after-work purposes: a gentle stroll, a scenic detour, the pleasure of a friend's company.

It's times like this that spark envy in my mind. I'm almost thirty-four, working a six-figure job as the northeast regional V.P. of Johnson Apparel Group, proud and smug to have worked my way up from lowly sales trainee to one of three upper management positions. Of course, it didn't hurt that prior to his retirement my stockbroker father once had the CEO of Johnson as a client, earning him nearly seven figures and me a career in fashion. Insert wink-emoji here.

Despite a great career and the ego massaging that comes with it, it's not as rewarding as taking photos. As taking the perfect photo. Taking photos makes me happy...

(...you look out the window HE is with her you point and click...)

...but happy photographer plus unhappy marriage equals, *You were out every night this week taking pictures. Pictures of what? Skies and birds and storefronts and ugly people? It must really get you off when you click that little button. What the hell do you do in your darkroom anyway? For God's sakes pumpkin-eater, throw that stupid fucking camera away!*

I know this sounds cruel, and dear God I love my daughter *(love?)*, but sometimes I wish I'd never met Jolie. Everywhere I go there are so many pretty girls. Single ones. Married ones. Younger ones. Older ones. Thin and hard-bodied ones, curvy and buxom ones. Many of them looking for a handsome, well-to-do, driven, passionate man—like me—to love and respect.

It's a battle that wages in my head every day.

(...sex helps you REPRESS without it you feel six-seven-eight...)

Time and time again I remind myself how blessed I am to have such a darling little angel in Rachel. But I wonder: what would've become of my life had I not gotten Jolie pregnant? Would I be pursuing my dream as a professional photographer, exhibiting in village galleries with no binding ties and unreasonable demands draining me of my time, energy, and money, a beautiful woman by my side who loves and cherishes and respects me? *Would I?*

I peer at my phone again, an unwanted habit forced upon me by way of Jolie's shitty-ass attitude. Her *shassitude*. This morning she texted that our nanny Carmen called in sick again, third day in a row, and *when are* you *going to take a day to watch your daughter, pumpkin-eater*? Two hundred bucks a day for childcare, and what do I get? Fuel for the inferno that has torched my marriage, that's what. With client meetings and luncheons packing my calendar, it was Jolie who *volunteered* to play the sick card from her sales position at Saks Fifth Avenue to take care of Rachel. The events that followed are still fresh in my mind: Jolie complaining about how her day was "completely fucked," me eating a bowl of oatmeal and wondering how the world could keep on spinning without Jolie there to straighten up the racks in the Saks Fifth Avenue dress department. I finished my breakfast and walked out the door, cold-shouldering her final words about needing to leave for a 6:30 abs class, and *"you better be home before then pumpkin-eater, so help me God!"* As mentioned, just as photography is my means for escapism, exercise is Jolie's means for blowing off steam. And she has a lot of it.

In a way I feel sorry for her. She's only twenty-six. Twenty-two when the pregnancy test disclosed *two lines*. And when the girl you're fucking is a millennial with a right-to-life patch on her backpack, and when the girl you're fucking turns up the volume during infomercials of starving Ethiopian children, you suck it up and plan to grow old together. We hadn't even gone to the movies yet and there we were, planning for parenthood.

The road was bumpy from the get-go, but I navigated every turn, filled every pothole, armed and ready with an easy-going attitude, loving (albeit judgmental and cynical), more than willing to make it all work because I only want to love (and be loved by) someone. But that was then, and this is now. Today I'm a frustrated jellyfish, drained of vigor and sapped of virtue. Who wouldn't be with a shitstorm of post-partum depression and busted-condom resentment raining down on their parade?

I look at my phone. The minutes…they're crawling by like bomb-ticks as my mind sweats out with crystal-ball clarity what must be happening at home: Jolie sitting in the kitchen, eyebrows furrowed into a headache, fingers intolerantly tap-tap-tapping the table as a bathed and fed Rachel fidgets on her lap.

I'm not asking for much. I just want to take pictures. All by myself. With no one to bother or distract me or curse me out.

(…or stir up six-seven-eight…)

Some Renaissance artist—not sure which one—once said that solitude is the foundation for ingenuity. That's smacking the nail right on the head. An artist and his solitary thoughts make for the greatest achievements in creativity, not one hampered by an angry, depressed wife and a three-and-a-half-year-old that still doesn't have the whole potty-training routine down yet.

Damn you Peter, don't you ever do anything right?

Daddy, I just did number-one in my panties.

I walk out onto the lawn and position myself in front of the band. The spraying fountain behind the stage glimmers in the sunbeams and provides an array of natural light like that of a rig in a concert hall. It's a magical scene, a perfect moment in time. And I'm about to capture it forever. This picture is going to make my day.

I remove the lens cap, raise the camera, and peer through the viewfinder.

The image comes into view, flawless.

My finger finds the button and…

Someone bumps into me.

Click.

No need to continue peering through the lens to know I've missed the shot. As if punished by God for my selfish thoughts, I watch the dazzling display of watery light behind the band disappear as the sun dips behind a gray cloud.

The moment is lost forever.

CHAPTER 3

"Are you okay? I'm so sorry."

A woman's voice.

A hand grabs my bicep as I regain my balance. The camera joggles in my grip. For a second I think it's going to drop to the trampled grass, but thankfully I manage to secure hold of it. Anger blooms in me and I have to bite my tongue. Confession: I've got a bit of a temper, inherited from my Sicilian father Nick Delmonico, whose old-world rage might've sent my mother to an early grave. But that's a story for another chapter.

As I check the camera for damage, the voice says, "I really am sorry..." The hand on my arm squeezes gently.

I look up and lock eyes with a woman who blows me away. Okay, a lot of women blow me away. But this one is touching my arm. And the pouty look on her face—eyebrows arched over crystal blues ringed with black, clear-glossed lips gently downcast—tells me she feels bad about having messed up what I considered to be an idyllic moment to capture on film.

She says apologetically, telepathically, "I messed up your shot, didn't I?" Her voice is Downy soft, delivered on a breath of fresh air, gentle south-of-New-York accent adding an extra layer of femininity to it.

Her hand is still on my arm.

"No...well...it's okay." My words struggle to surface because, simply put and rightly so, I'm captured by this woman. Late twenties, faded denims, pink baby-tee, four inches of tan-cut abs exposed for the world to admire, silver navel ring a cherry on top. She's *yum* on a stick.

(...a distraction from six-seven-eight...)

"You sure?" she asks coyly.

"Yeah, no, it's okay." Still the only words I can find, idiot out-of-practice me. Her eyes, they're so blue and they're looking into mine...not just *into* my eyes, they're a double-shot of cliché bulleting into my *soul*. I can *feel* it: that unmistakable shudder of pleasure that runs up and down your body before settling in the heart like an electrostatic charge.

She's *still* holding my arm and I start counting in my head, *one one-hundred, two one-hundred, three one-hundred,* a spectrummy self-stimulatory rumination I perform to keep focus.

(...it keeps you calm, one one-hundred it's dark and dusty and stinks of mothballs, two one-hundred the door opens harsh light his silhouette, three one-hundred the BELT, the business end, you count and count until it stops...)

"Well...okay then." She smiles, exposing twin rows of pearly whites behind a pair of moist, lustrous lips. A gentle breeze tosses a drift of sandy brown hair across her blue eyes, bringing to light the makeup on her face, nothing out of the ordinary for New York, but enough of it to make me wonder if she's hiding a bad complexion.

"It's all right," I say, fidgeting with my new lens. "Camera's fine."

Her stare lingers, *one one-hundred, two one-hundred,* and then her hand finally releases.

In my world, the unexpected happens and I never expect it. With a slight narrowing of the eyes that might allege an attraction for me, she leans forward and kisses me on the lips. My shudder oozes pure delight as the kiss lingers *one one-*

hundred, two one-hundred, three one-hundred until she pulls back, wiggles her fingers at me, and paces away, revealing a *tramp-stamp* tattoo highlighting a cursive *LD* amid a bouquet of symmetrically positioned roses.

Devil on my left shoulder, pitchfork raised high.

Angel on my right shoulder, halo fading.

I should discuss them, my good and evil counterparts. They're bound to me every step of the way, have been since *(...six-seven-eight...)* I was nine years old, light and dark companions riding shotgun, offering opposing viewpoints given any scenario, any situation. Cliché but omnipresent companions, reliable even if their advice occasionally sucks.

In a move more instinctual than purposeful, I raise the camera and bring her into focus. I shout, "Hey!" and watch through the viewfinder as she twists around and smiles at me, this beautiful girl in Bryant Park who just kissed me more passionately than my supposed life partner has in over three years; she smiles, this beautiful outsider who has promptly incorporated herself into all my near-future wet-dreams; she smiles, as if happily posing for the picture I'm about to take.

She smiles.

My sweaty finger presses the button.

Click.

CHAPTER 4

The ensuing seconds flicker by like frames of stop-action film. *What just happened?* To the casual observer—if anyone had been paying attention—what just occurred between me and Ms. Pink Baby-Tee stands to look like any other casual event taking place in Bryant Park. But to me? It's much more than that. It's fate taking a front seat in my life, making sure I'm *distracted.*

(…from six-seven-eight…)

The devil on my left shoulder, shouting: *Go! It's what you need!*

I shake off my what-just-happened-to-me reverie and follow my hard-on in the direction *LD* just walked away. I shoulder across the lawn through the crowd of jazz-band enthusiasts. No sight of her. Over the gravel walkway. Nothing. *Where did she go?* I skim the entire scene in a semi-circle, striving to glimpse a fragment of her tight pink top.

The angel on my right shoulder: *Let her go. Go home and be with your wife and daughter.*

It's not every day a young Barbara Eden materializes in a veil of pink and kisses you in the park. This could be a once-in-a-lifetime opportunity. I can't just trudge away with my head hung low, back to my groundhog's-day-in-hell life. I need to talk to her. I want to know why she kissed me. I want to kiss her *again.*

(...she's steering you away from six-seven-eight...)

I step up the pace, moving back and forth across the graveled path, weaving between and bumping into aimless nose-in-phone meanderers. I turn to look at each one, hopelessly optimistic, but all I get are dirty looks.

Near the kiddie carousel I catch a flash of pink. I dart in that direction but realize, despondently, that it's just a child atop a fiberglass horse wearing a pink shirt. I turn, look back over the lawn toward the 41st Street exit. A continuous stream of bodies moves in and out of the park, but none are wearing pink.

Fuck! She's gone, lost in the crowd, this strange woman who kissed me at random, who gave me a minute taste of *everything* I've been missing out on the last four years of my life.

My hopelessly loveless life.

CHAPTER 5

Before I have a chance to collect my thoughts, or even think about looking at my phone to see how late I am, my cell phone vibrates. I pray it isn't Jolie. I pray it's a solicitor promising me a surefire way to consolidate my debt, or an affordable timeshare in St Lucia. Promising me anything or anyone other than *her*.

I put my camera back in its case, harness it over my shoulder, then dig out my phone and check the display.

Jolie's cell. Joy to the fucking world.

I take a deep breath, counting *one one-hundred* in my head because the tempest is real, then press the green phone icon and there's no chance to say "Hey," or "I'm on my way," because when I put the phone to my ear, I'm greeted with my daughter Rachel's unbridled, tear-bursting, snot-blubbering cries.

At least it's not Jolie.

I possess the innate talent of setting calm into my daughter. Could be that I just understand her needs, could be that she's just plain scared of her father *(...you get that...)*. "Baby...baby, what's wrong? Why are you crying?"

More crying, tapering, tapering, tapering, *see I told you so*...into a bewildering wail like something heard on Friday the 13th Part VIII. I stand corrected.

"Honey, Daddy can't hear you if you cry really loud like that in my ear." Sometimes I think Jolie has a sixth sense that informs her when I'm up to no good. I wonder if she's sitting idly by right now, a Dr. Evil pinkie lodged in the corner of her mouth as she employs her toddler to inject anguish into my magic moment. "You need to stop crying so Daddy can hear what's wrong, okay?"

Her stream of cries stagger into intermittent, hiccupping sobs. Amid the gloom and doom, a sad child's voice emerges like a bright star on a cloudy night. "Wh-when are you…*hiccup*…coming home, da-da?"

My ears are listening, but my eyes are searching. I feel like a snake because it's no easy feat going from a beauty's kiss in the park to a counseling session with my almost-four-year-old daughter.

"Soon, baby-doll. Real soon, okay?" I'm craning, glimpsing, standing on my tippy-toes. Still no pink.

"I want you to come home."

"I'll be there soon. Where's Mommy?"

"In her room."

"And where are you?"

"In her room."

"Can I talk to her?"

I hear my baby-doll (not to be confused with baby-tee) fumbling with the phone. Her slightly muffled voice says, "Da-da wants to talk."

Jolie's voice, also slightly muffled: "Tell da-da to get his ass home."

More phone fumbling. "Mommy says get your ass home."

Nice. I say, "Okay," but am suddenly distracted by a glimpse of a pink shirt across the street, about a hundred feet away. Like a dog to its owner, I start jogging toward it, saying in a choppy voice, "Rachel, baby, tell Mommy that Daddy's on his way home, okay?" I disconnect the line, then move down the adjacent walkway leading to 41st Street…and *there it is*! The very symbol of all my present aspirations: a pink tee-shirt—hardly the back of one shoulder, but as pink as the sky is blue—disappearing into a storefront.

I slow to a brisk walk as I exit the park, thinking about what to say to her, if it is her. There's my camera and her captured image inside, and then her LD tattoo, which given the situation can be used to melt the broken ice. *So, what does LD stand for?*

I scurry between a pair of gridlocked taxis, step onto the curb and move through the door the glimpse of pink went into. I'd been far too distracted to notice what kind of place this is, and promptly grind to a halt before a makeshift wooden partition with a stop sign and faded capital letters that demand my exit if I'm under the age of twenty-one.

Uh-huh. On the other side of the wall are adult videos and toys.

I'm no stranger to sex, have had my fair share of it prior to getting married,

(…it distracts from you, six-seven-eight…)

a significant portion credited to my undergrad years at Fordham. And while college was a playground for experimentation, I emerged a man who loves and admires and appreciates sex in a mature, gentle, respectable manner. Ergo, count me out for anything that might cause pain *(…BELT…)* or get me dirty *(…dust…)* or smelly *(…mothballs…)*; my kink pretty much stops at the widespread male fantasy of having a threesome; what man doesn't want to be sandwiched between two beauties? Right? But I digress. I've never really understood the allure of the kinky stuff, which, as I step past the wooden panel into the store, is what most of the clientele here are looking for.

Tall rows of shelves like those in a library present my choice of path to take, each offering a plethora of colorful DVDs, none of them labeled with anything I'd have with my morning coffee.

There's an old/young section, a hairy section, and an amputee section. As I move deeper into the store, more lively brands emerge: water-sports, granny, midget, and a few other deviant fetishes I have no familiarity with. Apparently, the farther in you go, the more extreme the videos get. Please don't ask me what they keep against the back wall.

Denying my curiosity to know what a furry film is, I tear myself away from the DVDs and head to the register. Here there's a glass tabletop display running fifteen feet long which under normal circumstances, like in department store, might be filled with women's jewelry or men's cologne. But here? You've got vibrators and dildos and fleshlights, plus a whole other host of "toys" that come in more shapes, sizes, and colors than Bryant Park does people. The variety is staggering.

"Help you, honey?"

The rugged, cigarette-abused voice belongs to the awful-looking elderly woman behind the register. She's a horror show, overly tanned, overly wrinkled, sleeved in tattoos with one on her neck that identifies her in flowing script as *Marge*. "Marge" loops a matted gray curl behind one ear and smiles, her beady black eyes sizing me up and down over a graveyard of yellow stumps for teeth.

The angel on my right screams: *Get out of here! Marge the Garage is going to get you!* but my lips speak for the devil and its simmering libido. "I'm looking for a…friend. She just came in here, wearing a pink tee-shirt."

The woman—Marge the Garage—uses her fat jaundiced fingers to snuff out her cigarette in the ashtray on the counter, ignoring at least one law, then shrugs her rounded shoulders and says, "Maybe in the back?"

"In the back?"

She motions with a yellow toe-thumb toward a curtain of beads hanging in the doorway at the rear of the store. A red neon sign above it indicates, among other things, what's going on back there:

PEEPSHOW

Marge clears her throat, then deposits the spoils in a wastepaper basket behind the counter. At least I hope there's one back there. "Need any singles?"

"I'm sorry?"

"Singles. For the slot in the booth." She winks and flaunts her cemetery smile.

"Of course." I reach into my wallet and pull out a twenty, thinking that LD, who may or may not be the glimpse of pink I just saw, may also not be a customer, but an employee. I'm suddenly disillusioned, but the pieces fall into place, offering a realistic explanation to what just happened to me. LD, cutting through the park on her way to work, bumping into me while texting, using her up-close-and-personal career skills to earn my attention and extract my forgiveness—the very same skills she uses here to extract dollar bills from the slot in the booth.

Marge sticks another cigarette between her lips and hands me a pre-made stack of singles, well-worn and well-handled. I accept the bills from her before considering where they've been. Gag.

Feeling unsure and nervous, I slink away, clutching the singles tightly and fighting my insecurity by pretending I'm Tony Montana with a fistful of c-notes. I peer over my shoulder to see if anyone is watching me, considering where I am. That I am a married man, this apprehensive move matters, but it doesn't stop me.

One one-hundred, two one-hundred, three one-hundred, heart galloping, blood racing, I spread the swaying curtain of beads and pass beneath the glowing *PEEPSHOW* sign.

CHAPTER 6

The beads rain and clatter behind me.

I'm in a dark, dingy vestibule, maybe ten by ten feet, nondescript with moldy gray paint peeling away from the wall. Ahead to the left is a hallway that runs into the darkness beyond. From its mysterious, shadowy depths come the diverse chants of women pretending to be horny. I swallow past the lump in my throat and wonder what in the hell I'm doing here.

Angel on my right: *You're looking for trouble…*

I've never been to a place like this before. New York's got its share of strip clubs and I've visited a few of them *(…they help repress six-seven-eight…)*. But a peepshow? Is it simply what I imagine it to be? Or is there something more to it? Something I've been missing out on my entire life?

No better time to find out.

I step into the deep, shadowy, mysterious hallway and am startled by a male voice. A deep, croaky one.

"Hey brah."

I turn and behold a mountain of a man, a bouncer from the oversized looks of him, so black—and wearing all black clothing—that he's hard to make out in the musty gloom. If not for the whites of his eyes, he'd possess the power of invisibility over anyone deciding to misbehave back here. Maybe that's why they hired him.

"What's in the bag?" he asks.

At first I'm confused because I've got no bag with me. Then I realize he's referring to my attaché, forgetfully looped over my shoulder. *It's not a* bag, *it's a Tenba Transport Attaché for cameras. Pfft!*

"A camera. Some prints."

"Can't take no pictures." His eyes roll toward the case and they bulge out of his skull proptosis-style and I freak out because that's not supposed to happen, ever. But it *just did*. And I have no words, other than his mugshot would reign supreme in my Freaks & Geeks portfolio.

"No...of course not. Don't plan to."

"Open it up." His breath reaches my nose and it's rancid, like death only worse because it's *warm*. Which is what he'll make of me, warm death, if I don't comply. So, I open the case. He looks, says "Aight," then goes back to waiting for more perverts to harass.

I say, "There was a girl I saw come back here. She was wearing a pink tee-shirt?"

He nods, slowly, guardedly, seemingly poised to kick my ass should I make a wrong move, but doesn't say anything.

"I want to see her. Do you know where I might find her?"

"Pick a room."

I grin uncomfortably, snap the case shut, then move down the dark hallway, passing five closed doors before locating one that's available. Room six. Sounds good to me.

I step inside.

CHAPTER 7

What in the hell am I doing?

It's an abrupt question I have no answer for other than *"I've reached a new low."* I notice a sliding bolt on the door and wonder who in God's name would want to lock themselves inside this dark, sticky prison. Ugh. I hope in the end, after this mission impossible of mine is completed, that LD appreciates all I'm doing to track her down.

There's an exposed lightbulb jutting from the ceiling casting twenty-five watts at best, gloomier in here than in the hallway, but not by much. To my left sits a patent leather loveseat that's seen better days. The surface is torn in no less than a dozen places and the exposed stuffing, what's left of it, is yellow and moldy. I can't help but stare at the thing and be blown away by the fact that grown men decidedly plant their bare asses on it to take care of business. The room stinks of sweat and Clorox, and if I had to guess, cum. There's a scratched plastic window in the wall with a painted-black panel of wood behind it. On the right is a slot for accepting dollar bills, like those found on a soda machine. I step forward and peel a GW from the stack. As I ready it for deposit, my heart shifts into high gear and my brain starts asking questions: What will I find on the other side of the window? Will it be my lady-in-pink, once again in the flesh? Do I really want to pursue a woman who works in a joint like this?

When I think about those blue eyes and how they looked at me, those soft lips and how mouthwatering they were, her gentle touch and how it electrified the skin on my arm, the sad answer to my last question is an indisputable, resounding *"Yes."*

Hand trembling, I slip the dollar into the slot. It churns out an unhealthy grinding noise and spits it back out. Fabulous. I try another bill. This time it works. A rough motorized sound starts up and the black plank of wood, the barricade between me and the secrets in the room behind the scratched plastic, slides up.

The room is well lit, reaching about eight feet back and extending on both sides beyond my line of sight. There's a pair of timeworn sofas in the room, both in similar condition to the loveseat behind me. Sitting on them are three bored-looking women, none of them the girl of my dreams. Not even close.

A middle-aged European-looking woman eating Lo Mein from a white carton swallows what's in her mouth and rises from the sofa. She appears annoyed that I've interrupted her dinner, and nearly stumbles in her four-step journey to my window.

"Hi honey," she purrs in an accent that might be Ukrainian. The string bikini she's got on is so small you could floss with it, her ridiculous-sized boobs supported, but hardly covered by, a matching teensy-weensy top. She reaches behind her neck, unties the knot, and tosses it aside.

I smile uncomfortably, and give her a feeble little wave.

She grabs her monster boobs and rubs them together in a tiresome manner, mashing them up against the clear partition and cooing through greasy lips, "You like these baaaabby? I'm Sugah, what's your name?"

Not "Sugar," but "Sugah." I tell her my name is John and ask her if I can ask a question and she says *Shooya honey* and all of a sudden it's too hot in the room and I take a deep breath of urine-Clorox-cum-infused air and say, "I saw a girl come back here. She was wearing a pink tee-shirt. Is she working now?"

The wood slides down (much faster than it went up) before Sugah can reply. I stick another dollar in the slot and the window grinds back up. Sugah is still present.

She says, "Tair are more girls at de udder end, honey." She motions to her right, then traipses back to her Lo Mein.

I escape the confines of room six and almost bump into a guy returning from the dark end of the hallway. He's middle-aged, bald, wearing glasses that magnify his eyes into fishlike peepers. He says nothing as he scoots past me, making a noble effort to cover the stain on the front of his pants. What a place.

I go to the end of the hall. The door here has a number "10"on it. Ten rooms for ten perverts. Do they have ten Sugahs here to service them all? I open the door…and it occurs to me all too late that the door to the last room I was in—Room 6—had been ajar. And this one, Room 10, had been tightly shut. And now, as a result of my inattention to detail, I'm facing a man with his dick in his hand.

CHAPTER 8

See? I'm not the only one. He didn't want to lock himself inside the cum-coffin either.

What happens next goes down in slow motion, or so it seems. The guy yells, "What the fuck!" and my mind informs me that if *he* doesn't feed me my asshole, the bouncer will. I backpedal into the hallway, leaving the door to Room 10 open. It stays that way too: with his right hand still occupied, he's struggling—quite hysterically, I might add—to grab hold of the doorknob with his left.

In this fleeting moment I peek through the dirty plastic window behind him, into the hot-and-mangy den of girls, and see a flash of pink.

The barricade slams down, covering the window. Damn it! I didn't see her face! Which doesn't matter because I'm facing the more pressing issue of pants-down guy wanting to kill me. He's a businessman from the looks of him, white dress shirt, unknotted tie, slacks crumpled around his ankles, and women's red lace panties bunched at the knees. Finally, he lets go of his dick and uses both hands in a comical attempt to work his panties up back up. As he tugs on the soft fabric, his erection bobs up and down and it reminds me of those little birdie toys they sell in Spencer's Gifts. You know, with the red hair that dips in and out of a glass of water? I want to laugh, but this is no laughing matter. The look on his face is clear. He wants to fucking kill me.

I hold my hands up, palms out. "Sorry. I didn't know anyone was in here." *Now* I know what the lock on the door is for: it's to keep the morons out. I about-face and pace back up the hallway toward the bouncer. He's off his stool with a look of concern (and not-so-guilty pleasure) on his huge round face. Thankfully he makes no move for me as I skate by. He's got his sights set on the other guy, who much to my advantage has stumbled into the hallway in his struggle to pull his panties back up.

The beads rain as I pass through them back into the brightly lit perv-atorium. Marge the Garage is ringing up a rubber shlong the size of a water pipe for a guy who must weigh 120 pounds soaking wet. I zip back through the shelves of assorted DVDs, making eye-contact with no one. Some guy is perusing the furry films. I still don't know what they are and don't stop to find out. I've had my share of debauchery for one day.

From the back of the store, I hear a shout. It might be Marge. Could be the bouncer. Maybe even be the panty-wearing businessman. Doesn't matter. I'm gone, past the barricade with the warning sign, back out into Manhattan's vibrant sea of life.

Like the girl in pink who managed to elude me, I become elusive myself. I'm at least twenty-five feet away from the storefront when the bouncer emerges looking for me. Mr. Panties must've pointed a defensive finger in my direction because he's coat-tailing the bouncer outside, also looking every-which-way. It's a déjà-vu moment. Gridlocked cabs. Me, skipping between them. Only this time I'm racing *away* from the place I saw my glimpse of pink.

I stop at the corner of 41st and 6th, long enough for me to remove my camera from its case. I quickly focus it on the video store and…*click*, then hurriedly race down 6th Avenue into the subway entrance a block away, thinking only of LD, and her image captured inside my camera.

CHAPTER 9

I exit the subway station at 7:00 p.m., an hour later than I'd promised to be home, and a half-hour after the start of Jolie's abs class. Batten down the hatches, I'm about to get an earful.

I enter my Upper East Side building and stop to get the mail from the glass box in the lobby, mostly shopping circulars for Jolie and a utility bill for me. As the sole breadwinner, I've been duly elected to handle our finances. Jolie's job at Saks brings nothing to the fold, primarily acting as means for her to earn spending money which, on the 15th of each month—Employee Appreciation Day—goes right back into Mr. Saks's pocket. It's a vicious circle, one that doesn't warrant the cost of our nanny, but rather keeps Jolie away from me, and keeps me from having to provide her with a weekly allowance. Something like that.

Garvin Mooney, the old man from 4F, is waiting by the elevator. I choose to take the stairs. He's about 150, smells like cauliflower, and has ear hair like cat's eyebrows. He sees me and holds the door open, but I wave him on.

I take the three flights two steps at a time, huffing and puffing as my footfalls echo off the white cement walls: the most exercise I'm willing to exact upon myself in a single day. Someone hand me a Zone bar. As soon as I enter the hallway, I hear Rachel crying. Great. I pause in front of my apartment door and take a series of deep breaths and sometimes when I get really nervous I involuntarily verbalize my self-stimulatory rumination: "One one-hundred, two one-hundred, three one-hundred."

So you're thinking, "Peter, just get out of the marriage. Pay your dues and lawyer fees and move in with your dad." The problem is *(...your dad...)* I'd have to give up seeing Rachel every day, and that's a sacrifice I'm not willing to make. Sometimes I wonder if in a court of law I could prove Jolie unfit for custody. Maybe. But that would cost me time and money, and to what effect on Rachel? So many children today fall victim to their parents' incompatibility—they grow up wearing heavy black eyeliner, cover themselves in tattoos and dye their hair purple, maybe do internet porn. I can't have my little girl be one of them.

I slip the key into the lock, turn the knob, and wince as I enter my apartment. Silence. Well would you look at that, my little girl isn't crying anymore...

Strike that. From my daughter's bedroom comes an ear-piercing wail fit for a TV-MA horror flick. I must've walked in on one of those "not-breathing" moments toddlers have when they cry, when their faces turn three shades of purple as they gear up for the next shriek. Jolie typically hides in bed when this happens, unwilling or unable to attend to Rachel's immediate needs, a tirade clutched tightly in her fists, primed and readied for my return home. Welcome to my nightly routine.

What I get instead is something completely unforeseen: Jolie appearing from our bedroom in full gym gear, makeup and hair done, bouncing a sobbing Rachel in her arms, calmly coo-cooing her—a job typically reserved for me.

The devil on my left offers a bit of worldly advice: *she suffers from a personality disorder.*

Tell me something I don't know.

"Our baby has a belly ache," she utters in her rarely-spoken *soft-and-gentle baby-speak* voice, and not her usually-spoken *hate-*

venom-scream-shout-crying voice. Jolie's out-of-nowhere good-naturedness is really throwing me for a loop.

But what really *gets me* is what she's wearing.

Black leggings and...*pink* sports bra.

Jolie is a head-turner: shoulder-length blonde hair, big brown Snapchat-filter eyes and trim golden body that'd snapped back into place right after giving birth. She accredits her slender form to countless hours at the gym. I'm convinced it's genetics. More than likely it's a lotto-winning combination of the two. She doesn't look much different than the day we met four years ago, a chance crossing of paths at an Ed Sheeran concert. I was offered a free ticket and went expecting to be tortured by shitty music (I was), but the pretty blonde seated next to me made up for it with good conversation and a make-out session in Washington Square Park that lasted until sun-up.

I'm still physically attracted to her *(...it distracts you from six-seven-eight...)*, and now that she's unexplainably decided to be nice to me, she's become even more beautiful in my eyes. *This* is the Jolie I met at the concert four years ago.

Or maybe it's the pink sports bra.

Rachel's cheeks are a canvas of tears and snot. I take her from Jolie and baby-wipe her face, then hold her against my shoulder and savor in her warm embrace. It's moments like this where everything wrong in my world—my flaws, my desires, my flawed desires—seems not to matter now that I have my little girl seeking comfort in my arms.

"What's the matter baby-doll?"

"I have a boo-boo belly. I want you to stay home with me."

My little girl, laying it on thick. "I'm home now. I'll take care of you."

Jolie then does something she hasn't done since Rachel's first birthday. She bear-hugs us. Her warm body presses against mine and our heartbeats interact, big browns looking at my lips, face leaning in, *wait, what's happening?*, landing a mellow kiss *(...you begin to fade now...)*, another kiss, a little longer, gooseflesh smacking my skin in this *unexpected* moment that instantly soothes my ails *(...represses six-seven-eight...)* and makes everything appear right in the world. Confusing, but right.

Rachel shouts, "Ewwwww," to which we all giggle. When was the last time we all shared a laugh together? I place her down and she chases her bouncing shadow into the family room.

Jolie says, "I'm sorry I've been such a bitch. Rachel can be very challenging at times..."

In a world where apologies are scarce, you embrace them willingly. I say, "I get it," but don't really. Her apology...it feels a bit contrived: a stopgap implanted where animosity and dislike usually dwell. This isn't routine Jolie. This is her best possible version, a throwback to her pre-pregnancy days. My guilty conscience kicks in: is it possible she knows where I was less than an hour ago? Did I take on the scent of Clorox and cum from Room 6? Is this her sixth-sense thing making an appearance? The angel on my right thinks otherwise, so I side with my virtuous half and give in to coincidence and consider it an opportunity to work things out with the woman I exchanged vows with four years ago.

She smiles, touches my face, my chest, sweet honeysuckle essence. Her warm breath fills my ear: "I missed you today." She nibbles on my earlobe, then kisses me on the cheek, mouth partially open, teasing me with the tip of her tongue, one one-hundred, two one-hundred, three one-hundred.

And I'm thinking: *I kissed two women in one day!*

(...you REPRESS six-seven-eight, the closet, the belt, the shame, the pain...)

I say, "You missed me...is that for real or make believe?"

She giggles. "This time it's for real." Her hand roams. Things stir.

My smile is real, but it's charged with skepticism. "Jolie…what is this?"

She finds my erection, airing her sexiest smile, the one where her eyes narrow and her lips thrust into a gentle pout. "What is what?" Her words are English, but mostly incomprehensible coming from *her* lips.

I say, "You're in a good mood today…" but I'm awash with incredulity. Don't get me wrong, Jolie has her moments. Good days where we remain civil and keep our detestation cloaked beneath forced pleasantries. But this is different. She hasn't come on to me in over two years. So, what gives? "It's really good to hear you say such nice things to me." I mean it, too.

She leans back with our pinkies locked…and then they're not locked, and with no closure to the arousing development, she retrieves her phone and water bottle from the kitchen table and makes for the door.

Wait…what's happening?

"I missed my abs class so I'm gonna take a spin class at eight. Okay?"

"Ok…" I say, feeling suddenly abandoned. "When will you be home?"

She shrugs. "Couple hours, I guess?"

Good. Just enough time to develop the photo of LD.

CHAPTER 18

Two storybooks after Jolie leaves, Rachel falls asleep. It's now 7:55, giving me around ninety minutes, more than enough time to do my deed. I feel a degree of guilt developing today's shots, my everyday hobby now a pretense to erotically charged motivations. But I remind myself: from the outside looking in, it's just another darkroom session, even if driven by something secretively carnal.

Devil on my left: *You're doing nothing wrong.*

It's human curiosity, fervor. Scientists strive for greater knowledge and so do I. *Ms. pretty-in-pink-in-the-park* kissed me today. So did *Ms. pretty-in-pink-at-home.* Both incidents shoulder the same unanswered question: *Why?*

Our two-bedroom apartment boasts a pair of walk-in closets, one in our room overflowing with Jolie's things, the other in Rachel's room, converted into a darkroom complete with a cheap plastic *Do Not Disturb* sign on the door. It's my densely crowded man-cave, steel shelves packed with supplies, a half-dozen prints of Central Park on the opposite wall, a table in the corner providing thirty-six inches of tight but practicable workspace. People ask me why I even bother, and I tell them this: developing via darkroom in today's digital age is music's equivalent to listening to records, and we all know that vinyl has made a comeback. So yeah, that.

Time to get to work.

After a few minutes of prep, I tug the beaded chain to the overhead 15-watt red light and close the door. I grab a clean developing tank from the shelf and fill it with distilled water then feed the film from my camera onto the spool alongside the tray. Once the film is loaded, I submerge it in the tank filled with water. While it soaks, I retrieve a second tank from the shelf and fill it with developing chemicals—careful to measure correct amounts of each—then pour it into the first tank with the film. I set the timer for fifty seconds, cap the tank and gently shake it. When the timer *dings*, I remove the film, dunk it into a tank of fresh water, and hang it on the line to dry.

And I wait, *one one-hundred, two one-hundred, three one-hundred...*

The images fade into reality. I skim past those of the library and...*there she is*. Even in the dim red light, I can tell: the shot came out perfect.

It's a body shot from the knees up, exposed waist turned toward me, below-the-shoulder sandy hair framing her face, her *whole* face, smiling at me, blue eyes sparkling, teeth beaming. I can't stop staring at her, captured not just by her looks, but her perceived demeanor as well, her *attitude* toward me in this suggestive moment: pure sexual chemistry bleeding out through space and time, from our shared moment in the park to her striking presence here in my darkroom. Even if I never see her again, I'm quite happy to have this small remembrance of her in my life.

Then things take a slight turn.

I see something. Not in this perfectly modeled photo, but in the one I took before it, when she bumped into me.

What I thought was an accident at the time. Now, I'm not so sure.

I unclip the photo from the line and turn on the lights.

Surprisingly, it's in focus. It's a close-up of half her face, a woman suiting up for a physical encounter: brow downcast, clenched teeth, one squinting eye fixing me with purposeful intent.

I know faces—I have portfolios full of the expressions and emotions of countless subjects. This is the face of a woman who seconds earlier must've said to herself *There's the guy!*, then forged ahead with deliberate aim to physically confront him. Why, though? Did she have a host of friends nearby putting her on a dare? *I'll give you twenty bucks to mess up camera-boy's shot.* What other reason could she have to intentionally bump into me like that?

I keep looking back and forth between the "angel" and "devil" versions of her and it's starting to give me a headache. The darkroom chemicals aren't helping either. Plus, it's late and I haven't eaten, and this is what happens when you get overly obsessed with something, you stop eating and start sniffing chemicals, like a fucking rock star.

The clock strikes nine and I'm famished. I go into the kitchen and open the fridge and there's a takeout box from La Fontana with pasta and meatballs and a post-it note in Jolie's flowing script: *Peter's Dinner.* Alongside that is a six-pack of Porch Rocker I didn't buy. I chase down two Advil and devour my meal, pondering Jolie's personality disorder as I stare blankly at her note.

After eating and polishing off my beer, I unclip the photos of the library, the model-shot of LD, and the photo I took outside the video store. The video store shot is gently out of focus, but I can still make out the bouncer and the panty-wearing businessman (now with pants on). I slide them into a manila envelope, date it, and file it among the countless other envelopes lining my shelves.

Like a sucker punch from out of nowhere, exhaustion moves in, promising me a good night's sleep. I glance at the row of envelopes before shutting the door, vowing with *fingers crossed* to never look at the photos of LD ever again as long as Jolie continues to be nice to me.

CHAPTER 11

I awake to the chime of my alarm. Jolie is still asleep on her side of the bed, breaths even and undisturbed, a sleeping beauty dreaming of shitstorms and insecurities. Sorry, one night of refinement does not undo three years of bitch.

I sit up on the edge of the bed and *whoa*! I'm dizzy. Something feels *off*, not fever-sick off, just all-around *off*. Headachy. Confused. Vision blurred with the remnants of sleep. I'm still in my clothes but my pants are open and there's a dried cum stain on my CK's.

Angel on my right: *You and Jolie* your wife *shared a tender moment last night.* Kisses, hugs, apologies, La Fontana, Porch Rocker, Advil.

Devil on my left: *Your subconscious mind went full-monty on the pink lady last night.* No recall of that, however a more likely (and believable) rationalization for splooging my Calvin's.

I stagger into the bathroom and piss for an eternity before taking a long, hot shower. It clears my head, but weariness lingers hangover-style. Maybe I'm getting sick after all? Maybe I picked up something from the peepshow room? Or Marge's stack of dollar bills?

After dressing for work, I go into the kitchen where Jolie is now up feeding Rachel a bowl of Cheerios. She looks like I feel: hair mussed, red-rimmed eyes, face pale and swollen as if out partying all night. A half-finished mug of coffee with the catchphrase *May Contain Alcohol* adorns the table.

"Morning," she mutters, indifferent.

"You look like shit." It's never my intention to ruffle her feathers, but I'm curious to see if last night's guest from the land of benevolence stayed the night, and pushing one of her buttons is a surefire way to find out.

She closes her eyes, upper lip twitching as if readying to lash out at me (if it were her lower lip in motion, tears would ensue). "Too much coffee plus too much workout equals up all night. And you snored like a motherfucker."

"I don't snore," I reply, but she would know better than me. I put an Eggo in the toaster, still unsure of which version of Jolie is in attendance.

"Next time I'll record it." She spoon-feeds Rachel another mouthful, washed-out eyes avoiding my scrutiny.

"Can we talk? About last night?"

Eyes still averted: "What about it?"

What about it? She rips me 364 new assholes a year and last night's jaunt to pre-pregnancy days is followed with an unenthusiastic *what about it?* I say, "The hugs, the kisses, I mean, when was the last time we—"

She looks up at me with a hint of tears in her eyes. "I'm sorry, Peter."

Sorry? A cautionary mechanism goes off inside me. Not a defensive trigger, but a *warning* of sorts, as if she might be apologizing for something I don't know about yet.

Her cell rings. She wipes her eyes and answers it. *Saved by the bell.* Says hello. Listens. "Uh-huh. Uh-huh. Okay, feel better. Bye." She disconnects. "That was Carmen. She's still sick."

"That's what…four days in a row now?" Carmen's been our nanny for nearly two years, and I can't remember the last time she's called in sick, if ever. "What's wrong with her?"

"Flu, something, I don't know. Said she's going to the doctor today."

Despite the offset of saving a few hundred bucks, it's fucking annoying having to fight with Jolie over who's going to stay home with Rachel. I pull my phone from my pocket. "I want to talk to her. If she thinks she's gonna be out next week, we're gonna have to come up with a plan."

Jolie swoops in, "Peter!" then slams the spoon on the table, startling both me and Rachel. Tears begin to flow, and not just from Rachel. "I told you, she's *sick*."

My waffle pops from the toaster. "I just want to—"

She closes her eyes, eyelids trembling as if in deep thought. I've seen this look before. She's reining in her anger, for Rachel's sake, for her own sake. Rachel's tears aren't fun to deal with, and Jolie knows it. "Peter. Just stop. I said she's sick."

Butting heads is how Jolie and I roll, so I retrieve Carmen's number from my contacts and hit dial and give Jolie a dirty look and she shoots me poisoned darts as if trying to hocus-pocus the call straight to voice mail, which fucking happens. I disconnect the call. "I guess the next question is, 'Are you working today?'"

"Supposed to."

"Meaning—?"

"Meaning I'll stay home with Rachel so you can go do your fucking job, pumpkin-eater."

She knows I hate it when she calls me that and the tension mounts, not at fighting level yet but within sniffing distance. I take a deep breath and hold it (my anger-dampener), then express my gratitude: "Thank you for staying home to take care of our daughter."

She fakes a smile and I pour myself a cup of coffee and circle back to her cryptic apology. "So…you were apologizing—"

"Were you in your darkroom last night?"

What? "I was…"

"Get any good shots?"

Does she know? I take a bite of waffle. "The only thing I developed last night was a headache."

She nods, then motions toward the clock on the microwave. "You're running late, pumpkin-eater. Better get a move on."

At this point it's safe to say our close encounter last night was an anomaly, so I decide not to push it (and her mysterious apology) any further. I kiss Rachel on the head. "Daddy's got to go to work now, honey."

She exclaims proudly, "I did peeps on the potty all by myself!"

"Wow! That's fabulous."

Out of habit I look at Jolie with disdain and regret…but all my thoughts lean toward the only other woman that's kissed me in years. I shoulder my attaché, trying to convince myself to leave yesterday's photos on the shelf to go down in history as, and I quote myself, "a few more random memoirs diluted amidst chronicles of mediocrity and eccentricity." But like an addiction *(…your need to repress…)*, I am drawn into my darkroom to retrieve my latest masterpiece. I grab the envelope, tuck it into my attaché, and leave for work, duly ignoring Jolie on the way out and thinking, *Sorry for what?*

CHAPTER 12

The N-line is more crowded than usual for a summer Friday. I still feel groggy and queasy and pray I don't puke on someone's shoes before my stop. The doors open and I escape onto the platform with Starbucks on my mind. Starbucks is a cure-all, the Oxycodone of coffee.

It's a five-minute walk from the subway to my building. A pitstop for a Grande Sumatra puts me at about the thirty-minutes-late-for-work mark, but no one seems to notice or care as I skirt past Amy's desk into my office. Amy is our receptionist. She's tiny and insufferable and lives life out loud, a good person to avoid when you're low on caffeine.

Once behind my desk I dig into my attaché and pull out the envelope containing the photos I took yesterday. I flip past the ones from the library—they came out well—then remove the two more interesting shots and ogle the woman who for a moment in time caused all my thoughts to fuse into one; whose mere essence invaded my sleep and automagically extracted my seeds. Two very different shots, one simulating happiness, the other truer: decisive, driven…*angry?*

There's a wall of paperwork on my desk that needs attention, but I ignore it and just stare at her, her image springing to life under the office fluorescents, bright as day and hotter than hell. Eager to find out who LD really is, I bring up Google on my desktop, type in the letter "F" and let autocomplete bring me to Facebook. I start surfing the friends lists of people I know, women whose names begin with the letter "L," but quickly realize how needle-in-a-haystack futile this is. I try Instagram, then Tinder, searching by state, city, zip, age, hair color; so many pretty faces to swipe, all of them yearning for attention.

My social media lifestyle is a marginal affair, a few clicks away from off-the-grid, hence Peter D's faceless and mostly unproductive Facebook photography page, bragging 46 Manhattan landmark shots and 143 likes. It's here I exchange tips with frustrated photographers who also use cameras as a form of escapism from everything that's wrong in their lives. Photography is my first true love, my perfect time waster, exceedingly more rewarding than the hour I just lost throwing digital shit against the wall. Babe shopping is an exhausting process, all those pretty selfies tempting me to click on them.

"Petey-boy…how is my bubby doing on this fine Friday morning?"

The voice belongs to Dave Fisher. Dave's been with Johnson Apparel for sixteen years. Like me, he started out of college and worked his way up to a prominent position on the company's totem pole. We hold parallel positions, working hand-in-hand to make sure our territories are covered. Dave and I have a lot of common interests: Italian food (Dave's one of those New York Jews who not only looks Italian, but acts and dresses the part too), NY Yankees baseball, and of course, women. I live the single lifestyle vicariously through Dave. On mornings following a "hot date," he divulges T-M-I right down to how he fucks all night and comes to work the next day on no sleep, and *"do you know how difficult it is running on fumes after a half-dozen orgasms, Petey-boy?"* I've always been suspect to the integrity of this number. I haven't been able to top three in one session.

"Hey," I reply, voice cracking. I gulp down more caffeine.

He sits in the chair opposite my desk and in all his stinking-of-alcohol glory relates his Thursday night escapade to me. It's a sordid tale, one enhanced through an array of inappropriate hand gestures.

"So, Pete, get this, I'm at the Villa in Garden City. It's ladies night and there's these three women at the bar…"

Like Dave's *pop count,* I suspect his other reports to be exaggerated as well. For example, there's his dubious claim of having had sex with over a thousand women, a self-serving boast typically reserved for the likes of Gene Simmons or Harry Reems, although Dave does have one killer pornstache.

"…so, I bring the brunette back to my apartment. She's wearing black pumps and a miniskirt with legs up to her ears and…"

Dave's thirty-seven going on twenty-two looking forty-eight. Once a dead-ringer for Selleck, the bags and jowls he's developed have transformed him into Hitchcock. He's led a fast life, one filled with vices (coke) and temptations (hookers) that most men don't give in to.

"…and that's when she stands up on the bed, takes aim, and—*whoa!*"

"Whoa, what?"

He grabs the photo of my lust-woman. "Who's she?"

Dave knows things about me that no one else does, like all the sex I had when I was single and all the sex I don't have now. He's my confidant, the only person in my life I can "tell it like it is" to. "I took a picture of her in Bryant Park. Yesterday, after work."

He croons, "Brother! Who is she?"

I shrug. "No clue."

"Just some rando in the park?"

"Sort of…"

"Sort of? Fess up, Peter. You *schtupping* her?"

"No. Dope. She bumped into me while I was taking a picture. My camera went off and this is what I ended up with." I hand him the picture of her evil twin.

"Yikes. Cinderella's stepsister. She looks pissed."

"Right?" He performs a side-by-side comparison just like I did last night, bloodshot eyes darting back and forth between the two images. I point to the model-shot. "I took that one immediately afterwards."

"Looks like two different girls. Any others?" This isn't the first time I've shown Dave photos of my better-looking *subject unawares.*

I hand him the envelope and disappoint him with the photos I took of the library, then spill every detail about what happened, from the moment she bumped into me up to and including my impromptu escapade at the peepshow.

He says, "I've been there before. They've got a dancer there named Sugah, and for forty bucks, she'll—"

I put up a time-out signal with both hands. "Please. No." I point to the Cinderella-version of LD. "Ever see *her* there?"

He hands me back the "evil twin" photo, but holds onto her hot twin. "No…she's way too pretty for that place."

"My thoughts exactly."

"You get her number?" He pinches his nose and sniffs loudly.

"I told you everything that happened. Besides, I'm married."

He laughs. "Right. And you have her picture on your desk why?"

"Admiring my work."

He nods and grins and holds up the photos of the library. "Actually, Rembrandt, these are kind of cool."

"Rembrandt was a painter. You can have a couple if you want."

"Cool, thanks." He takes the top two photos of the library, then holds up the photo of my current obsession and says, "You know, Petey-boy…if you want, I can tell you how to find this girl."

CHAPTER 13

"Missed Connection," he says.

"What's that?"

"A dating app.

"Like Tinder?"

"Kind of, but different."

"Okay, I'll bite."

"All right. So…let's say I'm at a club. And I'm talking to this woman, right? But there's *another* woman there who keeps eyeing me up and down. But I can't talk to her because I'm busy with the first woman. The other woman is your *missed connection*. All you have to do is upload a photo to the app, and hope that someone else either uploaded a photo of her, or recognizes her. I've used it. It works. Everyone knows about it."

"I don't."

"That's because you're a married loser." He stands, circles around the desk, and grabs my phone. I roll my eyes but still let him download the app. After a minute he hands it back to me and says, "I put you in the 'Manhattan Missed Connection' group. There's one for every city. We're in New York."

"Really?"

"Fuck off, I'm still drunk. Now complete the profile."

I do, caffeine deprived, flying on auto-pilot and not quite sure I'd be doing this if it were late in the afternoon. I type in my personal details, location, email address, yada yada. The background wallpaper is a picture of a sharp looking dude and an attractive blonde woman nuzzling. They look happy, like they're about to get laid. I really miss that lusty-flirty pre-sex feeling you get with someone new and strange, when your blood races and your skin ripples and your stomach gets all tingly, and you just *know* it's only going to get better once your clothes start coming off. What an injustice to think I could very well spend the rest of my life not feeling my God-given gift of being really, really, horny.

"Okay," Dave says. "Now hit the 'post' button and write about your encounter."

"That's it?"

"Yep. After your ad goes live, three buttons will appear below her photo. One says *I know her!* and another says, *I am her!* If either one of them gets clicked, you'll get a notification. The last button, scan, uses facial recognition to search the database. It will tell you if anyone else posted a photo of her."

"Seems like long shot, Romeo. Even if she knows about this app, then who's to say she'll use it to find me…which in and of itself is a long shot, right? The odds seem way too stacked."

"You're posting on here, aren't you?"

"Haven't yet."

The angel pleads, the devil goads.

"But you're going to."

"You trying to get me divorced?"

"I'd be doing you a favor. C'mon, do it, just for shits and giggles."

"It says to upload photo."

He positions my lust-woman's photo on the desk, and I take a picture of it; bachelor Dave, directing the show with me in its starring role, just for shits and giggles. I lean more toward the devil's encouragement and spend the next few minutes neglecting my job to write the following:

Missed Connection in Bryant Park

Thursday July 26th, 6:00 PM

I was taking a photo of the Jazz Band. You were wearing a pink tee. You bumped into me and ruined my shot. You have a script LD tattoo on the small of your back. I looked for you as you walked away but could not find you. I would love to thank you for the parting gift you left me.

A pop up on my screen asks if I want to save the ad. The devil tells me to click YES, so I click "YES," and LD's photo fills my phone's screen. I stare into her digital eyes, evoking how they narrowed when they looked at me; her glossed lips, how they gently pressed against mine, leaving behind the faint aroma of cherries.

The app asks: *Do you want to publish your ad?* I click "YES" and am informed that my ad is now live on Manhattan Missed Connection.

CHAPTER 14

After the Missed Connection app fails to locate LD in its database using the facial recognition feature, I close it and spend the rest of the day in meetings reviewing surplus inventory and how much of a bath the company is going to take on markdowns this fall. Upscale department stores are nearing extinction, with "dressing professionally" having ungraciously surrendered to "dressing unprofessionally" in the last five years.

As the day comes to a close, I check the Missed Connection mailbox and find two colorful offers, one for Viagra and the other for Russian Brides—a match made in spam heaven—but no response about my lady-in-pink. I delete the spam and set the app to notify me if another reply comes in. After that, I check my voicemail and find two messages. The first one is from Jolie:

Hey. It's me. I have to tell you something…I…I'm… A rustling sound, like sheets on a mouthpiece, followed by Rachel crying in the background and Jolie saying *shit!* before disconnecting. *Were you going to tell me that you're sorry?* I erase Jolie's message and listen to the second message. This one's from UNKNOWN NUMBER. UNKNOWN NUMBER whispers *Peter* before disconnecting. I listen again and go on the notion that it's a misfired robocall. I don't think twice before erasing this message too.

Time to kiss the workweek goodbye. I pack up my camera and prints and escape into the hallway where I bump into Bobby Rabinowitz, CEO of the swimwear company we share the floor with. Bobby has spent years tanning himself into a new species of human with shoulder-length gray wisps of hair and tobacco-stained gravestones for teeth. "Boychik!" he calls me.

"Hello Bobby."

"Half a day?" Oldest joke in the "garmento" handbook.

The elevator opens and there's just enough room for the two of us. I let him enter first—age before beauty—and he *"boychiks"* someone else. I snake in sideways alongside a pretty redhead who skillfully implements her right to ignore me.

Outside, hurry-home people are on the move, eager to hit the Jersey Shore or the Hamptons. For me, the best kickoff to any weekend starts in Greenwich Village, that playground of potential offering scores of independent shops and loitering characters to shoot. I open my attaché and check my camera: new roll of film, cocked and loaded, two-dozen blanks waiting to be shot.

But first, Jolie and her half-cocked effort to apologize for…for what? I'm curious and decide to give her a chance to finish what she started.

She picks up on the first ring. "I was just going to call you."

"You were going to call me…"

"Yes."

"About…?"

"You first."

I pause, then say what I always say, one of the half-dozen niceties I keep in reserve in the event of a rare, composed exchange: "I just wanted to see how your day was going?" Simple is the path of least resistance with Jolie; one wrong word and the gates of hell could open. I've been there before and it's a painful place to be.

(...Polaroid, dark, dusty, mothballs, BELT, pain...)

"Good...took a spin class, put Rachel in the sitting room—she made a new friend—then went to lunch with the girls. Rachel as usual was the center of attention."

I say, "And you called because...?"

A beat: Jolie collecting her thoughts. "I...I'm going to my mother's for dinner tonight. It's been months since she last saw Rachel. Do you mind?"

Do I mind? Most Friday nights we ignore each other, and *do I mind?* "No, I don't mind. Say hi to Susan for me." Susan the cunt, that pompous all-white-wearing, bourbon-guzzling matriarch of suburbia who specializes in day-drinking, narcissism, and killing off husbands. Susan the cunt, who *doesn't* specialize in her only daughter whose emotional years are forever lost, and I can count on one hand how many times she's seen her granddaughter, and I don't need a single fucking finger to count the nice things she's said about the man who married her daughter. Susan and I don't jibe, if you haven't guessed.

"You started to leave me a voice message earlier—"

"Yeah, uh...about going to Jersey." But then Rachel peed all over the kitchen floor, so I had to hang up. *That makes sense.* Then she surprises me: "You should go out, take some pictures. Maybe go back to Bryant Park?"

There's a first time for everything: first sex, first job, first time Jolie has ever told me to go take pictures without the word "fucking" before the word "pictures."

"O-kay...I was thinking of St. Marks Place."

"Where the music stores are."

"Right."

"Have a good time. When you get home, you'll find dinner in the fridge."

A beat, me thinking: *what the fuck?*

"You want La Fontana again?"

I step up and take a swing. "Jolie…what is this?"

A pause, an uncomfortable one. Then, "I'm…I'm *trying*."

(…he's been TRYING since you were nine…)

Three years and four shattered lamps later, and *now* she's trying? Jolie is a heartless, complex creature suffering from multiple forms of MS: PMS, DMS, and AMS. Pre, during, and after in case I stumped you. But…there's this rare and magical moment in time when all her stars line up, and I get *this* version of her: a semi-annual display of humanity that's appeared two days in a row now (putting aside this morning's hiccup). Is this the start of a better life together?

She says, "Rachel's crying…I have to go. *Love you.*"

"I…"

She abruptly disconnects the phone, saving me the anguish of having to return the proclamation, *her* words (not mine): she loves me not because she *loves* me, but because she never loved me and has guilt to shed, *I'm sorry*. It's what couples say when they break up, *I love you*, but love is conditional and when they part ways they're fucking relieved to be rid of one another.

I join the school of after-work foot-traffic, thinking in Jolie's voice, *why don't you go out and take some pictures? Maybe go back to Bryant Park?* and in my voice, answering, *I never told you that I went to Bryant Park.*

CHAPTER 15

Greenwich Village is Manhattan's colorful tattoo, unsightly but beautiful, strange but charming. The shops are curious, offering an eclectic variety of materials for those looking to quell out-of-the-ordinary tastes: ink parlors, foreign cinema shops, music stores, restaurants with seating for ten, all dark and crumbling and magnetic in their capacity to attract.

On St. Marks Place, I stop by a smoke and novelty shop, aptly called Smoke & Novelty. Like the adult video store, there's a red *STOP!* sign alerting potential customers to be at least twenty-one years of age before entering.

I open the door and enter. A tiny bell above signals my arrival, its tinkle meshing nicely with the jam of Grateful Dead and jasmine incense pervading the small space. Three round faces greet me, one red-eyed, one gape-mouthed, and one framed in a Grizzly Adams beard and Bob Marley dreadlocks. "Grizzly Marley" is leaning against a glass counter-display like the one in the adult video store. At first I wonder if it too is filled with adult toys (thus the *novelty* portion in the name), but soon realize that the elongated objects in the glass counter are bongs. For smoking *tobacco*. The guy next to him is a sight: undeniably stoned, munchies-portly, black tee-shirt too small, worn Lee's halfway down his ass.

Sitting on a stool behind the counter (and of the same flock as the two customers) is a guy wearing all black down to the mascara enhancing his beady, inset eyes. His nose is in a book whose title I can't see but there's a picture on the cover of a dragon looming over a partially clad Viking Goddess. She's got great big boobs, and they're mostly out. The guy's almost-one-eyes never leave the page as I watch him pick his nose and park the booger under the stool he's seated on.

The crew here at Smoke & Novelty would make for a great addition to my Freaks & Geek portfolio, if only for *shits and giggles*.

Dave's witticism reminds me of my missed connection, my love story prologue who may or may not have seen my ad by now. The angel and devil begin to wage war, the devil telling me that someone in the city will see her photo and respond to my ad, the angel telling me that in a city with nearly nine million people, the odds of that happening are slim to none.

"Help you?" The guy behind the counter.

"I was wondering if I could take a photo of the store, with the three of you in it."

Grizzly Marley shrugs his shoulders and says, "Why not?" then steps into position in front of the display case, twirling a dreadlock that makes a soft *scrunching* sound like soft rubber tearing. The nosepicker puts down his book and skirts around the side of the counter and squeezes in between his two amigos. He's got a look of witless amusement on his face, as if he just clocked in for his 15 minutes of fame. He smiles and his inset eyes almost (and quite disturbingly) merge into one. The two dudes flanking him look like photo-op cutouts, unmoving, blank stares, and open mouths.

Point.

Click.

I grin and share my thanks, and then, as if on cue, my cell phone sings a tune I've never heard before. It's a sexy little jingle, *Chimey-chimey-chime-chime, Chimey-chimey-chime-chime, Chimey-chimey-chime-chime.*

The Missed Connection alert?

I look at my cell, preparing myself for disappointment.

I'm not disappointed.

> *To: PeterDel13*
>
> *From: Response@NYMissedConnection.com*
>
> ***Hi, I saw your ad and the picture you posted. I recognize this girl. I'm a barista at Stafford Coffee in the Village, on Houston between 4th & 5th. For the last week she's been coming in here every night, between 8:00 & 9:00. She's always alone. Good luck!***

Heart pounding. Blood pumping. I could go on and on—the list of involuntary responses is a long one. I read the message again. And again. Out of nowhere, guilt begins to bloom. *I really shouldn't go…*

The devil sticks me with its pitchfork: *Stafford Coffee is within walking distance, and you're in the window.*

The angel argues: *Don't Peter…*

"Dude…"

I go from the tiny, mesmerizing words on my cell phone, to the cyclopean nosepicker staring me down as if *I'm* the most interesting person here. Grizzly Marley and the high school dropout have moved on to the rear of the store. They're standing alongside a doorway with, get this, a beaded curtain. There's no peepshow sign, but there *is* a shadowy darkness beyond, one gently lit by a blue neon bulb. What do the folks at Smoke & Novelty keep back there? The sign next to the entrance says *Watch Your Language!* Maybe they keep kindergarteners back there. Maybe Sugah's back there.

He asks, “Help you with something? A new pipe? Smokes?”

Some of Marge’s singles are still in my wallet and I wonder what would happen if the nosepicker got his paws on those? A science experiment would no doubt ensue, one the kindergartners behind the beaded curtain could learn a lot from. I shake my head, and politely decline.

Next stop: Stafford Coffee.

CHAPTER 16

I immediately put in a call to Dave Fisher. He'll want to know the good news. But his cell goes direct to voicemail. I consider leaving a message, but don't because it's happy hour, and if history repeats, Dave is out somewhere being happy. I disconnect the line and set out for Stafford Coffee.

The sidewalks are busy but everything's a blur as I consider what to say upon "accidentally bumping into her." My capacity for dating has plunged since meeting Jolie and my ideas are vapid. Dave once told me that breaking the ice with women is easy, so long as you "keep it simple." *"It doesn't matter what you say, it's how you say it. They're the fish, your words are the bait, and you Petey-boy are the studly captain that reels them in!"*

I memorize this grand bit of insight and practice my best smile, thinking about what to say. *"Hello—remember me?"* No. Too egocentric. *"Hey, you from the park!"* Too stalkerish. What if she looks at me and doesn't remember me? Then it'll be just me, myself, and I, all alone in the world, holding my latte with my flirty-turned-to-stupid grin, waiting *one one-hundred two one-hundred three one-hundred* for a reaction that'll never come, while the world crowds in on me, while everyone in the busy café stares at me, my heartbeat quickening as the seconds slow, slow, *slooooow...*

I obliterate the daymare and place my trust in fate, knowing that if I do *bump into her,* the ensuing events could run the gamut, from smiling to talking to flirting to fucking to downright rejection. Whatever happens, happens. Right?

But…do I want to cheat on my wife?

I'm married. Took a vow. Remained faithful despite the storm and okay, *one time* I wadded up my jeans during a lap dance, but that gets a pass for inconsequence. Jolie and I live out our lives in defiance of what a marriage is supposed to represent. We exist as opposites. We flip each other off behind our backs, sometimes in our faces. We coexist and don't fuck. What good is faithful if faithful doesn't do any good?

The angel, whispering in my ear: *Cheating is not the answer.*

The devil, pitchfork up my ass: *The coffee shop is a block away.*

So, I make a deal with both. If she doesn't show up at the coffee shop, I'll go home and enjoy La Fontana for the second night in a row. But if she *does* show up, then I'll sign on the devil's dotted line and see where the fine print takes me. Nothing more than few minutes of simple conversation is likely, anyway. And maybe, if I'm lucky, another middle-of-the-night wingding in my Calvin's.

She's been coming here nearly every evening, between 8:00 & 9:00. She's always alone…

An evening gust picks up, mining gooseflesh from my arms and back. I shiver, chilly and anxious like a goof on a blind date, jacked with nervous energy, butterflies hatching in my gut. I check my watch. 7:55.

Stafford Coffee is one of the few independent cafés left in Manhattan that Starbucks or Gregory's hasn't digested. It's got an eclectic clientele, arsty-fartsies who eat granola, save the whales, and shackle themselves to rainforest trees. It's the anti-corporate, anti-Starbucks crowd, of which I don't fit in. I like creative things, but also wear a suit Monday through Thursday, and drink a dark Venti Sumatra every morning.

I turn the corner, and here I am. Stafford Coffee. Big. Crumbling. Hand-painted windows. I begin to count, *one one-hundred, two one-hundred, three one-hundred…*

Devil on my shoulder, pitchfork up my ass.

…four one-hundred, five one-hundred, six one-hundred…

Angel on my shoulder, praying for salvation.

The door opens and a man appears with mountainous shoulders and an impressive set of man-boobs, holding a cup of steaming something, and I can't decide if he's muscular or fat. He holds the door for me and…fuck it, I'm going in.

The angel: *This the beginning of the end…*

The devil: *It's the start of a new beginning…*

(…REPRESS…)

My conflicting emotions weigh heavily on my thoughts. I'm an errant piece of a puzzle I don't fit into, *where am I?*, under circumstances I don't completely understand, *what am I doing here?* The angel and devil have never fought so hard with each other. And it's confusing me. I feel lost, unsure of what to do, a stranger in a strange land. You know that dream you have when you're naked in the produce section of the supermarket taking an exam you didn't study for? That's how I feel right now.

I scan my environment. Stafford Coffee is big and rustic, walls full of weather-rusted license plates and repurposed signs, two-dozen tables and counter seats filling the front, patrons circling a glass display case filled with tempting high-calorie desserts (the butterflies in my stomach aren't hungry), an equal share of men, women, gatherers, sketchers, readers. Most of the men have beards. The women could if they tried, one has. Makeup is scarcer here than Starbucks logos. *Now* I know how the barista was able to recognize LD's photo. Like me, she's not one of *the tribe*.

I get in line and look around, but don't see her. The line moves quickly and I keep firing glances at the door as it opens and closes. I order a latte from a barista who's so shiny he could lead spelunkers through a cave. He's bald with over-tweezed eyebrows and red lips that smile way-too-cheerfully while taking my order. He tells me my order will be right up, winking three times in succession as if burdened from a dusty contact lens. When my latte is served (again with a smile and a wink), I thank him and move over to the coffee bar.

While creaming my coffee, I take notice of a highly shootable jamboree: two men sporting scraggly Pearl Jam haircuts and two women with brightly colored buzz cuts. Leaves of sheet music hide the table between them as they discuss their latest magnum opus. One of the women hums a discordant melody that doesn't mesh well with the blues piping in overhead, while the bohemian across from her taps out a rhythm on the table using a pair of plastic spoons. Listening to this confirms three things in life that are certain: death, taxes, and me not purchasing tickets to see this band play.

Point.

Click.

Time passes. I'm antsy and nervous and all this caffeine isn't helping. Back and forth (and out and in) I go, checking the time every few minutes. A stool opens up in the corner and I snag it, watching the foot-traffic through the window, holding my empty cup of latte.

Alone.

Counting.

And then…

CHAPTER 17

The sea of people outside flows evenly and consistently, human bodies melting into one another like minnows, colorless and identical. From amidst them comes an aberration, a rainbow fish separated not only from its own kind, but from the sea it once swam. Bursting with color and beauty, the woman who kissed me in the park enters the café, gets in line, and checks her phone.

And I'm counting *onetwothreefourfivesixsevenone-hundred*.

Here. We. Are. Me: the café's walls closing in. Her: my twenty-four-hour mind-light, set in my sights. Both of us: sharing space and time together *again*. She's dressed differently. Gone are the tight jeans and pink baby-tee, replaced now with clothing more suited for the milieu: worn Levi's, holes at the knees, blue plaid shirt, untucked and unbuttoned, white ribbed tank underneath, less makeup and *still* beautiful, uniquely sexual unlike anyone working at Marge the Garage's peepshow.

She places an order with Shiny Guy (now no longer weathering a contact lens issue), then pays and steps to the milk and sugar station. I watch her every move, not caring if anyone is on to the thirty-something guy leering at the twenty-something girl from the corner of the café. I'm really taken by her: the way she looks, the way she stands, the way she stirs her coffee. It's love and lust at first and second sight.

Love.

Devil on my left: *Keep it simple.*

With sleight-of-hand dexterity—and a shred of guilt—I yank the wedding band from my ring finger and make it disappear in my pocket, then step to the milk and sugar station, *counting, counting, counting…*

She snaps the lid back onto her coffee cup…

…four one-hundred, five one-hundred, six one-hundred…

…and turns.

Sees me. Stops.

I take Dave's advice and keep it simple. "Hello."

"Hi…?" she says, eyes narrowing, wheels spinning, thinking *I know this guy from somewhere.* Then, like a flower in stop-action bloom, she smiles and her face lights up and she points an unmanicured finger at me and says, "The guy with the camera. From the park."

Her voice is beautiful, softly southern, medicine for my damaged soul. I say, "I *thought* I recognized you."

"What *are* the odds?" Her suspecting eyes linger, screening me, making sure I *am* the nice guy she met in the park, and not some random coffeehouse douchebag. Part of me senses sarcasm in her voice, part of me watches her ponder how this second meeting in as many days could have happened without some external force driving it.

I spew, "Millions-maybe-more-to-one?" Embarrassment paints my face, red hot—would have if I'd said anything cleverer. And like two friends exchanging small talk after bumping into one another, I say, "What are you doing here?"

She toasts her cup. "Evening pick-me-up."

"Right…" She's so beautiful, so feminine. I want to place my hand on her LD tattoo and usher her in, taste her lips. Again. But it's too soon for that. *But soon.* "I was just gonna get a refill. You…expecting anyone?"

She smiles and she's so damn good at it. I may be out of practice, but I know what a flirt looks like, and the grin on her face is conveying her enthusiasm for this sudden encounter. She says, "Just you." Her eyes lose their guarded focus as she points to an empty table near the restroom. "I'll be over there, okay?"

I'm a newbie at flirting and my words are unskilled so I hold them back with a smile and toast my empty cup, then rush to the counter where shiny guy awaits, customer-free.

"Can I get a refill?"

"For you, anything." He winks and look at that, he's got something in his eye again. I turn around and watch my *date* take a seat at the table for two. She's head-to-toe hot, less slutty than yesterday, lips licking, fingers tapping as she checks in on Facebook or Instagram, texting her boyfriend to not wait up because *I want to make out with the cute guy from the park.*

The angel: *You're getting ahead of yourself.*

I still have her photos in my attaché, again thankful that I grabbed them before leaving this morning; had I not done that, I wouldn't be sharing space with her right now. The barista hands me my refill. "Here you are, handsome. I hope things work out for you and your…missed connection."

I nod and say, "Thanks." This time I'm the one who winks and I salute my new friend, *thank you for responding to my ad.*

I start my passage back toward the woman of my dreams, weaving past the band of songwriters and the coffee bar. I catch a whiff of B-O and it sends the butterflies in my stomach back into a fluttering frenzy…but they're quickly soothed by the sweet scent of vanilla surrounding the table my date is sitting at.

She smiles. "Hi again."

I take the seat across from her, heart beat-beat-beating ferociously, blood rush-rush-rushing hotly. "Hi again. I'm Peter." I offer my hand and she takes it, warm and soft and lingering much like her touch on my arm in the park. I count to myself *one one-hundred, two one-hundred, three one-hundred,* so neuroatypical and compulsory. I'm distracted,

(REPRESSING)

and it feels really fucking good.

"I'm Lily," she says. "Lily Dahl."

LD. "As in baby-doll? Or doll-house?"

She fake laughs—she's heard it before. "It's D-A-H-L. Like Roald. But don't worry, it wouldn't be the first time."

I laugh automatically and if I had a curl I'd be twirling it. "Dahl, got it…like in the chocolate factory, and the giant peach."

"Correct." She takes a sip then, "So Peter…what *are* the odds?"

"Even more so…" I reach under the table and open my attaché. In the envelope containing the photographs, I finger past the shots of the library, past the Cinderella-stepsister version of Lily (she's got a name now, stick a fork in LD), and slide out the photo of her walking away. I show it to her and her face lights up, palm-over-mouth, a brilliant blush of red coloring her cheeks. She likes what she sees.

"Came out good, huh?"

"Better than good…never in my wildest dreams…"

"…did you think you'd ever see this," I finish. *Someone did,* but she won't hear it from me. That would shatter the coincidence of us running into each other, a key element to making this conversation work. Plus, getting my number blocked before she even has it isn't high up on my priorities list.

"Never in my wildest dreams did I think I'd be showing this to you." *My dreams of her are already wild, cum-in-my-Calvins wild.* She tries to hand it back and I tell her to keep it and she says "Really?" and I say, "I have the negative," and don't mention anything about it being on a dating app for stalkers.

"Thank you, Peter." Cool silence passes and we sip and smile and my mind races for something witty to say, but my tongue is bound. Eventually she breaks it, and does so in an epic way: "Peter...do you have any plans for tonight?"

Plans? I peek at my phone. 9:20. Jolie is at Susan the Cunt's and isn't likely to question my whereabouts. But I've also never stayed out to any unreasonable (or inexplicable) hour. Plans? Yes, my *plans*...they're unfolding in real-time, right here, right now, and I *plan* to stay right where I am, with Lily Dahl, because the feeling I've got is exactly how Mick Jagger feels when he sings "Wild Horses," and I fucking love that song.

"I do now."

CHAPTER 18

We spend the next hour walking the village, effortless dialogue drifting between us, from Bryant Park to our favorite village boutiques, our literary tastes and photography, even the grainy clientele at Stafford Coffee, some of whom we laugh out loud over, judgmental us. We talk about music, and she loves grunge and we agree that Staind sucks and Puddle of Mudd has two decent songs and there's no topping Nirvana. Ever.

I give her the brief 4-1-1 on my job—intentionally omitting the name of the company because phone calls from a girlfriend in an office full of co-workers who know you're married doesn't align any stars—with which she seems quite impressed, despite having never worn anything even remotely corporate.

She professes to have spent two years studying residential health care at Miami-Dade Community College. After that she moved to New York and worked as an aide in a Queens nursing home, but the meager hours forced her to take an in-home assistance gig to help pay the rent on her 4th Street studio.

She apologizes for bumping into me and messing up my shot, which I in turn thank her for. She laughs and a little snort comes out and she laughs harder and turns red and it's splendid just how human she is. I think of the evil-version photo of her…but the image fades like mist in a flame, because when you're holding hands with a woman who's always smiling, who flirts with you and makes you feel special, nothing else matters.

Everything is perfect. Except *I'm married*.

She asks, "Are you sure there isn't someplace else you need to be?" She arches her right brow, the eye beneath it scrutinizing me carefully, seeking honesty.

"No…I need to be right here with you, Lily Dahl."

The inquisitorial eyebrow settles and her smile returns. She takes hold of my hand and it's damp and I don't care. She says, "You're sweet," then kisses me on the cheek, *one one-hundred…(…six-seven-eight is now a distant dream, REPRESSED…)* and my heartbeat shifts into high gear, one because it feels wonderful to be kissed, but two because the risk of bumping into someone I know, the risk of them seeing me holding hands with a woman that isn't my wife, the risk of them witnessing the huge smile on my face and huger hard-on in my jeans, is just so fucking worth it as long as it's with Lily Dahl.

Touring the village hand-in-hand with Lily is paramount; us, new friends sharing an attraction for lattes and Nirvana and window shopping. Never have I been so attracted to someone, so *fulfilled*. Our connection is chemical, robust, satisfying, *(…distracting…)*. She hooks an arm around my waist and her head rests on my shoulder and we slow our pace, one embodiment, magnetic in our embrace as though here and now I've finally met my soul mate, my female half, the woman I'm supposed to be with. Yes, I know it's only been two hours and it's cringy as fuck, but I don't give a shit, it's how I feel.

We get ice cream cones from a Mr. Softee truck. We talk, we laugh. And all throughout the evening, I take pictures of Lily.

Point.

Click.

Lily eating ice cream. Lily on a park bench. Lily doing anything at all because Lily is beautiful no matter what. We pretend to be *together*, and get to know each other fast. She's single, and for the moment, *so am I*; sometimes the truth is worth lying about. We smell the flowers in Washington Square Park and silently agree—in my mind, anyway—that we are a *thing* now. I look into her blue eyes and run my fingers through her beach-sand hair and hum Nirvana's "No Apologies" to myself.

The angel and devil are at a loss for words but agree I'm in trouble, *good* trouble, the kind that fills your heart with promise, but promises to empty it if the truth comes out.

We sit on a bench in Washington Square, the full moon spotlighting us as Manhattan's most intimate moment. An ocean of activity surrounds us but it's not there and as a clock tower chimes twelve someplace else, our phones come out. She texts. I don't. I want to ask her who she's texting. *At midnight*. But I don't. My notifications show zero texts from Jolie, a rare occurrence; her visit to Susan the Cunt's was a well-timed distraction.

I finally ask, "Why did you kiss me in the park yesterday?"

She smiles, mouth closed, *amused*, crimson cheeks purple under the blue moonlight. "I guess because I felt bad about messing up your shot." She pauses, looks down, then adds, "And because I think you're very handsome."

She brings her gaze back up and we lock eyes, a magnetic tango of *want* connecting us. "I'm so happy you messed up my shot."

"I. Am. Too." Her ringed baby-blues hypnotize me as she leans in and kisses me. She stays close and whispers, "I'm *drawn* to you. But…"

"But…?"

"But you lied to me. You're married."

She pulls back—not all the way, but far enough—watching my face as my heart melts and drips into my gut, the butterflies feeding on it until there's nothing left to drive my happiness.

All my wants and desires, my positive emotions, they're gone now, replaced by sadness and heartache. Is this how my life's most perfect love story ends?

(…glimpses of six-seven-eight trickle back…)

"How did you know?"

She grabs my left hand and points to my ring finger. "There's a white circle on your finger where the ring you were wearing yesterday used to be."

Angel on my right: *She noticed your ring yesterday, and walked away.*

Devil on my left: *She noticed it was missing today, and didn't walk away.*

I suppose now would be a good time to take my wants and desires (and my hard-on), and go bury them with my head in the sand on some far-off beach. I touch the white circle of untanned skin on my finger. "I suppose there is…" I rarely remove my ring and being the awful criminal I am, didn't realize I'd left such clear evidence behind. Throw the fucking cuffs on, I'm guilty as charged.

She places a hand on my cheek, turns my face toward hers, and pulls my head (and hard-on) back out of the sand. "I'm still glad you found me…" Her lips press against mine, a little longer this time, and with a flicker of tongue. She knows I'm married and it's not stopping her from becoming a willing participant in my crime of infidelity. *Yes.* I can literally feel my heart being stitched back together now, pumping, pumping, pumping blood down, down, down.

(…glimpses of six-seven-eight, wiped away again…)

We kiss again. And again. Her lips are moist, delicious, cherries with cool traces of vanilla ice cream, our tongues meeting eagerly now, passion escalating, closing out the world around us. I cup her face in my hands, nibble her, lick her, all of space and time crumbling away as lonely bystanders silently tell us to *"get a room."*

And then, as if mindreading them, she puts her hand on my swollen dick and whispers: "Would you like to walk me home now?"

CHAPTER 19

Her apartment is three blocks away on West 4th Street. We take to the sidewalk in giddy silence, holding hands, *anticipating* like the nuzzling couple on the Missed Connection home screen. I'm nervous and tired, head in the clouds *(am I about to get laid?)*, brain in my pants *(I'm going to get laid!)*, the only uncomplicated thing about me my hard-on, here to stay and please don't judge me, I haven't had sex in nearly two years.

As we walk my eyes roam every inch of her. She's perfect, everything I could ever want in a woman: clean, pretty, shapely, the type of girl guys eat their hearts out for. She's a princess on my arm and I'm her prince. And here we are, at her castle.

The building is your archetypal Greenwich Village eyesore, heavily barred door, well-rusted and well-locked. On the left side of the crumbling alcove sits a column of nine buzzers alongside tiny, cracked panes covering barely legible scrawled names. I search for *Lily Dahl* but can't make out anything. To the right of the building sits a Chinese takeout joint, the air saturated, deep-fried greasy stench, the type of place Sugah gets her dinners from.

"I'm on the third floor."

"Walk up?"

"Yes."

"Sucks when you forget something."

She rolls her eyes. "*Yes…*" She unlocks the door, then stops and kisses me.

"That's nice," I breathe, eyes closed.

She points upstairs. "You up for a bit of exercise?"

I laugh. It's an uncomfortable laugh. I want to go with her. But I'm scared. It's like this: I'm strapped to a rocket and I'm traveling through space, but it's only been a couple of hours and I'm not quite ready to plant my feet on the moon's surface yet. Lily's apartment is the moon and me going up there is my world's one giant leap for mankind. Something like that. You get the picture.

I have to ask, "Does it bother you at all that I'm married?"

She grips the front of my shirt with one hand and faces me with a cocky smile. "You only go around the block once…might as well stop at a few houses along the way. Just pretend I'm one of those houses…" She leans and whispers in my ear, "…and that my door is wide open."

Poetic. I shiver. Nod. Oh. Yes. But… "You didn't answer my question."

"You know Peter, some things are just best left unsaid. Wouldn't you agree?" Her voice engages a serious tone, and she nods her head as if trying to get me to agree with her and I see, ever so faintly, a smidgeon of the Lily from the Wicked Witch of the West snapshot on her face. But like the afterglow of a camera's flash, it fades and Pretty-Lily returns. She leans forward in her ever-so-proficient manner, and with her lips touching my ear, whispers, "Now come upstairs and fuck me…"

CHAPTER 28

Who was it that said, *be careful what you wish for, you just might get it?* I'd love to tell that guy to go fuck himself. I wished for it. And I got it. And now I've got to take the fucker's advice. But I don't want to be careful. I want to wallow in my good fortune. I want to forget about the first thirty-three years of my life and start things anew, right here, right now, with Lily Dahl and her invitation of carnal pleasure: a first step toward real *love*.

We take the wooden steps slowly, Lily in the lead. The angel on my right shares a quick common-sense reminder to use caution. It knows there's no chance in heaven I'm turning back now. The lure is too strong with Lily's booty see-sawing inches from my face, her beltline an inch below the pink—*pink!*—straps of her thong panties. I feel like a fish, worm dangling inches from my lips, pain-in-the-ass angel tapping me on the gills, urging me to be mindful of the hook.

We reach the third floor and pass two doors in a nondescript hallway before stopping in front of 3C.

"Welcome to my abode," she says, and opens the door.

Remember the list of three things in life that are certain? Well, make it four. Add in me having some fun with Lily Dahl.

As Lily pees in a bathroom with no door, I scan her paltry apartment. It's a studio, roughly the size of a single-car garage, full bed to the left, floral-patterned comforter sheathing a rectangle frame, no headboard. The walls are gray and pictureless, a single paint-chipped window with sheer drapes looking out over West 4th. There's a dresser in one corner with a running portable fan, and a small nightstand and clock-radio alongside the bed. Two feet of kitchen sits to the right, hotplate, small fridge, doorless bathroom warning me not to get the urge. That's everything I notice before she emerges from the bathroom, and her lips find mine.

I could go on and on about how nice her kisses are, how scrumptious she tastes, how our bodies come together so effortlessly, how my blood rushes, my heart beats, my nerves jangle, my…clothes peel off.

The angel: *He's self-conscious of them…*

The devil: *The lights are out…*

And strangely, I feel calm *(…you're distracted…)*, this moment in time the therapy I need to combat the emotional torment I've suffered in my marriage.

(…you REPRESS…)

We settle on the bed, bare limbs intertwined as we kiss, skin on *(…damaged…)* skin. She takes me in her mouth and my eyes find a gap in the curtain and I observe the full moon's light branching into the room, striking the bed, irradiating her fanned out hair. I can't keep my eyes off her. If I pull them away, I'm afraid I'll wake up and find this whole dream-come-true scenario the result of some very intense midnight encounter with myself.

She climbs on top of me. I cup her breasts, soft, damp, golden. I can feel her heartbeat through them, a rhythmic pounding intensifying the physical pleasure of the moment, adding consolation to my life—a means to quell the lonesomeness and so much more. I accept her giving approach and press my shaft against her silky-smooth wetness.

For the first time in forever, everything is *perfect*, pure intimacy and infatuation taking hold of me, *saturating* me. Our eyes lock, her perfect crystal blues ringed with black absorbing me passionately, her sex hot, sopping against my shaft. Her hand roams, positioning me for a fitted thrust.

We become one. Me, within her. She, filled with me.

It's the first time all over again, cherished memories of that momentous event (her name was Emma Jayne and we were sixteen and awkward, but that's a story for another day) now renewed with a fresh, exhilarating sense of awareness, of expertise, emotional pain fading (REPRESSING) as I submit to the pleasures of Lily Dahl, to the coital rhythms connecting us, with no awkward Emma Jayne-like attempt to work it all out.

My senses heighten to levels previously unfelt: I can hear the rumble of a distant generator in the walls; can feel the cool breeze of the fan blowing across the edges of the draped window. It's as though I'm in a chamber of pure pleasure, hidden from the harsh certainty of the real world, this moment of ecstasy a shroud of protection from the despondency that's consumed the last four years of my life.

(...memories of six-seven-eight...)

In an adept move, I grasp Lily's smooth thigh and bring her leg over my waist, twisting myself on top of her. I admire her face: eyes shut, mouth drawing in quick gasps of air. Her features trigger an eroticism in me, one born of creativity: perfect lips pouting to taste, eyes like cobalt, nose quivering with want and desire. She's irreproachably sensuous, unparalleled in her beauty, the *real* Lily Dahl, giving herself to me physically and *emotionally*. This is what I've always wanted: a spontaneous joining with a woman that breaks through the boundaries of simple sex, toward an incalculable, satisfying display of *love*.

She opens her eyes and looks deeply into mine. I'm hyper-energized under the dazzle of her intimacy and desire. But I want to absorb *all* of Lily Dahl, so I lift my torso up and explore her smooth shoulders, her damp breasts, taut waist, the twinkle of her navel piercing. Our fucking *surges*, we're panting heavily now, heat and sweat and more heat and more sweat until the moment of no stopping arrives and I can no longer endure the crescendo of bliss overrunning my body.

YES…!

We cry out in unison as I thrust one final time and release myself inside of her.

One one-hundred, two one-hundred, three one-hundred…

Everything making up my world flows into quiet bliss. The room settles into breathy silence. We remain in an unmoving position for minutes, holding each other tightly…

(…her hands on your scars…)

…until she eventually allows me to withdraw. I roll onto my side, facing her, our foreheads touching but barely, breaths commingling, her wet sex cooling on my still-throbbing cock. Delicate silence dominates and we relish the laughter bubbling inside, and the promise of sleep drifting toward us.

I close my eyes and roll onto my back, body begging for rest. But rest doesn't come. Post-orgasmic alarms are now ringing in my head, firing questions, one after another: *Is she going to stalk me? Is she on the pill? Does she have any diseases? Does she have a crazy ex-boyfriend?*

All questions I don't want the answers to.

CHAPTER 21

I don't want to disturb her. She's sleeping, like Snow White, like Sleeping Beauty, with no trace of the Maleficent counter-ego present from photo number two. My oxytocin blindfold has dissipated and I'm wondering if there's more to this woman I've fallen hard for. If there's an underlying motive to her actions tonight.

If I should be worried about what just happened.

The angel: *You should.*

Immediately, instantly, and every other overused synonym that means *all of a fucking sudden*, I'm sick to my stomach.

I just cheated on my wife.

My *insane* wife.

I leave the bed and get dressed, tired and tripping over myself, body awash in Lily's scent. I should clean up before leaving, but don't.

The angel on my right, crying.

The devil on my left, grinning.

And all of a fucking sudden (much too late after the fact), I'm worried about my swimmy-seeds, now paddling upstream toward her finish line (this happened once before, you know). And now, on top of that, I'm wondering if she's done this kind of thing before, with other men, too many times to count, and as a result has something replicating inside of her, and I wonder (now way too fucking late after fact), if it's inside of *me*, partying up an infectious storm.

My eyes roam over her naked body, lying prone to the stalker she brought home tonight. Does fate have this pinned as a one-night stand? Or do I want to see her again? Use her as a catalyst to end the marriage I've been fantasizing about getting out of for so long?

(...REPRESS...)

I open my attaché and quietly remove my camera.

Point.

Click.

She stirs. I spin and slip it back into its case, peer over my shoulder, and watch as she moans...but remains asleep. *Thank you.* I tiptoe to the door, unlatch it, and at eye-level notice a small dry-erase board with a note scrawled on it:

CLICK ED IN MOON

I stare at the odd note-to-self, overtired mind blind to clear-headedness and unable to formulate a translation. A familiarity exists in it though, so I make a mental note of CLICK ED IN MOON, and give no second thought to scrawling my cell number down beneath it.

Without knowing who Ed is and why he needs to be clicked in his moon, I abandon Lily Dahl's pictureless, paint-chipped, hotplate world, reflecting on the events taking place therein and hearing from behind me, from behind her closed door, the melodic chime of a cell phone.

CHAPTER 22

It's 3:17 a.m. when I slip the key into the lock of my apartment. I took a cab home (I've never been one for the New York subway system between the hours of 12:00 a.m. and 6:00 a.m.; the meager crowds, despite being photo-worthy, are decrepit and drunk and stink like piss) and as expected, my tired attempt to formulate an excuse as to why I stayed out until 3:00 a.m. without a text or phone call finds nothing but a brick wall to slam face-first into.

Angel on my right: *Confess your sin, Peter. Tell her the truth.*

I enter our dark and silent apartment and place my attaché on the kitchen counter. Like a burglar in a tacky Lifetime flick, I tiptoe to Rachel's bedroom door and crack it open. Beneath the soft amber glow of her nightlight, she sleeps like an angel, every gentle breath a guilt-ridden reminder of my transgression tonight. *Ugh.*

With my hand on the wall next to the door, I feel more than see a web of hairline cracks branching away from a baseball-sized indent. It isn't unlike Rachel to hurl a toy (or Jolie a lamp), but this looks and feels like more damage than just that, as if my darling wife tossed something *heavy.*

I peek into my bedroom. Jolie's in bed, the rise and fall of the covers matching the even sound of her dragon breaths. I slip into the bathroom, shrug free of my Lily-scented clothes and stuff them deep into the hamper before using a half-dozen baby-wipes to freshen up my parts. I brush my teeth, muss my hair (so it looks like I've been sleeping), then don my bathrobe and creep into the kitchen.

Bullet dodged.

It hadn't occurred to me till now that I'd only eaten ice cream for dinner; isn't it amazing how the male constitution can forego food (and sleep) for sex? I open the fridge and find, as promised, takeout from La Fontana. Fuel for the flames of guilt burning my conscience. I peek in the tin. Chicken Parmigiana and penne, my favorite. Jolie's *trying*. And what did I do? I cheated on her, and there is no relief in that, even if she sucks most of the time. I'm exhausted and remorseful and despise myself, *let's-take-a-detour-into-Bryant-Park-and-take-some-pictures-before-going-home.* And I'm ravenous after having sex with a woman who isn't my wife, now about to eat the dinner my wife bought for me. It's a fistful of gut-wrenching irony, isn't it?

I remove the foil and place the tin on the kitchen table.

The angel: *Did Rachel deserve what you did tonight?*

The devil: *Burned a lot of calories tonight, eh Petey-boy?*

I devour my dinner cold, recognizing in this moment of self-loathing that if Jolie is in fact trying to make things right, if she's finally recognized that Rachel and I are the best thing to have ever happened to her, then I'll chalk up Lily Dahl as a one-time fling, a mistake, a what's-done-is-done in the rearview mirror.

The devil: *you wrote your number on her dry-erase board.*

Fuck. I did, didn't I?

I finish eating and put my dish in the sink…and see movement out of the corner of my eye.

I turn and it's Rachel, standing in the entrance of her bedroom, number-one dripping down her legs.

I stutter and stumble. "Oh…honey, baby, come here. Let me clean you up." I usher her into the bathroom and run the shower. Fuck—is this day ever going to end? Ten minutes later she's cleaned and back in bed and I'm tiptoeing into my bedroom. The floor creaks and Jolie stirs and in her unconscious movements the comforter slides away. Her nightie is bunched up, every-day-at-the-gym abs exposed, moving up and down. She's wearing *pink* lace panties, or maybe they're red and my eyes are seeing what they want to see in the darkness. Does it even matter? I shrug into a Soundgarden tee and settle into bed alongside her.

She stirs. I shudder. She turns over and her hand gently comes to rest on my chest as she sleep-talks: "Did you get up?"

"Yes," I whisper. "I changed Rachel."

She murmurs, "You're the best," before going back to sleep.

Fuck.

CHAPTER 23

I jolt awake, unsure of the day, or time, or where I am. My eyes are dried shut and it takes a gentle rub to unglue them. The room arrives in dim focus and okay, I'm home, right where I should be. Good.

I sit up and the world see-saws and I have to squeeze my eyes shut and hold my head in my hands for a few minutes. I'm dizzy and nauseous and unusually exhausted, like yesterday morning, only worse. Much worse. The clock on the cable box comes into focus: 1:25 p.m. Damn. I haven't slept this late since I was in college.

I use the footboard of the bed to prop myself up, waiting *hun hun-hundred two hun-hundred three hun-hundred* until the dizzying feeling fades. The apartment is quiet. Jolie and Rachel aren't here.

You're the best…

I take some deep breaths, and with my eyes closed, practice reciting last night's events in my head: *After work, I went to the Village and lost track of time. Got home later than expected. Ate the dinner you got me—thank you for that, it was delicious—went to bed, and come to think of it, I think I changed Rachel during the night but…but everything seems a little vague to me right now.*

The devil appears like a magician in a cloud of smoke: *Is Lily vague?* Lily is all I can think about. Lily at the park. Lily eating ice cream. Lily sleeping naked. I don't *want* to think about her, but she weighs heavily on my conscience, the burgeoning remorse of what I did and the uncertainty of what may come eating me from the inside out. I need three Advil, two Tums, and one *venti* cup of coffee.

The devil, more awake than I am, gives me a jab: *Stafford Coffee, open 24 hours a day!*

I'm strong-willed and don't need the angel to deny the devil his due. What I need is caffeine, and a time-out from my extra-marital deviltry to help assuage the guilt. I slip into jeans and a Tool tee-shirt and drag my corpse into the kitchen. My attaché is still on the counter, right where I left it, the camera inside fully loaded with Lily. The display on my cell is dark, so I slap it on the wireless charger in the kitchen and hold the "power-on" button until the Samsung logo appears. It's here I notice a post-it note on the fridge:

Went to the gym. Took Rachel. Having lunch afterwards. Sorry I fell asleep last night. Visit with mom tired me out!

Fancy that. I'm not the world's worst criminal after all. I committed the crime, cleaned up the evidence, and seemingly got away with it. I fist-pump the air, halfheartedly because I still need to know for sure, and because I'm an idiot and can't leave well enough alone. With my phone still on the charger, I tap on *wife from hell cell* and put the call on speaker. It rings three times before she picks up.

"Hey," she says, huffing and puffing.

"You at the gym?"

"On…on the treadmill. Y-you see my note?"

I pretend to look and say, "I do now. Thanks for dinner last night. How's Susan?" *The cunt.*

"Self-absorbed…talked about herself the entire time." Heavy breathing.

"Par for the course."

"Rachel going into beast-mode the minute we got there didn't help either." Lungs gasping sexually. Pounding sounds. *Treadmill?* She asks, "What time did you get in last night?"

It's a good thing she can't see my face right now because *I Fucked Lily* might as well be written all over it. I'm a terrible liar, no matter how many times I practice my defense. "Eleven, or thereabouts." An English professor once told me never to use the word "thereabouts." *It hints at dishonesty*. So, I activate my brain's auto-correct and say, "Hit a few shops in the village (the truth), took some pictures (the truth), stopped for a cup of latte (the truth), I guess I lost track of time (the truth). Sorry (Or thereabouts)."

I hear a disturbance on her end of the phone. Indistinct voices. A man's voice? She huffs, "I need to get back to my workout, okay?"

"Sure. What time will you be home?"

She says in time for dinner and informs me that Rachel is growing like a weed and needs new clothes so they're going to hit Bloomingdales after lunch, and do I want Greek or Thai for dinner? I say Thai and we exchange goodbyes and disconnect. Jolie...she's acting so abnormally normal, making me wonder if her sixth-sense thing is causing her mental eyebrows to rise—if all this nicety is merely a smokescreen hiding some massive shitstorm brewing deep down inside her. It's so painfully confusing! Last night I slept with a strange woman, and today my wife is acting strange. Regardless, I had my cake and ate it too, and I'm still alive to talk about it, and guilt is only real when you get caught, right?

My cell phone vibrates. The display reads: *UNKNOWN NUMBER*.

I answer it: "Hello?"

"Peter? It's Lily."

Fuckfuckfuckfuckfuck. "Hi...Lily..." I say, voice cracking.

"Hi..."

The devil on my left, evil laughter, flipping off the angel.

She says, "Sorry I fell asleep on you last night."

My eyes turn toward Jolie's post-it note on the fridge: *Sorry I fell asleep last night.* Fate, destiny, kismet, call it what you will, it's fucking with me. I say, "I'm sorry I just upped and left. I didn't want to wake you, and I needed to get home, and—"

"You don't have to explain yourself to me, Peter. I understand. I just hope it's okay I called, given your situation, you know? But...you did leave your number, and I wanted to hear your voice again, so..."

I smile. My dick enters semi territory and the soreness in it calls out to me: *You got laid last night!* It's a pleasant pain, like that tenderness you feel in your muscles after working out. I worked out my dick last night after a long off-period, and it's a muscle, so yeah, *that!* I say, "I wouldn't have left my number if I didn't want you to call."

I can hear her smiling. "Can I see you again?"

The devil on my left: *Jolie won't be home till dinner...*

The angel, desperate: *Peter, end it right here, right—*

I shove the angel aside. "Meet you in thirty minutes?"

So much for a time-out.

CHAPTER 24

New York City's subways are a playground, and this amateur photog has made a habit of snapping its dwellers and visitors on a near-daily basis. Humans are creatures of habit, their strap-hanging tendencies no exception. Every day, same time, same seat, same dull expression: work-weary eyes staring emptily at the advertisements lining the upper walls. Weekends offer the best pickings; gone are the cardboard cutout commuters, leaving ample room for the eclectic to shine.

The R-line pulls into the station and for a hot second I consider hightailing it back uptown, far away from my second-life world. But I don't. I experienced Lily Dahl once, and despite feeling like a landfill of shit—both physically and emotionally—I think, consider, and decide: *I want more.*

(…to REPRESS six-seven-eight…)

Sex is like dessert for most men. It satiates in the moment…but when the *crave* hits again (always sooner rather than later) the urge to feed it is strong. The female libido is a more complex affair: five course extravaganzas with appetizers (dating), salads (foreplay), main courses (relationship), dessert (love-making), and after dinner drinks (cuddling). Could I bear living with Jolie as my main course, so long as there's Lily for dessert? Food for thought.

I step out of the train and the first thing I notice is the piss-stench, compliments of a young druggie who at some point in his teens must've shrugged off life for needle and spoon companionship. He's sitting on the platform with a battered Casio keyboard on his lap, aggressively punching out an off-tune rendition of "Country Road," gloves of street-grime and infection hitting too many wrong keys. He's got a small plastic sand pail, yellow with black smiley face and crudely drawn speech-bubble—"*tips*"—sloppily duct-taped to the side of his cheap instrument.

I sidestep several faceless people, drop five bucks into his smiley-pail, and ask him to stop playing. He responds by pounding the keyboard even harder, earning me the chagrin of those standing nearby.

I ask, "Can I take your picture?"

He doesn't stop playing and sings his response, still to the melody of country road, and still more out of tune than his dying instrument: "*Take my picture! Sure you can! Thanks for the tip! You da man!*" He laughs, green teeth bared, receding gums oozing a malady only the bravest of dentists might examine. He'll make a fine addition to my Freaks & Geeks portfolio.

Point.

Click.

I nod my thanks, holster my camera, and walk upstairs into the heart of Greenwich Village, away from the piss-stench, and into the waiting arms of Lily Dahl.

She's even more beautiful than I remember.

It's odd—in the first few days of dating someone, it's always difficult to remember what that person looks like when they're not around. I can't explain it. It's a weird circumstance even the laws of nature have no rationalization for. Ask me what the guys in Smoke & Novelty look like, and I'll provide you with enough details to give a police sketch artist a hard-on. But Lily...despite knowing her intimately, the perfect whole of her parts hadn't truly come back together until now. *Now* I remember the piercing intensity of her crystal blue eyes, the rosy hue of her cheeks, the glossy shine of her full lips. She's wearing a short khaki skirt and white collared blouse like a model in a J.Crew catalogue, perfectly preppy.

We go to Stafford Coffee and order lattes (shiny guy has the day off) and sit at the same table as last night. We talk and giggle and reminisce about our night together and the pleasures and gratifications we shared. We laugh more and she takes out her phone to text someone and I get jealous and clench my fists, now reminded of the ringing phone I heard in her apartment after leaving. It comes out of me unbidden: "I thought I heard your phone ringing as I was leaving last night…"

Her eyes widen. *Panic?* "Peter…!"

I stop talking.

"Would you…like to be with me again?"

I do not hesitate. "Yes."

"Right now?"

Despite my hesitation, I do not hesitate. "Yes."

By the time we're back at her castle on West 4th Street, the topic of the phone ringing in her apartment is a distant memory. As soon as the door to her apartment closes, our clothes come off. We kiss and stroke and she is *wet* and we sink into her sheets and suck and fuck and cum twice. Afterwards we talk about *The Exorcist* and *The Omen* and how Regan kicks Damien's ass, and how dark chocolate is the diamond to milk chocolate's coal, and how next time we want to shower together and soap-fuck.

When I stand to get dressed, she scooches up on her elbows and says, "Tell me about your wife."

I shudder. Fuck. No. I don't want to talk about Jolie. I don't want to think about Jolie. When I do, anxiety swoops in like a vampire and sucks away my dopamine, making everything as un-fucking-fun as possible. No. I'm with Lily now. Lily is spectacular. A willing distraction to everything wrong in my life. Jolie is not spectacular. Jolie is a buzzkill. And I can't talk about dinner when I just finished dessert.

"I plead the fifth."

Her face flickers into something nearly reminiscent of the Lily in photo #2. She looks out the window. "You don't have to say anything, Peter. Just like I don't have to fuck you."

Aggressive. *Hostile?*

"She's a handful."

Her frown vanishes. *She knows how to manipulate.* "Is she pretty?"

"Depends. On the outside she's angel cake. On the inside, torpedoes. She was wonderful when we first met…"

…like you…

"…but fell in hate with me after our daughter was born." The angel pilfers the devil's pitchfork and pokes my heart, making me think out loud: "You know…what's really strange is, and I don't understand why, but for the last couple days, ever since I saw you in the park, she's been *okay*. Doting, even."

Lily nods. She gets it. She's a woman. "Could be she feels guilty about something. Did you guys have a fight recently?"

"When do we not fight?"

"That bad, huh?"

I nod. "She's not well. Got pregnant at twenty-one and was sucked into a marriage with a man she wasn't in love with, all without her mother's support. A few months after having Rachel, she changed." *Changed.* "Went postal-partum. Batshit crazy. It was as if the pregger-particles in her brain just took over and turned her into a fucking madwoman, the very same Jolie I know and hate today."

She laughs and shifts her body and the sheet spills down, revealing a nipple. She pulls it back up, then taps the bed. I sit next to her, and she takes my hands in hers. "What do all women need?"

"If I knew that…"

"Love, Peter. We need love. And if she's not getting it at home…"

Wait. "Wait…are you saying that Jolie is being nice to me because she's having an affair?"

"Let me ask you a few questions. Does she often go out for hours at a time?"

"Well…sure. Besides work, she goes to the gym, has lunch with her friends, shopping, which is all fine by me. We do our best to stay away from each other."

"The gym?"

"Every day. She's got the goods to show for it too."

"Does she shop every day too?" She air-quotes "shop."

I shrug. "I don't know. Almost every day, I guess."

"What does she buy?"

Another shrug, the start of a pattern. "I don't know…clothes for Rachel, stuff for the apartment."

"Whose money is she spending?"

"What does this have to do with anything?"

"C'mon—humor me."

"She works at Saks. The money she earns is her spending money. I pay for everything else, the rent, nanny, bills."

"Ever see her paycheck?"

I shake my head. "She has direct deposit into her own account."

"What about credit cards? She have any?"

Lily's line of questioning is peripheral, bordering on nosy. But I'm in lust, so I continue to *humor her*. "Just one. Ours. We have a shared account which she uses to buy food and clothes for our daughter. She pays cash for everything else. Look, I really don't care what she does with her money, as long as there aren't any lavish charges on our shared account, which there aren't. We have a system, and it works, despite our mutual loathing."

"You ever give her any cash?"

Do I give her cash? Alarm bells ring. Uh-oh. Am I being played? Is Lily looking to get paid for our sex? Is that what this is about? A big fucking smoke-and-mirror show to earn a few bucks? Am I a fucking *john*?

The devil: *She works at Marge the Garage's fucking peepshow. What did you expect?* Fuck me. The devil is right. I've been had. And yet I can't ask her about it because our meeting at Stafford's was *coincidental*. "What are you driving at, Lily?"

She doesn't hesitate, immediately (and thankfully) proving my shotgun theory wrong: "I don't think either of you have any idea what the other is doing. Not that I'm complaining—we wouldn't be together if this weren't the case."

The devil: *When was the last time you and Jolie had sex? She has needs too.*

I nod. "Hmm…that's definitely something to chew on."

"You need to get proof."

"Proof?"

"Don't you want to know if she's screwing around?"

"I guess…" But finding out if Jolie is cheating (or not) doesn't really matter to me, even if up until yesterday I stayed faithful. I mean, I just slept with another woman; if she's fucking someone else behind my back, then mark it as the only thing we have in common besides Rachel. Besides, the only way into her private life is through her phone, and I don't have her PIN. "If she's been having an affair all this time, then why hasn't she left me?"

She laughs. "Hello? Peter? You're her cash-cow. Free rent, free support. She does what she wants, when she wants, and Peter, that question goes both ways. If you're so unhappy, then why haven't you left?"

"Because she'd suck me dry, and not in a good way. She'd also keep Rachel from me, and I can't let that happen."

I look at my phone. 4:45. Approaching the gray area Jolie might consider "dinnertime": the time she'll be back home from her day of...what? Working out? Shopping? *Fucking?* I excuse myself to the bathroom and unzip with the *no-door* wide open, then lean sideways and peer out. Lily is texting (*who?*) fast and furious, an *important* message. It occurs to me that I don't know anything about anyone else in her life. She never mentioned parents or siblings or friends or even a *boyfriend*. So, who? I zip up and exit with the realization that I really don't *know* her, and *who is she texting?*

She places her phone face-down on the bed, solemn face fast exchanged for a pleasant one. I could analyze that shift but I've neither the time nor the headspace for it right now.

"I've got to go."

"Meeting Jolie for dinner?"

I nod. She makes a pouty face. The devil is tired (but always inspired) and gives it a damn good try anyway: *Give her one more for the road. You've got it in you...*

The angel, energy preserved, gets right up in my face: *Go home and be with your wife. Now!*

I lean over and kiss Lily, then turn away from her before I'm tempted to give in to the devil's provocation. The dry-erase board I saw last night is still in my face. My phone number is there, but the oddly familiar phrase, CLICK ED IN MOON, is gone.

CHAPTER 25

I enter my apartment in silence. As an anxious newbie cheater, an intelligent, inconspicuous entrance is my only play.

Jolie's in Rachel's room, fussing with our little angel, chatting in toddler-speak. I find it humorous, the pitchy gibberish adults employ when conversing with a baby; fun fact: the idiocy of adult baby-babble is directly proportional to the age of the child; the younger the baby, the more delayed the adult sounds. For a moment I wonder (rather ludicrously) what might happen if I spoke in baby-tongue to an adult with the mentality of a three-year-old? Probably get my ass handed to me by his caretaker.

They didn't hear me come in, which is good because I'm not used to hauling so much dishonesty and guilt into my personal world. I take a deep breath, place my attaché on the kitchen table, heart pounding *one-one hundred. Just be yourself, Peter. Everything will be okay.* I can't tell if it's angel or devil speaking, but it's good advice. I break for the bathroom, lock the door, and lean against the sink for a minute, lips pursed, breathing…breathing…breathing. Once my heartbeat begins to settle, I drop trou and squat on the toilet, a place (and position) where solid, rational thoughts usually come easily.

Today, however, only thoughts of my afternoon with Lily play out.

Would you like to be with me again?

Fuck me Peter.

Are there times she goes out for hours at a time?

Fuck me Peter.

Is she spending your money?

Fuck me Peter.

I think Jolie is having an affair.

I baby-wipe my business (we're running low again and Jolie will positively yell at me for wiping my ass with them, *don't flush fucking wipes down the toilet*!), and exit the bathroom. She's still in Rachel's room. I call out, "How was your day, Jo?"

I cringe, expecting a verbal blow, but receive a humane response instead: "Good. Went to the gym—that's when I spoke to you—met a couple of the girls from Saks, shopped for Rachel, went for Thai."

"What did you buy?"

"Told you—some clothes for our daughter. She's growing like a weed." She changes the subject. "I brought you a dish from the restaurant. It's on the stove."

Dinner again? Three nights in a row now, this after zero nights in a row for over three years.

The devil, being a dick: *Three dinners, one for each time you came inside Lily Dahl. Insert devil emoji here.*

"Thank you," I say. It's all I can think of as I sit at the kitchen table before a still-warm tin plate.

She asks, "How was your afternoon?"

Here we go. I run my hands through my hair, hearing naivety in her voice. Or is it antipathy and sarcasm? Wishing and hoping for sincerity, I say, "Good." Went back to the village," (the truth), "grabbed a latte," (the truth), "took some pictures," (the truth). I open the plate from the restaurant. Smells delicious. My stomach growls despite being laden with anxiety. I didn't eat breakfast or lunch.

Just dessert.

After eating only half my dinner, and washing it down with a Porch Rocker (compliments of my *wife*), I shower and scrub away Lily's remnants for the second time today. *Déjà vu* from what…fifteen hours ago? I slip into a pair of lounge pants and enjoy the ego-boost of having heroically equaled my pop-count record of three times in one day. Dave Fisher would be proud. *I'm* proud.

I emerge from the bathroom feeling unexpectedly weak and drowsy, arms like dumbbells, feet like sandbags. Jolie and Rachel are on the sofa in front of the TV, watching *Blue's Clues*.

I give Rachel a half-dozen smooches on her head, then look at Jolie.

Does she know?

She beckons me with a *come here* finger and a pucker. I (cautiously) lean over. She kisses me on the lips and, like magic, my fear is washed away. I'm at peace, *PHEW!*, here in *my* castle with *my* wife and *my* child, enjoying a quality moment.

Our evening of *togetherness* progresses peacefully (free of all MS-types), and thoughts of Lily fade into a dim notion. Rachel is all giggles and kisses. Jolie, despite having a micro-tantrum over half my Thai going in the garbage, is being mostly pleasant. This familial scenario is everything I've always wanted: a refuge of love and security. *Love.* Given the excitement of the last couple days, spending time with this repaired version of Jolie is a welcome relief.

She's having an affair…

I can't stop thinking about it. I shouldn't give a shit, but I do, and my suspicion rises, with a demented part of me wanting to spoil the moment with an argument over who she's fucking. But that would make me the worst kind of hypocrite. So, I don't. Instead, Jolie surprises me with a man-sized portion of Ben and Jerry's vanilla bean topped with whipped cream and chocolate syrup; she and Rachel prefer chocolate and enjoy smaller helpings. *Dessert.* I savor every bite and use a napkin to wipe away the chocolate running down Rachel's chin.

After we finish, Jolie gets Rachel ready for bed and I clean the dishes. I feel abnormally spent, *exhausted;* I suppose this is what happens when you have sex three times in one day. By the time Jolie returns from the bedroom, I'm a useless jellyfish. She's wearing a *pink* negligee and a lace corset that lifts her golden 34B's into perfect velvet half-moons. I look and I *want* (it's been two years...no, wait...two *hours*, but *still*), but my eyes are starting to close and...I think I'm seeing a trend here. *Pink.*

She starts a movie on Netflix and snuggles with me. I put an arm around her and she kisses my neck and I cup a breast through the lacy fabric of her nightie. This is the first time I've touched her in a long time...but it's futile. I'm tapped. Can barely stay awake. My consciousness drifts, eyelids turning to lead, the opening credits to the movie blurring into snowflakes until there's only blackness that willfully surrenders to nightmares of Lily calling my cell phone, and Jolie picking up.

CHAPTER 26

I wake up, sleep-stoned. It's mostly dark, save for the beam of light bleeding in at the curtain's edge: just enough daylight to reveal I slept in the TV room all night. I sit up…and my head spins, *again!* Nausea tosses my gut. I've got another mysterious hangover, just like yesterday morning, and the morning before. I don't feel feverishly sick, there are no body aches. It's not like I'm coming down with anything. It's more of an *askew* feeling that's nudging me off-balance, making me feel sick to my stomach.

I struggle to my feet and have to take hold of the sofa to recapture my balance. I watch the time, 12:45 p.m., breathing *one one-hundred two one-hundred* until the headspins subside. I stumble to the fridge, grab a bottle of Poland Spring, and chug it in seconds.

When I close the door, I see a new Post-it note from Jolie:

Took Rachel out for breakfast.

Lily's affair theory flashes back to me, but I'm hypocritical and vague and incapable of pondering any sense into it right now. So, I focus on more immediate matters, for one, coffee. As it brews, I steal into my darkroom with my attaché. There's a two-foot space behind the filing cabinet where I sometimes keep my camera out of harm's (Jolie's) way. She's thrown things at me in the past just because they were within reaching distance, so best be safe than sorry.

The front door opens.

Rachel's little pitter-patter, then, "Daddy?"

"I'll be right out..." I hide my camera away (filled with pictures of Lily), then meet my family in the kitchen. Rachel leaps into my arms, smothering me with hugs and kisses. Jolie helps herself to the fresh brew I made.

"I had Froot Loops at the diner with Mommy."

Jolie, mug of joe in hand, saunters over and grants me a peck on the cheek. "I need you to watch Rachel this afternoon—no sitter at the gym on Sundays." She disappears into the bedroom.

The devil bursts in: *She's having an affair.*

The angel intercedes: *Spend some time with your daughter.*

On a whim, I say, "I was thinking of visiting my dad today." Rachel hasn't seen her papa in a few weeks, and a beautiful day poolside at Nick's place could do me some good.

"Great! Please give Nick my love."

Your what?

She calls out, "I haven't been able to get in touch with Carmen all weekend. Can you try her?"

Now she wants me to call? "How many days has she been out?"

"Four, and she's playing hard to get."

"Not a good sign."

"No shit, pumpkin-eater. I'll legit lose my job if I have to take another day off."

I pick Rachel up, her baby-butt soft in my fatherly embrace. "Do you want to visit with Papa today?"

She nods, puts a finger in her nose, and shouts, "Pumpkin-eater!"

Great. "Let's try giving Carmen a call first. See how she's feeling." Questioning our nanny's dependability is something I've never had to do before, but she's called in sick more in the last week than she has in the past two years.

I grab my cell…

(…the devil moves to speak, but I already know what it's thinking…)

…and power it down.

"Jo…my phone's dead. Can I use yours?"

No response. She heard me. She's fifteen feet away, and the door is open.

"Hello? Jolie?"

"What is it?" Her getting-angry voice, edging into frame.

"You just told me to call Carmen, but my phone is dead. Can I use yours?" Again, no response. Time to push a button: the only way to get immediate action out of her. "Jolie—?"

She emerges in full gym gear, cell phone in hand. "Forget it…I'll call."

I watch closely as she punches in her PIN and brings up Carmen's number. When she turns and puts the phone to her ear, I react fast and snatch it out of her hand. The look on her face (mouth agape, eyes stunned wide-the-fuck-open) is priceless, as if the threat of me smashing it on the floor is real. She lunges, barking, "Give it back!" then grabs my wrist and we begin wrestling like movie foes fighting over control of a gun.

Rachel screams, "No, Mommy!" She charges at Jolie, tears on full blast, stomping and clawing at her yoga pants. Jolie lets go of my hand, takes a weak swing at me and misses, then utters *fuck* under her breath before stooping down to pick up Rachel. My window of opportunity has arrived. I dart into the bathroom and lock the door.

Holy shit. Jolie's unlocked phone is in my hand.

Don't you want to know if she's screwing around?

One one-hundred, two one-hundred, three one-hundred…

There's a rapid knock on the door. Of course there is. "Peter…what are you doing?" She joggles the knob, knocks again. "Peter!"

I shout, "Keep it down, I'm calling Carmen." I put it on speaker so Jolie can hear, then tap the messenger icon. Jolie's texts come up and I start scrolling. I go back almost a week, looking over a long list of names, Debbie, Kelly, Susana, Marcy, all familiar work-slash-gym friend names. I'm included among them, *Pumpkin-Eater*. What a bitch. I check her call log. Same list of usual suspects.

But no texts or calls from (or to) Carmen.

...she called in sick again...

So, Jolie lied. She may have deleted the record, but what's the motive in that? Meanwhile, the call to Carmen goes to voicemail and I hear her recorded voice from when she used to return our calls. I'm about to move onto Jolie's photo gallery when I notice something odd in her call log. On Saturday, 2:42 a.m., she made a call to a number with no saved contact name, a 646 exchange, New York City.

I dial Carmen's number again, keep it on speaker.

Another knock on the door, this one more aggressive. "What the fuck, Peter?" Rachel's cries are growing more aggressive as well and Jolie shouts at her, "Just a minute honey! Okay?"

The second call also goes to voice mail.

Now she's pounding on the door. "PETER!"

I yell, "I'm leaving Carmen a message!" which I do, then disconnect the line and repeat the 646 number over and over in my head, like one one-hundred, two one-hundred, three one-hundred, only with an actual phone number. My brain tic, finally coming in handy.

I open the door and a familiar visage is there, one filled with piss, vinegar, and exasperation. I've encountered this face too-many-times-to-count over the last three years. It's usually followed with an argument I can't win. With dexterity, she snatches her phone from my hand and spins away, no doubt choking back a choice range of vulgarities. "I'm leaving," she hisses, and then, like the Jolie of all-the-time, slams the door on the way out.

And…here I stand, in silent rejection, casting away all inklings of Jolie being a changed woman. I repeat out loud the 646 number from her outgoing calls, once, twice, three times…then power up my phone and tap it in. As the call connects, it hits me: Jolie made the call at 2:42 a.m. Saturday morning…around the same time I heard the phone ringing inside Lily's apartment.

Can't be, can it?

The phone number rings once, after which a familiar *do-do-do* chime notifies me that the number I just dialed is no longer in service.

The angel and devil agree: *Jolie lied to you about Carmen calling in sick, and it's preposterous to think the outgoing call she made at 2:42 a.m. was to Lily Dahl.*

CHAPTER 27

Just for the record, I'm a good dad. I've taken every bit of energy typically reserved for being a husband, and have diverted it toward nurturing Rachel. Today is no exception. After a cup of coffee and quick shower to help erase my lightheadedness, I feed her, put her in a sundress of pale pink and yellow flowers, then race from room to room packing a day-trip bag: panties, diapers (just in case), swimsuit, snacks, kid books, and a sippy-cup filled with cold milk. I have a little trek in mind, one quick stop before heading out to Nick's place in Long Beach.

Jolie's gym.

The seeds Lily planted in my head have budded into something worth watering. Time to see what Jolie is really up to.

You need proof…

One foot out the door and I almost forgot. I've missed opportune moments in the past and have vowed to be forever armed and ready should something point-and-click worthy cross my path. I retrieve my attaché from behind the darkroom filing cabinet and shoulder it along with the diaper bag. With Rachel in one arm and a fold-away stroller in the other, we exit the apartment to the gap-toothed grin of the ancient man in 4F. You know, the one that smells like cauliflower and has ear hair like cat's eyebrows?

He says (shouts, really) to Rachel, "Well hello there, young lady! My name's Garvin! What's yours?" She rightly buries her face in my armpit. I would too; his breath has a chicken-soup waft to it and the corners of his mouth are white with foamy residue. The thought of getting into the elevator with him makes me want to kill myself. But my hands are full, and I need someone to push the button for me.

"Rachel, be nice to our neighbor."

She shakes her head vehemently, smearing spit in my pit.

The old man laughs and presses the button. The door dings and we enter and from this moment forward I vow to never eat cauliflower again. Or chicken soup. I place Rachel down and, ignoring her clawing pleads to be picked back up, remove my camera and ask Garvin for his picture. He obliges with a fervent "Sure!" and a rictus grin only a corpse could love. If I'm going to torture myself in this moment, I might as well get something out of it.

Point.

Click.

Once outside, the fresh air hits me like, well, a breath of fresh air. Couldn't come any sooner. The Central Park Sports Club is only three blocks away. I've never been one for working out; to me the reward is not worth the effort, or the sore muscles. Unless, of course, that workout involves Lily Dahl. Grins.

With Rachel secured in her stroller, we pass Jolie's coffee shop of choice, The Busy Bean. I peer through the window but there's no sign of her, just a long line of uppity-ups—like myself—waiting to pay eight bucks for a venti Sumatra. No Stafford Coffee granola hippie activist types in this neck of the woods.

The Central Park Sports Club is home to more than just state-of-the-art weightlifting equipment. It's a theme park for healthy adults. They've got a smoothie bar, a sitting room, a health-food eatery, aerobics rooms, spin rooms, yoga rooms, rooms that cater to all kinds of self-improvement pursuits. With a half block of floor-to-ceiling windows looking out from the second floor, at least two-dozen patrons can absorb a sun-kissed view of Central Park while treadmilling to nowhere.

My hands are full and with Rachel in her stroller, my only option is the elevator. I wonder who I'll be sharing personal space with this time? I enter the vestibule to the gym. Alongside the elevator are a set of steps, a high-traffic area of overly fit gym-bunnies coming and going. Sometimes I wonder if the world might be a better place if certain people were purged. Now is one of those times.

The elevator doors slide open, promising me a solo trip to the second floor. Who was it that once said promises were made to be broken? Well, shoot that guy. As soon as the doors begin to shut, a hand the size of a baseball mitt wedges in, granting access to a man who's as wide as he is tall. Rachel looks like a Cabbage Patch doll next to him.

"Sup," he grunts. He's wearing a way-too-small spaghetti-strap tank top that does nothing to cover his massive muscles, obscene layers of thew and sinew stretching his way-too-tan skin (and tank top) to the limit. He's a walking tree-trunk, a human mountain with meandering tree-roots for veins.

We make eye-contact. He nods. Again says, "Sup."

"Sup," I respond, knowing but then not knowing what I'm actually saying, or for that matter, what he's saying. Is he saying hello? Is he designating me for dinner? Taking his picture could very well be one of the bravest things I've ever done. But I'm too afraid to ask, too afraid he might use me for some awful pre-workout ritual. *Sup.*

So, I do the dirty on the D-L.

Point.

Click.

He shoots me daggers, anabolic pupils big, black, and drilling. Thankfully the doors glide open, and he departs, bobble-head shaking up and down, beefsteak neck pulsing as he vanishes into the land of muscles, tendons, and sweat.

Before me is a desk with two pretty girls behind it. They could be sisters with their matching Central Park Health Club tees, lean figures, and chinaware skin. Healthy living has done these two good.

Rachel protests, "I don't want the gym. I want to see Papa."

Both of the girls smile. One of them says, "Oooh, I'm sorry. We don't have sitting services on Sunday."

I smile back as charmingly as I can: a guppy spreading its tail. "I'm not here to work out."

The gravity falls from their faces. Does not being one for the lifestyle make me less interesting? Probably. "I'm looking for my wife…Jolie Delmonico? She's not answering her cell, never does when she's pumping iron." I simulate working out by thrusting my fists in the air: a very poor impersonation of someone more fit than me. That, or a 1970s *Soul Train* dancer.

"Oh sure!" she says, then peeks over the counter to Rachel. "Hi there, cutie-pie!"

Rachel wriggles her fingers shyly then takes a swig of milk from her sippy-cup. Before her brain tells her mouth to swallow, her eyes narrow and she sneezes. Tepid milk sprays my knees: dairy buckshot.

"Peter? What are you doing here?"

Jolie emerges from the sea of healthy people bearing three dark sweat-circles and a white hand-towel around her neck, blonde tresses tied up into a bun, no makeup under bright overheads seeing beyond her anger, toward her natural beauty. It's simple moments like this where I am reminded of the ardent feelings we once shared, days long surrendered to three years of vitriol and disgust.

She crouches to Rachel's level. "Is everything okay, honey?"

"I wanna go to Papa's."

She looks at me, confused. "I thought you were going to your dad's?"

Devil on my left: *Fake it till you make it.*

"I...*we* wanted to surprise you." I lean down into her. "I didn't like the way we left things off this morning. You've been so nice to me these past few days. I just want to keep things moving in that direction."

Her *what-the-fuck* look moves into uncharted territory: the type of face one might make after hearing an alien abduction account. She stands, wipes the sweat from her forehead, then feigns happiness with a fake-as-fuck, "Awwwwwwwa."

It's how we roll.

So, to twist things up a little more (because why the fuck not?), I lean forward, cup my hand on her damp waist, and press my lips against hers, marking my territory, one one-hundred, two one-hundred. To everyone, I'm just a husband or boyfriend kissing his better half. But to Jolie, my kiss is an uncertain ploy, the look of confusion (and perhaps disgust) on her face demonstrable evidence of this. Whoever thought kissing your wife could do such a thing?

She looks over her shoulder into the gym area, then peers back at me. "What the fuck was that?"

I ignore the question and turn my thoughts into an impulse, demanding more than asking, "Where are you going after your workout?"

She squints and grins. "Probably home to enjoy some quiet time without the two of you to fuck it all up." Tears well in her eyes. "Anything else? I have to get back to my workout."

You cold bitch! "You cold bitch..."

She hunkers down and kisses Rachel. "I'm mad at Daddy, honey. Not you. You know I love you, right?" She looks up at me with poisoned daggers. "Daddy not so much." She stands and walks away and if there were a door between us, she'd be slamming it right...about...*now.*

Moral of the story: she's here, doing what she said she'd be doing.

Being Jolie.

CHAPTER 28

Back on 5th Avenue, I cast my gaze through the second story window and watch as Jolie takes an open spot. She's speaking to someone through her Air Pods, phone clutched in a gesturing fist, head shaking back and forth. The conversation screams of *intense*. I keep my eyes on her until she backs off the treadmill seconds later, out of my field of view.

Who the hell is she talking to? I try calling her, but it goes straight to voicemail. Better off. I have nothing left to say to her that wouldn't result in another argument.

The devil goads: *She's having an affair.*

We grab a cab to Penn Station. The driver, a grizzled Middle Eastern man, spends the entire twelve minutes unveiling the benefits of smoking Beedi, a type of hand-rolled herbal cigarette consisting of cloves, ground betel nut, and tobacco. A perfect conversation piece to share when a toddler is present. Once at Penn, with Rachel in her stroller and my camera around my neck, we enter through the 34th Street access. Like the subway, weekends are best for securing shooting prospects without throngs of commuters clogging the view. As soon as the escalator touches down, I hit the jackpot.

My focus is on one of Manhattan's mentally ill nomads. He's made Penn Station's pavilion his stage to the world, performing an almost-in-tune a cappella version of "Unchained Melody," all the while doing a zealous jig, arms spread helicopter-style beneath a stained and tattered raincoat, bare leathery soles beating a choppy rhythm on the dirty floor. He's holding an empty coffee cup, vain hope for a handout.

Point.

Click.

We stroll into Duane Reade for drinks, snacks, and a pair of socks for the homeless guy. I'm a judgmental goof, guilty as charged. I like poking fun at others. It adds to my creative stamina and empowers my sense of humor as I decide whose images should be captured in time. But when I set all that aside, I maintain a soft spot for those less fortunate than me. Armed with water bottles, protein bars, and a pair of tube socks, I head back to where our crooner is performing to his audience of none. I hold out a water bottle and motion for him to take it. He two-steps toward me, snatches it in mid-dance, and shoves it into his raincoat pocket. I hold out the socks. He dance-takes those too, but leaves the protein bar behind.

"You can have this too," I say, extending my hand.

He croons, "I don't like strawberry!" then dances away, laughing.

An overhead announcement informs me that the train to Long Beach is boarding, track 20.

I ask Rachel, "Ready to go see Papa?"

She replies with a vigorous nod.

The train is crowded, and I'm resigned to standing in the vestibule by the doors. Rachel is seated alongside me in her stroller, happily munching on a strawberry protein bar and washing it down with milk from her sippy-cup.

I look around.

A couple clandestine shots are imminent.

Subject one: seated diagonally from me is a guy in his mid-thirties, positively overweight with clusters of pockmarks marring his patchy-haired face. He's wearing a too-small denim jacket and attached to his jeans is a worn leather thing that's attached to a chain that's attached to a withered belt loop in the back. He's a near-middle-aged disappointment who's probably never been laid but can give you detailed directions to every porn site on the internet. He's one of *those guys*.

Subject two: sitting next to our disappointment is his diametrical opposite. She's in her late twenties, raven hair with matching lipstick and broad eyeliner. Ashen breasts oozing from a gray leather tank top, pewter ankh slung from a chain around her neck, nestled in the heart of it all. Face like the beautiful dark goddess she is.

Subject one's beady eyes twist into a sideways glance, drilling lasers from subject two's raven hair down to her milk-toned calves: a desperate attempt to develop x-ray vision. He picks up the small gym bag nestled between his ankles on the floor and situates it on his lap. Presuming her familiarity with this predicament, and of course that female sixth-sense thing, one can assume that subject two is indisputably aware of what subject one is up to. But she doesn't flinch. She's been through this before. She's a champ.

Point.

Click.

The click of the camera reminds me of my distraction, Lily Dahl. The stranger I had sex with three times yesterday, whose image crowds the film in my camera, whose phone number is as much a mystery as she is. I mentally inventory everything I know about her: Twenty-seven years of age, graduated Miami-Dade Community with a two-year nursing degree, worked at an assisted living home in Queens, currently employed by an on-call at-home elderly care service. She likes horror movies and grunge, is hot and likes to fuck. Other than twice visiting her 4th Street studio, my knowledge of her is limited to the few hours we've spent together.

Devil on my left: *Search her ass on the internet, moron.*

I am a moron! Eff me! I recap the last seventy-two hours and realize that I'd spent most of my free time either in Lily's midst, or in a fatigued stupor. There hasn't been an opportune moment to dig until now.

As the train pulls into the Jamaica station, I pull up my phone's browser and begin the hunt. There's a couple dozen Lily Dahl's on Facebook and Instagram, half of them in Europe, none are my girl. There's a movie with a main character named Lily Dahl, and a mid-tier actress with the same name, just enough not-my-Lily to clog up the search results.

I look down at Rachel. She's fast asleep now, a half-eaten protein bar in her hand, strawberry smudge on her lips. I peek at subjects one and two. His hands are missing, and he's sweating up a storm. She's using a mirrored compact to apply another gothic layer to her lips. The conductor comes through, checking tickets, announcing Long Beach as the next stop. In the few minutes it takes to arrive there, I wonder if I'll ever hear from Lily Dahl again.

CHAPTER 29

Let me take five to tell you about Nick Delmonico. He's my favorite person in the world *(...your practiced lie...)*. He used to share that distinction with my mom, but cancer ate her stomach and took her away from us a few weeks shy of her fifty-fifth birthday. That was fifteen years ago. Since then, Nick has been my ride-or-die *(...will be as long as he keeps on TRYING...)*.

Nick has lived well. Spent thirty years killing it on Wall Street then cruised the world with my mom till her dying day *(...she never protected you, six-seven-eight...)*. He lives alone with his golden lab Brutus who provides all the companionship he needs. He prefers it that way, and I can't say I blame him.

(...anticipation triggers memories of you, six-seven-eight...).

His home at 426 Beacon Lane is a gorgeous Dutch Colonial with five bedrooms, four baths, and a sunroom with attached pool landscaped out of something you'd see in *Better Homes and Gardens*; he's got the good life, money, health, and happiness. Yes, he can get curmudgeonly at times (post-Mom, he's eased to just-a-little curmudgeonly), but he's still my dad, and I love him *(love?)*. Aside from Rachel, he's all I've got.

(...he's been TRYING, ever since nine, six-seven-eight is a blur and with distraction, disappears...)

We catch an Uber at the Long Beach station. The driver is cordial with no extreme mannerisms or peculiarities, which is fine by me. Thanks to the LIRR, I've met my quota of "Freaks &

Geeks" for the day. We pull onto Beacon Lane, and I roll down my window and take a deep breath of crisp Atlantic Ocean air, savoring Long Island's beachfront ecology; gulls squawking in the distance; ocean waves crashing against the sand; the gentle taste of salt on my tongue. You can't buy this feeling in the city.

I call Nick from the head of the driveway because it's sometimes tough getting a signal so close to the beach. No doubt he's spending this gorgeous Sunday afternoon poolside, working on his tan. The driver pulls forward and that's when Nick emerges from the front door with the phone still attached to his ear. He's wearing white swim trunks, an aqua tank top, and flip-flops. He stomps down the walkway grinning ear-to-ear *(…guilt…)*, arms spread wide *(…forgive me…)*. That's because I have his granddaughter in tow today.

Rachel screams "Papa!" from the back seat, waving energetically with both hands. I open the door and she races out, blonde curls bouncing up and down like little Slinkys. Brutus barks excitedly from behind the storm door, tongue and nose painting a viscous smear the glass.

"Come here you little cupcake!" His smile is all veneers, glimmering against a tanned face. She launches herself into his arms, unbothered by the tufts of hair sprouting from his shoulders. He groans as he picks her up and something goes *crack!* inside his body.

BELT.

I tip the driver and we all head inside for a day of "R and R," something I desperately need. Brutus keeps up his gleeful woofing and performs a clumsy pirouette around us as we head into the kitchen.

Nick purchased Beacon Manor (as I like to call it) soon after my mom passed. All the wonderful *(…painful…)* memories they shared for twenty-eight years turned into heartrending reminiscences for Nick, compelling him to make a lifestyle change before depression earned the upper hand. He keeps everything in pristine condition, hiring a variety of workers to lift fingers for him: landscapers, pool maintenance, in-home assistance to cook, clean, and run errands. Nick has a Range Rover, but still prefers others to do his bidding. Why not? He can afford it.

Rachel points out the back door and shouts, "I want to go swimming!"

Nick replies, "Lunch first, honey."

"I'm not hungry!"

"She ate a protein bar on the train." I look at my daughter and remind myself to be thankful she looks more like me than Jolie. I know. It's a skewed thought. But can you imagine having to be forever reminded of the one person you can't fucking stand when they're not around? "How about you go watch TV, and after we eat we'll all go in the pool. Sound good?"

She nods and heads off into the living room. Nick and I sit at the kitchen table and catch up over egg sandwiches and coffee. We talk about my career, Rachel and her frequent bedwetting, and finally Jolie and how she and I haven't been getting along. I've kept my despairing relationship a secret from Nick, too ashamed to share my troubles with the very man who took care of my mother till her dying day *(...six-seven-eight...?)*. But now I feel the need to divulge, to reveal my ongoing problem. It's as if my brief time spent with Lily, an initial step toward escaping my toxic marriage, is also acting as a catalyst to making my personal dilemma known to my father.

"Divorce just isn't in the cards right now," I say. "It wouldn't be fair to Rachel."

"It's also not fair for her to be brought up in an environment filled with resentment and hostility. Why do you think she still wets the bed?"

Nick's right. If there ever was a catch-22, this is it. I plead my case: "The number-one problem is money. Jolie doesn't bring anything to the table. She can't afford to raise Rachel without my support. Not in Manhattan, anyway. She could move in with her mom in Jersey, but then I'd rarely see Rachel anymore," *because I can't bear to look at Susan's wrinkled cunt-face.* "And she won't go down without a fight. On more than one occasion she's threatened to 'drain me dry,' minus a few indecorous words." It's hard to imagine the battles that would ensue should Jolie and I start making moves to divide our (my) assets. Money—or lack thereof—can bring out the worst in a person, and if I have yet to see Jolie at her worst…

"I know a good divorce attorney—"

I raise my hands into a time-out. "That would complicate everything, and I can't go there right now. It's hard enough just making ends meet. The rent on the apartment, the bills, the nanny…"

"The nanny is an expense you can do without. If Jolie isn't using her paycheck to contribute, then what good is it to have hired help? There's nothing wrong with her being a full-time mother and housewife."

That gives me a chuckle, and for all the wrong reasons. "She wouldn't agree. But something's come up. Our nanny Carmen. She called in sick last week, and now isn't returning our calls."

Nick nods. "There you go. Problem solved. Cut Carmen loose and pay Jolie instead. I'm sure it's more than what she's making now, and all she has to do is stay home with her daughter."

"And clean the house, which she'd rather pour sand in her eyes than do. I agree it's a good idea, but I've broached the subject before, and it didn't go over very well."

"I went through a similar situation with Gail, my housekeeper. She decided to move back to California to be with her parents a few weeks ago."

"No kidding?" I look around. "Your place is clean, though."

"New help. Linda."

"Where'd you find her?"

He hesitates, looks down, then says, "A recommendation. From a friend." He stands up and starts clearing the table. "She works three days a week, cooks, cleans, does everything Gail used to do." He pauses…then digresses with an awkward wink: "You know, she's a real looker."

"Nick. Eww. No."

The angel: *You've got more women in your life than you can handle right now, anyway*. True story.

While Nick puts the dishes in the sink, I go into the living room where Rachel is preoccupied with *PAW Patrol*. It's here I notice for the first time a small security camera above the front door, looking over the living room and kitchen. "Nick…when did you get that?"

He comes into the living room. "Had it professionally installed a couple months ago. Got a full system with cameras in the backyard, driveway, there's one upstairs too. They record movement. Come on, I'll show you."

He leads me upstairs to where three of the five bedrooms and two of the four bathrooms are located. One of the bedrooms acts as an office, one is a furnished guest room: my future home should I ever need it. He unlocks the office. *Why is there a lock on the door? There never used to be.* Inside is a desk supporting a computer monitor, a standing lamp, filing cabinet, and other workspace accompaniments. He dons a pair of readers, enters a pin on his phone, and performs a few leisurely swipes.

"Look," he says, showing me a live image of Rachel on the couch in the living room. The video is crystal clear. She's watching *Sponge Bob* now, much to my chagrin.

"Great clarity."

He swipes again to another camera's point of view. Now I'm looking at an image of me and Nick, looking at the phone. I glance around but don't see a camera.

"It's in the lamp. Pass your hand in front of the shade."

I wave my right hand across a row of faux jewels circling the lampshade. The close-up image of my face on Nick's phone turns dark. I lean in close and notice that one of the jewels is slightly different, a fish-eye lens.

"Each camera on the property keeps a record of all movement." He scrolls through what looks like a long list of links and randomly taps one. "This is from two weeks ago." The video shows a man wearing cargo shorts and a white tee, cleaning the pool.

"This is cool. You should've done this years ago." I'm impressed with Nick's resourcefulness, and am pleased he's taken measures to protect himself.

(...he didn't protect six-seven-eight...)

He's TRYING.

"I never had a reason to get it done till now."

Okay... "What are you talking about?"

He steps to the closet and opens it. Inside are wool winter coats, cashmere sweaters, and a few lightweight parkas. He spreads them aside to reveal a wall of painted sheetrock. With both hands, he slides the wall to the left, revealing a combination safe about the size of a mini-fridge. Now I know why he keeps this room locked.

"Who installed that for you?"

"Did it myself, and for good reason." Nick was damn handy back in the day and could fix just about anything requiring hand tools. He punches in a seven-digit code on the digital keypad and the door pops open. My jaw drops when I see the contents. Cash, and lots of it.

He removes a bundle of hundreds and tosses it to me. "That's ten grand."

It's heavy, as thick as a brick and sexy as hell. I peek past my dad into the safe; there's a lot more where it came from. My heart picks up speed. This is way too much cash to keep in the house. There's also a black velvet bag in the safe, which he tells me contains all of my mother's jewelry.

"Now you know why I had the security system installed."

I hand him back the ten-grand stack, which he promptly returns to the mother lode. "Why do you have all this here?"

"There's five hundred fifty thousand in cash, and about eighty grand in jewelry. Should something happen to me and I end up in hospice like your mom, I don't want my money to go to waste. More than half my liquidity went to your mother's treatments and nursing home bills. If I get sick, let the state pay for it. What I have left, I want you and Rachel to have. If anything, it'll help pay for your divorce."

(…he's TRYING he regrets six-seven-eight this is his final plea for forgiveness so you six-seven-eight have to TRY as well…)

"Dad…" *Dad.* Tears well in my eyes. What a jumble of emotions I'm feeling, the gratefulness of my *favorite person* stirred together with thoughts of losing him one day. It's a lot to absorb. Still fixated on the cash, I say, "You can't feel comfortable having all this money in the house."

"The safe is well hidden, the door is always locked, and you're the only person I've ever shown it to. It's wedge-anchored to a cement foundation with a threaded rod and epoxy running through the center. It's not going anywhere. If anyone tries, I've got them on video." He points to the lamp, then folds his arms and says, "You'll never have to worry about money, son." *Son.* His voice trails off and his eyes turn toward the closet, face steeped in what could be sadness.

Or guilt?

"Nick?"

He flaps a hand in my direction and changes the subject. "Do you remember our old phone number? From when you were growing up?"

"Sure. Four-two-three-seven-two-six-nine."

"That's the combination to the safe."

"Is that smart?"

"It is if you don't want to forget it."

From downstairs: "Daddy…I want to go swimming!"

Nick reaches into the safe, peels off five C-notes and hands them to me. "Here's a little wallet money for you. Now c'mon, let's go for a swim."

The rest of the afternoon is spent sunning, swimming, and playing fetch on the beach with Brutus. We share a ton of laughs, snacks, a pitcher of iced tea, and before long, dinnertime rolls around.

I wonder what Jolie is doing.

The devil exclaims: *She's having an affair.*

I wonder what Lily is doing.

The angel replies: *Not thinking about you.*

As we head back into the house, I look up at the security camera above the sliding doors. I wave to it, then enter the sunroom, where I left my phone.

No texts, no missed calls.

CHAPTER 38

After packing up Rachel's things, we bid farewell to Nick and Brutus. Rachel shuns a kiss from her papa but happily allows the lab to make a mess of her face. I baby-wipe her clean (for the most part), then give Nick a power-hug. He's never been the touchy-feely type,

(...unless the BELT was in his hand...)

but today allows me all the time I need to tell him I love him *(love!)* and that *maybe* deep down inside *I forgive him*.

The return trip to Manhattan is uneventful and I turn my thoughts back to Lily. Lily and her hotness, Lily and her loving touch, Lily and her relationship advice: *Does she go out for hours at a time? Ever see her paycheck? Don't you want to know if she's screwing around?* As my mind wanders and considers, Rachel sleeps; a few hours swimming in the sun will do that to a toddler. From car to train to taxi to apartment, she awakes only as I seat her in the stroller for the elevator ride back up to 4C.

"We have to get you into the shower, dirty-bird." God knows I need one too.

Upon entering my building, I'm reminded of Nick's security system by the camera peering down at me from the entranceway. It's been there for as long as I've been here, and I wonder for a moment if it works the same way, if it too records the comings and goings of everyone passing through the door…but my wonderment doesn't last very long because, *shit-for-brains,* of course it does.

It's a little after 6:00 p.m. and the elevator is jam-packed with tenants heading out for dinner or a stroll through Central Park. With no one behind us, we luck into a solo trip to the fourth floor. To our home. Where Jolie awaits. I wonder which version of her I'm in store for tonight? I hope it's *Nice-Jolie* with another dinner, maybe some dessert, and maybe, just maybe, we can finish what we almost started last night. Maybe. I unlock the door and enter the apartment. All is quiet, save for the sound of running water in the bathroom.

She's in the shower.

Sitting on the kitchen table are her gym bag and purse.

Don't you want to know if she's screwing around?

Her gym bag is usually locked away at the sports club, and only visits home to swap out the dirty for the clean. This is me getting lucky, the opportunity before me a rare one, my mind's eye seeing a marquee spotlighting my wife's things: *Important stuff here! One night only! Don't miss out!*

"Rachel, why don't you go to your room and read some books while Daddy makes dinner?" *While Daddy rifles through Mommy's shit.* "Grilled cheese sound good?"

She gives me a spit-coated thumbs up and skips off into her room.

Sometimes life offers us choices and it's so easy to take the path of least resistance, where blind eyes turn, and suspicions are swept under rugs. But in my head I hear Kennedy's moon speech, *we do things not because they are easy, but because they are hard,* and with that veer not toward the path of least resistance, but toward the path less-traveled, the path of *this-could-really-fuck-things-up.* And really fucking things up, without really trying, is a really hard thing to do. Really. But you know what?

I'm gonna do it anyway because that's what I do. Fuck things up.

It's like this: with the shower still running, I unzip Jolie's gym bag and find bike shorts, leggings, and sports bras, an empty water bottle, a combo lock, a membership card to the Central Park Sports Club. Running the length of the inner lining is a zipper with a visible bulge. I open it. Inside I find a small faux-leather handbag.

It has some weight to it.

I unzip it...

...there are papers inside.

I start leafing through them...

...oh my god...

Does she have credit cards?

...it must be an illusion, what I'm seeing, it has to be, because no one with even a shred of sanity would choose to amass the mountain of debt I'm looking at: credit card bills, charge card statements, late notices, collection notices, enough of them to choke a fucking shredder.

Some are in Jolie Delmonico's name, and some are in my name. Some are variations thereof: Peter Jo-Delmonico. Jody Delmonico. Jolie Demonic, that one's so fucking fitting. The balances are petrifying: Saks Fifth Ave, $12,683. Bloomingdales, $7876, Macy's $9403. The list goes on and on, statements from dozens of retail locations, Visas, Mastercards, the pile is thicker than one of Nick's ten-grand stacks, the balances an endless path disappearing into a horizon of debt. They're all addressed here, my home, and I'm the one who takes in the mail at the end of each day, so how the fuck did I miss all these?

The angel and devil, in unison: *She checks the mail every day before you do!*

Fuck! I'm choking, bracing for puke. If my adulterous wrongdoing is heartburn, then this is mother-fucking stomach cancer. I keep flipping through the bills, counting out loud, "One fucking-one-hundred, two fucking-one-hundred, three fucking-one-hundred," only now I'm counting all the dust motes replacing my father's inheritance. *What the ever-loving-fuck Jolie, you destructive calamity-cunt!*

There's another zipper in the bag. Inside, another black pouch. Here I find all the credit cards that match the statements, two rubber-banded stacks fifty-some-odd-deep with embossed logos to almost every fucking retailer in Manhattan, with more variations of Jolie's married and maiden names, of *my fucking name,* and if there ever was a rock-bottom to be hit, there's even one in Rachel's name. What. The. Fuck.

I'm beyond pissed and for sure will puke in the short term, but my anger somehow helps me choke it back. I keep digging and unearth no bonus gym-bag goodies. But her purse is now fair game. I dump all the contents onto the kitchen table. Items clatter and fall, cell phone, makeup pens, two twenties, three singles, some spare change. Inside, another a side zipper. I open it.

Something in here…I remove it.

A…*burner*?

Is she having an affair?

I flip it open, and it asks me to "scan fingerprint." *No time.* I shut it and quickly shove it into my front pocket. I keep searching. At the bottom, concealed by yet another secretive side zipper (side zippers: the zippers that hold secrets), I find one last item…and it just fucking blows me away, forces me to reevaluate my position as Jolie's husband. As a human being in her midst.

In my hand is a pill bottle, partway filled with 10mg Ambien tablets, a prescription sleep aid. Printed on the bottle are a list of side-effects: drowsiness, nausea, dizziness, confusion, disorientation, et al. The prescription is in Jolie's name.

The angel: *It's simple math. Put one and one together.*

And when I do just that, I become more troubled than I've ever been in my thirty-three years. Jolie (the nice version) made sure I had dinner three nights in a row. On all three of those nights, I fell fast asleep and stayed down for at least twelve hours, and each morning after, experienced the side-effects that are listed on the bottle. Fuck. The road leading to divorce just became a fucking expressway demanding I shift from zero to sixty as quickly as fucking possible.

The devil, the angel, and I are for once all in agreement. Jolie wasn't being nice. No. She was being evil, *poisoning me* with a smile, a kiss, and a heavy dose of sleeping pills. But…was it her intention to keep me asleep, or actually kill me? If she wanted me dead, she could've ground up the entire bottle in my food. So, what then? Is she building up her courage? One or two pills on the first night, more on the second and third nights, increasing the dosage little by little so to slowly poison me to death? And *why* is she doing this to me? What is her endgame? It's one thing to hate someone, it's another to try to kill them.

The water in the shower stops running.

Time to find out what the fuck is going on.

CHAPTER 31

I'm seated at the kitchen table, staring at the bathroom door, reining in my anger, my fear, my disgust. On display are Jolie's bills, credit cards, and fucking prescription bottle. Each represents a law broken by the mother of my child: defaulting on credit card payments, fraud, and...*attempted murder?* She drugged me without my consent and that in and of itself is a crime punishable by jail time. Talk up motive (like I hate my fucking husband), and she's looking at years behind bars. First two pills, then three, then four. How many more before I go into cardiac arrest? Add a beer or two into the mix (Porch Rocker, thanks Jo!) and my coma-slash-death will go down as an accidental overdose. And then what about the spending? I'm facing a quarter-million in debt bound to smolder longer than Centralia, PA!

The door opens. She emerges from the bathroom, wrapped in a bath towel, hand-drying her hair and not looking my way just yet.

Rachel teeters from her room, rubbing her eyes. "Momma...I'm hungry."

Jolie looks at me, fake-smiles, *one one-hundred*...then sees the table with her once-secretive mementos on full display. The color drains from her face, as if she just saw her dead father, fake-smile now a very real frown, wide eyes bearing out her thoughts with clarity: *This isn't happening! This can't be happening!* Silent seconds pass. I growl, *"One one-hundred, two one-hundred, three one-hundred,"* all the while shooting her poisoned darts and fighting the urge to deepen the crack in the wall with her head. She crouches in front of Rachel. "Honey, go into your room. I need to talk to Daddy really quick, okay?"

Our toddler stomps her feet in protest.

The anger is real, and I can't help myself. I bolt up. The chair slams against the tile floor, startling both Rachel and Jolie. I point and shout, "Rachel, go to your room now!" I feel shitty for having to raise my voice, but my emotional dam is about to burst and there's no way of halting the deluge of anger behind it. Rachel howls and races back into her room. Jolie peeks her head in and says, "Stay in your bed honey and do not come out, ok?"

She closes the door, muffling Rachel's hysterics, then turns to face me with a look of imbalance in her face that wasn't there before: lips and eyelids twitching, cheeks purple, brow deeply furrowed.

"Where the fuck do I start, Jo?"

What I get in response isn't the nice version of Jolie…but isn't the bitch version either. It's an all-new third version of her that tells me how fucking mentally ill she is, how I never really knew her, and how repentant I am for saying "I do." This third version of my wife, we'll call her *Out-Of-Her-Fucking-Mind-Jolie,* calmly releases the towel and lets it drop to the floor, and just stands there bared-assed naked, trying way too hard to look sexy.

Awful seconds pass. I'm speechless. Finally, I manage a slight deviation from my initial response, "What the fuck, Jo?" My *wife* (the bare-assed lady in my living room) must be thinking, *distraction will erase the butt-fuckery of the moment,* because there's no other believable explanation for what she's trying to do. I pity her and fear her and desire her all at once:

tear-soaked eyes, wet hair draped over smooth shoulders, slow beads of water underscoring the feathery trajectory into her gap. She licks her lips (more childishly than sensually) and begins running her hands all over her square-cut abs and muscular breasts (also un-sexily), moaning as she exclaims, "Peter, I want you to fuck me."

It worked with Lily Dahl. And if things were normal with Jolie, my man-mind would tolerate her unbearable negativity for a quick romp. But things aren't normal, the irrefutable evidence of it spread out on the table and standing naked and pathetic before me. I want to scream, rip into her like I never have before. But I can't. Rachel's in the next room, hysterical, dejected, and alone, and I don't want to frighten her any more than she already is.

So I temper my temper and ask, ever-so-calmly, "Jo…what are you doing?"

Dripping wet, she steps over to me and stands close enough so I can smell her rosewater and cream body wash. She gently places her trembling hands on my face, smooths them through my hair, lips closing in on mine. My thoughts go to war over how physically attracted I am to her, and how we haven't had sex in over two years…and how her eyes are just fucking overflowing with *crazy*. She licks her lips again (this time with a little more sex-appeal), looking at mine, *wanting to taste them,* smiling. I'm growing hard for her, and I lean in as the devil screams for me to grab her around the waist and pull her in close…

…and then with a dense shudder that comes out of nowhere, I think about how she tried to fucking kill me, and I scream in her face, *"One-one-hundred-two-one-hundred-three-one-hundred!"* and forcefully swipe her hands away.

And then, all breaks loose.

Her face turns red like a summer sky after a deluge, and then, from out of thin air, an open-handed crack-of-thunder strikes me across the face, a bolt-of-lightning shriek chasing it: *"How dare you go through my things!"*

(…how dare you watch me BELT it's my business BELT you're six years old BELT you need to learn how to keep your nose out of other BELT people's BELT business BELT…)

(…REPRESS…)

She bends down, snatches a sports bra, leggings, and tee from the floor, while blabbering an inglorious tirade as she cries and shrugs into them. "You are such a fucking ass-asshole! We are fuck-fucking done!" The diatribe ends and now she's a schoolyard bully: *"Going through my things?! Ohhhh, I'll kick your fucking asssss!"* Gasping for air, eyes rolling crazily, she snatches her cell phone and money, tears streaming fiercely as she searches the empty gym bag for…

"WHERE IS IT?"

I shift a hand over the burner in my front pocket, appreciating the routine of lying and diversion that's crept into my life. "Where is WHAT Jolie? Your fucking quarter-million in bills? Your credit cards? Is that what you're looking for? Or maybe it's *these*?" I hold up the bottle of Ambien and shake it like a tiny maraca.

She freezes but for the slow shake of her head, looking at me with peculiar eyes, *not all there,* a jumbled expression of confusion and madness distorting her good looks. Without warning, she howls and attacks me, fisticuffs launching left and right like missiles. But I'm more prepared this time and I parry and roll and evade the onslaught—practice makes perfect—and she screams, "WHERE IS IT YOU FUCKER?!" Blue veins I've never noticed before puff out of her forehead like birthday ribbons. Her throat swells and flushes, Rorschach splotches. The whites of her eyes burst red, twisting with swollen veins.

I'm a captain lost at sea, facing a monolithic swell in uncharted territory with Moby fucking Dick trying to sink me and my ship.

Rachel's cries are growing louder now, more desperate for attention. I grimace and growl, "I don't know what the fuck you're talking about!" She backs me up against the kitchen counter. I face my palms out, *calm down*! "For god sakes please, keep your voice down, the neighbors will hear!"

Arms flailing, she screams, "FUCK YOU PETER! I HOPE ALL THE NEIGHBORS HEAR!"

(…neighbor…)

Like a tornado ripping through a farm, she spins and starts throwing stuff at me, anything within reach, the stack of bills, the credit cards, a small plant from the table that explodes against the cabinets, raining soil. The combination lock from her gym bag finds my cheek, adding sting to the slap. One sneaker hits me in the ear, the other strikes the fridge and sends post-it notes fluttering like frightened pigeons.

Amid the turmoil, I move the pill bottle from my hand into my pocket. "Christ Jolie! Stop hurling shit or I swear I'm gonna call the police!"

She paces and breathes—a caged animal. I can only stand and stare in silence, watching her, wondering who the fuck she is and what she's become. She grabs a couch pillow and flings it at me, more an afterthought than an attempt to inflict injury. "We're done, Peter…I'm getting my things and I'm going to my mom's." Her voice, still seething, drops a few decibels: a hopeful shift back to civility for Rachel's sake. She hurriedly collects her mostly-crushed makeup off the floor and shoves it every-which-way back into her purse full of secrets, all the while telling me how much my ass will hurt after she "drains every last dollar out of it."

I welcome her departure; extracting ourselves from each other is the only "right now" reaction to what our relationship has evolved into. It destroys me to have to put myself before Rachel, but there's a limit to how much I can take, the wealth of patience I've exhibited over the last three years drawing the line at attempted murder.

She storms into our bedroom and starts aggressively opening drawers. Clothes soar. Objects crash. She moves on to the closet where she rummages and shouts, "Where's the fucking luggage, Peter? Is it in your idiot darkroom?"

I want to curse. I want to retort. I want to hit her in her pretty fucking face. Oh. Ah. Oh…I can…I can feel myself *changing*: a subliminal boost into something I'm not, something I'm *becoming*, something angry, *violent*. "It's in the storage locker, I put it there a long time ago." With derision (and a spike of gladness), I add, "I'll *happily* get it for you."

One of the perks of our building is the basement storage facility, $200 a month and worth every nickel. It's here we keep our seldom used items: bikes, winter coats, beach chairs. About a year ago I relocated our luggage down there to free up more space in my darkroom; I didn't see any romantic vacations in our future.

I about-face and grip the doorknob.

"Wait…!"

I stop, turn, face her. Her stunned gaze is nowhere on earth, eyes wide and vacant, damp hair a tangled mess. She looks like an escaped psychiatric patient. Or someone soon to become one. She pleads, "Don't go down there, pumpkin-eater."

"Why not, Jo?"

She looks around at nothing, uttering blankly as her eyes float everywhere but in my direction, "I just…there's got to be a suitcase or duffle bag up here somewhere…?" Her words are tragic, less a question than a ruse.

And that's when I realize.
It's been a year since I've been in the storage unit.
Time to see what's inside.

CHAPTER 32

Her final scream to *WAIT!* is drowned out by the thump of the door slamming in my wake. The anger and adrenaline I'm feeling is strangely unique to me and I let it propel me into the stairwell and down two steps at a time. The images assaulting my mind—Jolie's neck in my hands, Jolie eating the floor, Jolie in a world of hurt—seem feasible as I accept my waking world's new nightmare. It's so fucking hard to be positive, so fucking hard to retain a glimmer of hope, but I'm trying. Because if I'm right, the contents of the storage locker will be my only hope of defusing the bomb that's seconds away from obliterating my financial freedom.

I reach the basement and skate through the laundry room…and nearly collide with one of the building's tenants. I've taken note of the guy before in passing: thin, handsome-ish with Ted-Bundy-like eyes that stare into you as if you're next on his hit list. I offer a quick "excuse me" (and regret for a split second missing this opportunity to grab a full-color moment in time), then skirt around him into the storage area.

There's a dozen self-storage lockers down here, all of which, judging from the padlocks, look to be in use. I find mine, number 4, and dial in the combo. One one-hundred (if I'm right, this thing will be bursting with merch), two one-hundred (if I'm wrong, I'll return with Jolie's suitcase just in time to watch the door hit her in the ass on the way out), three one-hundred…

...I open the unit and turn on the light.

I'm both right and wrong.

I'm right because before me is what I'd hoped for. A treasure trove of department store purchases: jackets, clothing, more clothing, home decor items, a chandelier (a fucking chandelier!), a splendid variety of designer sunglasses displayed on a swanky mirrored coffee table, unopened boxes of God-knows-what crammed into the unit like Monday morning commuters on the 1-line. I can keep going, and in the interest of locating our luggage (new or old), I start aggressively excavating, unearthing lamps and frames and figurines until...

Until the mine becomes a minefield.

I'm wrong because even though most of Jolie's purchases are stored here, there's something else in here too, marked by a revolting stench that intensifies the farther I go in. I've never smelled anything quite like it...and yet, it's dreadfully unmistakable.

It's now, in this terrible moment, that I comprehend how short-lived my hope for financial salvation was, because everything here, *everything*, is steeped...

...in the stink of death, the devil finishes.

Everything is unsalvageable, unreturnable trash.

Dizzied, I shift aside a full-length cheval mirror, yank away a patchwork quilt, and behold the source of the wretched stench, my worried-sick mind praying—*praying*—that the twisted form in the clear plastic, duct-taped bin—recently containing my daughter's coloring books and crayons—is not what my eyes are telling me it is. That the terrible moment I tear away the tape and lid and behold the crammed body inside...the moment I pray it's a prop or a mannequin even though I know props and mannequins don't stink like corpses, do I realize, now and forever, that my life, as complex and complicated as I thought it was, just got ten times more fucked-up.

Crammed inside the bin—beaten, broken, and bloodied—is the body of our nanny Carmen.

CHAPTER 33

Panic swoops in. I backpedal recklessly and stumble over boxes and spin-fall into the glass coffee table. My shin screams and sunglasses fall, and I trample them, barely escaping the unit before bumping into Ted Bundy.

He says, "Whoa there, champ. Ohhh…smells like something died in there."

The next moment is exceptional, takes me to a place where pure horror and common sense convene—a rare joining of conflicting emotions fueling the expulsion of my lunch. My vomit hits the floor in a large yellow spatter, splashing my pants and Ted's sneakers. I heave again, and in the fleeting moment of lucidity that follows, come to the realization that all my thriving anguish has but one crucial underlying purpose: protect Rachel from Jolie.

I back away from Ted, sprawling, gagging, Carmen's grisly form forever imprinted in my brain: her diminutive remains folded in half, arms inhumanly twisted, left pelvis peeking through a rupture in her waist.

My legs buckle and I trip and stagger, momentum carrying me from Ted Bundy's arms into the locker across from mine. I must look unhinged in the uncertainty of my actions: tears bursting from my eyes as I gag and cower next to the steel door, haunting myself with *the* question: *Did Jolie kill Carmen?* I beg my mind to consider otherwise as I question how the woman I married, the mother of my daughter, could have erased all emotion from her heart, and discretion from her brain, to take a human life.

With Ted's assistance, I struggle to my feet, feverishly sick with worry: *Rachel is alone with her…*

"You okay, pal?" My building mate—who may or may not be a serial killer—attempts to console me, unmindful of the dead body laying mangled in a box fifteen feet away.

I glare at the guy. He really does look like Ted Bundy. In this critical moment where my next decision could forever alter my life, I stammer, "Dead rats, nest, maggots…" I really should go to the police, but my first concern is Rachel's safety. Her mother, who may have tried to kill me—and allegedly succeeded with Carmen—is alone with our daughter at this very moment, broken thoughts formulating a next move.

I thank Ted, apologize for my performance, then promptly lock up the unit and drunk-walk back through the laundry room with its more favorable scent of Tide PODS. I'm dizzy with fear as gray-veiled shapes edge into my field of view, generating tunnel-vision. I stumble into the elevator, misfiring muscles and nerves unable to confront four flights of steps. The voices in my head belonging to my good versus evil counterparts express rolling opinions that break away like talus from a cliff, impossible to hold onto, and quickly forgotten.

I'm hyperventilating: One one-hunh, two one hunh, three one-hunh…*(…your memories are no longer REPRESSED you're at the bottom of the closet cowering choking gagging dust mothballs you've been here the entire night it's been months since you took the picture he still hasn't forgiven you he opens the door the light is blinding you hear your mother crying "please not again!" he is angry the BELT comes out and you didn't realize at the time this would go on for another two years…)*

Riding up is always less congested than riding down, and if I can make it past the lobby…

Ding!

A kid steps in—late teens, hair greased back, skateboard tucked under one arm, half-smoked cigarette behind one ear—and presses the button for the third floor. Before the doors close, I look out through the front door of the building and see a man leaning against the *No Parking* signpost outside. He's bad-boy handsome, full black beard, neck tattoo, Risky Business sunglasses that seem to fix me from thirty feet away. He lifts a cell to his ear as the elevator doors close, the inventive part of my mind—remarkably still operational—informing me that he's annoyed the person he's waiting for is late.

Skater-boy exits the elevator on the third floor, leaving me one more floor to resolve how to deal with the suspected murderer I'm married to. I beseech the angel and devil for assistance, but they remain silent witnesses, leaving me to drift alone in the world of shit the *path less-traveled* has led me to.

She knew, I tell myself. *She didn't want me to go down there because she knew.*

The devil: *She knew because she did it.*

The elevator doors open. I say aloud to myself, "No, she couldn't have…" But she could have. Occam's razor decides this for me. No one else had the combination to the storage padlock outside of Carmen, Jolie, and me. The problem is, suspecting fingers will point at me first, then *maybe* Jolie.

That's not a good spot to be in right now.

I breathe in the air outside my apartment and hold it, deciding that blind ignorance is my only hope because I like being alive and love my daughter and those are two monumental fucking reasons not to get murdered by my wife. My balls shrink into my crotch as I inch the door open, my planned lie of ignorance already a failure because creeping into my own home wishing I had a weapon isn't something I typically do. The door creaks. One foot inside. Still eerily quiet. Rachel isn't crying anymore.

Fuck it. I burst in. Two AAA batteries slide across the kitchen floor, and why the fuck did she have those in her purse? Then I see the mini vibrator minus the battery cap under the kitchen table and yeah, *that's why*.

I'm met with silence as I call out, "Jo?"

I shut the door behind me. "Rachel? Baby?"

Nothing.

Fuckfuckfuckfuckfuck! She left and took Rachel!

I was gone maybe fifteen minutes, plenty of time for her to get lost in the city. Panic sets in. I call out, "Rachel?" over and over, looking for her in the bathroom, my bedroom, under the bed, in the closet *(...the closet...)*. There are clothes everywhere and I'm kicking them aside hoping, *praying* my little girl is hiding beneath them somewhere. Tears fall, terrors rise. Fear begs me to call the police, but my common sense says not to because they'll no doubt take me in and question me all night and pressure me into confessing to a crime I didn't commit, because that's what they do, and how many housewives murder their nanny anyway? *It's always the fucking husband!*

My cell is still in my back pocket, and I pull it out and call Jolie's number. Straight to voicemail. I race into Rachel's room, "Rachel? Are you in here?" No reply. I look under her bed and now I'm starting to sob because I failed my daughter, was fucking blind to the insanity building in her mother's head, and now she's gone, and I let it happen on my fucking watch. How could I not see it coming?

I bolt into my darkroom, one last-ditch hope for her salvation. She's never stepped foot in here. She's learned *off-limits* well because *honey it's dangerous.* Everything appears to be in its place, which I suppose I should be thankful for; Jolie used her short time fleeing instead of revenge-trashing my place of worship.

Fuckfuckfuckfuckfuck! My camera! I left it on the kitchen counter. If Jolie took it, if she has the film developed and finds out about my summer fling, she'll use the photos against me in…in what? Divorce court? No. That's a joke. This undoing has risen to levels far beyond the nastiest of divorces. This is a clusterfuck of secrets caught in a tangled web of murder and lies, and that will be the tagline of my biography if Lily's photos ever see the light of day. Thankfully, my camera is still where I left it, and even though there's a dead body in my storage unit, and even though my murderous wife just kidnapped our daughter, I experience a small wave of relief knowing that Lily's pictures will not air for public consumption. Until Carmen's murder is solved, they will dissect our lives piece by piece, and those photos could unnecessarily cloud the truth of what really happened.

Fuckfuckfuckfuckfuck. I really should call the fucking police. *Butbutbutbutbut* there's no happy ending in sight if I do that. Choosing to have the NYPD breathing up my ass 24/7 before taking a breather to consider all my options is not a prudent strategy. I need to *think* first.

Angel, depleted and on the verge of collapsing: *Destroy the photos of Lily.*

Devil, cajoling and full of corruption: *You want to see her nude photo, don't you?*

Now is not the time to focus on my hobby. Now is not the time to focus on my other significant other. But Lily stepped into my thoughts and now, there's no way to eradicate her, even if the angel insists I delete her from my life. She has *nothing* to do with this. She's an innocent, guilty by association. I think about it…but then freely choose to do nothing and leave the film right where it is. She's a distraction *(…from you, six-seven-*

eight...), and at the moment these photos are all I have to keep my head on straight.

My attention is drawn to the kitchen table and Jolie's scattered effects. Among them is a pressed powder compact, broken open, the fine beige dust broadcast across the table's smooth surface. In the midst of it all, a partial handprint. Jolie's handprint. I'm no stranger to shows like *The Forensic Files* and *Cold Justice* and know that clear fingerprints can be lifted and utilized in a variety of ways. Time is short and I want to find Jolie and get Rachel back, and the burner in my pocket could lead me to them.

Using my cell phone camera, I grab digital images of the hand and all the fingerprints because developing photos in my darkroom isn't in the cards right now. Finding Rachel is. The problem is: where to start? Again, I try calling Jolie, and again it goes to voicemail. I move out of the kitchen and back into my darkroom, where normalcy still (sort of) exists. It doesn't help. Rachel is still gone, and my heart and mind have become uncertain if I'll ever see her again.

I wish I could go back to a simpler time where the stress of co-existing with a bitchy wife was the worst of my problems. With my simple past now obliterated in the wake of murder and kidnapping and *what the hell else*? I'm starting to feel my sanity and judgment slip, my anger and antagonism rise. I'm *changing*. But then I think of Rachel and that helps me locate the wisdom to keep it together. She needs me, and I need her.

I reach across the side of the file cabinet to hide my camera...and freeze as my heart explodes in my throat.

In the tight space where I usually store my camera is Rachel, fast asleep.

CHAPTER 34

I reach into the gap and gently retrieve Rachel. She's warm and sweaty. *Familiar*. Her little heart is racing through her damp onesie, each micro-beat absorbed by my larger, galloping one. She's been through more in one day than any child should have to endure in a lifetime, the fighting, the cursing, the throwing of credit cards and padlocks and sneakers.

Words alone could never express the relief I'm feeling in this moment with her in my arms...and words alone could never express how fucked-up it is for a mother to abandon her only child, even if abandoning Rachel was the only thing, the *right* thing for her to do. Jolie knew that taking our daughter out into the wild (after leaving a dead body in her wake) would only place her in harm's way, and I have to give her that.

I tuck Rachel in beneath the Ariel comforter on her bed, grateful I didn't call the police. With Jolie gone—a fleeing person of interest—I'll be (by default) the primary person of interest. I'll be summoned to *the station* for questioning where they'll put me inside a dank two-way-mirrored room and spew incriminating allegations at me. They'll cordon off my building, my neighbors-in-passing rubbernecking the comings and goings of the NYPD while Rachel finds herself whisked away by Child Protective Services and processed in a room full of police, then placed in a foster home because Susan the Cunt won't be able to retrieve her with a bottle in her hand. I can't let that happen. First thing in the morning, I'm going to take Rachel to Nick's place. She'll be safe there…

(…are you sure about that, six-seven-eight…?)

…at least until I can speak with the police.

In the moments before arriving home tonight, I felt happy. Optimistic. Hopeful for another night with my *new-and-improved* wife. But those hopes were dashed faster than a speeding bullet. I feel extracorporeal now, not more powerful than a locomotive, partly detached from my body, not *all there,* inanimate and unable to leap over anything, skeletal in the wind. Forgotten. All of that. Life is fucking cruel.

(…you're changing, just like he did…)

I change out of my vomit jeans and go into the kitchen to clean up the mess, tossing all of Jolie's remaining mementos in the trash. Once everything is wiped spotless, all evidence of our battle erased (except for the dent the plant made in the cabinet door), I check to make sure Rachel is still asleep, then exit the apartment and take the stairwell back into the basement to clean up the puke (evidence) I left behind. It's here I run into Chico, the building's maintenance man, who (thankfully) has already begun the process of mopping it all up. Chico is short, fat, and angry. His English is limited. He swears in Spanish, "*malditos gilipollas borrachos!*" and I don't know if his outburst is directed toward me, but he's doing the deed for me, and that's all that matters right now. The stench of bleach is really strong too, enough I hope to mask the stink of death behind storage locker number four.

"Hola Mr. Peter," he says.

"Hi Chico."

"You need go in?" he asks, pointing to the lockers.

I shake my head vigorously. "No, no, I…I heard you back here and…and just wanted to say *hola*." I grin feebly.

He smiles back and says, "Ah, ok Mr. Peter."

He waves…and I'm off the hook. I race back upstairs and straight away check on Rachel because paranoia is invading the gaps in my mind where rational thought usually dwells. She's still here, good, a butterfly in a cocoon baby-snoring.

Fuck, I'm exhausted.

But the promise of sleep is a lie.

The devil on my left: *there's a bottle of Ambien in your pocket…*

Fuck you. What I need is for time to pass. The night will be long, and I have to stand watch. As long as Rachel remains in the thick of her parents' calamity, I'll remain by her side and hope for morning to arrive quickly. Jolie returning in the middle of the night to retrieve her daughter is a fearful possibility, and over my dead body will I let that happen.

So.

I put up a pot of coffee, wedge the door, and enter my darkroom.

CHAPTER 35

Two hours later, after midnight, I turn on the overhead light and survey the twenty-four images I took over the past couple days. Here are my friends from Smoke & Novelty, the druggie keyboardist on the subway platform, the homeless crooner in Penn Station, the will-never-be-married couple on the LIRR, and *hello Lily*.

Eating, drinking, smiling, posing, laughing, *sleeping naked* Lily.

I take down all the not-Lily photos and file them in the sea of manila on the shelves, then arrange the rest to my liking. I center the *sleeping naked* photo on the line, clip the full body shots on either sides of it, and surround those with a half-dozen candid portraits. Eighteen photos of her in all, my life's compulsory distraction, two days ago a remorseful pleasure, now the only sanity left inside my head *(…six-seven-eight begins to fade…)*. Without her, I'd be in pieces.

I crack the darkroom door. Rachel is still dreaming. Three hours ago, I glimpsed my first dead body, and as soon as the cops discover it, I'll go from "innocent" to "prime suspect" in a flash. Jolie might be guilty of the crime, but they won't see that because nine times out of ten, it's *the husband*. They'll put me behind bars during which our lives will be torn apart as they uncover our debauchery and lies, where in the end we'll go down in flames as one. The depravity of the situation eats at my logic, my lucidity, my constitution—I don't need to be poisoned to feel wrong, off, *not right*. I'm doing it all on my own.

I'm not the same man I was four days ago. I'm *changing*. There's a part of me that feels as if I'm unraveling at the seams, regressing into something else, something *primal*. I need a distraction. Now. So, I do what I always do when distraction becomes the only means to dissociate my pain.

(…you, six-seven-eight…)

I spin the chair and face all eighteen portraits of Lily. Before I start, I check my phone. She hasn't texted or called and I'm guessing *this is it*, what I have in front of me is the most I'll ever get out of her again, and that terrifies me because she's been the most effective distraction *(…from you, six-seven-eight…)* I've had in years. I unzip, and if you ever need a diversion from all that's wrong in your life, find the object of all your desires and put every ounce of your being into it, because trust me, whether you're a guy or a gal or something in between, *it works*. The moment is a short-lived affair, but an effective remedy to help whiten the dark clouds hanging over me. *Now* I feel as if I can look toward tomorrow. I clean up (yes Jolie, *that's* where the baby-wipes are going, *what did you expect?*), tiptoe into the kitchen to make sure the chair under the doorknob is still secure, then return to Rachel's room and lay on the floor next to her bed…and in minutes or hours I nod off and dream of you, six-seven-eight…

(…of that first night, you were so excited about the Polaroid camera your mother bought for you at the garage sale, there were three packages of unused film, and you didn't even make it through the first one when you looked out the window in the middle of the night at the neighbor's house and saw your father there with HER, the neighbor, not your mother, and you POINTED and CLICKED, and from the very moment the flash went off, you changed and he changed and your mother changed and you, six-seven-eight came to be…)

I awake with a start in the middle of a nightmare of dead bodies in storage units…into a waking world of dead bodies in storage units. It's 6:43 a.m. I scramble to my feet and without delay begin to get ready. I pack Rachel an overnight bag and in less than thirty minutes we are both cleaned and ready to flee apartment 4C. It's Monday and I'm supposed to be at work, and I should go and feign normalcy because, isn't that what you're supposed to do when there's a dead body in your storage locker? Feign normalcy?

I say to Rachel, "Ready Freddy?" and she says, " Ready to go, Geronimo," but says *Germomomo* and as I un-wedge the chair from beneath the doorknob, there's a knock at the door.

The angel wakes up and says: *Jolie…*

The devil wakes up and says: *Jolie…*

I send Rachel back into her room. If it is Jolie, she doesn't need to be witness to the murderous accusations I'm going to unleash upon her mother. I clench my sweating fists. "I'll be just a minute honey, okay?"

She asks, "Is that Mommy?"

"She's at work, honey. Now go."

She goes, and I look through the peephole.

It isn't Jolie.

It's the NYPD.

CHAPTER 36

It's 8:00 a.m. on Monday morning and 5th Avenue is overflowing with revving cars and honking horns, rush-hour packed after a sleepy weekend. But I'm not rushing anywhere. There are two cops at my door, blocking the way.

"Who is it?"

"NYPD."

I open the door. Standing before me are two of NY's "finest." A male cop, mid-thirties, pale with orange freckles and tufts of ginger hair sprouting from the brim of his hat, nametag Murphy, and a female cop, hot for a cop and sorry, I can't help it, my mind just goes *there* whether my body wants to or not *(...it helps you repress...)*, fair with red pinned-up curls, green eyes, nametag: Molloy. He has a beer-belly and his uniform is too tight, she has an athlete's body and her uniform is just right.

Officer Murphy smiles and speaks. "Sorry to bother you so early, Sir." His voice has a slight Irish *twang*. "Are you Peter Delmonico?"

The politeness they're exhibiting is more than just a formality, it's the calm before the cuffs. My mind screams *they must've found the body and now they've found me!* and I'm strangely grateful to have puked last night because if there was any food left in my stomach, I'd be unloading it on their shoes right now. In my peripheral vision I see Rachel peeking out from her room and pray that no painful memories are created for her in this moment.

"I'm Peter," I say, brow furrowed, lips pursed, me doing my damnedest to appear perplexed with their unannounced visit.

"May we come in?"

"Sure, of course." I show them to the kitchen table, inwardly thanking God I power-cleaned the remnants of last night's gym-bag fiasco. Rachel is still watching, and they notice her and say hello but do not ask for privacy, which has to be a good thing, no? I offer them coffee, but they decline. I swallow two tepid mouthfuls; I'm parched and more non-Ambien tired than a bear in the dead of winter.

Officer Molloy—the hotter of the two—says, "This should only take a few minutes."

We sit at the kitchen table, and I immediately ask what all suspects innocent or guilty ask when the *fuzz* shows up on their doorstep: "How can I be of help?"

Murphy speaks and Molloy watches, eyes on me and not in a good way. "We received a missing persons report from the family of Carmen Rodriguez. We understand that she worked for you?"

Okay…so she's still a *missing* person and not a *murdered* person, and in the grand scheme of things, that's good for me. What's bad is that I know where she is and by not saying anything could be charged with obstruction of justice, a crime punishable of up to five years. With Rachel looking on, it's best to feign ignorance (lie), at least until I can get her to Nick's place.

"Yes, she's our nanny. But she hasn't shown up for work in almost a week, and we haven't been able to get in touch with her."

"When was the last time you saw her?"

"She was here…last Monday, a week ago today. But she was a no-show for the rest of the week."

"Did she call at all during that time?"

"According to my wife Jolie, yes, she called in sick."

"So, Jolie's the one that spoke to Carmen?"

"Yes, that's correct."

"Did she mention if Carmen called in every day?"

Yes, she told me Carmen called in sick every day and fuck, now that I think about it, she took a call on Friday morning right in front of me, said it was Carmen calling in sick again. But…if Carmen was already dead at the time, then who the hell was that on the phone?

I keep my answer vague: "I'm not entirely sure. I can only go by what Jolie told me, which is that she called in sick."

"Where is Jolie now?"

Good question. "Either at the gym, or at work. She's always up and out early during the week." Am I really lying to the police for the woman who *poisoned* me, maybe even tried to kill me?

Molloy says, "So…Jolie just up and left this morning without knowing if the nanny was going to show up?"

I rely on my ruse to create a believable half-truth in record time. "We just assumed she wasn't coming today, so last night we…"

FUCK YOU PETER!

"…made the decision that I'd drop off Rachel at my dad's place for the day."

He nods. "Rachel is your daughter?" She's still watching the goings-on from her room and when Molloy peeks at her, she dips out of sight. This innocent little move puts a faint smile on the cop's pretty face, and a damper on my slamming heart.

"That's correct."

"Where does your father live?"

"Long Beach."

Murphy nods and scribbles in a tiny notebook, and how come cops don't use iPads nowadays? He asks, "Where does Jolie work?"

"Saks Fifth Avenue, flagship store."

There's a pause as Murphy points to something he scribbled down. Molloy nods. He then asks, "Did Carmen say anything out of the ordinary, maybe about leaving town, or having an argument with someone?"

"Not that I'm aware of. As mentioned, I really don't have any contact with her. I work a nine-to-five-thirty in the garment center, even later if I have clients in town. Jolie's hours are more flexible so she's the one who usually deals with the nanny. Except when it comes to payday." I grin. They don't.

"Does Carmen have a key?"

"She does."

The devil chimes in: *One for the apartment, and one for storage locker,* and in my head I tell the devil to *fuck off, it's a combo lock.*

"Is it possible for you to get your wife on the phone? We'd like to speak to her."

My heart sheds its damper and ramps back up again. Calling Jolie is at the very bottom of my to-do list. What if she picks up screaming and cursing? I say, "Sure, no problem," but it *is* a problem, a big problem, and I look at the time and tell them I'm expected to be at work at ten for a meeting (another lie), and that I still have to get to Long Beach to drop my daughter off (the truth), and then I tell them that I'm very worried about Carmen (a half-truth, a white lie) before dialing Jolie's number and putting it on speaker.

Please don't pick up, please don't pick up…

It rings twice and goes to voicemail. *Yes!* She rejected my call. And they know it, too. "Par for the course," I say. "She's either exercising, or working the floor. I'll try texting her."

Molloy puts her hand on my phone. Her fingertips brush against mine and my skin tingles and if given the chance, *I would*. She says, "Don't. If you could just provide us with her number, we'll get in touch with her later this morning."

I do, and they thank me for my cooperation. As they stand to leave, Molloy looks at me and I smile and she doesn't and asks, "When you say, 'working the floor,' do you mean at Saks?"

"Yes, she works in the dress department." What else could it mean?

The devil: *They want to surprise her, just like they surprised you.*

Thing is, Jolie won't be there. They thank me for my time and leave.

After the door closes, the angel and devil speak in unison, and scare the shit out of me: *They will be back with detectives to search the building.*

CHAPTER 37

I've said it before: In my life the unexpected happens, and I never expect it. Only now the unexpected is evolving, having gone from a stranger's kiss in the park to a nanny's dead body in my storage unit. And I wonder, will the bar continue to rise? In my mixed-up, muddled-up, shook-up world—so befitting, thank you Mr. Davies—it will. Lily said, *fate has an odd way of revealing itself*, and in light of this I must prepare myself for the next odd wave of fate, anticipate it, ready my response. Step up my game, confront ugly with uglier.

Before leaving, I grab my camera, load it with a fresh roll of film, then crowd all eighteen images of Lily into my attaché; it's tight and heavy, but I don't want to leave them behind because broken Jolie might come home and see them and hand me the same fate Jessica Walter did Clint Eastwood in *Play Misty For Me*.

Rachel and I leave. I'm tentative, paranoid even, peering back and forth and over both shoulders because I wouldn't put it past Jolie to be spying on us from some discreet, sniper-like location. I'm also on the lookout for uniforms and blood-detection dogs, but don't see any, thankfully.

We immediately luck into a cab. Today's driver is Phuk. That's what it says on his displayed permit. Phuk. He tells us he is Vietnamese and that his name is pronounced *Fook*. He's wearing a white jacket and a red hat and he must've taken a wrong turn on his way to Benihana's. While driving, he points out his favorite food carts and tells us how much he loves smoking rice, and I can't decide if he's smoking-curing or smoking-combusting, but then I consider his outfit and decide he's eating it, not inhaling it. We arrive at Penn Station a few minutes before 9:00 a.m. I bid farewell to Phuk, using the phonetic pronunciation for just, yes, shits and giggles. Rachel echoes my sendoff and *Phukin' I* both get a charge out of it. Insert cheesy-grin emoji here.

Like yesterday, we enter Penn Station through the 34th Street entrance, and like yesterday I'm graced with someone remarkable to photograph, a street musician whose banner promotes him as *Blanco de Maia, "world famous" didgeridooer.* Blanco is starving-thin, crusty dreads darting every-which-way from his head and face. He's hairy. Very hairy. Hypertrichosis hairy. He's seated on the floor, huffing and puffing into a four-foot wooden trumpet, shaggy cheeks ballooning out Louis Armstrong-style. The instrument bellows in a way that makes me wonder what an elephant having an orgasm might sound like, low-toned, throaty, and lamenting. If not for the techno-beat emanating from the boom box behind him, the riveting sounds would be lost amid the ambient chatter and footfalls of Penn's Monday morning commuters, and that would be a shame because Blanco rocks.

Point.

Click.

We find the platform for the train to Long Beach. I accidentally sideswipe Rachel's stroller into a portable bar offering cans of beer and mini wine bottles to reverse-commute night-shifters. The display beverages tremble, earning me an unpleasant look from the faux bartender.

We get on the train and take a seat. I call Nick and he picks up on the first ring and I lie about Carmen being out sick and ask if I can tender his services. He says no problem, but before hanging up reminds me—with a *dammit!*—how his new housekeeper doesn't work on Mondays, and *isn't that too bad*? Yesterday Nick called Linda a looker. To a seventy-five-year-old, lookers must be plentiful. The figurative *they* say: Beauty is in the eye of the beholder. I say: I'm probably not missing much. Dave Fisher says: different courses for different horses. And Nick, one old Italian stallion, will no doubt take a swing on any course. So yeah, that.

Next, I call the office. Amy picks up on the first ring.

"Hi Aimster. It's Peter."

"Hi Peter! How was your weekend!? I hope you're not calling in sick! My dog has a cold! Are you on a train!?" Amy is a human exclamation point. She's annoying and exasperating but answers a good phone so we keep her around.

"I should be in around eleven—is Dave in?"

"He *just* walked in!" She lowers her voice to a discreet whisper, still loud enough though for those within proximity to hear. "He's a little wobbly, if you get my drift." She then turns it back up to eleven and yells, more so in my ear than across the office, "Dave? Peter's on line one!" Cost-effective Amy came equipped with a built-in intercom, and she uses it frequently. "I'll connect you! See you later Peter-Peter-Pumpkin-Eater!"

I say with no gratitude, "Thanks Amy," but the call is already ringing in Dave's office.

"Wellllllll?" he says upon picking up. I can almost smell the alcohol on his breath. "Did you hear anything?" Dave, not wasting any time.

I say, "I did," and immediately regret it because he's going to want to hear *all the details,* and I don't have the time nor energy for *all the details*.

His excitement and expectation *breathes* through the phone. I can practically feel the warmth of it on my ear. "Oh snap

Peter!" He says snap. "When are you getting here? It's after nine and you know I won't be able to get any work done until you fess it all up. All of it! I need *dem deets Petes*!"

He's come to work drunk. Again. I can almost see the red in his eyes, and the muss in his hair. Typically, I'd get a charge out of Dave's nonsense, but today I'm not in the mood, and rightly so. How can I be with a dead nanny in my storage locker? "Sorry…not much to divulge."

He Bronx cheers, "*Booooo*," just like he does when the Yankees are trailing, only this time *I'm* the one that's losing: my grip, at life, at love. He shouts, "You're a liar!" and he's right, I am. I'm getting good at it too. I've been practicing.

"Listen, can you tell the boss I'm running late? I have to take Rachel to my dad's. Our nanny ghosted us."

"Oooh, that sucks. I'll let her know. By the way…"

I look over at Rachel. She's keeping busy with *Where the Wild Things Are.* My heart bleeds for her. She's such an innocent little cherub, unknowingly trapped at the core of her parents' inexcusable fuckupalooza. *Where in God's name are you Jolie? How can you just up and abandon your daughter like that?* Not that I'm unhappy she did. My first priority is Rachel's well-being. That's what matters most. But what happens then if Peter and Jolie Delmonico's dirty laundry is aired? At three-and-a-half years old, her brain is overly ripe with the ability to shed soon-to-be-formed negative memories. If Jolie and I are whisked off to prison, and are no longer able to nurture her, who will step up to ensure she matures into a supportive member of society, and not some post-traumatic drug-addled *Pornhub* queen? I need to prioritize her safety, and bringing her to Nick's is my best and only choice.

Dave says, "So…this morning I was looking through the photos you gave me, you know, the ones of the library? You have them handy?"

"I do." They're in the envelope next to the eighteen portraits of Lily I squeezed into my camera bag this morning. I slide them out and Lily's original nice and nasty portraits meet my gaze. I shift them to the bottom of the pile.

"Ok, look at the crowd."

"I'm looking…" I glance over the two hundred some-odd bodies standing and sitting and talking. "What am I looking for?"

"Top step, center, standing next to the third column."

Now I see it.

A pink baby-tee.

It's Lily.

And she's staring directly into the camera.

CHAPTER 38

"Holy shit."

"My sentiments exactly."

The image is small, but it's clear. It's *her*. Human faces are easily identifiable even when only a portion is visible. We're hardwired to *recognize* who to be attracted to, or what might be dangerous. Lily fits into both categories. It's a proven fact that humans can read words with the vowels removed, and it's also a proven fact that I *recognize* Lily's tiny face floating above a tiny pink tee—a flash of color in a tight sea of neutrals, center stage, *tiny but distinguishable*—in the photo.

"Pete? You still with me?"

"I am…I'm just trying to decide…" *What does this mean?*

Angel on my right: *You ended up in the same place by coincidence.*

Devil on my left: *She's looking at you, she was following you, purposefully.*

Dave says, "You gave me two photos, and it looks like she's looking at you in both of them."

I lean heavily on the angel's opinion of coincidence, examining the facts and making sure I'm not brushing it off as something I don't want to be true. I took nine photos of the library, all of them from different angles as I walked up 5th Avenue toward 42nd Street. Not only is she looking at me in each and every one of them, but in the last two shots she moved down the steps *toward me*, much closer than in the others: *physical* proof the devil is correct. That she was *following me*, expressionless eyes staring directly into the camera's lens.

"Petey-boy, you still with me?"

"I have to go..." I'm too spooked now to continue the conversation and disconnect the line, at once coming to terms with the facts (coincidences?) revealed to me in my photos. She followed me. Chose *me*—the guy with the camera—to mess with. The evil-stepsister photo hinted at it, and these photos confirm it. But why? Now I'm leaning in agreement with the devil: that her actions were intentional.

Random or not, it's *true* that she followed me from the library into Bryant Park and it's *true* that she bumped into me, and it's *true* that she kissed me and fucked me three times, and women don't just fuck randos three times in a twenty-four-hour period, do they?

My brain hurts and Rachel is bitching that she's hungry and with all the left-field distraction in the last twenty minutes, we nearly miss the stop for Long Beach. My life has been torn apart over the past four days, and now wrong signals are firing in my brain. I feel less-than-human, *off*. I'm *changing*. My wife tried to kill me and my nanny is rotting in my storage locker and I'm in debt for a quarter-million and my summer fling is a breathtaking dilemma. Less than a week ago, I was an unhappily married man whose problems centered around finding time to take photos. Now I'm an unhappily married man in the eye of the perfect shitstorm, and no matter which way I turn, the eye-wall is closing in on me, promising further despair.

We grab an Uber with "Pierre" who claims to be a professional mime and talks (ironically) the entire way about a vocation he never talks at. In ten minutes, we arrive at Nick's place. I call from the end of the driveway and in seconds he's out front greeting us with that shiny smile of his, and shinier Tommy Bahama shirt. On the outside I'm all grins and laughs and pleasant surprises, but on the inside I'm in hell, fear and anxiety *(...of you, six-seven-eight...)* smoke-screened parasites eating me from the inside out. We go into the house and all is quiet and for a moment I hope to meet Nick's *looker*, but then remember: she's off today.

He asks, "What's happening with Carmen?" *She's dead*, but I tell him that she's "moved on" for personal reasons, and he repeats his semi-matching experience with Gail, making sure to mention how much of the "slack Linda has picked up." He goes on to remind me how easy on the eyes she is, forcing me to conclude that all my girl-craziness must've been handed down from my father, because if I were doing the hiring, "easy on the eyes" would be a legit resume bullet-point too.

Rachel skips through the sunroom into the backyard and gives Brutus a big hug. The dog yips and hops, excited to see her. It's after ten now and I decide that going to my job isn't in the cards today because, nothing trumps murder and poisoning and financial ruin. And somehow, amidst the thick of it all, I remain strangely calm; my *changing* mind has found a way to *merge* with the darkness fighting for control of my life. I've lied and cheated and have gotten away with it. I've clashed with my housekeeper's corpse. And if circumstances demand it, I can take it up a notch and...and...

OH NO FUCK-FUCK-FUCK! It just occurred to me. My fingerprints. They're all over the plastic bin (and tape) holding Carmen's corpse! And the bad person—*the devil?*—blooming inside of me knows: I have to get it out of there before the cops search the building! Circumstances demand it.

I'm gravely tired, not *crushed-Ambien-in-food* tired but *murdered-nanny-in-storage-unit* tired. I ask Nick for a cup of coffee, and he pours it just how I like it, dark and bitter. I take two steaming mouthfuls and confirm to myself that no, work isn't in the cards for today. *Getting rid of Carmen's body is.* I say, "I need to use your computer," because calling in sick at Johnson Apparel is an online thing and I'm not getting a signal on my phone, and even though Nick the Ancient has snazzy security cameras, he doesn't know the Wi-Fi password because *the guy* set everything up for him.

"You know where it is," he says. He reaches into his pocket and tosses me two identical keys on a flimsy ring. "Password is taped to the inside of the middle drawer, under the green folder."

Rachel and Brutus come inside, and I head upstairs to the office. I let myself in and wave to the hidden camera in the lampshade. The closet is closed. Behind it sits more than enough cash to level my newfound debt. I'm suddenly curious: what does 550k in cash look like up close? The new part of me simmering deep inside—the *changing* part—is impulsive, fueling my hasty decision to open the closet. I shove the coats aside, then the back panel, well camouflaged to the untrained eye, good job Nick. I punch in my childhood phone number. The safe beeps, the door opens, and ta-da, I'm gazing at my future, numerous stacks of neatly bundled cash, a velvet bag, and a few manila envelopes. My heart beats a rhythm against my chest and the cash smells rich and I breathe it in, holding the plush aroma in my lungs for as long as I can, whispering *"One one-hundred, two one-hundred, three one-hundred,"* until I close the safe and lock *Banco Delmonico* back up.

From downstairs I hear Rachel squeal and Brutus yip and Nick laugh, everyone that means everything to me, unaware of the utter detriment in my life. So much has happened, so much will happen; I'm still in the eye of the storm but it will soon pass and new worlds of shit will rush in and fuck everything up even more. Bet on that.

Calling in sick to work seems so trivial and unimportant right now, but I have to keep up with appearances. I sit at Nick's desk and touch the mouse and Windows asks for a password, *middle drawer under the green folder.*

I open the middle drawer, lift up the green folder…and if I didn't think things could get any more twisted, I realize now just how fucking wrong I was.

CHAPTER 39

CLICKED IN MOON.

These three words, Sharpied in all-caps on a 5 x 7 index card in Nick's desk drawer, strike my senses like an M-80 blast, loud and clear in my head. I repeat them to myself as my worlds collide head-on, the pieces drifting toward a space where logic doesn't exist.

The oddly familiar statement, once scribbled on Lily's dry-erase board as *CLICK ED IN MOON,* is the password to Nick's computer.

My skin crawls and I start clawing anxiously at my shirt, struggling to tame my roaring heart. I want to scream but start dry-heaving instead, my mind no longer able to put one and one together because everything just went from simple math to fucking calculus. I want to be wrong. I'm *praying* to be wrong. But no. The words continue to stare at me from inside my father's desk drawer.

Lily was *here.*

You should meet Linda, she's a real looker.

I'm trembling and it's really fucking hard typing these letters in, *CLICKED IN MOON,* still unusually familiar to me and I don't know why. But…this is proof. I wasn't chosen at random. She one-hundred percent tracked me down as the photos at the library suggest, followed not *the guy with the camera,* but *Peter, Nick's son,* and with purposeful intent. I peer over at the treasure closet, and even though I can't perform calculus, I can add, and one-plus-one equals a *much bigger picture*, one that more than likely has to do with the cash in my father's safe.

Through the window, I watch as Nick, Rachel, and Brutus move into the backyard. Nick opens the shed and grabs a few plastic balls and tosses them on the lawn. Brutus chases after them and Rachel jumps up and down, clapping and cheering the dog on.

My father's Windows desktop is clean, only the most basic Microsoft icons visible plus a couple others, Bank of America and Argent Security Cloud, which is where I'm guessing all the security camera recordings are stored. I double-click it because I'm on a mission now to obtain irrefutable evidence, because *scrawled password* and *looker* are circumstantial and so is the long gone CLICK ED IN MOON from Lily's dry-erase board. I'm clicking and I'm thinking: she didn't intend to meet me at the café, and she didn't intend to take me home, or those words would not have been there, and I'm thinking: she was so distracted when we got there that she forgot about them, and it's my pure dumb luck I saw them before she wiped them clean from existence. Add in the library photos—*one-plus-one*—and I see circumstantial evidence of predetermined knowledge, of fixed intent. The devil was right. And now my brain is hurting me even more, because *who the fuck are you, Lily?*

The Argent Security Cloud loads and his password auto-fills and I'm sure *the guy* handled that too. It looks like Nick is paying for a terabyte of space, so everything is here, dating back to when he first had the system installed a few months ago. *She's off on Mondays* so I click on Tuesday, six days ago.

Four folders appear. I click on *Main Room Interior* and…

The Devil: *It's her.*

The Angel: *It's her.*

Me: *IT'S HER!* There's a fist in my mouth and tears in my eyes as I stare at security footage of Lily—*Linda*—from a time before we fucked. She's cleaning Nick's living room, dusting tables, fluffing pillows, dressed in jeans and a plain black tee. She looks up at the camera and I click *pause* and we lock eyes across time, from when we existed as complete strangers, a time before my life was FUBAR. She's wearing no makeup and doesn't have a poor complexion and she's still fucking beautiful and the worst and best fucking thing to have ever happened to me. I open the window and shout for my father to come inside.

As I wait and stare at Lily, at *Linda*, the longest less-than-two-minutes in my life passes where I should be stuttering *one one-hundred* but discover my tic to be gone, vanished, the need for it completely obliterated. *I'm changing.*

Nick walks in holding Rachel.

I point to the screen and ask, "Nick…who is this?"

And Rachel answers, "That's Mommy's friend."

CHAPTER 48

My life's focus has transitioned from bored-with-it-all amateur photographer, family provider, effusive wife-despiser, into seeker of answers, sedulous warrior, plotter of retribution. The gentle and kind person in my shell once adhering to all the angel's appeals has shed its protective layer and now remains vulnerable to the devil's command of action, its every move. It's official. I'm *changed*.

I ask Rachel, "Honey…what do you mean?" I point to Lily-slash-Linda and ask, "This woman here, she's Mommy's *friend*?"

She nods happily, smiling, little chiclet teeth.

"Dad?"

He puts Rachel down, then faces me, hands on hips, visibly nervous. "That's Linda, my new housekeeper."

"Yeah, that much I've got…but why is Rachel saying it's Jolie's friend?"

"Jolie introduced us."

Nick and Jolie have never had any kind of relationship beyond the one that includes me, his decision to keep it hidden a legit enough reason to be nervous now that it's out in the open. *What else are you hiding, Nick?* "When did this happen?"

"About a month ago. You seem upset, Peter."

My words trip over my tongue as I stare him down, thinking out loud: "I-I am upset because, for one, I-I didn't know about this, and two…well let's just say it's a problem. A *big* problem." *And three because this woman right here? It turns out she's an enemy masquerading as a lover: a showy but true depiction.* "Why didn't you tell me about this?"

He licks his lips and drops his gaze to the floor. He looks ashamed, perhaps even remorseful *(…you've seen this look many times before, six-seven-eight…)*. He should be. He fucked up *(…again…)*, so much more than he realizes this time *(…again…)*. Finally, he confesses: "She asked me not to."

I don't have to think before I say, "Why am I not surprised? Did you ask her why she didn't want you to tell me?"

He flaps his arms up and down, as if trying to physically deflect the question. "Of course, I did. She said you wouldn't approve of her getting involved, and Pete, in all honesty, she was doing me a favor, you know? Gail was already gone, and I've gotten used to having someone around the house, you know?"

It's a valid response, I suppose; if I were in Nick's shoes and *Lily* showed up as an immediate option to fill the gap my former housekeeper left, I'd say *YES* in a heartbeat because there are worse things in life than watching Lily Dahl fluffing pillows.

But we're talking about my seventy-five-year-old father, not girl-crazy, still-functioning-like-a-teenager me, so I retort loudly, "She's right I wouldn't approve!" He startles. My *father*, old-man Nick, sleeping with the enemy, with me a fucking interrogator now, the tension between us thick as a brick. I yell *"FUCK!"* and slam the desk and Rachel flees across the hall into the spare bedroom—my future home so long as the chink in Nick's armor doesn't crack wide open.

So *fuckfuckfuckfuckfuck,* Lily and Jolie know each other and there's a clandestine drama between them involving me (the roadblock?) and Nick (the keyholder?) and…and *Carmen*? How the hell does she fit into whatever *this* is? And if there is a God *please help her*, Rachel.

Nick sits in the corner high-back, bowing his head shamefully, forehead to palms, thin wisps of gray hair jutting between his fingers like corn silk from a cob. I take a deep breath, hold it, blow it out, unsure of what to do next. Just as the room is about to fill with awkward silence, he says, "You want to tell me what's going on, Pete?"

I clutch handfuls of my hair and pull hard. The pain of it is relieving, bringing a dash of lucidity to the surreal development. "Nick..." Tears form in my eyes and when I feel sad my brain leaps back to *(...six-seven-eight cowering in the closet, in the darkness, dusty shoes, mothball scent, tears falling, BELT...)* the vague distant past. A chill hits my bones and I shudder and say, "I...I have a big problem, and it involves the woman you know as Linda." I use a knuckle to tap her image on the computer screen. "Promise me you will never let this woman into the house again."

He nods vigorously. "Okay, I promise...but you gotta tell me what's going on."

He's pressing and *I just can't right now* so I ignore him with my eyes closed, lips pursed, head shaking; divulging everything would take time and energy and wasting time and energy is only going to hold me back from getting the answers I really need. So, I open Google on his computer and ask, "Did you do a background check on Linda?"

"No." He's visibly shaken, and I'm visibly pissed, and as I voice my frustration with an under-the-breath *fuck,* he comes at me with a predictable line of defense: "I never would have done this if I knew you and Jolie were having problems."

The devil, pushing buttons: *An attempt, inadvertent or not, to turn the blame on you. After all these years, you're still at war.*

The angel: *You're complicating things. Please stop thinking for him.*

"What's Linda's last name?"

"Davis."

"Linda Davis," I say, *LD*, a digital needle in the worldwide haystack, but I ask anyway and am presented with 203 million results that start and eternally carry on with country music star Linda Kaye Davis. *Shit, shit, shit, shit, shit.* On the image search tab, hundreds of LKD's smile at me, all of them a…a hot older blonde, a MILF, and…and *would I*? Yes…yes…yes, I most enthusiastically would. Sorry. Women are, were, and will always be my ambition, my distraction, my downfall, even at the most critical of times.

I spin in my chair. Nick looks at me with tear-glossed eyes and my tears build, not because I feel sorry for him, but because of how lost a soul I am, of how alone I am, *again*. Lily, who I thought was my saving grace, isn't contacting me, and now I know why. She is manifestly linked to Jolie, with me the monkey in the middle of their manipulative game. I motion toward the closet. "Are you sure no one else knows about the safe?"

"I swear to it. Those are the only keys to the room." He points to the keyring on the desk.

I go back to scrolling and move past all the Linda Davis faces, way down into uncharted territory, but the effort is futile. Nick's housekeeper isn't *Linda Davis*, and she isn't *Lily Dahl*. She's someone else, someone whose real name Jolie might not even know. Fucking Jolie. *She's* the catalyst in all of this, not Nick, and not Lily. "Has Jolie been here recently?"

"Just the one time, when she introduced me to Linda. About a month ago."

"How did this come about?"

He squirms uncomfortably in the chair, breathing more heavily now, halfway to hyperventilation, tanned forehead glimmering with beads of sweat. If he dropped dead right now (a plausible scenario given his reddening complexion), it would be the equivalent of dumping salt into my life's gaping wound. "It was on Memorial Day weekend, when you were all here. You and Rachel were in the pool and Jolie was with me in the kitchen, helping me with the snacks. She mentioned that she had a friend who once worked as an H-H-A in Florida, and that if Gail ever left, she'd be a great fit."

"And Gail left when?

"A few weeks later."

"That's a little convenient, no?" The devil, my main go-to now, deals a frightening consideration: *Carmen vanished and look what happened to her*. I say, "You said that Gail left for California, to be with her parents?"

"Yes."

"Did she tell you this herself?"

He pauses and I can practically hear the rusty gears in his head grinding as he thinks this one through. He mutters, "She texted me."

I make a *what the fuck* face and exclaim loudly, "She *texted*! Your tried and true for two years just ups and leaves you with a text? And you don't find that strange?"

He takes a deep breath and his eyelids flutter and he's turning purple and for a moment I think he's going to pass out, but he doesn't. "Of course I did, but…but she would always talk about how much she missed her family, and who am I to argue with that?"

The devil says: *California my ass*, and with this astute reaction consider that Gail's timely fate may have followed the same path as Carmen's. That their *disappearances* are inextricably connected with the same person (Jolie?) or persons (Jolie and Lily?) being responsible for both.

I nod in silent agreement.

He says, "I think it's time you tell me what's going on."

I have to give him *something*, so I improvise and edit: "Jolie and I, our marriage, it's worse than I've let on. We've been fighting." *She wants me dead.* "Remember when I told you that she wants to take me for all I'm worth? Well with what I just discovered today, it's easy to think that now includes you."

The devil: *Nick's stash will pay for all those bills.*

"No, Pete, that can't be. Like I said, no one knows about the safe except me, and you now."

The proverbial light bulb illuminates my headspace. I spin and face the computer and with shaking hands pull up the *Argent Security Cloud* window. I click on the folder entitled *office* and a series of subfolders appears. I skip past the file dated today—that's me snooping in Nick's safe—and scroll back through a few dozen folders until I locate the one I'm looking for, dated Saturday, May 28th, Memorial Day Weekend. I double-click on it. Inside is one file.

Staring at the computer screen, I say, "I'm assuming that all of the files in the office folder, the recordings made by the lamp-camera, are of you going into the safe?"

"Yes, should be."

"Did you watch them all?"

"No, only a few. But they're all of me walking in and opening the safe and depositing or withdrawing money, then locking up and leaving."

"You sure about that?" I'm confident that the images on the file dated Saturday May 28th will prove my out-of-the-blue theory correct, so I double-click on the file and immediately look at the running timestamp, minutes before noon, just after we arrived and around the same time Jolie brought Rachel's diaper bag up to the guest room. We're greeted with the now familiar wide-angle shot of the office. The door swings open and Nick walks inside. He's wearing cargo shorts and a tank top. He reaches into his leg pocket and pulls out a white envelope and we watch as he opens the closet and slides the coats aside.

And then we spot Jolie, emerging from the guest room across the hall, holding a change of clothes for Rachel. She peers into the office, stops, soft-steps to the entrance and cranes her head inside. The video is as clear as day. I watch as she furrows her brow and purses her lips, the same face she makes when her wheels are spinning, and I can almost smell rubber burning as she watches Nick open the safe and deposit the cash from the envelope. As soon as Nick closes the safe door, Jolie ducks away.

Nailed it. Jolie knows about the money. Has for a while now. And it's my guess that sometime after this video was filmed, Jolie joined forces with Lily/Linda and formulated a plan to rob Nick…a plan that is still sloppily unfolding today. I say, "Will you get a safety deposit box now?"

Nick's face is a blend of *what did I just see?* and *holy shit.* "First thing tomorrow."

"Call an armored car company. You can't walk around with that kind of cash." I want to tell Nick not to worry, that this will all be over soon, but I'd be lying. Whatever's happening is far from over. In fact, it's just beginning, with very few answers and a mine of sordid details yet to be unearthed. I step across the hall to the guest room where Rachel is playing with the stuffed animals my dad keeps there for her.

"Daddy, look!" she exclaims, holding up a fluffy white tiger with black stripes.

"He's so cute." I sit on the bed. "Honey, I have a question for you. That lady on papa's computer, the one you said was Mommy's friend? What's her name?"

"I dunno."

"Where did you see her?"

She shrugs her shoulders and begins to toy nervously with the stuffed tiger.

"Rachel, honey, it's really important you try to remember. Where did you see her?"

"The park."

"Ok, good, honey…anywhere else?"

She hesitates, nods.

"Where honey?"

"The house, with the man."

Nick and I exchange glances. "That's good honey. Do you know the man's name?"

She shakes her head.

"How about the house? Was it at our house?"

She shakes her head no.

"Was it at a house like Papa's, or one in a building like ours?"

"Like ours," she says.

"Okay, good. And how many times have you seen her, the lady in the picture?"

"I dunno."

"Was it just one time?"

Rachel shakes her head *no.*

"Was it lots of times?"

She nods.

"Okay. You did great, honey." I could press the issue, but there's not much more I can bring to the surface grilling a three-year-old. Her words corroborate my assumption that Lily and Jolie have known each other for a while now, and that's what I was after. I walk out of the room into the hallway, my head still dumbly focusing on Nick's hiring of Lily as the root cause of everything that's happening. But he can't be blamed. He had no idea that there was any strife between Jolie and me. Jolie, now more of a super-fucking-bitch than I ever imagined her to be, she came to Nick with a golden opportunity saving him a finder's fee and the grief of interviewing strangers for the three-days-a-week position. Why wouldn't he trust a friend of his daughter-in-law's?

I say, "I'm sorry I got upset. This isn't your fault. You didn't know." The apology is empty, but acts as a preamble to what I really need to get across to him. "But please listen to me carefully, this is very important. Be vigilant. Keep your eyes open, and don't let *anyone* into the house. If you see anyone on the property, call the police."

He nods and frowns. "Pete, you're scaring me now. What's happening?"

Jolie murdered Carmen, and possibly Gail. "Just do as I say."

"Which is what? What do you need me to do?"

"Keep your doors locked and make sure Rachel is safe. I'm probably over-reacting, but it's best to err on the side of caution." I stand up and shoulder my attaché. "I need to go now. I'll call you when I'm on my way back to get Rachel."

"Where are you going?"

"I have to go to work." It's a weak lie, but he buys it with a nod.

"You really think Jolie is planning to rob me?"

I don't want to get him any more involved than he already is. Undue stress on a seventy-five-year-old can't be good for the heart, and if my offspring-senses are accurate, he's not in any condition to do anything other than sit by the pool and work on his tan. But he also has to know what he's gotten himself into, so I settle for middle ground: "I'm not a hundred percent certain, but if I had to guess, I think Jolie was, *is* using Lily, uh…Linda, to rob you."

His mouth drops and his bottom lip trembles, face paling but still more tan than I'll ever be. "What makes you so sure?"

"For starters, about a quarter-million in debt."

CHAPTER 41

I sit back down and spend the next ten minutes providing Nick with limited details about my battle with Jolie last night: her cache of bills, her compilation of credit cards, and the chaos that ensued. I edit out the Ambien-related sequence of events, and don't mention the burner with its unknown arsenal of evidence. The discovery of Carmen's corpse doesn't even enter into the equation. As the legendary philosophical duo Hall and Oates once said, "Some Things are Better Left Unsaid," and poor dead Carmen is one of those things.

The devil: *What about poor dead Gail?*

The angel manages a faint whisper: *She left to be with her family*. Maybe. But I need to keep expecting the unexpected. Ready myself for the worst. Nick the Ancient goes on to tell me how the three of them had lunch in the kitchen—it's all coming back to him now, *what else are you hiding, Nick*?—but he had a dentist's appointment and left them alone in the house. He shrugs. "I was gone for about an hour. When I got back, they were both gone."

I'm angry but keep calm as I ask, "Do you remember the exact date?"

He pauses, thinking. "The appointment is written on my calendar…" He opens the top drawer to the desk (*CLICKED IN MOON*) and removes a Town of Long Beach calendar complete with color images of nearby beaches and roads. Amid cartoon images of smiling newspapers and bottles on recycling days are scribbles in Nick's handwriting, one in particular, the word *dentist* written on July 15th. Almost a month ago. "Here it is."

I see it. Fuck. Lily and Jolie were here *alone*, plotting…and voila, I find the date in the Argent Security *office* folder and when I double-click it, the unexpected happens *again*. But this time, I expect it. Kind of.

It's like this: I expect it because in the video, the office door opens and I immediately say to Nick, "I thought you were the only one with a key?" and he tells me that he sometimes keeps it open, *I'm the only one here and there's a camera*, and we watch with intense interest as Jolie and Lily enter the room, open the closet, and view the safe. There's no audio, but it's clear from their hand gestures that they're brainstorming. The conversation lasts a couple minutes during which they point to the safe numerous times, unquestionably trying to figure out a way to get into it.

It's like this: I don't expect it because what happens after their muted discussion…*well*, let me start by saying that what occurs next is one of those fundamental things that all men hope and wish for on a daily basis but never experience…and yet, as I watch it—*the unexpected*—unfolding, it unnerves me and confirms to me how wrong I am when I think things can't get any more *(intertwiningly interesting)* twisted, any more fucked-up. *Again.*

Jolie and Lily share a laugh. They hold each other's hands, facing each other and smiling, after which a few tense seconds pass (normally I'd be counting here) before they lean in and…kiss. It's an uncertain moment between them, a first time encounter that lasts less than a minute during which they gaze at each other in wonderment, perhaps trying to decide if the liaison should continue. It does, the second kiss a bit more eager and a few seconds longer than the first. Soon the exuberance of the moment ignites into *passionate* and it's *hot* and I can't look away as Lily's tongue finds Jolie's, just as it found mine.

Lily's words bullet back to me, *Jolie was having an affair*.

Spot on, girl. You got me.

Nick feigns embarrassment but can't look away either. Of course he can't. He's riveted and we're speechless and if there was any doubt of collusion between Jolie and Lily, this quashes it. I say, "Email me these videos. At some point we're gonna have to look through the rest." The two women break away just as Rachel totters into the room, and they all hurry out, shutting the door behind them.

We mirror their exit in stunned silence, too ashamed to look at each other, my lovely wife now adding unfaithful to the long list of ways she's managed to tell me to go fuck myself, Nick's housekeeper colluding with the mastermind behind everything that's *wrong* in my life, *our* lives. More veils have been lifted.

Before I leave, I ask, "How did you come up with the password for your computer? Clicked in moon?"

He huffs and shakes his head. "I suppose I need to change it now, huh? Clicked in moon. It's an anagram for Nick Delmonico."

I *knew* there was something familiar about it.

CHAPTER 42

Once outside, I tell Nick to get in touch with Gail, thinking, *we need to find out if she's still alive*. He nods and stares, eyeing me suspiciously, but doesn't say anything, which I'm grateful for. I'm all fresh out of lies.

I grab an Uber back to the Long Beach station. The driver has a voice like a muted-trombone, like a *Peanuts* adult, sonically annoying. I flex some brain muscle and manage to keep her babbling out of frame and mind as I *don't count one one-hundred* and ponder my options for wiping down, and possibly getting rid of Carmen's plastic coffin. Innocent or not, no one gets off scot-free with a dead body in their storage unit.

Problem is, I'm not familiar with the surveillance in the building. I know about the camera at the front entrance, and the one in the elevator, but don't know if there are any in the stairwell, laundry room, or storage area. *Shit, shit, shit*, I really need to figure all this out before I get impulsive again and find myself in more trouble than I'm already in.

The angel on my right, feeling weak and uninspired: *Every move you make is impulsive now.* Once my go-to voice of reason, the angel has become an impediment to the devil's determination, my *now* better half, my new whole. If I take the angel's advice and go to the police and tell the whole truth and nothing but the truth, I'll fry, in spite of my innocence. If I want to stay out of prison, I'll have to follow the devil's path, and fight evil with evil.

For the first time in my life, the devil has taken full command of my mind and body. I can feel it. *Sense* it. And it's telling me to deal with Carmen's corpse, but to do so later because it's *daytime*, and no one moves a corpse while the sun's still out.

The angel: *If you wait, the cops might get there before you do.* Indeed, they might. But what else can I do?

The devil: *Find Lily.*

Yes, Lily. Fucking Lily. She fucked me good, took me for a ride both literally and figuratively and now, because of this, she'll always be with me, a tattoo on my brain clawing at my subconscious. I want to let her go, but there's no way I can. She is my meth. My meth with answers.

I catch a train back to Penn Station. Long Beach is the last stop before Jamaica and the car I'm in is full. I sit facing an old man. He's asleep, head back, mouth wide open like a burst-the-balloon clown at the carnival. I wish had a water gun. If I had any popcorn, I'd try to see how many I could get into his mouth before he wakes up. My thoughts make me chuckle aloud and nearby commuters leer at me. But I don't care. I remove my camera for a quick shot.

Point.

Click.

The train pulls into Penn Station. An announcement blares through the overhead speaker and the old guy startle-wakes with a honking-snore sound. I chuckle again, then make my way back through Penn Station. Another street act is performing in the pavilion, this time it's a duo of folk singers wearing tie-dye t-shirts and ratty jeans, perfect Stafford Coffee candidates. STP's "Pretty Penny" is currently in rotation, and I'd stop if I didn't have more pressing matters at hand. The homeless crooner from yesterday is back to doing his thing, but not as spasmodically. He's still barefoot, the socks I gave him nowhere in sight. No good deed goes unpunished.

Once outside, I start walking down 7th Avenue, mind still spinning over conniving Lily-Linda, whoever the fuck she is. The devil tells me: *she's dangerous* and I respond out loud, "No kidding." She could very well be with Jolie right now, formulating a plan to stop me from getting in their way, from disrupting their predatory task. Isn't that what they've been doing all along? But it's not going to work out for them because now I know what they're up to. My brain is functioning differently now. I no longer need to *count.* I feel shrewd and daring and no longer bear any guilt. Everything feels *right.*

My thoughts trigger back to yesterday when I envisioned myself at Lily's side, wanting nothing more than to be with her, protect her, *love* her. That's all I've ever wanted in life: to love, and be loved. But once again love has eluded me, shunned me, *fucked me,* my world's lack thereof shaping me into someone I'm not. Someone I'm forced to become in order to survive. And as I persist in fending off the feelings of rejection plaguing me, I feel more and more *right* about my pursuit of happiness and everything I need to do in order to remain a man free of Jolie's mammoth clusterfuck.

For the first time ever, *I'm taking control.*

I reach downtown. Stafford Coffee is in one direction and Washington Square Park is in the other. I'll never look at either the same way again. Despite having walked thirty blocks, I'm bursting with nervous energy as I pace up 4th Street, blood rushing, legs pumping. I skid to a stop in front of Lily's building—*is she up there right now? What if Jolie is with her?* The whole area stinks of greasy Chinese food. I peek through the steamy window of the takeout joint. Lots of cooks in the kitchen, but still no sign of Sugah. Heh-heh.

I check out the column of names alongside the buzzers, nine in all. Next to 3C is a name I do not know: Claire Benson. It's very American and have you ever noticed how movies and television shows overuse the character name Claire? *Outlander* and *Lost* and *House of Cards* and I can see Lily being *Linda,* but I can't see her being *Claire.* She doesn't look like a Claire. Plus, her LD tattoo doesn't fit the narrative. Maybe it stands for something else? Loves Dick? Insert crying-laughing emoji here.

The angel, still trying: *It's her real name* and it's ungoogleable but I open my phone's browser and try anyway, and the results are only slightly more surfable than Linda Davis, only 112 million results to browse through, an internet's worth of pretty-smiling Claire-faces. A young guy enters the vestibule and I smile and grab the door as he pushes out, nose in phone with not a sideways glance in my direction as I slip inside.

You ready for some exercise?

Three flights. Right. I take them slowly, thinking of a million different things to say, none of them pleasant. It's easy when you're a fucked-over lover and you're barking hostile words at your mind's eye image of the woman you wanted to fall in love with—*Claire,* that's going to take some getting used to—but it's much harder when the same woman, who also fucked you six ways to Sunday, is standing right in front of you.

I reach the third floor and stand in front of apartment 3C, hesitating, listening to Rihanna's *We Found Love* thumping behind the closed door, and *I thought you liked grunge, Lily, uh…Claire?* My heart chokes my throat.

The angel, or the devil, I can't tell: *Jolie tried to hurt you, so be prepared. Lily-Linda-Claire might try something impulsive.*

Just like I am now.

I knock.

The door opens.

It's not Lily.

CHAPTER 43

It's Claire.

"Yeah?" Claire says. She's a twenty-something Stafford Coffee hipster, pale with red frizz up top, cut-off denim shorts and sleeveless Guinness Dark Irish Stout tee. She's the strong bitter type who enjoys dark ale, dark coffee, and judging by the guy standing behind her, dark men.

This is *unexpected*. I'd tried to *expect*, but didn't expect *this*. I say, "I'm looking for..." and almost say "Lily" but it's safe to assume that "Lily" is a fictitious handle, so instead say, "I was here, uh, last week. With the girl who lived here. And I was hoping to surprise her, but...you aren't her."

"No, I'm not." No smile. The guy behind her isn't the threatening type, but he's standing guard and staring me down because this is New York City. "How did you get in here?"

I white-lie it: "I hit your buzzer and a guy came out and I thought maybe you sent him to let me in, so..."

Claire rolls her eyes. She's no pushover. "Sorry pal, can't help you."

"But...I *was here*, with a girl, and she had a key, and I slept here two nights in a row." I make a peace sign with my fingers.

"Did you try calling her?"

"I lost her number."

Her eyes roll again and damn, she's good at it. She's losing patience and I can't blame her. "The landlord Airbnb's the place when I'm not around. Whoever you were here with, her time expired yesterday."

Airbnb? No shit. "Okay..." Hmm. Was I just Lily's last hurrah in New York City? A final fling before heading back to where her accent came from? "Would you happen to know her? The girl that was here before you?"

"I thought you slept with her."

She has a point and the guy behind her steps forward. He's also wearing cut-off Levi's, only with a Slayer tee, and somehow that concerns me. "Okay, look. I had the greatest time of my life here, with a girl I'd only just met. She took my number, but I never got hers, and I only want to get in touch with her again." I wink at the guy. He doesn't wink back, gives me a dose of stink-eye instead. "We don't know who was here last week. Sorry." He moves to shut the door.

I put my hand against the door. "Wait...how about the person you're renting from? Can you give me *their* contact info?"

The devil applauds my aggression, but they shake their hipster-heads in unison. *Shit.* Now it's Claire's turn to try and shut me out. "Wait..." I reach into my wallet and pluck out one of the hundred-dollar bills Nick gave me yesterday. If I had a twenty I'd start with that, but I don't and I *need dem deets*. I hand it to her, and she doesn't hesitate. Money talks.

She says, "Hold on," then whispers something to the hovering boyfriend. He removes a cell phone from his back pocket, and in a C-note flash, I have the landlord's number. "They live downstairs, apartment 1A."

The door slams shut and *poof,* I'm out a hundred bucks. Great. I race to the first floor and knock on 1A. A monotone voice emerges from behind the closed door: "Who is it?"

"Uh, hi? My name is Peter. Claire up in 3C? She told me to come speak to you about..." And it's here I try a different approach because honesty hasn't really proven to be the best policy. "...about renting the Airbnb upstairs?"

The door opens and I'm faced with a buzzed-cut gender-neutral thirty-something who looks exactly like *they* sound. They/them invite me inside and I step into a studio apartment only slightly larger than 3C, with a small stove, a pull-out sofa, and bathroom with a door.

"I'm Morgan," the landlord says. Morgan is distinctly non-binary. They were born a female but now outwardly identify as both (neither?) sexes. They're wearing khaki pants and a Ralph Lauren polo buttoned to the neck, a man's dress belt and woman's loafers with shiny little pennies tucked in. Morgan says, "I'm leaving for work in ten minutes, so make it snappy."

Morgan is no nonsense and I'm thinking they have the right idea: create a life for oneself that encompasses the best of all worlds. There's no keeping up with the Joneses, no saving faces, no airs or posturing. Just all truths put out there for the world to take or leave. I say, "I was here last week with the girl that rented 3C, and I liked the place."

Morgan scoffs. "What's there to like? Bathroom has no door."

"Yeah, I noticed that. But I only need it for a short while, and I was wondering if you might have her contact info? The girl who stayed there?"

Too soon?

Definitely. Morgan is a pragmatist and can see right through my clear-as-cellophane intentions. They say, "Really, dude? Do I look *that* naïve?" They walk to the door and hold it open. "Like I said, I have to leave for work."

"Okay. I get it. But please..." I make a cute face, big eyes, fake pout. "I had the two greatest nights of my life with the girl from 3C," (the truth), "but I lost her number," (a lie), "and I just want to connect with her again." I pull another one of Nick's

Benjamins from my wallet and Morgan must've seen the others because they say, *"make it three hundred,"* and it makes me sick, but I really need to find Lily. So I peel off another two and fork them over. Morgan smiles and grabs. I mini-puke in my mouth.

"Hold on..." They search their phone, then say, "Sorry to be the bearer of bad news, but the person who rented the place last week is a guy."

CHAPTER 44

"You still want the name? I'll give you back a hundred if you don't."

How sweet of you, Morgan. "No, keep the money. I'll take the number." They show me the name in their phone—Gregory Strand—along with a phone number, a NYC 646 exchange that I type into my phone's notepad with no concerns of being scammed. The number looks familiar…and then, like a jolt of electricity, it hits me as my phone's history completes it for me. My heart starts thumping and I'm still not counting, *yes!* I thank Morgan, unsure of how in my search for Lily I ended up with a man's number in my phone and moths in my wallet. But I'm expecting the unexpected now, and for a passing moment wished Morgan was Julie Chen and this was all just *Big Brother*. But it's not. It's my life, where the unexpected keeps rearing its ugly head in the most unfortunate of ways.

They reply, "Do not make me regret giving that to you."

"You'll never hear from me again," I say, a partial truth if there ever was one. They'll either never hear from me, or they'll be subpoenaed as a witness in my murder trial. Before I leave, I hold up my attaché and ask, "Would it be okay if I take your picture?"

They fire a look at me that screams of *are you fucking kidding me?*

I ask, "No?"

They reply firmly, "No."

I exit Morgan's apartment and for a hot second consider spinning and snapping a shot before they close the door, but don't chance it. I don't need to draw any more attention to myself, and getting into a hubbub with Morgan the landlord isn't a good way to keep things low profile. Once outside, I open my cell's phone log and whoop, there it is: the same number Morgan gave me—*Gregory Strand*—is the same number Jolie called last week at 1:42 a.m. I try it again with familiar results, *do-do-do the number you have reached is no longer in service.*

I walk back up 4th Street, sidestepping pedestrians as my thoughts bounce to and fro: the renter's number belongs to a person named Gregory Strand. But Lily was the only person in the apartment. The devil chimes in, planting seeds: *He could have been hiding in the closet, watching*. The thought of that makes me shudder. And Jolie had called someone in the apartment—either Lily or Greg—as I left. Why? The devil waters the seeds: *Gregory Strand purchased Lily's burner and paid for the weekly rental. He also purchased Jolie's burner, a small investment into a potentially lucrative opportunity.*

Nick's stash.

I attempt the simple math: Jolie finds out about Nick's treasure-chest and sees it as a way to get out debt. Somewhere along the line, she meets Lily. Lily introduces her to Greg and together they formulate a plan that begins with Lily getting Gail's job, and ends with Nick's money in Jolie's (and Greg's) pockets. But something must've not gone as planned, because between then and now, Lily slept with me, and Carmen ended up dead in my storage locker.

Christ Jolie…what the fuck have you gotten us into?

The time on my phone says 1:13. It vanishes as a call comes in from the office. Shit. I never checked-in sick. I answer. It's Annoying Amy.

"Peter! I told the boss you would be in at eleven, and now I look like a liar, where are you?!"

"Uh…something came up—I won't be in today."

"Oh no, Peter, I hope everything's okay!"

"Everything is fine. I just need to take care of a few things with my dad."

She keeps on talking and I keep on hating her voice, so I hang up. I've never done that before, and should feel bad about it, but don't. In fact, I feel *good* about it.

The devil: *You're a changed man. You're taking control now.*

I continue walking up 4th Street, a smile on my face, the *now* me pressing on.

Next stop, Stafford Coffee.

CHAPTER 45

I'm back and nothing's changed. The aroma is still pleasant, the clientele is still grainy, and shiny-boy still has something in his eye.

"Welcome back," he says, grinning so widely I wouldn't be surprised if a canary's feather fluttered from his mouth. "What can I *help* you with?" Emphasis on *help.* His eyes are twinkling, and I want to take his picture because my creative piece always goes there but, I also don't want to lead him on and *can I take your picture* won't do me any favors right now. So instead I say, "Large and dark," and yeah. Now Shiny-boy is thinking *there is a god,* and he smiles and it lingers and I smile and turn away because, well...let's just say I have enough relationship drama in my life. Once my caffeine is served, I find a spot near the window and reminisce about better times when it was just me and *Lily* and our splendid, flirt-filled conversations.

I sip and google *Gregory Strand* and you guessed it, there are 25 million clickable options. I click and tap and tap and click, but find nothing. I tap the image search (I should've done that first) and scroll and scroll and scroll. A dozen pages down, one photo jumps out at me. Of a man's face. A *familiar* man's face.

A mugshot.

No doubt about it. I've seen this guy before. But I can't place him. I'm really good with faces, have about a thousand of them in my darkroom, and could just swear this guy has popped up somewhere in my recent travels. The person I'm staring at is not of my flock: jacked to the gills, badass and grizzled, thick neck inked, a hummingbird in flight. *Where the hell do I know this guy from?* I click on his mugshot and am brought to a page on the Pinellas County Sheriff's website. Gregory "Greg" Strand, aged 35, a drifter half his life, multiple arrests in Florida: grand larceny, breaking and entering, assault, drug possession. A real winner, the type of guy you see on *60 Days In*, the type of guy you wouldn't let your daughter date, even over your dead body.

I scroll and click and understand now with dread that Jolie is linked to this guy, *your wife is having an affair*, and it makes me want to pull out my hair and scream. I mean, she consciously chose to let this scumbag into our (already dysfunctional) lives! And then Lily. Enter her into the equation and my life becomes one of those betrayal-greed-murder-love quadrangles Netflix films documentaries about.

There's no short supply of his image on the web, a half-dozen mug shots, two walk-of-shame photos, and a few from long ago when Myspace was still a thing and he had a profile, when promise and potential still endured in his life. The photo I'm looking at is gently out of focus, pre-HD age. He was a handsome youth back then, cleaner-cut (despite the tattoos), an ordinary-looking twenty-five-year-old with a girl at his side. She looks to be six or seven years younger than him, a future *looker* offering her long-lost genuine smile to the camera.

Lily as a beautiful eighteen year-old, blind to the ugliness soon to be introduced into her life, smiles from a time when innocence and naivety still dominated her persona. And as I stare at her photo from the past, an upwelling of strength and fortitude rises in me. I can *feel* it. What once made me weak and guilty now empowers me. Yes, I'm a *changed* man, ready for anything the fuckhead standing next to her in the photo throws at me.

I've uncovered a great deal today, and it's all starting to gang up on my emotions. My eyes gloss over. *What have I gotten myself into?* I've made poor decisions in my life,

(...Polaroid...)

marrying the wrong woman was one, making the choice to stay with her is the other. A couple years ago Google told me what bi-polar disorder looked like, so I suggested to Jolie (with kid gloves, of course) that she see a doctor. All throughout the three-day tantrum that followed, I heard *there's nothing wrong with me, you're the fucking problem Peter!* about a thousand times. So, I never mentioned it again.

(REPRESSED)

Now I'm in a moment where all my life's decisions have converged, giving me no choice but to veer from the path of *least resistance,* and onto the path *less-traveled.* It's what the devil wants, what the devil *needs.* I touch Lily's muted, pixilated face. She looks the same...but *younger,* bleeding innocence on the arm of a man who would soon force her into a world she has no understanding of. Ten years have passed since this photo was taken. It must've been a happier time, before their lives slipped into an orbit of drugs, lies, and greed. *Lola.* I tap the photo and it leads me to the Myspace graveyard, where images of the past remain like poor forgotten souls. Under the photo is a comment from the pictureless profile of one Lola Dawson, a single heart emoji. I click on it and find a profile completely purged of its content.

I want to, no...*need* to rescue her from the degenerative life she's trapped in. I know, I should just walk away, go to the cops, tell the whole truth and nothing but the truth, end this scandalous drama. But I can't. She gave herself to me, her *true* self, and in those moments we shared, she *loved me.* I felt it. No one has ever made me feel that way before. And if it means I can have her in my life always and forever, I'll do whatever it takes to keep myself out of prison so I can love her back.

The angel: *She's been using you, playing a kept role for him.*

Fuck him, that fucking fucker. Who the fuck does he think he is?

The devil: *He's their puppet master. He's got Jolie's and Lily's strings knotted and tethered just the way he wants them.* Greg. *Fucking* Greg. I don't know him, but I'm jealous of him. He's everything I now want to be: a bad-boy with *two* beautiful women at his beck and call. Instead, I'm a lonely and desperate cuckold.

But I'm a *changed* cuckold, one with a burning sensation that's encouraging me to stand up for what I want. What I *need*.

You better be ready, Greg.

CHAPTER 46

Time keeps passing slowly on this longest day ever.

I google *Lola Dawson* and she's as off-the-grid as Lily Dahl, making me wonder if *this* LD is as made up as the others. This time I conduct an image search first and find exactly zero links to any social media (even the barren Myspace profile doesn't come up). Nothing even remotely identifiable as her. I keep scrolling anyway and start to lose interest until, way down in the results, beyond a dozen or so other Lola Dawsons, I spot a single low-res photo of my Lily-slash-Lola. It's a mugshot, from a time when she was not much older than the Lola in the photo with Greg. There are tears streaming down her young, photogenic face, red eyes staring blankly into the camera, heartbroken over a first offense riding shotgun alongside her new boyfriend. I touch her picture, sensing her soft red lips, her damp cheeks, wishing I could reach into the past to rescue her from the last ten years.

To distract myself from the woman I love, I move on to the woman I hate.

I pull up the digital photos I took of her hand impression, then zoom in on each fingerprint. The index, middle, and ring fingers are clear and swirly, a nail in any murder suspect's coffin if this were a crime scene; I can't say for certain if Carmen was killed inside my apartment, but I'm cautiously optimistic she wasn't. There was no blood anywhere, none that I could see, and didn't notice anything out of the ordinary except for the crack in the wall near the entrance to Rachel's room. I size up her index fingerprint to actual size, *Joliefinger-sized,* then open the burner and place the image against the scanner. It doesn't work. I try the middle finger and then the ring finger, cursing my futile effort because no one uses their middle or ring finger to unlock their phone. Possibly the thumb, but the image of her thumbprint is an unusable smeary partial. I try the index finger again. Nothing.

My frustration builds and my head gets hot...but my *changed* self starts to think outside the box and it's saying that I'm much better off in the world of *now,* where my novel identity *understands* that the digital image of Jolie's fingerprint is a reverse-image to her real fingerprint. I quickly flip the image in my phone, place it against the scanner on the burner, and...

...it flashes once and...holy shit. I'm in!

At once a message pops up from the carrier informing me that the phone is no longer in service. No surprise there. It's like this: Jolie loses the burner. Tells Greg. Greg cancels the phone's service...then slaps Jolie around for being irresponsible (this part is a wishful, icing-on-the-cake embellishment, but I just can't help myself right now.)

The devil: *Then what happens?*

With her smile (and maybe her body), she convinces Greg that *"there's no way he can get into it,"* adding something like, *"he couldn't figure out his way into a car without an instruction manual."*

Yeah, no doubt I'd enjoy seeing Jolie in a world of Greg Strand's hurt right now.

I tap the text icon and I'm disappointed. A blank log. She either deleted everything, or followed seasoned criminal Greg's lead by *never ever EVER putting unlawful intentions in writing*. I check the call log and it adds a couple of nuggets, two 646

Manhattan exchange numbers with a dozen short calls going back and forth between them, none longer than five minutes. I google the phone numbers—one of them is the familiar number Jolie called in the middle of the night last week from her cell—and they appear in crowded lists of previously activated Manhattan burner numbers, more than enough evidence for me to know that these two numbers once led to Greg Strand and Lola Dawson.

I've been multitasking the entire time, peering through the tops of my eyes at every Lola-looking woman (stick a fork in *Lily?*) coming in for a midday caffeine fix. But she's a no-show, my hour at Stafford Coffee not entirely wasted, but the hope of running into her a failure. I get up…and I can't help myself. I remove my camera, point, and click. First at a nerdy chess club, and then at a random Tinder couple who may (or may not) fuck and never see each other again.

I head back outside into the hustle and bustle of Greenwich Village and make it one block before my cell rings.

The caller ID screams and spits in my face.

NYPD 19th Precinct.

CHAPTER 47

They want to talk about Carmen. Poor dead Carmen, the nanny who for two-plus years earned $600 a week to clean my home and watch my daughter. Now she's *missing*, and I'm a person of interest, a *lying* person of interest, a soon-to-be suspect. My prints are on the plastic bin (and the tape that once sealed it), completely of my own doing, and if I don't remove them, I'm fucked. Simple as that. I need to create a diversion, lead the cops away from me, toward Greg Strand. But how do I do that when they don't even know he exists?

What the fuck are you mixed up in, Jolie? Twice she'd said to me *I'm sorry*, and I can count all the times she's ever apologized to me on two fingers, each one a lie. I'm guessing it's like this: she's *sorry* because she's involved in Carmen's death, and in her inescapable position realized the only way out of it was to pull me in.

Frame me.

I'm sorry…

The next chapter of this saga has me on the E-Train uptown. It breaks down, a common occurrence in the summer when everyone is ripe for the picking. The smelly masses transfer, too-close-for-comfort commuters momentarily hating their lives. By the time I get to the 19th, I'm hot and stressed and on the verge of a possible all-nighter that won't be nearly as fun as the one I had with Lily Dahl (I'm pulling the fork back out, she will always be Lily to me).

The *old* me from last week, he'd be shitting his pants about now, stooped with anxiety, fingers clawing nervously at his belly. Do-or-die situations weren't his thing. But the *now* me? The *changed* me? He thinks differently. He's smarter and wiser and will do whatever it takes to make certain the wool is pulled completely over the law's prying eyes. If he doesn't, he'll earn a non-stop, first-class ticket to Riker's Island.

The 19th Precinct is a four-story Italian edifice of red brick with bluestone copings and terra cotta trimmings, a beautiful building home to over 150 of NYC's finest, and no place I ever wanted to visit.

But here I am.

I step into the bustling precinct and approach the reception area. They have their very own Amy manning the lines, desk plate: Amy Adams. She's a twenty-something plain-Jane short-cut newbie with a cadet corps badge, low-key and brooding, the antithesis of Johnson Apparel's Amy. She's on the phone, disdaining the unfortunate caller with an utterly mediocre tone. She hangs up and duly ignores me, stiff unmanicured hands shuffling papers into a variety of metal trays. She's a multitasker. She's Amy-dexterous. She eventually acknowledges my existence with a silent glare that could freeze a snake in its track. "Can I help you?"

"Hi—Peter Delmonico here to see Officer Molloy." Murphy had called but I asked for Molloy because she's a sight *(…for distraction…)* and Murphy is not. Plain Amy pages Molloy and Murphy shows up. His smile is wide and threatening. We shake hands and he offers me coffee and it's cold and bitter, like Claire. I'm led into a back room, you know, the dank one with the lights and the camera and the two-way mirror? There's a detective here, archetypal NYC gumshoe fare, fifty-something-looking-sixty-something, drab blazer with beige faux-suede elbow patches. His hair is mussed and his beard is grizzled, cheeks and nose flush with twisting spider veins. He looks as if he just crawled out of bed after a night working *undercover*. Grins.

I peek around for Molloy but she's nowhere to be found. In this intimidating moment, I could use her as a distraction as this unexpected second visit with the police slackens the devil's grip on me and produces a trickle of pain *(...six-seven-eight...)* deep inside my mind.

The detective introduces himself as Detective Lerner, and "You know Officer Murphy." He searches my attaché, somewhat inefficiently, then drapes it over the back of my chair.

I sip, grin, and...*focus*.

They're going to pry.

The devil: *Stay the course, utter only truths. Except the inconvenient ones, of course.*

"I've been assigned to the missing persons case of Carmen Rodriguez. I understand Carmen worked for you?"

So, it begins. The first hour mirrors the hour I spent with Murphy and Molloy in my kitchen, simple questions asked simply garnering simple answers. I know I appear calm right now, but on the inside I'm freaking out. What if Jolie is in another room doling out a completely different series of events? One that tosses me head-first under the bus? They refill my coffee—they want me to be nervous and alert.

Murphy says, "When we first spoke, you said that Jolie worked at Saks Fifth Avenue."

"That's correct." His eyes are awful, his nose a big fat punchable tomato.

"How long has she worked there?"

"About two years. She got the job a few months before Rachel's second birthday. That's when we hired Carmen." I glance at the two-way mirror, and it judges me back.

Lerner replies, "Well…we stopped by Saks, and there's no one by the name of Jolie Delmonico employed there."

What? My heart stops, turns itself inside-out, then starts beating backwards. I look back and forth between the two cops, reading the painful truth in their eyes.

He continues, "We also spoke to the store manager. You know what she said? That no one by the name of 'Jolie' has ever worked there, at least in the last eight years she's been there. We also showed her Jolie's photo, just in the odd chance she might've been employed under a different name…" *(Jolie Demonic?),* "and…well, guess what? Your wife, the woman you're married to and currently *live* with, has been lying to you about her job for…how long has it been?"

"Two years…" The shock is real. A painful throb starts up in my head and I rub my temples with both palms, an unsuccessful attempt to ease the ghostly pain. My stomach wrenches into a dense tangle. The devil: *Your marriage is a LIE!* Then, Lily's voice in my head, a faint echo from Saturday afternoon: *Ever see her paycheck?*

My mind momentarily digresses toward the painful truth: Lily already knew the answers to the questions she was asking me, about me and my baggage and my insane wife's spending habits. I say, weakly because Jolie's mother-of-all-lies just sucked the life out of me, "I assure you, Detective, I-I didn't know. I…I…" My words emerge broken, rock-shards in a tumbler. "Two years ago, she told me she got a job at Saks and I swear, if she's never worked there, then she's been lying to me about it all this time."

Lerner grimaces, either feeling my pain or struck with incredulity. It's here I notice a large skin tag on his neck and from this point forward it will be hard to look at anything else.

"Do you have any idea where she might be now? The number you provided us goes straight to voicemail."

I shake my head, and this is where I might be able to steer their prying eyes away from me, and onto Jolie. "I don't...we had an argument last night and she stormed out and I haven't heard from her since. Have you tried her mother's place in Jersey?"

"We have...she isn't there."

Part of me is thrilled Jolie is "missing." It pulls their attention away from me, and also gives Susan the Cunt something to worry about (not so much about her missing daughter, but how she might appear on the *Six O'clock News*). Still.

Lerner asks, "What did you fight about?"

"The usual, money, *bills*. Look...we have our fair share of arguments, I won't deny that. And they usually end with her slamming the door in my face." I pause and rub my face with both hands, solely for effect. "But there's something you need to understand about Jolie. She's not well. Hasn't been since Rachel was born. She was diagnosed with post-partum depression that, over time, has progressed into something much worse."

"Something *worse*?"

"My Google-educated guess is bi-polar disorder. I've begged her to see a doctor, but she refuses."

The devil reminds me: *She has a script for Ambien, and that came from a doctor, which means they're going to find out about it.*

"Do you see her as a danger to your daughter?"

I nod slowly and assuredly, a well-deserved toss under the bus if there ever was one. "I never thought so...but with

Carmen missing, and Jolie not answering my calls, I'm concerned."

"She stopped answering your calls?"

Uh-oh. "Yes, since our fight."

"Fight? You said argument."

Fuck. "Argument, then. No punches were thrown." *Only plants and sneakers and stacks of bills.*

Murphy nods and takes a sip of tepid black brew, burps: coffee and street-vendor hot-dogs. "Last night was the last time you saw her?"

"Yes."

"So, she slept out."

"She said that she was going to her mom's. That's where she usually goes after we argue, so I didn't think anything of it."

"Where's Rachel now?"

"At my dad's in Long Beach. Which reminds me, I should let him know that I'm going to be late picking her up."

They agree and say they need a bathroom break, but that's just a ruse. They're going to watch me from the other side of the looking-glass to see if I keep to the storyline with Nick: Carmen is missing and the cops want to speak to me, and *no* I can't talk about it, and *yes* I'm a person of interest, and *obviously* I had nothing to do with it. I ask him if he wouldn't mind keeping Rachel overnight, and he's happy to do it. Nick, continuing to *try*.

Before we hang up, he says, "I tried calling Gail a few times, but she hasn't picked up."

The devil pokes me with its logic: *Gail was taken out of the picture so "Linda" could get in.*

I say, "Okay, no worries." But there's a lot to worry about and on that note, I end the call. Lerner and Murphy return with an open laptop and if I didn't think my heart could beat any harder, it surprises me by muffling my world, *boom-boom-boom.*

I have no sense of what they're going to show me, but it must be relevant. Lerner sits alongside me and positions the screen so all three of us can see it.

He says, "We obtained the security footage from your building."

Fuck fuck fuck fuck fuck. Here's where I find out if a security camera caught me rifling through my storage unit, and puking on Ted Bundy's shoes. This moment in the questioning room at the 19th Precinct could very well be my last free one on earth.

The detective blows his tomato-nose into a coffee-stained napkin, then clicks into a folder containing a long list of files. He opens the first one and at once I'm looking at a black-and-white image of the lobby in my building. He states, "On Monday, 9:03 a.m., Carmen is seen walking into the building." I watch as Carmen's five-foot-nothing frame appears through the revolving door. She waits for the elevator and enters when the doors slide open. No other people are visible. He clicks on the next file in the queue. This time I watch as she takes the elevator to the fourth floor. She exits and the doors shut behind her.

Lerner says, "That's the last time anyone's seen her."

The *now* me is *now* realizing: Carmen always dropped our trash in the dumpster, and to get there you have to walk past the storage units, and if the elevator footage is *last* time anyone's seen her…

The devil: *That's what they want you think…*

"Were you there at the apartment when she arrived?"

"No. I left for work around eight and was at my desk before nine. I remember I worked until after six because I had a Zoom call late in the day."

Lerner and Murphy jot and whisper and tap the notebook for emphasis. Lerner nods and Murphy asks, "So you'll have no problem if we call your office to confirm your hours?"

"No, not at all, I'm happy to help." I am. This might be starting to look okay for me.

Lerner gets back into the driver's seat. "We searched through hours of security footage. She doesn't appear again. So, unless she exited down a fire-escape, or left through the freight entrance, she never left the building."

One one-hundred, two one-hundred…NO! STOP!

Murphy says, "Peter…it's important you understand that we have probable cause for a search warrant, not only for the building, but for your apartment as well. Knowing this, it would be very foolish for you to not tell us everything you know." He deepens his tone to level serious, but I've watched enough true crime to know interrogator stock verbiage when I hear it. I broadcast my version of the truth with a *fine-by-me* shrug. "I'm here to help." Cooperation keeps the innocent free.

They nod in unison and the video clips continue. They show me a clip of myself leaving at 8:07 a.m., dressed in a jacket and tie. Then, they play one showing Jolie leaving at 9:13 a.m., decked in full gym gear. Lerner asks, "This is Jolie, correct?"

"Yes."

"Ok, fast forward to 11:43." He opens another file and this one shows Jolie returning, still in gym gear but less kempt. It's a familiar look, fading sweat-circles at the neck and ribs, humidity-frizzed hair tied back into a pony.

And then I see *her.* Lily, Linda, Lola, stepping in behind Jolie, not in gym gear but in jeans and a tee. She has a downcast grimace on her face. She appears to be nervous, perhaps even scared.

Wait for it…

Lerner asks, "Do you know this woman behind Jolie?"

I squint as if trying to make out her image. "No. Jolie has a lot of gym friends and it's not uncommon for them to stop by during the day." I could have told the truth, but don't want to throw Lily under the bus (a trending endeavor, it seems). Finding Lily has rescued me, wrenched me away *(...distracted you...)* from my ills *(...six-seven-eight...)*, comforted me in more ways than anyone ever has. I must protect her at all costs.

The detective continues, "Jolie doesn't leave again until 5:15 p.m., with Rachel in a stroller." He shows me the video and I look closely at the black-and-white footage. It's a little grainy but clear enough to show me that my wife of four years had been crying. If this were any other day, I wouldn't think twice about it—she's a pro at shedding tears. But when you consider Carmen's murder and her probable connection to it, those tears have meaning.

Lerner says, "She looks upset."

I nod.

"Any idea why?"

I shrug my shoulders, shake my head.

Murphy clicks into another directory on the computer. Lerner says, "Peter...I'm going to ask you to assist us with one more thing. It shouldn't take too much time."

The devil: *They're trying to wear you down.*

The angel: *They're doing their jobs.*

"Okay."

He says, "I'm going to show you a number of photos, one at a time. They're stills taken of everyone entering and leaving the building on Monday August 3rd, a week ago today, the day of Carmen's disappearance. I want you to look through them and let us know if you see someone or something unusual. Anything at all that you think might help us. Can you do that?"

I can and I do. I look and click and can feel them examining me as I scan through dozens of comers and goers. "Some of these people are tenants in the building."

Murphy replies, "Let's just stick with anyone who may seem out of place, or anything that just doesn't look right to you."

I feel like they're guiding me. Why wouldn't they want to know who lives in the building? The devil: *Because they already spoke to everyone there.*

All of a sudden the atmosphere feels changed. *Charged.* As if something big is coming. I can feel it. I click and click and click and...*THERE.* Lerner doesn't give me a second's chance to speak. He sees it on my face. "Does this person look familiar to you?"

The person I'm looking at *is* familiar. But he doesn't belong here, in my building, my world, my universe.

And yet, here he is.

The devil shouts: *You don't know him, Peter!*

I almost tell the truth, but what ends up coming out is, "No, I don't know him."

But I do.

The person I can't stop staring at in the surveillance image is the bulgy-eyed bouncer from Sugah's Peepshow.

CHAPTER 48

"Are you sure you don't recognize this man?" Murphy asks.

"I'm sure," I lie with all my heart, and with blind hope it sticks; they're pros and know what a liar looks like. "I thought I did…but now I'm thinking he's just a messenger, or a delivery guy. Someone I've crossed paths with in the building."

They confer in whispers, then ask me to keep going. I do so uneasily, unable to contain my recognition of the man following the bouncer through the door.

Greg Strand.

This is where I saw him before. It's all coming back to me now. My mind had been agitated at the time because moments earlier I'd found a dead body in my daughter's toy box and had completely forgotten about the elevator doors opening; about skater-boy joining me for the short ride up; about the bearded man with the neck tattoo standing outside, leaning against the *No Parking* sign. In Greg's online mug-shot, there'd been no beard and no Risky Business sunglasses, but the hummingbird sailing across his neck had been visible—the very same one in the black-and-white image I'm looking at now.

"This guy," I say.

"What about him?"

I tread lightly. I have to know him, but not *know* him. Cops are no different than cats—you can dangle the string and let them take a few swipes, but give them too much play and they're going to snag you. "I've seen him a few times, outside my building. I think I recognize the tattoo."

"Do you think Jolie knows him?"

Yes. And in an effort to steer the cops toward Greg Strand without actually pointing any fingers, I say, "With Jolie, nothing's out of the question." *Meow.*

The conversation continues. They move on to Carmen's possible whereabouts, *she has to be in the building somewhere*, and Jolie's possible whereabouts, *does she have any friends she might be staying with?*, and then how I should stay in the area because *we're certain to have additional questions for you*. After four hours of too much caffeine and no food, I'm fried, but also somewhat comfortable with how everything went down. Without them coming out and saying it, it feels as if they're looking at Jolie as their primary suspect, not me. That's my takeaway, anyway.

I haven't eaten all day and my stomach rumbles as the interrogation breaks. Lerner and Murphy thank me for my time. I ask to use the bathroom and on the way see Officer Molloy seated at a desk. I smile. She doesn't. When I come back out, I smile again. Again she doesn't. I shoulder my attaché, then try my smile on Plain Amy. Nope.

"Peter..." A woman's voice from behind me.

I turn and lo and behold Officer Molloy is walking toward me, parting Lerner and Murphy like they're the Red Sea, and I'm thinking: if I'm going to get cuffed, let it be Molloy, because under the most stressful of circumstances, my mind needs *distraction.*

(...from six-seven-eight...)

She shows me a slip of paper with lots of small print. "We just received the search warrant for your apartment, and we expect the warrant for your building to come through very shortly."

My heart leaps, but outwardly I remain steadfast and calm. "Are you coming by now? I…I just wanted to grab a quick bite first, but afterwards…"

"We'll come as soon as we receive the warrant for the building."

I nod. "Two birds, one stone?"

She smiles, just a little, but not enough to *distract.* "Something like that. It would be helpful if you were there to let us in."

"Understood." Deep inside, a faraway echo, the angel counting: *one-one hundred, two-one hundred, three one-hundred.*

When I turn to leave, she adds, "Oh…and just one more thing."

I face her and she steps in close as if to whisper something in my ear. She's so pretty, pale, lightly-freckled face, emerald eyes with red curls tied neatly into a bun. She says, "Your camera."

I put both hands on it, as if to protect it. "What about it?"

"Your hobby?"

"My passion." *Is she flirting with me?*

She utters slowly, "Can I see it?"

Okay. Lerner and Murphy watch on curiously; they appear as perplexed with this line of questioning as I am. My fingers and toes are crossed for her being genuinely interested in me, but…the mood quickly changes, her interest not the kind of interest I'm interested in. Something like that.

I open up my attaché and remove the camera and she calls a young cop over. "The camera. Bag it, and the contents."

Within seconds, and for the first time ever, my camera is in someone else's hands…

(…he took the Polaroid from you, and you never saw it again…)

…and it feels as if my heart was just ripped free of my chest, still beating in the hands of my assailant. "What do you need my camera for?"

Scribbling a note in her stupid pad, she says, "We're going to examine the contents, then dust it for prints and test it for DNA. Once we're done, you can have it back."

"No one other than myself has ever touched that camera. The only prints you'll find are my own." I bullet my gaze back and forth between Molloy and my camera, feeling alone, disconnected, a refugee whose child was just taken away.

Molloy smiles. I don't. She can take her pretty smile and shove it up her ass. "Then you have nothing to worry about, right?"

"Right," I say.

But I do.

Not only did they take my camera, but they also took the envelope, filled with pictures of Lily.

The woman I denied knowing in the security cam stills.

CHAPTER 49

Connecting the dots in this drama has been an arduous task. I've jumped over hurdles, knocked down roadblocks, and managed to construct a believable series of events in my head leading up to this point. But now? With the presence of someone previously insignificant playing a role, an extra in passing now a puzzle piece that doesn't fit, I've taken a step backward.

What the fuck was the bulgy-eyed bouncer from Peepshow doing in my building?

The devil: *He was with Greg Strand. They're all connected. Lily and Jolie too.*

I exit the 19th Precinct into the Upper East Side's manic flow. Without my camera, my security blanket, I feel lost, the urge to whisper *one one-hundred* nagging my subconscious. But...I remind myself that for the first time since *(...six-seven-eight...)* I was a child, my need to count vanished today. That has to count for something, no?

A central part of me for as long as my memories go back, the intensity of my tic has always been directly proportional to the nerve-racking situation driving it. The worse the experience, the more intense my counting. Earlier today, pressured above anything even remotely akin to my everyday anxieties, it peaked, and then unexplainably vanished, imploded, changing me into the person I am now, the *now* me, the person that always lived inside of me but I never knew existed. *Hello me, nice to meet you.* At an intersection, I pause with my hands on my knees, taking in deep controlled breaths while staring into the gutter and begging myself not to count. *Please don't count, please don't count. REPRESS and take control. REPRESS and take control. I am the NOW me…*

The numbers fade. Okay. Better.

I haven't eaten all day and I'm famished. Lightheadedness is kicking in and if I don't put something other than coffee into my system, I'll hit the ground hard. I stop by a random salad bar, one of those get-whatever-you-want kind of eateries exclusive to NYC, and decide on breakfast for dinner. I sink into a back corner seat and devour a wrap bursting with eggs, potatoes, and sausage. It's hell on my constitution, but heaven to the rest of me. Interesting people come and go and I want to capture them on film, but I can't, and it *hurts*. It's as though part of my soul has been torn away, the urge to count continuously pressuring me behind the scenes like an itch that can't be scratched.

I exit the eatery and walk in the direction of my home. Smiling people come and go, oblivious to the news-worthy injustice tearing me apart. Tears fill my eyes, not of sadness, but of anger and frustration. In less than a week, almost everything I've ever identified with has been stripped away: my family, my nanny, my finances, my camera, my *lover*. I do still have Rachel and Nick, and of course my job, but could easily lose them too—along with my freedom—if things don't go right for me. What did I do to deserve this?

The angel: *You cheated on your wife.*

The devil: *Everything would've happened anyway.*

I turn the corner and pass the entrance to the Central Park Sports Club, Jolie's home away from home. I try her cell again and again it goes to voicemail. She has her phone turned off so it won't ping, *smart*; the cops won't be able to pinpoint her location—guidance from Greg Strand, no doubt. It's cool out now and the second-floor row of windows is steamy, making it difficult to see the queue of treadmillers. I consider stopping in to look for her, but in my heart of hearts know she's not there. She's got bigger fish to fry than to squeeze in forty-five minutes of cardio.

It's getting dark and the time for me to make my move in the storage area is fast approaching. I can do it too. I know I can. All I need is ten minutes of alone time, and the promise of getting there before the cops do.

The angel asks: *What are you planning to do with the body?*

I answer aloud, "That, I have no fucking idea."

In minutes I'm back in my building and can't help but peek at the camera in the lobby. I do the same in the elevator as I ride up to the fourth floor, knowing that they're watching my every move. When the doors open, Garvin the ancient man from 4F is in my face.

"Well, hello there!" he says, smiling broadly as if tooth-gaps were something to be proud of.

I say, "How are you?" *Are we pals now?*

He leans in close as if to divulge a secret, *ugh he smells,* and whispers, "They told me not to say anything, but the cops were at my place this afternoon."

True Crime lesson number one: question everyone in the building. The devil called it. "What did they say?"

"They were asking about that little lady who watches your daughter. Told me she was missing, and that they were speaking to everyone on the floor."

The devil: *See? The cops didn't tell you that. They also didn't say anything about watching the security footage from the storage area. They are withholding information.*

The seconds pass like minutes. I really need to make my move downstairs, and soon. I change the subject. "Heading out for dinner?"

He nods vigorously, ear-to-ear grin stuck as if his batteries just ran out. "Gettin' some breakfast for dinner! Sometimes the body needs a good omelet to hit the spot, you know?" I give him a thumbs up as the doors close, thinking how easy it is, despite appearances, to have something in common with just about anyone.

(...even HIM...)

I enter my apartment. It's way too quiet, so I put the TV on to a local spot from *The Bathroom Buddies,* who promise to be my "buddy in the business," whatever the fuck that means. I empty my pockets and put my phone and Jolie's burner on the charge pad. The kitchen is exactly how I left it, wiped clean, but the bedroom is still a mess, Jolie's things yanked from drawers and half the closet's contents strewn on the floor. I need to tidy up before the cops get here.

I put in a call to Nick to check on Rachel—she's doing great, they had Chick-Fil-A for dinner—and provide him with an edited summary of my visit to the 19th Precinct. After our call, I open the fridge and see the last three bottles of Porch Rocker on the top shelf. I'm fairly certain I only drank two, and could've sworn there were four left this morning, but I'm too tired to think past *I must've had three* and am thankful they're not screw-tops, meaning I don't have to worry about them being Ambien-infused. I hope.

And thus begins the slow build of willpower toward moving Carmen's corpse. The first beer goes down in five minutes, during which CNN bashes today's political idiot in the crosshairs. I'm not much of a drinker (or a political guy), so two beers gets me good and buzzed. I pop my second, hoping the last one in the fridge will give me the balls I need to make my move.

In less than thirty minutes, I've downed all three beers. I never thought I could be *that guy,* you know, the one who uses alcohol to bolster his courage? But I'm *changed* now, my buzz (and balls) not game-ready yet, but getting there. I need something else, something a little stronger. I go through the cabinets and find a couple of unopened wine bottles that were gifted to us some time ago. Jolie and I aren't wine people. We don't even own a corkscrew. So I grab a steak knife and get to work. Half of the cork crumbles into the bottle. I drop the other half into the garbage pail…on top of an empty Porch Rocker bottle. *I knew there were four bottles in the fridge this morning.*

The devil asks: *Who drank it?*

I shrug my shoulders and take a swig, spitting out tiny pieces of cork, the warm and cloudy effects providing the determination I need to ignore the empty beer bottle and handle the unscrupulous task ahead. I check the time, 9:43, not late enough, but getting there. With at least another hour to kill before I can think about making my move, I decide to straighten up the bedroom.

Thump.

I startle and spin and nearly drop the wine bottle. It came from Rachel's room. I turn off the TV, firm up my grip on the bottle, and take another gulp. Now I know why people like wine so much. It dulls the senses and provides the balls one needs to do something one wouldn't normally do. *Like move a corpse.* It also makes walking in a straight line a challenge. I zig-zag to Rachel's room and lean against the doorframe and flip on the lights. The room is quiet and empty. Of course it is.

I slur out, "Jolie?"

No answer.

From behind the closed door of my darkroom comes a light *thud.*

"Jolie…is that you?" *Who else could it be?*

The angel: *Could be a water pipe delivering a hot shower to another apartment, or a…*

Thump.

Louder now, definitely not a water pipe. The door shakes and my cheap *do not disturb* sign sails to the floor. I take another swig, warm and awful-tasting.

The door knob begins to turn.

The fuck! My breath quickens. This is it, no time for deliberation. I thank God for alcohol and decide that from this point forward, I'm a drinker. The door begins to inch open and with no hesitation, I take two steps forward and karate-kick it shut. The person inside—a male voice—goes *oomph*! A hidden ruckus ensues, someone crashing into the table, the clatter of metal developing trays on the floor, the door trembling as the fallen stranger flounders behind it.

I yank the door open. The overhead bulb in the darkroom is out, but the reaching glow of the bedroom light is more than enough to expose the two large bulging eyeballs staring up at me from the floor.

It's the fucking bouncer from Peepshow. He tries to get up, but can't, his arms and legs thrashing uselessly, failing to leverage his massive girth. He looks like a giant tortoise upturned on its shell. I'm drunk, in auto-self-preservation mode, do-or-die, kill-or-be-killed, everything inside of me begging me to react or lose.

The wine bottle is still mostly full, the red liquid spraying out as I swing it in an overhead arc down onto his skull. It shatters into an alarming burst of glass and wine, the upper half of the jagged bottle still in my hand as blood and purple liquid creates a hideous mask on the bouncer's face, freakish eyes protruding from their sockets like a twin amphibious vocal-sacs. He emits a pig-like squeal and attempts to wipe them with his hands, but it's too late. They're wine-doused, and amazingly, still terribly wide-the-fuck-open.

I look at my hands. There's blood on them, his blood, my blood, who the fuck knows? My head is hot and I'm charged with adrenaline and a surge of might compels me to drop the broken bottle and grab a steel developing tray from the floor. I don't hesitate. With both hands, I raise it over my head and slam him in the face and dent the tray into an almost-L shape as I scream my tirade's words between each strike, "How *(whack!)* dare *(whack!)* you *(whack!)* drink *(whack!)* my *(whack!)* beer!" When I finally stop, his reptile-egg eyes draw back into his blood and wine-sheathed face, and his eyelids close over them like membranes.

My shoulders are burning from the workout. From my lack of working out. I stagger back into Rachel's bedroom, tripping over scattered darkroom supplies, slipping and skidding in the spilled wine. The bouncer isn't moving, *thank you*, but his huge gut is still rising up and down like an air reservoir on a ventilator. He's out cold, but in minutes could come to in a rage, so I improvise in the art of subjugation and collect what I can to restrain him, belts and purse straps and duct tape. I grab him by his filthy boots and try with all my might to slide him into the bedroom where there's more room to work with (and heavier furniture to fetter him to), but my lifelong lack of faith in the gym doesn't let it happen.

He begins stirring and I begin subduing, moving as quickly as my inebriety will allow. I slip and slide in the wine as I bind his right wrist to the shelving unit with a strap from one of Jolie's purses. The shelf is anchored but it's not that heavy and I'm worried he could use his bulk to wrench it free. There's nothing close by I could cuff his ankles to, so I kneel alongside him and yank his right arm across his body, positioning the loose wrist next to the fettered one. Using the duct tape, I wrap them together as quickly and tightly as possible.

I move to stand...and lose my balance, treading in the spilled wine three times before falling right on top of the huge fucker (*thrump!*), face-to-face like lovers.

He comes to and his eyes pop out and they almost touch me and I startle and shout *ahhhhhhhhhhh!*, and he bellows too, his cry blooming not from a place of fear, but of anger. He starts squirming, and as soon as he realizes his wrists are trussed, begins thrashing like a shark out of water, feet slipping and sliding in the wine as they ineffectively attempt to gain purchase. I roll off of him and the shelf trembles and my very first Canon zoom lens tumbles onto his forehead, *clunk!* I scramble to my feet and step over his incredible bulk, then move in behind the fallen table and give his wrists another half-dozen layers of duct tape, just to make sure he doesn't go anywhere. There.

He stops thrashing and glares at me, eyes not in full pop-out-mode but quivering like they want to be. He's winded and snorting like a pig with every labored breath, fat face bloodied and swelling from the thrashing I just gave it.

I giant-step one leg over his huge gut and straddle him, hands on hips, drilling him with swagger. I stay like that while I catch my breath, savoring in the control I have over him now. Despite being winded, it feels great to be in a position of power. Like a million fucking bucks.

(...it's how HE felt, every time...)

He begins to sob. Whether faked or in defeat, I can't tell. Doesn't matter. I lurch unsteadily into the kitchen, grab my cell phone from the charging pad, and race back in.

It's not the same, but will have to do. I stand over him and recall his words to me the day we first crossed paths at Peepshow. "No one tells me I can't take no pictures."

Point.

Click.

CHAPTER 58

"Untie me! The fuck!"

"I ask the questions."

"Fuck you."

A moment passes in which the angel whimpers, *what's wrong with you?*, but it already knows the answer. The devil is running the show now, and together, we've become the *now* me.

"Let's start with how you got in."

"Fuck you," he replies, again.

I nod. Grin. Laugh, even. Being in control feels really fucking good *(…YES this is how HE felt…)*. I lean down, reach into his front jeans pocket—black denims residing halfway down his ass—and unearth Jolie's key to our apartment, still attached to the Coach keychain I bought for her back when she didn't poison people. I jiggle it like a tiny dinner bell and flaunt a tooth-bearing smile: a simple little pose to make me look unhinged. As expected, he doesn't like it, not one bit. His eyes bulge and a seizure-like dance ensues, filth-encrusted boots kicking surrealistic streaks into the puddle of wine and making *squelchy "thwack"* sounds. The shelf shakes and rattles, but remains anchored to the wall.

"Where'd you get this?"

"Fuckin' let me go!"

"After we talk." For now, I'm able to keep my cool, but the struggle is real. He blows out three times, then smartly follows suit with a scrunched face of resignation and a conceding relaxation of the arms.

"My hands. They're fucking numb. Cut the tape, man!"

"Tell me what I want to know, and I'll let you go. Fair enough?"

He blows out and nods, albeit tentatively.

"Good." I smile. He isn't going anywhere anyway, at least not by my hand.

The angel: *You're just going to leave him here? In your home?*

The devil: *This isn't his home anymore.*

He coughs, a loud and powerful *ORK!* sound producing a clot of blood that settles on his chin after he spits it out. "What do you want from me?"

"Who gave you the key to my home?"

He blurts, quite clearly, "I can't tell you that, man." He then starts hyperventilating, four or five drawn-out wheezes that eventually peter back down into quiet, normal breaths again. But no more words come out. He's too afraid to talk, no doubt terrified of blowing Greg's "cover."

I shout, "Speak!", my anger now beginning to rear its head.

His head pitches back and forth and doesn't stop until I grab another developing tray, hold it over my head like a trophy, and swing it down on his largely exposed gut. WHAP! He screams *owwwwwa!* like a kid falling knees-first into the street. His eyes bulge completely out of their sockets, so far that I can see the stringy muscle attached to the undersides. Teardrops erupt from them voluminously (two or three times the upwelling of a teen-aged girl), providing all the lubrication his eyes need to sink back down. I smack his belly again. Again, his eyes pop out...and then withdraw. I do it one more time (just for shits and giggles), but then stop because it's just too fucking hilarious a sight and laughing-out-loud while you've got a human tied up in your closet is just *too far gone*, unless you're a madman, or an evil genius, of which I'm neither.

The angel and the devil in unison: *You sure about that?*

I point at him and shout, "You're a human stress-ball toy! Literally!" I raise the steel tray back over my head.

"Okay, okay, okay! I'll talk! Untie me! Please. I…I can't feel my hands!"

The angel finds the strength to intervene: *Let the cops handle this.*

But the devil won't have any of it: *You're in control now. Do what you have to do, and when you're done, remove your prints from Carmen's plastic coffin.*

"Who gave you the key?"

"My boss."

"Greg Strand?"

He winces as if expecting another blow. "You didn't hear that from me."

"Where'd he get the key?"

"I dunno."

I raise the tray.

"He got it from one of the girls!"

"At the peepshow?"

"Yeah."

"Which one?"

"Don't know her name."

I raise the tray.

"Okay, okay! Listen…all I know is…Greg gave me that key and five bills and told me to wait here for you. Said to make sure you don't talk to the cops."

I feign ignorance. "What would I need to talk to the cops about?"

"His words, brah."

"Did he kill my housekeeper?"

His dead-giveaway eyes bulge halfway out, then settle back in. "Dunno nothin' 'bout that."

"Right. I don't either." I wink, but it's a taboo subject I don't want to discuss. Yet. I deflect, "Why were you in my darkroom? What were you looking for?"

"I figured I'd wait till you were in bed before…" He rolls his eyes past me into Rachel's room.

I laugh. "This is my daughter's room, you moron. So which girl gave Greg the key?" If I find out for sure that Jolie gave it to him (and that he didn't steal it from her), it will confirm her intended involvement with him to set me up, and quite possibly Carmen's murder as well. The truth about everything exists in the space between them.

"There's this new girl he's been hanging with."

I pull Jolie's photo up on my phone. "This her?"

"Yeah. They been spending a lot of time together. She's always at the shop."

"The shop—you mean the peepshow?"

He grins, ever-so-slightly, as if gently amused. "That your wife, ain't it?"

The devil delivers yet another morsel of truth: *Desperation sinks in when you've bitten off more debt than you can chew.*

"Does she perform there? At the peepshow?"

The bouncer nods and emits a quiet, guttural laugh. "All of Greg's girls work there."

Lily…

Imagine that. Jolie, my *wife*, working alongside Sugah and company at Peepshow. The only thing worse than the thought of Jolie rubbing her tits up against a scratched piece of Plexiglas for dirty businessmen jack off to, is the thought of me being the one on the other side of the glass, seeing Jolie there instead of

Sugah. If that'd happened, I'd be telling a completely different story right now.

Anger swells in me like a tornado about to touch down. I pause, savor the reaction, then shoot daggers at my nemesis-of-the-moment. "What's Greg's connection to the shop?" The more I find out about Greg now, the better off I'll be later, should I end up in the dank room again, or even face-to-face with the fucker.

He squeezes his eyes shut, an impressive feat, given his out-of-socket condition. "Fucking hurts man, cut me loose, c'mon brah!"

"Answer the question."

"Look, if I talk, they'll kill me."

I hold the developing tray over my head…

(…like HE did the belt…)

…and he trembles and screams and I scream and slam his gut. His eyes pop out and withdraw like a pair of corals in a reef.

"OwwwwOwwwwOwwww man, that really fucking hurts!"

I lean over him, baring my teeth for effect. "If you don't talk, *I'll* kill you." The threat is *almost* empty: there's a tiny piece of my *changed* self deep down inside that feels an intrinsic, conceivable willingness to commit murder. I embrace it and raise the tray again.

"Okay! Okay! Okay!"

"Speak now or I'll forever beat you to a fucking pulp." A good part of me is really enjoying this, but there's also a part of me that's doing this to kill time before heading downstairs to deal with Carmen. Wait. Maybe they're both part of the same part of me?

His breathing mounts, big, black, vile belly rising and falling, bloody sputum sputtering from his lips like lava from a volcano, labored words coughed out in fragments. "Greg's cousin Odie. Owns the shop. Got one Florida too. Greg moves the girls. Gets them from Russia. They earn for Greg. Odie washes it. Through the shop." He takes a deep wheezing breath, and then, finding his rhythm again, says, "Heard he was onto a big score. Something to do with his new girl."

His new girl.

I pull Lily's image up on my phone—the one from the park that started it all—and show it to him. "Tell me about this girl."

"That's Lola. She's been with Greg as long as I know him."

"How long is that?"

"Three, maybe four years. Look man, I can't lose this job. You gotta let me go. I won't say nothing to Greg, I promise."

I ignore him. "Tell me about Lola."

"You gonna fuckin' untie me?"

I raise the tray and…

…it keeps him talking. "Lola's Greg's girl. She's the one that brought your wife to him, and next thing I know Greg and her are spending a lot more time together, and Lola, she ain't hardly around anymore."

"How long have Greg and my wife been together?"

He bucks, squirms, twists. "Fucking hurts man, my hands, I can't feel them! I'm gonna die!"

"ANSWER THE FUCKING QUESTION!" *Damn, that feels good.* I'm in control and I'm *changed* and my pain…

(…six-seven-eight…)

…is REPRESSED. *This* is how I'm supposed to feel, this is the person I'm meant to be. Sex might be a distraction, but CONTROL is the *answer*. No more deluding myself with false promises. From now on, I live my truth. Like Morgan.

(…like HIM…)

He says, "She started hanging around 'bout four months ago."

Four months?

Somewhere deep inside my head, Lily's voice calls out to me, *Jolie's having an affair*, and I can almost hear the click of the light bulb turning on in my brain as one-plus-one makes another appearance: she told me that Jolie was having an affair, and I thought it was with Lily after seeing the footage on Nick's computer, but it was *also* with Greg. Lily's man. That's why Lily kissed me in the park, that's why she fucked me in the rental Greg paid for. She was getting back at the asshole, maybe even getting back at Jolie, the bitch who stole him from her. It's all starting to make sense now. Lily, spurned by two lovers: her man *and* her girlfriend. And through first-hand experience, I can confirm the words of "The Mourning Bride" to be an unquestionable truth: *Hell hath no fury than a woman scorned.*

CHAPTER 51

He's quieted down, thankfully. His hands have changed color, now a much deeper shade of black than the rest of him. His eyes remain closed, popping out only sporadically as if on a timer: two balls of what-the-fuck with a life of their own.

Ignoring the weakening pleads of…of Popeye, I move into the kitchen and with care, grind up the remaining six Ambien pills in a small bowl. I mix them into a cup of water until they dissolve into a gritty, milky-colored liquid; he's way bigger than me and will need more than one or two measly pills to stay the fuck down.

I'm still feeling the effects of the alcohol and it's aiding my drive to forge ahead, but my bid to walk a straight line has become a difficult task. Slowly, as if in a sobriety test, I place one foot in front of the other, using both hands to carefully hold the cocktail out before me like a peace offering. I can't let him go. If I do, Greg and his cronies will be here in a flash to inflict more cruel drama into my world. He has to stay right where he is: a pile of human trash, trapped in the midst of my former sanctuary, mere feet away from my daughter's room. It's a moment of finality that makes me realize, unequivocally, that I'm no longer in a home I can call my own.

He whimpers, "I-I can't feel my arms. It's spreading. Oh, God, I don't feel good. I think I'm gonna puke." He dry-heaves (and bulges) a few times, but thankfully the results are dry.

"You done? Cause I ain't gonna cut you free if you're gonna hurl on me."

He takes a massive wheezing breath, then dry-heaves like an asthma sufferer in desperate need of albuterol. I pick up the top half of the broken wine bottle...and as he takes his next huge gasp of air, I shove it funnel-like into his gaping mouth. His eyes pop out, of course they do, and I pour the Ambien cocktail into the jagged opening. He chokes and coughs and bulges. I press down on the bottle, as best I can without cutting myself, holding it in place until all the cloudy liquid gurgles down. When I yank it out, he coughs and spits (and yes, bulges), so loudly that the neighbors must be wondering why I have The Nature Channel on full volume in my apartment.

I stagger back into the kitchen, listening as his coughs taper down into weak, throaty croaks. By the time I wash up and collect supplies for the next chore on my to-do list, he's snoring. I open up another bottle of wine, knife-in-cork style because that's how I roll, and throw it back, swallowing cork-crumbs and all because who-the-fuck-cares at this point? I'm on a high! An adrenaline high! A CONTROL high! A fucking *changed* high! Never in my life have I felt so pumped, so in charge of my destiny. Fate swooped in and poured salt in my gaping wounds and I responded like a champ. I rocked it, man.

I chug a few more mouthfuls of red, then review the inventory of objects I've gathered: Playtex rubber gloves so I don't make the same mistake twice, check. Baby-wipes for my prints, check. Duct tape to reseal the bin, check. Foam earplugs for my nostrils, check.

I look in on Popeye. He's snoring up a stomach-churning storm. What I end up doing with him still remains to be seen. I can't move him because he's a fat fuck, and if I release him after he wakes up, he'll absolutely try to complete the murderous task he originally set out to do. Make sure I don't go to the cops?

Yeah, okay. So until the police search my apartment, he'll stay right the fuck where he is. They'll know what to do with him.

I tuck Jolie's key back into his front pocket, *God he stinks,* because it will help tell the story. The truth is my only ticket out: he let himself in and tried to attack me and it didn't work out well for him, an instance of self-defense if there ever was one.

The devil contemplates: *Maybe Popeye killed Carmen?*

Who killed Carmen doesn't matter as long as I remain innocent. And to do that, I need to deal with her corpse. The question of who did it will be answered soon enough via news video of either Popeye, Greg Strand, or Jolie being led away in cuffs. Or so I hope.

The devil: *Or Lily.*

That would knife me in the heart. In spite of her implicit involvement, in spite of her sidecar-life of crime, she has to remain innocent. I *need* her in my life. She is my motive, my passion, my influence. I will love her always and forever, and she will love me back. And together, we will persevere as *one.* Guilty or not, she *cannot* go to prison. She is my *distraction.*

(…from six-seven-eight…)

I shove the supplies into my backpack, don a hoodie, and take a few deep breaths before opening the door to my apartment. *Am I really doing this?* I peek out. No cops, no Jolie, no smelly neighbors. I skip the elevator, now more than ever looking back and forth and up and down for cameras. The devil may feel otherwise, but if there was any security footage from the storage area, I'm certain the cops would have shown it to me. There doesn't appear to be any cameras in the stairwell, the now inebriated devil slurring: *if there were cameras here, you would have noticed them long ago*. I tackle each step tentatively, five floors down into the basement, passing no one on the way and thankful none of the half-dozen washers and dryers are running.

I never checked the time, but it's late enough, Monday-almost-Tuesday, no better time to obstruct justice and desecrate a corpse. I stagger through the laundry room, stumbling over cracks in the floor, *I'm drunk*, then turn into the storage area. It's dim and empty, making me one thankful bastard.

I look up and around and notice a dome camera peering out from the uppermost right corner of the concrete room. Shit! Shit! Shit! I walk to it, focusing on the jagged crack bisecting the semitransparent eye. *That's a good sign.* From behind the device I see a half-dozen colorful wires jutting out, leading to nowhere. *A great sign!* So there *is* a camera and there *is* a God and in my slurred prayers for a best-case scenario, it's broken. *Rejoice!* I stagger back and peek into the laundry room. Still quiet, still empty. No tenants, no police.

It is with great hope that the next ten minutes secures my freedom.

What could go wrong?

The angel attempts a reply, but I shove a mental muzzle in its mouth.

I step to my locker, remove my backpack and place it on the floor. I fight with the combo lock, hands shaking, numbers blurred, back and forth I go, turning and pulling too many times before it finally falls open.

The stench hits me as the door slides up, ammonia and methane, denser than last time, conspicuous evidence of death. I open my backpack, shove the pliable earplugs into my nostrils, then slip on the gloves and pull the string to the exposed light bulb overhead, leaning out to make sure I'm still alone.

The devil: *it's now or life in prison.*

During my last visit, I'd made a burglar's mess, the once neat and orderly stash now a haphazard hodgepodge of stuff. My first step is on a box, *crush* go the unseen contents. I go deeper, trampling on jackets and shirts and pants, stepping over the fucking chandelier and nearly losing my balance. Sunglasses crunch somewhere down below and a pair of brass candlesticks topple from the mirrored table as I knock into it. I shimmy past the cheval mirror—it's about ten degrees hotter back here, the stench intensifying to tasteable levels—and circle around the rolling rack where I behold the plastic bin that once held Rachel's toys and books, but now contains Carmen's bloated corpse.

What was once recognizable as a body has metamorphosed into an expansive mass of reddish-pink pulp. The reek of it is nothing I've ever come close to experiencing before, a mixture of landfill rot and cat piss wafting past my nose plugs out into the common area. Might as well set up a fucking marquee. *Dead Body Here! One Night Only!*

I can't take the taste of the stench so I grab a scarf from the rolling rack and wrap it around my mouth and nose, then arm myself with a half-dozen baby-wipes.

When I first saw Carmen's body, she was identifiable. Now her once petite torso is only vaguely human, a gelatinous mass of biowaste digesting its clothing and leaking down the sides of the container in pulpy strips. Shit, this is gonna take much more than just a handful of baby-wipes.

The single light bulb overhead casts a dim light over Jolie's retail stockpile, items steeped in death casting dark shadows over the container, now spilling over more than I realize because the cement floor back here is *squelching* under my sneakers. As my eyes adjust to the dim light, an archipelago of blisters come into view, wriggling maggots pulsating beneath their translucent domes like tiny orbs in a lava-lamp.

Being drunk has given me bigger balls but hasn't done my objective of "getting the job done quickly" any favors. The sight and smell of it all makes my stomach cartwheel and forces my alcoholic gorge north. The devil and angel both weigh in with an immediate uncertainty: Can DNA be extracted from vomit? I came down here to remove my prints, not add more evidence to my faux complicity. In a déjà vu moment, I leap away from the corpse, but this time my sneakers skid and slip in the human muck, sending me careening into the cheval mirror, *crash*! I stagger past the rolling rack, over arbitrary boxes, and back out into storage room where I yank the scarf down and power-puke wine, beer, and breakfast-for-dinner all over the cement floor.

"Hijo de puta, hijo de puta chupapollas!"

With puke dripping down my chin, and earplugs clogging my nostrils, I look up to the scowling face of Chico, the building's maintenance man.

CHAPTER 52

"Ah shit, I'm sorry, Chico."

I'm panting and he's standing guardedly next to the locker across from mine, looking menacing with a pair of heavy-duty bolt-cutters in his hands, as if *finally* locating my pinkies after a long exhaustive search.

He asks, "You okay, Mr. Peter?"

"I'm fine," I manage but don't mean. With his eyes trained on me, he gently leans the bolt-cutters against the unit door and takes a hesitant step forward, as if trying not to set off a ticking bomb. His line of sight darts between my nose plugs, the yellow rubber gloves I'm wearing, and the open locker behind me.

"You sure got a lot of stuff in there," he remarks.

I pull my nose plugs out, then straighten my posture and, attempting *nonchalance*, feebly wave away his observation. But the tensed-up look on his face tells me he's well aware of me being *more off* than a few drinks too many. I deflect. "What are the bolt cutters for?"

His eyes never leave me as he twists ever-so-slightly toward them. "Guy forgot his combination, asked me to switch it out with a key lock."

He's gravely unsettled. I can hear the trepidation in his voice, not just because of the puke that needs cleaning up, but due to the stench emanating from my locker. I'm guilty of *something*, and he knows it. "I'm sorry about the floor. If you bring me some supplies, I'll clean it up right away."

He nods and judges and I don't need a translator to know the Spanish words going through his head aren't complimentary. He grumbles some of them under his breath as he trudges away through the laundry room into the janitor's closet.

This is my chance. My *only* chance. I can save myself right now. All I have to do is close up the unit. Conceal the evidence while I can and return later, when the "coast is clear'. But…I can't convince myself to do it. The *now* me guided me here in a now-or-never frame of mind. Blocked the angel from steering me in a safer direction. So I leap into the unit and trip and stagger over *all these fabulous prizes* and wipe out through the rolling rack head-first-palms-out into a puddle of what-used-to-be-Carmen. The rubber gloves shred at the palms, mixing pieces of my DNA into the hot mess. I move to stand and the headspins attack, forcing me back down. Fear swoops in on me from every direction like gulls on a bait-ball. I roll over on my side, but it's no use. I'm stuck, glued to the floor between the sludgy container and the rolling rack, instantly regretting my impulsivity to get the job done *pronto*.

"Hi, hi, hi, Mr. Peter? You okay? Something smells really bad in there." I look through the bottom of the rolling rack and see Chico holding a stained rag to his face. He's as white as a sheet save for the dilated uncertainty in his wide-open eyes.

"Hi, no, uh Chico, yeah, no I'm fine. I…I got a rat's nest back here." It's the excuse I made with Ted Bundy, so best to keep things consistent.

"Oh no, not good. You come out of there. I take care of it."

Fuck, no, no, no no no. "No, really, Chico, it's fine." I'm squinting and sweating and praying, my feet and arms slipping and sliding as I endeavor (quite pathetically) to stand. Now

Chico is making his way inside the unit. His voice goes from concerned, *are you okay?*, to suspicious, "That's no rat smell." He holds onto the mirror for balance, gagging and watching as I try to extract myself from the compromising position I've gotten myself into. He reaches out a helping hand, which I nervously accept, never minding the telltale residue on the Playtex glove.

"Thank you," I say as I arrive to my feet.

He cuffs the crook of his free arm over the rag covering his nose and mouth, then squints at the gunk on his hand. *"Peter…que diablos es eso?"*

Despite having struggled my way through Spanish in high school, I can still understand his legitimate question: *What the hell is this?* Deep in my subconscious the angel screams and cowers. At the forefront of my mind, the devil influences and goads, helping me push away my concerns and trepidations, my *(…six-seven-eight…)* fears.

"It's the rat nest. Right behind me." I point toward the bin using the same gloved hand he helped me with. His footfall squelches in the overflow as he steps in to investigate. He looks down at his shoes and I turn and straight away locate the object I'm looking for. He then sees the bin and immediately starts retching. His head turns and his eyes roll back at me, drowning in sheer terror…

(…you see through HIS eyes, you look at your hand, at the BELT white-knuckled in your fist, Mustang buckle dangling, business end dangling, you look into the closet and there he is, that cowering little shit, six-seven-eight, always crying, he sees the devil in your eyes, protecting his sad face with his scrawny arms, but you are in control, you're HIM, you're angry, you must not let him destroy the life you built…)

The terror in his *(…six-seven-eight…)* eyes moves into a clear awareness of what's happening. He sees the anger and the rage in me. He sees HIM in me *(...he took the photo, he showed it to her, you have to punish him, it's ALL HIS FAULT, HE TOOK THE PHOTO...)*. I *am* HIM, and the person before me is six-seven-eight, *this* is how HE felt, *this* is why HE did what he did to me, because of the way it felt. So fucking good! So fucking *right*!

I bring the BELT down on his head...but it isn't the BELT, it's one of the brass candlesticks that'd toppled from the table when I bumped into it, firm in my grip, base-end-up, *business end up*. I raise it and it appears as the BELT, *comfortable* in my hand as I swing it down on his head again. He wraps his arms around his face, expelling a whimpering sound, not so much a cry as the first jagged exhalation of death. I raise it up and *I can hear the jangle of the buckle* and bring it down *crack!* and up, *jangle*, and down, *crack!* He collapses into a heap alongside the plastic bin, in the same spot I couldn't get up from. I scream, "HOW DARE YOU TAKE A PICTURE OF ME! HOW DARE YOU SHOW YOUR MOTHER! YOU HAVE DESTROYED THIS FAMILY! IT'S YOUR FAULT! YOU DID IT! YOU!" The words escape my mouth unbidden as the blockade holding my repressed memories collapses, unleashing them into some kind of dark, twisted construct. He's choking, holding his wounded head, blood pouring into his eyes...eyes that silently plead *why*? I strike him one last time, an explosive blow that turns out a sickly wheeze through his lips, firming up his last breathing moment on earth.

I stand there for long seconds, heaving, staring at the body, and at the candlestick clutched in my bloody hand.

I can feel something move through me as HE leaves me. Alone. With him. It.

My first kill.

And I'm still not counting.

CHAPTER 53

A dark shadow in my head swoops in and momentarily blocks my recollection of what just happened. I look around and take in the grim reality, piece by piece. Lying beside the bin-of-death is another lifeless body, this one still pissing itself. In my gloved hand is the murder weapon, a brass candlestick, one of Jolie's impulsive purchases utilized in a most unfortunate, yet convenient way. *Mr. Delmonico in the storage unit with a candlestick.* The smoldering memory of what just happened soon breaks through the now dissipating shadow, rooting itself in my brain for easy retrieval for the rest of my broken life.

I'm a murderer now.

What shamed me with guilt last week, infidelity and lying, seems so inconsequential now in comparison. And yet, I feel no guilt. No shame. No fear. Contrarily, I feel empowered. In control. I *felt* HIM. *Became* HIM. And now, with the devil's aid, I *understand* HIM.

I am the *now* me.

I take one final look at the deadly mess I created, then stagger out of the unit. The basement is still empty, still quiet, middle-of-the-night-o-clock on a weekday. I peek around the corner. The half-dozen washers and dryers remain asleep. Somewhere outside, a truck beeps and brakes.

My buzz has dissipated slightly, leaving my thoughts less occluded to think through my next move. I peer at the bolt-cutters leaning against the locker across from mine. Perfect. I take hold of the oversized tool and use every muscle in my body to cut the lock on my neighbor's unit. *Snap!* I toss it in the dumpster near the freight entrance, then slide the unit open to a space that's holding about ten percent of the stuff I have in mine. Plenty of room.

I go into my locker, kicking and tossing items aside, clearing a path to the rear. Even though my Playtex gloves are torn at the palms, they still provide the extra grip I need to firm up a hold beneath Chico's arms. Chico is a small man, *gracias,* but is still dead-weight-heavy. I heave and rest, heave and rest, lugging his body twelve inches at a time through my crowded unit. When I first opened it and laid eyes on Jolie's trove, it was so neat and orderly, as if someone who worked in a department store had had a hand in organizing everything. Now all I can fathom is the irony of it all: Jolie never worked in a department store, and her treasure trove has gone from spoils to *spoiled*.

Once Chico's body is out of my unit (along with a few other random items), he slides more easily across the cement floor into the open locker. I drop him alongside a Schwinn ten-speed, then look out and notice a pink streak of fluid marking a path from my locker to this one. In the middle of it is the aftermath of too much beer and wine. I peer into the laundry room again because it's my only means of caution, then traipse back to the rear of my locker. The stench is impossible to get used to, so much more intense now without nose plugs. They say cats have smell receptors in their mouths. I can smell this with my mouth. Dead people really fucking *stink.*

Before I start set two with Carmen's bin, I utilize a couple shirts from Jolie's stash to wipe it down as much as possible. There's a lot of gunk that just spreads around in uneven swirls, but I'm ridding the thing of my fingerprints once and for all, and that's all that matters. From this moment forward, I never laid a finger on it.

Then there's the body. It's swollen so much that there's no putting the lid back on, and it makes me wonder if the container would've exploded had I not taken it off. I grip the indent on one side and lug it backward. The path is clearer and the container moves out more easily across the cement floor, like a garbage bin in a driveway. I waste no time, spending the next ten minutes racing back and forth, moving anything visibly stained into the other locker, clothes and shoeboxes and just because, the fucking chandelier. My heart pounds cardio-style the entire time, keeping in rhythm with the drumming in my head: a techno-beat of adrenaline and blood.

Outside, amid honking horns and faraway sirens, comes the rising volume of a truck beeping and braking. Hard thumps and mechanical churns identify it as a NYC sanitation vehicle. *Holy shit!* If my stars hadn't fully lined up with the presence of the bolt-cutters, they surely have now. I run to the janitor's closet, find a box of heavy-duty drum container bags, *yes*, then race them back into my locker, again acting impulsively and quickly: in goes the murder weapon (wrapped in a small throw), the lid to the container, the soiled shirts, plus a few random boxes. To dilute the evidence pool, I fill three additional bags with clothing and pillows and small unopened boxes, but don't pack away everything, just enough to make room for me to clean up. For a second I wonder if this could be a golden opportunity to get rid of the bodies...but the truck is on the street now and I don't have the strength nor the time to lift them up and over the edge of the dumpster, much less bag them up. My impulsivity has limits. The four filled bags go into the dumpster moments before the sanitation collectors open the freight door and empty it.

Back Inside my neighbor's unit, I shift a few things around, then cover the bodies with the quilt that once camouflaged Carmen's bin; my journey wouldn't feel complete if I didn't stage *something*, just for...well, you know. I root through Chico's jeans for the new padlock and *score*! I lock up the unit, then spend the next fifteen minutes using the industrial-strength cleaning supplies Chico retrieved to erase all visible remnants of something awful having taken place, neatening up what I can inside my locker, stacking boxes and salvaging sunglasses. It still stinks to high heaven, but all evidence of my crime(s) has been visibly erased, or so I hope. As I lock it up, I think about what I've just done and realize all too clearly that this, along with everything else I've done over the past five days, has been done solely in the name of love.

CHAPTER 54

I turn the corner into the laundry room just as a young female tenant I've never seen before emerges from the *dinging* elevator on the other side. She spots me and startles slightly and I mirror it with a feigned startle of my own, hand on chest for effect. She's lugging a large green laundry bag behind her, quick smile as fake as her press-on nails.

I fake-smile back and say, "Sorry I scared you," when I really should've just put my head down and paced silently by.

"My fault for doing laundry after midnight."

I stop, and I don't know why because I need to G-T-F-O, and it's here I realize that I never washed my hands, so I shove them into my hoodie pockets, and it's *now* I notice remnants of Carmen staining everything I've got on my body. And as I twist my body away from her, all I can think of saying is, "You know…it isn't safe for you to be down here all by yourself, so late at night."

She shrugs, indifferent on the surface, cautious within, my photog's eye giving her a quick once-over: mid-twenties, straight brown pixie-cut hair complementing her pocket-sized features, about my height but more torso than anything else. She's pretty, athletic-pretty, like Dorothy Hamill in her prime. As I walk to the stairwell hoping the back of my jeans and hoodie aren't stained as well, she says, "Something really stinks down here. You smell that?"

I think fast. "I do. I've got it all over me. The trash bag I brought down here broke open when I tossed it in the dumpster, disrespectfully reminding me how much I hate my wife's cooking. Plus, I think someone puked back there." Quick on my feet, thank you very much, *now me*.

She smiles and loads a washer, eyes still on me but slightly more relaxed now given our congenial exchange. *Nope, no murder took place here.* "Please don't ever invite me over for dinner."

Under ordinary circumstances I'd want to stay, flirt, *distract*. But with a sleeping giant in my apartment, and bits of Carmen on my hands, I nod and say, "Sounds like a plan," and make a speedy exit.

The steps confront me with an immediate (and unwanted) challenge, my energy draining rapidly as I tackle them one by one. By the time I reach my apartment, my meter's needle is almost flat, miles away from the red zone.

I remove my key, but don't need it.

The door is ajar.

Slowly and quietly and looking in all directions, I enter my apartment. I lean to the left and grab a steak knife from the butcher block, eyes scanning the living room, the open bathroom, and the two bedroom doors. I hold it pointed end out and move toward Rachel's room, assuming the bouncer somehow escaped, because if I were him, I wouldn't shut the door on my way out either.

But I'm wrong.

He's right where I left him.

Dead.

I have no idea who left the door open, but it must've been the same person who stabbed him through the heart with one of my kitchen knives. The convenient weapon is buried to the hilt, jutting like a land marker, a swath of fresh blood still running from the wound down his mountainous bulk into the tight gap between his body and the floor. If I didn't think my darkroom could get any more polluted, boy was I ever fucking wrong.

The devil chimes in with cautionary advice: *The killer might still be here.*

I spin around, gripping the murder weapon's twin, looking for the bouncer's probable killer: Greg Strand. I search Rachel's room, my bedroom, under all the beds, in the bathroom and shower stall. All clear. Whoever was here is gone now. I put the chain on the door and wedge the chair beneath the doorknob, ensuring my safety for now.

As the unforgiving reality of the situation sets in, *murder all around me,* I start to falter. I look at the clock. My ghosting vision barely tells me it's 12:26 a.m. My legs feel like wet towels, my breath shortened as all remaining energy disperses from me like air from an untied balloon. My mind leap-frogs between all my inner demons, from the devil-driven *now me,* to six-seven-eight, to HIM, adding utter confusion to the unnerving scenario. The knife drops from my hand and I start crying out loud, unbidden tears bursting from my eyes like spraying fountain drops. Panic overwhelms me and I use what little energy I have left to strip away my tainted-with-murder clothes, stumbling and falling through the simple process. On my hands and knees, I crawl into Jolie's ravaged closet where I, in all my utter nakedness, press my body against the rear wall amidst *my father's shoes, my mother's purses, the mothballs,* recoiling in the darkness and sighing out loud, "One one-hun, two one-hun, three one-hun," until I unconditionally submit to the obsessive force of *six-seven-eight* and relive what happened to me all those years ago…

CHAPTER 55

(…you're six-seven-eight again…)

…and your love for photography had been ingrained in you from the time you saw a program about landscape photographer Ansel Adams, and later Steve McCurry, whose *National Geographic* photos left you breathless at age five. You shared this newfound passion with your mother who, when not meeting your father's stringent expectations of cleaning and cooking and making sure the house was *up-to-snuff* and *germ-free,* would snuggle in bed with you, a bottle of bourbon in one hand, a satchel full of tears in the other. She was perfectly capable of providing you with love, you knew, but only when her well of dependency ran dry, which wasn't often.

You didn't see your father much. He worked long days and sometimes longer nights and in those rare instances when he was around, would tell you to *get lost* or *scram* because there were trades to make and gripes to air about your mother. You were six years old and you already knew everything in his life bore more importance than you, that he never wanted you in the first place, and by default (and as a consequence) you became the whipping post in his unpreventable marriage. Over time you reminded yourself that his love differed from your mother's, that it was perfunctory, demonstrated with material necessities like food on the table and a roof over your head. Her love for you was real, but forcefully burdened with fear and guilt and alcohol. You understood that, like their union, you were never supposed to be. He unremittingly reminded you of this, always making sure that she was within shouting distance: *If it weren't for you, I wouldn't be trapped in this useless marriage. It's ALL YOUR FAULT.*

One rare day, when your mother's well was dry, she found it in her heart to do something special for you. HE had just finished lashing into her about *something*, so to escape him, she took you for a walk, farther away from your house than you'd ever walked before. You passed a garage sale…and there it was, sitting atop a wooden snack table, a Polaroid Instamatic camera, that extinct species from another era you'd read about in those photography magazines from the library. With it came three twelve-packs of film, more than enough to get your photographic feet wet. A foundation for your discerning eye.

You spent the rest of the afternoon choosing opportunities to capture, a cardinal, a squirrel, a spider weaving a cocoon around the black carpenter ant you dropped in its web. You were so proud of the photos you took, and when you were called in for dinner that night, you told your mother that you wanted to show your captured-moments-in-time to HIM. But she hesitated, then shook her head nervously and told you "*No, he wouldn't approve.*" So you hid the camera under your bed instead, where it remained until the middle of the night, when you were startled by a not-so-distant scream.

You grabbed the camera and looked out the second story window. At first there was nothing to see, but then you heard it again. It was muffled, coming from inside the house behind yours. You watched as the door flew open and the woman that lived there stumbled out onto the patio, holding the handrail for support. There was a light on the porch and between that and the full moon's glow, you could see that she had no clothes on. You'd never seen a naked woman before, just the scantily clad ones in the Maidenform ads that came with the Sunday papers. So you raised the camera to take a photo of her, pinpointing her through the viewfinder, easy because you practiced all day. You clicked the red button and took her picture, *flash!*, just as a man was exiting the house behind her. You pulled the camera down, unable to make sense of the confusing scene.

What's happening…?

The man behind her, the man grabbing her by the hair, the man *hurting her*, was your father.

The woman must've seen the flash because her wet swollen eyes looked toward you. Your little heart beat-beat-beat hummingbird-fast, fresh blood chug-chug-chugging through your head like a freight train. You watched in dumbfounded silence as your father wrapped his hands around her neck and squeezed, and did not let go, and kept on squeezing and squeezing until her face turned a sickly shade of purple beneath the blue cast of the moonlight. Her arms pounded his shoulders and her nails raked at his face and you wanted to scream for him to stop but were too frightened, so you just sat there and cried inside until she stopped fighting back, those strangled eyes beseeching their very last hope from the window the flash came from.

You did the only thing you knew you could do.

You held up the camera.

Pointed.

Clicked.

Flash.

She collapsed onto her back. But he did not stop, his body jerking spasmodically as he climbed on top of her, forcing his entire weight into her, hands on throat, knees on lungs.

When he finally stopped, his lunatic gaze moved away from his victim, and toward your window.

You were petrified, too afraid to move an inch, entranced by his eyes, so wide and horribly unfamiliar, his thick hairy hands still wrapped around her neck, the woman, unmoving beneath him…the woman you'd seen in passing a few times while on neighborhood walks with your mother, the woman your mother once called *floozy* under her breath. The two of you stared at each other in deadly silence, enmeshed in a sudden event of murder now forever imprinted in your mind, an incident to burden and condemn you for as long as you lived.

You broke your trance, and like a gopher in a burrow, dipped beneath the sill, out of sight.

You prayed he didn't see you.

But you knew: he did.

You wasted no time. You ran to the bathroom, into the light, looking at the two photos you took as they developed into proof of his offense, a moment in time not meant for anyone's eyes. You didn't fully comprehend what just happened, but knew it wasn't good. Your mother heard you slam the bathroom door and she knocked and asked if you were ok and you said no and in tears opened the door and showed her the photos: the one of the neighbor alive, and the other of the neighbor dead, his silhouette a ghost in the doorway of the first photo, his clear image and even clearer intent fully visible in the second.

You heard the kitchen door downstairs crash open and slam shut. He screamed your name, voice a deafening mix of venom, hate, and regret. You hid behind your mother but it was in vain. There was nothing she could do to help you, now or for the next three years.

You listened as he launched up the stairs, two at a time, Timberland work-boots on hardwood, *boom-boom-boom-boom-boom*. The man you called Dad appeared, a trembling stinking mess, hair mussed, face quivering and bleeding in places, saliva coating his lips and stubbled chin like varnish. He screamed something indiscernible and launched at you with his arms outstretched, seizing you by the hair just like he did the lady. It hurt and you screamed. Your mother tried to intervene but was met with a quick and powerful shove into the wall. She crumpled into a heap, crying just like you. He dragged you by the hair into their bedroom and you held onto his wrists to alleviate some of the pain, and then the next thing you knew you were on the floor of your parents' bedroom closet, the big one with your mother's clothing and purses and shoes, with your father's suits and ties and belts. You shrunk against the back wall, screaming and trembling and not looking as he thrust the developed photos in your face, shouting crazy things like *you never took them!* and *you never saw them!* and *this never happened!* He screamed that he would never stop punishing you for taking them until he was one-hundred-per-fucking-cent-sure you forgot all about them. You tried to block out what was happening, crying as loudly as you could to drown out his voice, gagging from the stench of the mothballs. HE leaned down, and in a scary-calm voice, said, *Let me introduce you to a friend of mine.* This was the moment he introduced you to the BELT. You'd never seen it before, not in the closet and definitely not on him. An oversized brass buckle of a Ford Mustang made a jangle sound as it swayed from the end. He said, *This here is the business end.*

And in anticipation of the blow, you began to count, *one one-hundred, two one-hundred, three one-hundred…*

He took away your camera and the photos that night and you never saw them again. But you saw the BELT again, weekly at first, then more often. Sometimes it got really bad and he'd do it a few times a day. You endured his retribution (IT'S ALL YOUR FAULT!) as a six-year-old, (YOU DIDN'T SEE ANYTHING!) as a seven-year-old, (NOTHING HAPPENED!) and as an eight-year-old, and you became *six-seven-eight* and counted *one one-hundred* each and every time he delivered his dark justice upon you. At some point, you can't remember exactly when, your conscious mind split in two: one part innocence and naivety, one part wayward and wanton desire, forming two voices in your head, good and evil counterparts to help steer your decisions.

One time, the cops came by and your parents invited them in and you listened from your room upstairs while your mother and father pretended they didn't see anything that night at the neighbor's house. The cops left full of coffee and crumb cake and never came back. It took almost three years, but they finally made an arrest. A man from the next town over that *Floozy* once dated. You heard your father telling your mother to thank God the murderer was finally caught.

Later that night, he came into your room, and for the first time, told you he was *sorry*. He hugged you and kissed you then walked away with a look of relief on his face, muttering, *Thank God it's over*.

You hated him, wanted him to die. But still, you embraced the moment, for it seemed to mend what was broken between you. And it made the BELT stop. That was the day you began to REPRESS.

The angel inside you, your good half, reminded you that there was a dark truth being buried. But you didn't care. You saw an easier path to take, a *path of least resistance* the devil immediately put you on: a means to finally end the pain.

A week later, you turned nine and your mother bought you a Canon digital camera. An expensive one from the store. That helped you REPRESS even more, every shot you took another step away from…

(…six-seven-eight…)

CHAPTER 56

"One one-hundred, two one-hundred, three one-hundred, I don't remember anything!" BELT. "One one-hundred, two one-hundred, three one-hundred, I don't know what you're talking about!" BELT "One one-hundred, two one-hundred, three one-hundred, I was sleeping!"

Chimey-Chimey-chime chime.

My eyes open before I wake up. My ears never went to sleep; they stand at attention as the titillating Missed Connection ringtone leaps from my phone. My phone is still in my hand and through a muzzy haze observe the sexy notification-lady smiling back at me. Only as my finger taps her tiny image do I completely wake up.

I shift my body upright with my back against the closet wall, quick to notice the bandolier of puke across my chest and piss-puddle beneath my ass, both unsympathetic reminders of why I don't drink alcohol. I rub the sleep from my eyes and gaze at my inbox. *One message.* I tap it.

hey man saw your ad and your girl I'm looking at her right now she's at the artful dodger tavern on 43rd and 11th.

I check the timestamp. The message came in just now. *Lily.* I crawl out of the closet, scoop up my murder clothes and sneakers and shove them into one of Jolie's finer handbags, *fuck you Jolie.* The digital clock on my nightstand says 1:16 a.m. I was passed out for less than an hour.

While asleep my buzz morphed into a hangover. Thankfully my courage hung in there, giving me the strength to carry on. I take a two-minute shower, brush and mouthwash, then leap into fresh jeans and a hoodie. I've got my phone and Jolie's burner, and my wallet with every last bit of cash I've got. I check on the bouncer and he's still dead, of course, a carcass washed up on the beach to be cleared out by those who actually give a shit. I take one last look at my darkroom, my former sanctuary, my escape from reality, and blow it and my life's work—hundreds of photographs—a kiss goodbye. It will all be missed.

I shove the purse full of tainted clothes into my backpack, along with the steak knife I dropped before passing out in the closet. If Greg Strand were willing to send someone to my home to "rough me up," then it's imperative to be prepared for a second attempt, wherever that may be.

I exit the apartment and take the long way out, the camera-less way out, down the stairs and through the laundry room (outside of one running dryer, all is quiet) and into the storage area. I notice no evidence of murder, just a thicker-than-usual institutional smell covering up something *spoiled*. I wave goodbye to Chico and Carmen behind door number three, then pull my hood up and slip out the freight entrance onto the dark and empty sidewalk of East 72nd Street. I duck down and crouch-walk behind the queue of parked cars; with every inch of Manhattan's streets under surveillance, keeping my face hidden is the I-don't-want-to-get-in-any-more-trouble thing to do.

I luck into a town car on 5th Avenue, a not-so-easy feat at 1:30 a.m. on a Tuesday. In spite of the fatal circumstances distracting me, in spite of not having my camera, I gaze at the driver and his displayed medallion license and take mental snapshots of him, my mind's eye the only camera I have left.

Old habits die hard. He's a middle-aged Yankees-cap-wearing white guy named Jarvis Pinborough. Jarvis has a mask of acne, so thick that if you called him pizza-face, he'd thank you for the compliment. In the hundred or so portraits in my Geeks & Freaks portfolio, none come even close to the sad originality Jarvis's face brings to the table.

In my mind, I point.

In my mind, I *click.*

Drivers are bored people, more than willing to extend mildly interesting pleasantries into an otherwise awkward, mundane situation.

"What brings you out tonight?" he asks.

I think about it…and realize, with no indecisiveness, there's only one true answer to that question. I utter it proudly, with no qualms. Only faith, hope and…

"Love."

CHAPTER 57

Jarvis Pinborough talks, but I don't hear him.

My head is consumed with Lily. *My love.*

With the streets devoid of traffic, the ride downtown lasts less than ten minutes. Jarvis Pinborough (he *does* have an awesome name) drops me off outside the Artful Dodger Pub, and I give him two twenties, *keep the change*. He skillfully tucks them into his shirt pocket, then hands me a homemade business card (also from the same pocket) with a phone number scribbled on the back, should I "ever need a ride in a pinch." I slip the card in my backpack then jog to the corner and dump Jolie's purse-full-o-murder-clothes into an industrial-sized trash bin. It's a halfhearted effort to destroy evidence, but I'm a novice and my time and options are limited. I look around (I don't think anyone saw me), take a deep breath, *ready Freddie,* then cross the sidewalk and enter the bar.

The place is hopping for an early Tuesday morning, drunk college students getting in their last licks before summer shuts down. The Artful Dodger is a Manhattan dive bar if there ever was one, complete with neon beer logos, crudely painted walls, and a trio of overly tattooed barmaids in tight black tank tops serving drinks. Not the sort of place I'd typically be drawn to, although they are cranking Green Day at full volume, which helps bolster my confidence as I seek out my *love*.

Every seat at the bar is taken, clutches of teetering alcoholics squeezing in between them, twenties held high. Groups of four-plus fill a dozen wooden booths lining the wall opposite the bar, noisy and boisterous parties indiscreet about their tolerances for alcohol. A waitress from the same tribe as the bartenders gently bumps into me as she delivers a tray of apps to a table filled with pitchers, pints, and polluted people. There's a Red Bull on her tray and I offer her a twenty for it, *keep the change*, and she obliges with a monotone *tankyu*, seemingly annoyed that she has to go back to the bar to replace it. Better her than me.

I make my way through the crowd, gulping Red Bull, squeezing in between knots of partygoers buttressing the rowdy milieu with alcohol-fueled machismo and shameless skin-teasing. I bump and sidestep, carving a path to the rear of the bar where I stand on my tippy-toes to survey the crowd. No sign of her. I check my phone. No additional app notifications. *Shit.*

From behind me, cutting through the tang of stale beer and fresh wings, comes the faint, acrid scent of cigarette smoke. There hadn't been any smokers out front, which can only mean one thing: there's a courtyard out back. I turn and move down a hallway, passing three dingy unisex restrooms and a pair of grease-coated swinging doors. Ahead, a propped doorway leading into a small but fairly crowded outdoor area comes into view.

Not one foot outside, and I see her.

My heart leaps up into my throat and lodges there: a promise of broken words should I attempt to speak. In my mind's eye, I'm leaping forward and hugging her and whisking her away someplace safe and quiet where we can hash out everything that's happened between us, and discuss what could happen if we don't deal with Greg Strand ASAP.

But in the real world, I just stand in place and stare.

She's hunched on one of five wooden barstools, portable bar supporting her weight, bunched-up denim skirt flashing pink panties, wet-stained V-neck tee partly tucked at the waist. A good-looking, taller and more-muscular-than-me college-aged guy is invading her personal space with a grin that speaks volumes for his brawn. She's smiling too, but her wavering eye-contact and use of one forearm to (unsuccessfully) nudge him away broadcasts her disinterest in him. She's sipping red liquid from a cup with a lime wedge, twirling a hunk of hair that doesn't look like it's been washed in days. What little makeup she's got on is smeared around her eyes in bandit circles. She's a train wreck and so fucking beautiful and I can't stop looking at her, my mind restlessly obsessing, *she's not his, she's mine, mine all mine, not his, mine, mine all mine, not his, mine, mine all mine…*

The devil, perched confidently on my left shoulder, takes control of my mouth and mutters aloud: *"You're in love."*

Yes, in love, not just in my heart, but in all my organs and in my blood: an assembly of metaphorical tropes reaching for my throat as I make my approach. The *now me* has managed to separate himself from all incapacities to love, to be loved. He's taken control. And even though he's nervous, he's also confident and devoid of worry because he just murdered a man, and nothing fucking trumps that.

College-Dude doesn't notice me as he hogs the bar with his stupid Ralph Lauren shirt, Abercrombie shorts, and Teva sandals. He also doesn't budge an inch to let me squeeze in (of course he doesn't, he's *distracted*), so I move in behind Lily. My arm softly grazes her back and my entire body shivers, but she doesn't notice. She's too worse for the wear, teetering on her stool, groping the bar for balance.

I chug the rest of my Red Bull, take a deep breath…and then, just like she did to me at Bryant Park a million years ago, I grab her by the arm. She looks up at College-Dude (who's finally acknowledged my existence with a steaming glare), then looks at my hand before following the arm it's attached to all the way up to my eyes.

CHAPTER 58

"Hi, Lily."

College-Dude interrupts my twist-of-fate moment with a look of bewilderment, followed by an unsurprising interjection: "Wait a minute…I thought you said your name was Laura."

Lily-Lola-Linda-Laura smiles, swiping the air in front of him, *silly boy*. It's easy to smell the cloud of vodka surrounding her. She hangs a lazy arm over my shoulder and, with a deadpan face, runs her fingers through my hair, hypnotic eyes struggling to maintain their focus. It's not her finest moment, but I can relate. I'm in the midst of my own not-so-finest-moment.

She slurs, "Peter…I'm so glad you're here." With her arm still hooked around my neck, tightly so she doesn't fall off the barstool, she rests her head on my shoulder and breathes out an audible sigh, as though relieved I've come to her rescue. Her face is sweaty and her hair smells like french-fries and I put my arm around her waist and kiss the top of her head.

College-Dude doesn't like this, not one bit. I just cock-blocked him, after all. He scowls and shoves his juiced-up chest at me, purple-polo-shirt-dominance and dilated eyes functioning solely on instinct and cocaine.

I say to her, "We should go someplace else to talk. Okay?"

She nods, a simple gesture that brings a great deal of satisfaction and relief to me. I ease her off the stool with her one arm still hooked around my neck, as if I'm a life preserver. Which in a way, I am.

College-Dude shouts, "Where the fuck do you think you're going?" He can't just let it go. He just has to be a dick. Sullen and scowling and wide-eyed, he eventually gives up his spot at the bar and shoves his purple polo shirt at me again. "Who the fuck do you think you are, taking my girl?"

It's a good question, one I don't have a definitive answer to. *I'm a husband and a father and a son and a philanderer and a…murderer.*

And also, for the first time in my life, a man in *love*.

I stare at my moment's nemesis. He's bigger and taller, overflowing with testosterone; young, dumb and full of cum. Something not so deep inside of me wants me to pin him with crazy-eyes and growl, *I just murdered a dude tonight. Bashed his head in with a candlestick*. But I don't. Instead I go with a more acceptable confession. "I'm her boyfriend."

As if on cue, Lily kisses my cheek, leaving behind a moist circle of cranberry juice, vodka, and sweat on my skin.

College-Dude spreads his arms and exclaims, "What the fuck?" again shoving his much larger chest into mine, more forcefully now in defense of what he considers his territory. Lily and I break apart and the wall of testosterone skirts between us, arms still outstretched in that *come-at-me-bro* pose he's got down to a tee. I notice a stockade gate with a bouncer alongside it whose job it is to look menacing and let people out but not in. I reach around College-Douche (he's College-*Douche* now) and take Lily by the hand. He lunges at me—more than grazing Lily's breasts in the process—and grabs me by the hoodie, up-close-and-personal with both hands, like they do on TV. "I just invested a buck-fitty on this girl. No way are you going to reap my fruits."

The bouncer sees me in the much larger guy's grasp and promptly races over, dousing the incident with a scowl of disapproval. Lily appears confused, scared even. Who wouldn't be caught in the middle of a tug-o-war between a murderous lover and a drunk asshole? She's clutching fistfuls of her own hair, eyes darting back and forth in attempt to focus in on the action. The bouncer separates my hoodie from College-Douche's fists as a number of random partygoers watch on with shit-eating grins on their faces. He says to Lily, "Are either of these guys bothering you?"

She attempts a drunken hug on the bouncer, which he backs away from, then moves on to me, burying her head in my chest as if ashamed of the hubbub she's caused. I stick my tongue out at College-Douche. *I win, fuckface.*

That earns me a boisterous "Fuck you, asshole!" after which he throws his entire massive self at me. The bouncer rushes in, puts him in a chokehold, and drags him kicking and screaming out the back gate, producing fifteen seconds of front-seat entertainment for all those in attendance. When the bouncer returns—huffing as if this was the most exercise he's had in a while—he asks Lily if she's okay, to which she nods. He then suggests we exit through the front. We're being asked to leave.

Fine by me. I got what I came for.

With Lily holding my hand, I lead her back inside the bar. She hasn't said anything to me yet, leaving as much mystery to the situation as comfort in knowing she's with me now. Once in the hallway, she aggressively pulls me into one of the unisex bathrooms and shuts the door. Three times she tries to slide the latch shut, but misses, so I do it for her. With that done, she shoves me against the sink and deep-kisses me, wet, sloppy, passionate kisses. I kiss her back and we don't stop. Soon our hips are making out just as much as our mouths are, our feet producing sticky Velcro-like sounds on the floor as we bump and grind.

She whispers in my ear, "You…make…me…so…wet."

I unzip her jeans and she isn't lying. She's *drenched* and there's stubble down there now and I can smell her and my mouth waters. She opens my jeans and grips me with a clammy, heaven-sent hand. Her other hand joins my fingers as they bathe in her *love.*

Between kisses, I breathe, "I'm so hard for you…" and she responds by guiding my free hand under her damp tee-shirt. Her bra is loose, *when did she do that?* and I hold one breast in my hand and pinch her nipple. There's a knock on the plywood door, but we are animals in heat and I'm possessed by her silent control and there's no stopping us, heard or not. I slide two fingers into her and she fucks them vigorously and I vigorously fuck her hand that seconds ago was immersed in the slick between her legs. We stroke and kiss and stroke and pant and the crescendo builds and we get loud and ironically "Slow Ride" is playing in the bar and like practiced lovers we are in sync and cum in rapturous harmony.

Afterwards, we breathe heavily and hold each other tight in an embrace that I wish could go on forever.

CHAPTER 59

We take turns washing in the filthy sink. An awkward silence sets in between us, deepened by the shortage of elbow room in the space meant for one. She contemplates her warped reflection in the stained acrylic mirror and I watch as she attacks the bandit makeup around her eyes with baby-wipes from my backpack. Behind those eyes lives a forlorn woman hoarding a suitcase full of tears, and I plan on wiping them away the day she unpacks them.

"I hate that you're seeing me like this," she sobs, budding modesty hinting at the beginnings of sobriety. I ignore her and demand we immediately bridge the gap between us, hash out what's been happening in our prospective worlds these last few days, focus on the steps we need to take to ensure our safety and freedom. She nods and we emerge from the bathroom holding hands, the now near-empty bar spotlighting our indiscreet exit to a waitress stacking glasses nearby. Given her jaded eye-roll, one can assume that the Artful Dodger's unisex bathrooms regularly draw this kind of behavior. We grab a couple of water bottles from the bar and make our way outside into the cool summer night.

11th Avenue is dim, nearly devoid of life, off-duty taxis idling alongside empty sidewalks, faraway garbage trucks braking and banging in the distance. I peek toward the corner and bear witness to a homeless woman fishing Jolie's purse out of the trash can (along with a few empty water bottles). She adds the bounty to the rest of her possessions in the Gristedes grocery cart she calls home, then wheels away around the corner and out of sight. At some point she'll discover all the evidence needed to put me away for the rest of my life. Nothing I can—or should—do about it now.

Lily tugs me in the opposite direction. There's a diner a few blocks uptown and we agree to head that way, passing beneath a scaffolding hiding a lifeless construction site and dumpster alley.

"Hey asshole..."

The words are garbled, drawled by someone too close behind me. I turn and it's College-Douche, seizing the front of my hoodie just like he did in the bar. He shakes me like a rag doll. "You think you can just take my girl, eh? Well fuck you can!" He spits in my face and chases it with a head-butt straight between the eyes. I collapse to the sidewalk in a heap, blackness seeping into my vision. He grabs the waistband of my jeans and drags me like a sack of garbage into the alley. I hear Lily scream," *Let him go!*" and watch as she ineffectively double-fists a flurry of girl-punches onto his jacked back.

Ignoring the painless onslaught, he shoves me to the cement-littered pavement of the alley and straddles me, huffing and puffing, a predator on prey with coked-up eyes that don't bode well for me. He winds up with his right leg and delivers a slightly-off-aim kick against my ribs. I grunt at the grazing sting, then roll over and scramble to my feet, shrug out of my backpack, and toss it to Lily, who's taking in the scene from a safe distance, calmly and with great interest, as if getting a lay of the land.

He fast-jabs me in the jaw, once, twice, three times, my head jerking back with each painful strike. With my back now against the alley wall, Lily rushes in and wallops him across the back with my backpack, sadly no more a deterrent than her fists. He doesn't notice or care. He's tunnel-vision focused on me, scary eyes wielding joy as he punches me again, this time a hook across the side of my head. A black surge blankets my vision and I collapse to the dusty pavement, jagged shards of cement digging painfully into my knees and elbows. Lily swings the backpack again, this time striking him across the ribs. Again, he doesn't notice or care...but one of the zippers tears open and the steak knife from my kitchen tumbles onto the ground behind him. He drops to his knees and straddles me, leaning in with his stupid douche-baggy face six inches away from mine, close enough to smell the vodka on his breath. He squeezes my cheeks with his bloody punching hand and shakes my head back and forth, ranting and raving about how rude it was of me to steal *his* girl. How I fucked with the wrong guy, blah-blah-blah.

Yeah. I may have fucked with the wrong guy. But he fucked with the wrong girl.

Through the corner of my eye, I see Lily sneak up behind him. As she raises her arm, the steak knife (now in her hand) comes into view and he gets in one last glancing blow across my right eye socket before she plunges it into his back.

The face she's got on is the same exact one she wore in the park when she *messed up my shot*. I can do nothing but watch as she grunts and drools and uses her body weight to push the knife all the way in. Who would've thought that two of my kitchen knives would end up buried to the hilt inside two different assholes? And on the same day, no less? His coked-out eyes bulge almost as much as the peepshow bouncer's, black pupils reflecting moonlight as they swallow up all traces of color, red veins bursting into the whites like tributaries. His mouth drops open and he gropes for the hilt jutting from the unreachable part of his back, just as a loose string of saliva begins its quick descent toward my face. I roll out from under him before it lands, then scramble to my feet, my stunned gaze never leaving him as he continues fumbling for the knife like a frustrated poison-ivy victim trying to conquer an elusive itch. He attempts a cry for help, but all that emerges is a sickly wheeze. She must've punctured a lung.

Lily grips my arm aggressively—unlike the way she touched me in the park—and says, "We need to skedaddle. Like now."

Our attacker-turned-victim collapses against the side of the dumpster, gripping the fork pocket to keep from face-planting into the jagged concrete ground. The widening stripe of blood on the back of his purple polo glistens in the moonlight like a distant mirage.

In an ominously calm voice, she says, "*Now* Peter."

We peek out the alley and get lucky. No traffic, foot or otherwise. The scaffolding and plastic construction mesh surrounding it provides more than enough cover as we flee the alley and scoot away from the scene of the crime undetected. We emerge from our cover almost two blocks away, walking hand-in-hand as if we were just another couple on our way home from a long night out together. *Someone was attacked? Oh my god, that's terrible! No, I'm sorry, we didn't see anything!*

I pull her across 11th Avenue onto 46th Street, into the Midnight Moon Diner, a charming New York dive with bright lights and plastic menus, empty apart from a pair of construction workers eating breakfast at the counter. We grab a booth in the corner, complete with red vinyl seats and four pink ass-circles. The light is offensively bright, igniting Lily's natural blemishes, one perfect imperfection at a time, right down to the still-tacky blood on her hands. Before sitting down, she excuses herself and disappears into the ladies room.

While she's gone, I catch my breath, thinking of her, and only her.

We're together again, in this together. This time, it's forever.

It's a promise I plan to keep.

Five minutes later, she returns, face clean and alert.

Despite my pain, it's a happy moment.

Until she says, "So Peter…how the fuck did you find me *again*?"

CHAPTER 68

"Missed Connection."

"What's that?" she asks, hands still trembling, eyes tracking somewhere above my head. This is how I must've looked after *my* first kill, only a few hours ago.

I confess to how I used a dating app to track her down—twice—then swipe it up on my phone to show her how it works. She concentrates while watching, tense face judging the harass-the-girl-of-your-choice functionality it offers. *There's even a GPS locator and a facial recognition feature! Cool, huh?*

"It's stalker fucking central, is what it is." She tears off the lid to a grape jelly and slurps it noise and all and I think nothing of it. "I *am* glad you found me. Just not *how* you did it." She picks up her menu, impassively focused, eyes drifting aimlessly over her choices as she licks grape jelly from her lips. She's still a bit drunk and I can't stop my mind from going back over how I interrupted her aspirations to find a safe bed to sleep in tonight. How if I hadn't stepped in she'd be fucking College-Douche right now, instead of sitting here with me, just the two of us, beaten up and beaten down, caught in a nefarious love quadrangle, pale uncertainty worrying our faces, *I just killed someone*. Despite the predicament and the harm it has inflicted, I *distract* and take selfish delight in the puffy creases on her cheeks, the way her upper lip twitches, the slow, wayward drift of her eyes. She's perfection even under the most brutal of damaging conditions.

Considering this to be her first kill (I'd be shocked if College-Douche were still alive, given the generous flow of blood down his back), I wonder with concern if she'll be able to assess the mayhem (that I'm now so personally familiar with) going on in her head as something to embrace, to use as encouragement as she moves forward. Will she be able to understand the darkness blooming at the base of her thoughts? That it isn't something to cower away from, but rather to incorporate into her mind, body, and soul, just like I did after killing Chico? Knowing from my own recent encounter, the worse the offense committed, the more *accepting* one becomes of their wrongdoing. *That's how I feel.* It's in my genes, how I *am*. Accepting of fate and the absolute *need* for the immoral choices that got me here. I did what needed to be done to preserve…*this*. Carved my own path less-traveled and lived to look back upon it with glory. Saved myself. Saved *us*. She will understand soon. She will *feel*, just like I do.

The devil: *It's been in you since the day you were born. You've accepted your darkness and have evolved into what you have become.*

The waitress—thin, wrinkled, exhausted, indifferent—struggles with her aim as she fills our coffee cups. Name tag: Ethel. She looks like an Ethel with her faded yellow uniform and matching yellow hair and yellower nails that are almost brown. She's a character right out of a 1950s sitcom, remarkably still alive after having chain-smoked since then. I order a Hungry-Person's Special and Lily utters "*same*" and after the waitress leaves she looks out the window with worry haunting her taut, stricken face. The last few days of her life have been no less painful than my own, culminating with her own Clue-like accusation: *Lily in the Alley with a Kitchen Knife*. She's earned her catatonia.

After a period of silence I ask, "Are you okay?"

Her head turns to face me, slowly as if half asleep. "No Peter…I'm not okay. I…I need to tell you something. Something important…"

The waitress returns in record time with plates of scrambled eggs, bacon, home fries, toast, and even our own pot of coffee. We're starving and hold our thoughts as we eat. I watch and admire how she chews her food and sips her coffee and covers her lips when she burps. I love her dirty hair and how it frames her face in loose strands. Her faint un-showered scent. A lifetime ago I was taken by her beauty, confidence, and sway. Now that she's returned to my orbit in a more vulnerable state, stripped free of all her vanities, she offers so much more *human* to fall in love with.

With my food half-eaten, I say, "You started to say something…"

She nods, puts down her fork, and looks at me, face a mixed bag of emotions: angry, scared, sad. "You're not going to be happy about what I have to say."

I'm already not happy about it. Jolie. Nick's money. Greg Strand and his quote-unquote business.

The devil: *Don't forget Gail. How convenient was it for her to leave, just as Lily needed a window of opportunity to climb through?* I feign ignorance for now, and nod for her to continue.

She looks at her half-eaten plate of food and blows out nervously. "I really don't know how to tell you this, or even where to start, but something bad is going to happen…" She begins to sob, her confession hitting another brick wall. Is there something else happening behind the scenes that I don't know about? Something I should be gravely concerned about? Something that involves Rachel? Still in denial, I shrug off the possibility and look at her instead, *into* her, deeply, affectionately, *DISTRACTING*, wanting her despite my pain, despite our predicament, despite the terrible news she's struggling to drop on me.

Her sobs taper, and with an aim to set her at ease, I exclaim, "Whatever's happening, we'll get through it together." She stabbed someone coming to my defense and for that alone, she's gained my undying gratitude. Whatever it is she's worried about, we'll fix it, no matter what the cost. "And no matter what happens, I'll be here for you. For us."

She looks into my eyes. "Are we an *us*?"

"There's no escaping this if there isn't an us."

She attempts a smile. "You're the only good thing in my life right now."

I nod. "And you make me happy too. *Lola*."

My reveal interrupts her line of confession, but the window of opportunity inched open, so I decided to squeeze through. Her face blanches as if she just saw that proverbial ghost and when she moves to voice a reply her words get snagged in her throat. Outside, jarring sirens and swirling lights announce the charge of two police cruisers down 11th Avenue, and I use this small twist of fate to lighten the sudden discomfort between us. "Rumor has it they're on their way to assist with a stabbing victim."

Her face grows a smile as real as my pain, and I mirror it with one of my own. Despite our saga's painful chapter, despite the loveless pasts bringing us here together, it's a much needed (and openly embraced) lighter moment that once again demonstrates how much we belong together.

She asks, mostly to herself, "Why am I laughing? What's wrong with me?" Tears paint her cheeks, damp strips of unfettered emotion.

With her hands still in mine, I explain to her that she's laughing because of the change taking place inside her: this unstoppable transformation that will help preserve her life and keep her by my side as my partner in crime for years to come, despite our transgressions. I waste no time and implement the devil's therapy; it had helped me to understand what was happening inside of me, and now will help her understand that laughing at her *indulgences* can help ease the pain. Twist them into something *right*. "With trauma comes change. It affects everyone differently. Normal people cower from it, crawl into protective holes and wish it all way…"

(…one one-hundred, two one-hundred, three one-hundred…)

"…but you and I? We're not normal. We've experienced hardships sprouting from similarly dark sources…"

…lack of love, loss of love, pursuit of love…

"…and we've spent our entire lives responding to them in unique yet similar ways. We've been through more anguish than most, and not just for the past few days, but for many years. Like me, you've seen and experienced painful abuses that started when we you were a child. Right?"

She slowly nods.

"Do you see? I understand how you're feeling. It's like you're changing into somebody else, right? Someone that's *not you*. Lily, I'd like you to meet the *now you*. The tragedies you've encountered—that we've encountered—have forced you—us—to evolve into someone—*something*— unfamiliar, something terrifying and invigorating all wrapped up into one massive sense of *self*. It's as if there's this offensive instinct inside you hatching free, forcing you to live out your life differently, in a definitive 'kill-or-be-killed' manner. I can see it in your eyes, plainly as I see it in my own eyes when I look in the mirror, that it's there inside of you, changing you into the very same something I've already become." *The now me.*

She nods again. Anyone else listening would think I'm insane…

The devil: *You always have been.*

...but to her, I'm making perfect sense. She understands. She's like me.

The devil: *Like HIM.*

"I know this all sounds crazy, but I *know*. I've experienced what you're going through right now. On the outside you're beaten down, jaded, ready to give up on life. But on the inside, deep down, the opposite is happening. Tell me if I'm wrong—even given what just happened in the alley, you feel empowered and unafraid, as if you can do anything, take on anything you want no matter the circumstances, or possible consequences."

She breaks her silence. "I spent my whole childhood, even my teen years, being scared. But now, with you, I feel different. Like nothing I've ever felt before. Stronger. More powerful. In spite of what I just did, I feel good and right about it. Justified. No longer oppressed. But...it's also scaring me." She looks down at her hands...hands that moments ago were stained with human blood. "I mean, am I a monster?"

I shake my head. "I was scared just like you are, but only at first. I even asked myself that same question. But once you welcome it, listen to the devil inside, allow it to command you, you'll become the best possible version of you." I tap a fist against my chest and it hurts like hell. "I know this all sounds crazy, but you have to trust me. It's in me, and it's in you too."

The devil: *Evil...*

With the color creeping back into her face, with her eyes finally finding their equilibrium, she says, "You really do know me Peter, don't you?"

"More than you know."

She forks a potato into her mouth. "So then how did you get my real name?"

I don't hesitate. It all needs to come out anyway, sooner rather than later: "Same place I found out about Greg Strand."

She freezes in mid-sip, puts down her cup, and directs her gaze back out the window: a failed attempt to hide fresh tears.

I say, "I'm sorry, I didn't mean to—"

She waves a hand at me then wipes her eyes with a napkin. "No…it's fine. One less painful thing I need to tell you about."

It's painful for me to see her so upset. I shift in my seat and my ribs scold me for doing so, the smarting of just getting my ass handed to me in full bloom now. I take a deep breath then begin my sordid tale, starting with my encounter at the peepshow and the bouncer with the crazy eyes who came looking for me.

"His name is George but *everyone calls him Popeye.* And just for the record, I don't work there."

"Then what were you doing there?"

"Long story."

Here I go again: "I already know about Greg's business, and his cousin Odie."

She looks at me as if I'm a big fucking surprise party she just walked into, eyes and mouth stuck in an oval *what-the-fuck* shape. She shakes her head, looking scared for my life. "These are dangerous men into dangerous things. You cannot be involved with them in any way." She leans in, and with grit added to her tempered voice, utters, "I don't know what you know, or how you found out, but if Greg finds out, he *will* send someone to hurt you. That's a promise."

"That's how I found out," I say, my tone smug.

"What do you mean?"

"He sent someone to hurt me."

She slaps a hand over her mouth as if trying to keep her words from escaping, eyes darting sideways as if one of Greg's dangerous men might be seated nearby. "How are you still breathing?"

I answer cockily, "I handled him."

"Handled? What does that even mean?" Her voice is fully-sober-sounding now, and sharp with concern, as if I just revealed a terminal diagnosis.

I tell her what it even means, providing every detail about my confrontation with Popeye. How he had Jolie's key to the apartment, how I immobilized him and tied him up and made him talk about Greg. I tell her that I'd stepped out—*I'll tell you what I was doing in a minute*—and when I returned, my apartment door was open and Popeye had a steak knife in his heart.

This time she uses both hands to cover her mouth, waiting a moment before asking, "This was earlier tonight?"

I look at the time on my phone. 4:10 a.m. "About four hours ago, give or take. Has to be Greg, no?"

She shakes her head. "No. Popeye is loyal and Greg and Odie love him for it." She pauses a moment, then says, "Greg probably figured out you were on to him, and saw no option but to step in. Popeye is Greg's number one, so if Greg lost contact with him, he would have gone there himself to check things out. Bet you that Jolie was there with him, too. Those two are fucking connected at the hip! I can't say for sure what happened next, but I know Greg better than anyone, and know for sure he didn't hurt Popeye."

"Which means…Jolie?"

"Bank on it. You of all people should know how batshit crazy she is. Sorry to break the news to you Peter, but she's not just the bitchy housewife you once knew. She's very bad news now. Greg's gotten to her, just like he did to me years ago."

I'm having trouble wrapping my head around the 110-pound mother of my daughter stabbing a 300-pound bouncer to death, batshit crazy or not.

The devil: *Your girlfriend just stabbed a douchebag.*

Touché. I sure know how to pick them.

"Is it possible Greg sent someone else there to check on him?"

She shakes her head. "Popeye's the only guy Greg would offer a side job to. And Odie...he has no idea what Greg and Jolie are up to—he'd be pissed to no end if he found out Greg was onto a big score without him."

"Big score...as in rob my father?"

No longer surprised at my knowledge of Jolie and Greg's misdoings, she says, "And here I was worried sick about having to tell you all of this. Yes. That was Jolie's plan, right from the start. She knew about the safe and came to me with the idea of introducing me to your father for the housekeeping job. Told me she needed money to pay off some debt, and that she'd give me ten percent. All I had to do was get the combination to the safe. That's it. The problem is, I never got it. The only thing I was able to get a hold of was the password to his computer, and that got us nowhere. That's when Greg got involved. And that's when things changed between us."

"Between you and Greg?"

She nods. "And me and Jolie. Greg gets very impatient when jobs don't pan out right away. Eventually he convinced Jolie that they should brute-force the money out of Nick, and Jolie agreed, the fucking cunt. Your father is such a sweet man! That was last week. I wanted to warn Nick what was happening but Greg made me quit before I had a chance to. When I threatened to call Nick, Greg fucking choked me. Damn near killed me until he was convinced I wouldn't give Nick any sort of heads-up." More tears form in her crystal blues and her words break into sobs. "He told me he had no use for me anymore, that Jolie was his ticket to your father's money, not me."

Only yesterday I'd told Nick to call an armored car company and get the cash out of there. With Jolie at his side, Greg will have no problem getting inside the house.

"Fucking Jolie. Fucking Greg."

"I can't believe I wasted ten years of my life with that asshole!"

While she mourns a breakup that's the best thing to ever happen to her, I tell her about my first Missed Connection notification and how a shiny barista recognized the girl in the ad and thought it acceptable to let her creeper know about it. She echoes my stalker-fortified romanticism, telling me about how she followed me from work to the library, and then to the park. "I was doing it to get back at Jolie for stealing Greg from me. And vice-versa, I guess. I don't know! I honestly didn't know what I was going to do! I was just so pissed and scared and angry. So, I decided to follow you and bump into you, maybe hoping you'd drop and break your camera. It was the only thing I could think of at the moment to get back at Jolie."

"Guilty by association."

She nods. "But then, after I saw you up close, how handsome you were in your suit, and how you looked at me, I decided in that moment to kiss you. It was stupid. An impulsive way to get revenge, even if just in my head. But it was the only ammunition I had, you know? Then I realized you'd get the wrong impression…"

"Which I did."

"…and that I didn't need to get involved with you and clusterfuck everything up even more. So I just walked away as quickly as I could. The last place I thought I'd end up was back at the peepshow, but it was close by and I wanted to hide from you. Thankfully neither Greg nor Jolie were there."

"And thus begins chapter one of our saga."

"I'm so sorry, Peter. Everything is my fault."

"No. It's not. I could've just let you walk away. But I didn't. *I'm* the one who hunted *you* down. *I* got involved with *you*. "

She shrugs. "You must realize by now that us getting together wasn't supposed to happen. That night at the coffee shop, I was brooding badly over Greg and Jolie. When you showed up, I looked at it as my one and only chance to get revenge on them. But after that first night with you, I felt differently. I enjoyed being with you, and wanted to see you again."

"Blame me again for writing my number down." I go on to tell her about Jolie poisoning me with sleeping pills, *she did that so she could spend more time with Greg. Did you really think she was going to the gym all those hours?* and how three days later I found the pill bottle with her stockpile of credit cards in her gym bag. "It was the evening after our afternoon fuck-fest."

"Do you now understand why I was asking all those questions about Jolie after our…fuck-fest? I was trying to make you aware of what was happening around you, without actually letting on that I knew anything."

"You should have told me."

She pauses, then says, "I didn't want to reveal my real self to you. I…I just wanted to experience a loving moment in my life, without ruining it. I just wanted to be Lily Dahl, not Lola Dawson."

I understand.

As I relish in the thought of another fuck-fest with Lily, I explain how I discovered the body of our nanny in our storage locker; this type of uneven thinking—enmeshing sex and murder—should alarm me. But it doesn't. On the contrary, and with the devil as my witness, it *excites* me.

She bobs her head and runs her hands through her greasy hair and looks at me through the tops of her eyes. "I know what happened to Carmen. I was there."

My heart starts pounding heavily, and I hold my breath, waiting for her to start.

Her wet eyes flare and sparkle under the overhead fluorescent lamps. "That wasn't supposed to happen. Jolie told us that Carmen would be out with Rachel, that they usually go to Central Park from twelve and two, and that we'd have plenty of time to review Greg's plans to rob Nick. But they didn't go that day. Rachel must've fallen asleep and Carmen was lying in bed with her. We all thought they were out, but they weren't.

"So what happened?"

She purses her lips and blows out; this isn't an easy thing for her to discuss, and rightly so. *Embrace it, Lily. Let the devil guide you.* "Carmen heard everything, including how Greg would 'kill Nick if he had to.' She came out of the room white as a ghost and we all kinda freaked out when we saw her. But Greg…he totally lost it! He screamed 'Who the fuck are you!?' and…and then it all happened so fast…he just leaped at her and grabbed her by the neck and slammed her against the wall, and then…then he started ripping into her, saying stuff like 'You saw nothing' and 'I'll kill you if you say anything,' like he did to me when he thought I was going to tell Nick what was going on." *(…like HE did to you…)* "A few seconds later he stops and he's just standing there not saying anything and he still has his hand around her neck, and me and Jolie, we were just looking at each other like, 'okay, what's happening?' We were in shock, you know? Carmen's tongue was sticking out and her eyes were rolled up all white, and then…and then Greg just let go of her and she slammed to the floor. Dead. Just like that."

Now I know how the crack in the wall got there.

She says, "I was too scared to move. I'd seen Greg beat up guys before, but never anything like this. This was whole-other-level shit, you know? He was cursing and pacing and waving his arms around like a crazy man, and Jolie, she must have a magic vagina or something because she was able to calm him down in a way I never could. She just took him into the other room and sixty seconds later he comes back out a rational man. Just like that. She's the one who came up with the idea to hide Carmen's body in the storage locker and let you take the blame for it. Greg was on board, of course. He called Popeye to come help him move the body and then seconds later Greg and Jolie were stuffing Carmen into the plastic container." She starts sobbing. "I heard her fucking bones cracking! When I turned to look, they had her crammed into the bin with her legs bent backward so her toes were touching her face. Jolie was sitting on the lid trying to snap it shut and the whole time Rachel...oh my god, poor Rachel, she was sitting up in bed watching everything. I couldn't take it anymore, so I just ran out. They didn't see me at first and I was already on my way down when I heard Jolie calling after me. That was the last straw. I was out."

This was the day I saw Greg and Popeye on the security footage the police showed me. "Have you seen Greg since then?"

"Just once more, at the club. I went there a few days later because I was out of money. That was the day he choked me. I'm sure you can imagine how scared I was of ending up in a box like Carmen! But he spared me, probably because he'd already paid for the Airbnb he got me. He gave me five hundred bucks and a new burner and his last words to me were, 'You're on your own now.' He put his arm around Jolie and the two of them just stood there, looking at me, waiting for me to leave."

"Well, I'm here for you now." She smiles and wipes her swollen eyes and I go on to tell her about my two conversations with the police. She freaks out and starts crying again and Ethel the waitress is now paying attention to us from behind the counter, probably wondering if she should call the cops on the physically abused couple. Lily's scared and I can't say I blame her. She doesn't want to go to prison, and neither do I. I promise her that there's nothing to worry about, that they're looking for the guy with the neck tattoo in the surveillance footage. But the truth is, I'm freaking out too. They're going to find Carmen and they're going to find Chico and they're going to find Popeye and then they're going to want to talk to me about them, so, selfishly, I decide not to tell her that the cops kept my camera bag with *her pictures* in it.

Ethel comes by and asks if we need anything else. I say no and she makes a face and Lily and I go back to holding hands across the table. I look around. Early-risers are beginning to make their entrance, some peering suspiciously at the beat-up guy and torn-up girl in the corner booth. I finish my side of the story by telling her how I moved Carmen's body into another locker—that's what I was doing while Popeye was tied up in my darkroom—because I'm an idiot and left my prints all over it when I first found it. Again I leave out an inconvenient truth, this time of my kill-him-or-go-to-prison encounter with Chico.

The devil reminds me: *You didn't kill Chico. HE did.*

Lily says, "I was there once, in the locker. I was short on clothes and just got the job with your father, so she gave me a few things to wear."

I ask, "Did Greg have anything to do with Gail 'leaving?'"

Her eyes narrow and she shakes her head and says, "I don't think so…your father told me she moved back to California to be with her family."

I nod. I suppose coincidences do happen even under the most suspect of situations. I say, "That's it. I've told you everything that matters."

She looks at me suspiciously—I would too—and replies, "I have too."

"Well then, let's get out of here." I pay for our meals, and as we exit the diner, ask her, "By the way, where did you and Jolie meet?"

"Where do you think, Peter? The gym."

CHAPTER 61

A threesome.

A mother-fucking threesome.

My entire life has been upended because that mother-fucking-scum-sucking son-of-a-bitch Greg Strand wanted a threesome.

Lily and I walk through midtown, hand-in-hand. It should be a happy moment, but I'm steaming over that mother-fucking-scum-sucking son-of-a-bitch. She keeps talking and I keep listening and I understand her words but they're not soaking in at all, not one fucking bit. Greg fucking Strand—and I utter that with loathing. Lola's false knight in shining armor from *back in the day*, he took her in and *protected* her for years during which time she lived as a kept woman, complete with bruises on her body and scars on her brain. And now, after all these years, the asshole decides he wants a threesome, and what are the fucking odds that they cross paths with my exceptionally deranged wife?

It will be light out soon and I should be on my way to Nick's to get both him and Rachel out of there before Jolie and Greg barge in, but I'm pissed and dizzy and in a ton of pain and we're both exhausted so we take a breather and sit on a fountain ledge, thighs touching, arms hooked, hands clutching as if waiting for a meteor to strike, outside a garment center building three blocks from Johnson Apparel, where I'll never work again.

"I'm so stupid," she sobs. She pulls her shirt up and wipes her nose, exposing her pierced belly-button. In the dim early-morning light her abs look both soft *and* hard and her eyes dilate when she talks. "This is all my fault. People are dead because of me."

You don't even know about Chico. I demand because I need to know, "Tell me how you met Jolie."

She hiccup-cries, trying to explain how she and Greg started looking in cafés, and then in bars where their attempts to bring à trois into their ménage were met with drunken failure. Greg grew angry and impatient…

(…just like HE used to…)

Greg gets impatient when jobs don't pan out right away…

…so he sent Lily out on her own with a deadline to "get the fucking job done pronto."

"None of this would have happened if I hadn't met Jolie." She goes on to tell me how she toured the Central Park Sports Club one afternoon and found it full of bored-looking soccer-moms. She bought a trial membership and got dolled up and didn't need more than a few minutes before finding some good conversation with the pretty blonde bouncing on the treadmill next to her…

…and just like she did with me four years ago at the terrible Ed Sheeran concert, Jolie talked to Lily the entire time. Afterwards, they went for coffee at the Busy Bean and within hours were scissoring in my bed, and why couldn't *I* have been the lucky third they were prepping for? The simple thought of it starts getting me hard, until…

…she drops a fucking bomb. "I'm so sorry Peter. After our second tryst, I told Jolie about Greg and she was *all for it*. The next day, we were back. With him."

"Back? Wait…in my bed? *Him?*"

She sighs, and nods. "I'm sorry."

Just when I thought things couldn't get any nauseating, enter in the reality of having slept in my own bed with Greg Strand's fucking hair and skin cells and dried cum stuck to me. Fucking Jolie!

Lily is pathetic and hot with her dirty clothes and greasy hair and not enough money to last two days in Manhattan. She produces a burner from her rear pocket and asks me for my number. Seeing it in her hands reminds me of the one I swiped from Jolie, zipped up in my hoodie pocket, completely forgotten about until now. I pull it out and her eyes go wide, but don't pop out like Popeye's. She says, "Is that Jolie's burner?"

"It's Jolie's burner." She reaches for it and I pull it away, and she grabs at it again and I raise it over my head and she shouts, *"Peter…give it!"* and I shout, "What do you want it for?" and back and forth we go like two kids on a playground. The sun is reaching over the unseen horizon, accentuating her natural beauty beneath the painted stress and pent desire to get her hands on Jolie's phone.

She pleads. "Can I please have it? Greg's number is in there, and…and I'm sure he's worried about me and I…I just want to let him know I'm okay." Her gratuitous concern for him shows just how damaged her self-worth is—how as an abused woman she continues to function on fearful habit, misguided desperation succeeding through years of captive abuse.

"Greg is done with you. He's with Jolie now. And you are with me. We're an *us* now, remember?" She looks away and I use two fingers to gently pull her gaze back to me. "Hey…we're gonna get through this."

She nods and wraps both arms around my neck and hugs me tightly and I just fucking melt, a slave to her touch. She says, "You know I don't want to go back to Greg."

"Then let me handle this."

"Okay."

"I'll call him myself."

A beat. "What are you going to say?"

"I'm going to tell him to back off, otherwise I'm calling the cops."

She breaks our hug and looks at me with a smirk. "Really? Is that your big plan? Good luck with that. With or without Jolie, cops or no cops, he's gonna find a way to get your father's cash."

"Not without the combination to the safe he's not."

"Don't be so sure. He isn't known for being graceful."

I nod. His technique for finding a threesome is proof enough of this.

The devil: *You have to admit, his plan worked.*

I look at the two phone numbers and ask her *which one?* and she replies *the second one,* and I don't hesitate. I expect the robo-lady to tell me that the number I dialed is no longer in service, but that doesn't happen. Instead, a male voice picks up. "Hey pumpkin-eater…I was wondering when you'd call."

His voice is as derelict as I imagined, pack-a-day harsh. I start civilly. "I don't want any trouble. I just want you to leave me and my family alone."

"Your family?" He laughs like the fucking dick he's one-hundred percent endorsed himself to be. "Does that include your wife? The same woman you spoke to on the phone, who you thought was out of breath from the treadmill at the gym, but was actually huffing and puffing because my face was between her legs? That woman?" He laughs again then disconnects the call.

I look at Lily. She leans forward, breath bated. "Well? What did he say?"

"Let's just say you were right."

My phone vibrates, alerting an incoming text.

I check the display. One message, an image sent from Nick's cell. *At 4:45 in the morning?*

Lily asks, "What is it?"

"Something from Nick."

I open it…

…and nearly drop the phone when the photo pops up.

It's a selfie of Greg Strand, holding a crying Rachel in his arms.

CHAPTER 62

Jarvis Pinborough's town car pulls up less than ten minutes after I call. The last hundred-dollar bill from Nick's gifted stash is the right amount to get us to Long Beach. Lily and I hold hands in the backseat, silent as we pass into the sunrise over the Brooklyn Bridge. At the moment I'm calm and in focus…but my mind's eye can't stop staring at the nightmarish image of my daughter crying in the arms of that fucking monster.

The devil: *You are a monster.*

With her clammy body against mine, Lily's head falls upon my shoulder. I kiss her hair and allow myself—despite the caffeine racing through me, despite the immediate danger Rachel is in—to fall asleep for the forty-five minutes it takes to get to Long Beach…

(*…and in my subconscious I channel HIM and see through his eyes, think in his voice. I am of unsound mind, always have been, ever since I was a child. I look down at you and see myself at six, at seven, at eight. I hated myself then and hate you now! You ruined my life, just as I did my own father's life. You took that photo of me with HER and it* changed *me. And now I must introduce you to the BELT, the one with the Mustang buckle, the one that once belonged to HIM, my father, your grandfather. You will get to know each other well over the next three years, during which time you will be six-seven-eight. By the time you turn nine, I will be liberated and you will forget! You will REPRESS! Only then can we live our lives as if it never* *happened. As if SHE never happened. I will create a cover of love and for years it will seem like I'm TRYING, but I'm not. It's just a ruse to help hide my secret. We must keep up with the false pretense of love so that my secret stays hidden until the day I choose to reveal it to you…*)

"I remember! I remember!" I scream as I awaken from the dream. No. Not a dream. A…*resurfacing memory*. It was HIS voice I heard, HIS confession to me, repressed nearly all my life, now at the forefront of my mind. Crystal clear. *Secret*. My arms are autonomous, pounding the back of the passenger seat as I suck in salty air. I look around, confused. *Where am I?*

"Hey man," Jarvis says. "Please don't hit the seats."

Lily taps my cheeks and grabs my wrists until full wakefulness filters back. For a moment I don't know where I am, but soon see the familiar summer-morning charm of downtown Long Beach rolling by. I take another deep breath and run my hands through my hair with relief. She says, "You were having a nightmare. You scared the crap out of us."

My relief is fleeting. I look at Lily and the awful truth comes rushing back: a tsunami of real-world peril lying in wait inside my father's house. That this might be my last moment alive on earth, here alongside Lily in the backseat of Jarvis Pinborough's Lincoln. I shudder at the cruel thought, but realize things could be worse. I could be sitting next to Sugah.

Voice dry and broken, I tell the driver, "Leave us off at the foot of the driveway. We'll walk up."

The car pulls onto Beacon Lane and I roll down the window. Birdsong sonatas fill the morning air, accompanied by seagulls shrieking over the not-too-distant tide. Before we reach the house, an idea hits me and I roll with it because I've got nothing else. I tell Lily, "Duck down and don't let anybody see you." She puts her head in my lap and her cheek rubs against my dick and the instant fusion of danger and sex gets me rock-hard. She starts to bite me through my jeans and I don't stop her. Jarvis is oblivious and I remind him that it's house number 426 on the left. He pulls up at the apron and Lily is still biting me and I'm starting to *get there* and I tell her to stay down. The white picket fence surrounding the front yard glimmers in the early-morning sun, casting a queue of pointed shadows across the freshly mowed lawn. The home is pristine perfection, a *Better Homes & Gardens* cover, making it difficult to imagine the evil lurking within its walls at this very moment. My impulse is to charge from the car, break down the front door, and rescue Rachel from the hands of the derelict monster inside. But I'm not a fighter. And Lily is still working it through my jeans. And…

…fight fire with fire…

…I tell her stay hidden. That we don't want Greg to know she's here with me. "Have the driver drop you off at the end of the block. You can enter the beach from there. When you reach the shoreline, walk back and enter the property through the dunes."

She peers up at me from my lap. "Then what?"

"Then find a way to get Rachel out of there. The sliding doors by the pool might be open. There's also a set of steps in the back that lead down into the basement, but that door is usually locked."

"Your dad keeps a key in the shed that opens the basement door."

Really? "I didn't know that."

"I used to work here."

"That you did."

I pay Jarvis and get out of the car. I know I'm being watched, either through a window or from Nick's phone with the Argent Security app. The car pulls away with Lily inside and I step down the long driveway, watching every curtained window for movement. I've got my hands in my hoodie and my backpack full of nothing-that-can-protect-me, my only means of defense lost in the back of a College-Douche in a NYC alley. I stare at the house, thinking about Greg Strand, how my hatred of him must be rippling from me in visible waves. All I have to do is eliminate him. Then Lily and I can live as happily as my ever-after will allow. Simple as that.

I look at the house, quiet and non-threatening as though there aren't four people and a yellow lab inside in the midst of a takedown. My guard is up and my radar is on as I reach the paved walkway, the point in all my visits where Nick usually emerges in his cargo shorts smelling like coconuts. My gut is saying that Jolie wouldn't allow anything bad happen to Rachel, but I also didn't think she'd try to poison me, or fuck a lifelong criminal in my bed. I take a deep breath, pray these aren't my last precious seconds on earth, then shout out, "Rachel? Daddy's here!"

CHAPTER 63

No response.

I call for her again, louder this time, but all I'm met with is brooding silence. Usually I'm welcomed with a barrage of happy-barks from Brutus, but not today. I knock once, twice, ring the doorbell, shout. Seconds turn into minutes, but the curtained windows remain lifeless, the front door stoic in its capacity to keep me out.

The devil states the obvious: *No one's answering.*

I must look crazy when I reply out loud, "Oh, they're in there. He's just trying to figure out how to handle me. Hey Greg! I know you're in there! I know you can hear me!"

Eventually, the front door opens.

Jolie appears.

She closes the door behind her, gently like Rachel's bedroom door after putting her to sleep, then faces me with a sardonic grin that speaks volumes for her imbalance. In contrast to Lily, whose current fashion statement places her somewhere between mentally ill and homeless, Jolie is head-to-toe hot in white painted-on leggings, titty-tight tank top with no bra underneath, and black running sneakers. With a grin, I mumble aloud to the devil, "She killed Popeye. She's *changed* too."

Head shaking, and still with a smile, she says, "Talking to yourself now, Peter? It's about time you moved on from those stupid numbers of yours."

"Where's Rachel?"

"In good hands."

"Greg's hands?" She disgusts me with her power stance and convoluted thoughts and my head shakes and doesn't stop, one-one hundred on the outside but not the inside. "There's something so wrong with you."

Her creepy smile morphs into a *derisive scowl,* downcast brows completing that look I've seen so many times in the past: the same face she makes at the onset of a Jolie-fueled brouhaha.

I go on, arms flailing by design, "How can you expose our daughter to all this? The fuck!" Fighting over Rachel isn't going to help me in a head-to-head with the asshole trying to steal my father's money, so I attempt to get into Jolie's head instead. "Do you really believe Greg's going to stay with you after he gets the money? He's using you. Don't you see that? He doesn't give a shit about you, or Rachel for that matter. He wants Nick's cash, no thanks to you." I take another step forward, watching her hands and seeing nothing within grabbing distance she can use to defend herself against me.

Her face twitches: anger broiling beneath the surface. "Fuck you, pumpkin-eater, you—"

"And it was you, right, who killed Greg's pal Popeye? Huh? You really think he's gonna let that slide? That payback is gonna hurt like hell." I inch closer, enough to see the blood spatter on her right sneaker, red on black.

She ignores me, lack of denial and downcast gaze (and bloodstained sneaker) fully demonstrating her guilt. Eyes still averted, she changes the subject to further her cause: "You know, Peter, there's an easy fix to this."

"There's nothing easy about this. This is broken beyond repair."

On the top step now, she holds her hands out to me, little half-moons of Popeye's blood staining her cuticles. *That could have been me.* "All you have to do is take my hand, come inside, and open your father's safe. Once we have the money, we'll leave you *and* your little trailer slut alone."

"Who's *we* Jolie?"

"Me, Greg, and Rachel. You know that's the only way everyone lives happily ever after. That is what you want, isn't it? To live happily ever after? And as a bonus, you get to keep everything we...*you* have in storage." Her grin bleeds insanity, backed by the knowledge of Carmen's corpse being part of her worthless compromise.

I don't want to say it, don't want to portend my demise, but the words flee my lips before I can even think of stopping them: "Over my dead body will I let you take Rachel." I'm at the bottom of the porch now and she takes one step down—so brave—putting us eye to eye with one step between us. I lock my hands in faux-prayer and plead with her to reconsider what she's doing.

She says angrily, "You never had a clue, pumpkin-eater. You still don't. Now give me the combination so we can all move on."

Wait... "Didn't you ask Nick for the combination?"

She pauses, blows out nervously, eyes everywhere else. "Let's just say he wasn't very cooperative."

The devil: *She murdered Popeye...why stop there?*

She's changing, just like me, just like Lily...only with Greg as her mentor...

And Brutus still hasn't barked. Not a fucking yip. Nick is just as silent.

There's no other option.

Fight fire with fire.

And I do. I leap up the step between us and wrap my hands around her neck. Her eyes go wide and her teeth snarl and I press my thumbs into her throat and slam her against the front door, just like Greg Strand must've done to Carmen against the wall in my apartment. Only Jolie doesn't drop dead on the spot because she left the door ajar and it swings into the house with a forceful slam and we both crash onto the foyer floor, me on top barely glimpsing past her groping fingers into her going-purple face. I hear Rachel's screams bleeding through the chaos, followed by a man's incensed growl, "You stupid fucking bitch!" and another man grunting, *Nick*. I squeeze Jolie's throat for dear life and bang her head against the floor and *it feels really fucking good* and I can't see past her scraping fingers, and then…

CHAPTER 64

...a from-out-of-nowhere blitzkrieg of muscle swoops in and makes throwing all 165 pounds of me seem easy. I'm airborne for longer (it seems) than the two seconds it takes to crash into the wall leading into the kitchen, and thump on the floor in a crumpled heap. A wooden-framed painting of a fisherman falls onto the floor beside me, *crack!*, startling me. Dazed and confused, I'm helpless as the same strong hands grab me by the hood of my sweatshirt and haul me back into the living room.

My head *thuds* on the floor and when I open my eyes I behold *him*, towering in all his live-in-person, larger-than-life glory, Greg Strand. He's a big fucker, a *really big* fucker, six-foot-five, linebacker-wide, tattooed muscles exhausting the limits of his torn black tee. He's staring me down, breathing heftily through a thick black beard, needing only a ring in his septum to complete the ready-to-charge *toro* look he's got down. He fists my hoodie again and tosses me onto the loveseat across from the couch where Nick is sitting with his wrists and ankles duct-tape trussed, sporting a bruise on his cheek the size and color of a prune—evidence of having *not* divulged the combination to the safe, staring at me with dread in his eyes and it's only now that I notice one of Brutus's small rubber bones clenched in his teeth, held in place with the same black duct tape used to fetter his wrists and ankles. I hear Rachel screaming hysterically from the second floor guestroom as Jolie ineffectively coo-coos her between labored coughs: a perfectly nerve-racking soundtrack to the events going down at Beacon Manor.

Greg wastes no time. "What's the combo to the safe?"

I look at Nick and he shakes his head *no* and I look at Greg and he nods his head *yes* and says, "We can make this easy, or we can make it painful. What's the combination?"

"I don't know."

His slap is fast and furious and just as agonizing. Welts in the shape of his fingers swell on my face, I can feel them just as much as I can feel his hot breath on my ear as he leans in and says, "No more fucking games. The sooner we do this, the sooner me and Jolie get the fuck out of your life." I snag a peek out the window, hoping to catch a glimpse of Lily. He snaps his fingers in my face and blurts, "Hey, loser…I'm over here," following suit with his own quick glance out the window. He then looks back at me and I can almost see the word *eureka* light up behind his dilated eyes as he exclaims, "She's here with you, isn't she?"

"Who are you talking about…?" A lightning bolt of pain strikes me in the form of another slap, this one breaking my skin, pain flaming from cheeks to feet, pain on top of pain: the consequence of being hit too many times by two different assholes on the same day. The devil asks: *What the fuck are you waiting for?* and I have no answer other than *I just want to live,* which simply isn't good enough when your child is in danger. So without giving it any second thought, I leap up and start throwing hands, using all my might and all my strength: a flurry of ineffective love-taps instantly obliterated by one of Greg's black combat boots into my balls…

…and let me tell you, I'd forgotten how much it fucking hurts getting your nuts kicked in. It's as if your whole body is being turned inside-out, crotch on out. I roll onto the couch and curl up into a fetal position and cry-heave a few drawn-out seconds, the world around me dark, cloudy, flickering. As my vision filters back, his tattooed hands tighten the drawstrings around my neck and I watch as Nick huffs in a panic behind his dog-toy, eyes wide and soused with tears; I've witnessed his tears many times in my (REPRESSED) past, but those were borne of anger and hatred, not of fear and pain like these. My own pain melts into a blank numbness, and as I start losing consciousness, my beleaguered mind asks, *where is Brutus and why isn't he barking?*

Greg releases me and I plummet back to the couch, gasping for precious air; I can't hear Rachel crying anymore and pray she doesn't bear witness to any of this. Eventually I catch my breath and say, "I'll give you the pass code, but Rachel stays with me."

He grins smarmily, nodding before pronouncing, "Done deal."

Fucking told you so, Jolie.

I look over at Nick. He's gently shaking his head back and forth, *I'm sorry Peter* or *don't do it Peter,* as if it's all going to end right here right now in his living room, a strong possibility that becomes less of one if I open the safe.

He says, "You can keep your little brat. Just tell me where Lola is." *Lola.*

"She's not here."

Another slap across the face, not as hard as the others but just as painful. "Lying isn't one of your strong suits, pumpkin-eater."

"It's the truth, I swear it."

He nods and slides Nick's new smartphone out of his pocket, then swipes and taps and shows me the screen. "There's a tracker on the burner I gave Lola." He must've downloaded the app on Nick's phone because I'm suddenly looking at an aerial map of Long Beach with a single pink *(pink!)* dot with the letters LD in the center. He tramps into the kitchen and slides a large steak knife out of the butcher block on the counter, *sleek!*, then points it at both of us. "If either of you move, I'll slice the other open. Got it?"

Nick and I nod in silent agreement; my reckless leap at Greg didn't work to my advantage anyway, lesson learned. He disappears into the sunroom, muttering "Where the fuck is she?" and I answer in my head, *hopefully in the shed getting the key to the basement.* He returns to the living room, takes hold of the front of my hoodie with his free hand, and holds the knife in his other inches from my gut. When he yanks me up, my sweatshirt tears at the zipper from hood to waistband, and I thud back down to the floor. He rips it away and I flip over like a burger. He tries the same move with my tee-shirt, garnering the same result. Now I'm shirtless and shivering and even more pathetic than I was moments ago. He tosses my torn clothing at me and says, "Damn son, you ought to let your wife dress you. I hear she's got an outfit for every occasion." He laughs like an old-time TV villain then grabs my left bicep and I swear his fingers reach entirely around my arm. Nerve-like pain shoots from my shoulder into my hand as he drags me toward the steps leading upstairs. He shouts at Nick, "Let's go gramps!" but then screams "Fuck!", evidently forgetting about the duct tape around Nick's ankles. He shoves me down onto the bottom steps and shows me the knife. "Stay the fuck put or I'll fuck up your pa even more than he already is, got it?"

Got it.

He thuds to Nick and I waste no time. I race upstairs as fast as my beaten, bruised, *scarred* body will take me. I'm calling his bluff, sorry Nick. I scream, "Rachel!" and bang on the guest room door, but it's locked, and in a flash of memory recall a program I once saw on the Science Channel about the amygdala, the part of the brain that processes fear and drives the body to respond to dangerous situations by shutting down and taking away one's fear to combat life-threatening situations; when your child's life is in danger and your body goes into fight or flight mode, this shutdown allows you do whatever it takes to guarantee their safety, in this case giving me the strength needed to break down the guestroom door with one powerful, bone-rattling kick.

I burst in. Jolie is seated on the bed, knees-up with her back against the headboard, arms wrapped around a tearful Rachel who's looking at me like a fawn-in-the-headlights. She screams, "I want Daddy!"

"Rachel, honey…are you okay?"

I race around to the other side of the bed. Jolie pulls her in and growls, "Keep your fucking hands off of her!" Rachel shrieks…and then I do what I've always dreamed of doing, but never did.

I punch Jolie in the face.

Doing this in front of Rachel was never part of the plan, but Greg is pounding up the steps with Nick in tow, buying me only a few seconds. I take hold of Rachel. "Honey…Daddy's gonna get you out of here, I promise. But you have to stay with Mommy right now." I look at Jolie and mouth *cunt* at her and she glares at me and mouths *fuck you* and Rachel screams as Greg storms in and shoves Nick into the chair in the corner of the room. Something goes *crack*, either part of the chair or part of Nick, and he bites down on the rubber bone, wincing in pain.

As sick as it makes me, I hand Rachel back to Jolie. Rachel protests and Jolie hushes her with a hand over her mouth. I say to Greg, "Do you really need to gag a seventy-five-year-old man?"

He grabs me by the hair (because both my shirts are gone) and tosses Nick's phone to Jolie. "Lola is here somewhere. Keep tracking her. And make sure grandpa doesn't go anywhere." He leads me out of the room and I marionette-walk with my head tilted in his grasp across the hall into Nick's office, home of the safe-filled-with-cash. He shoves me into the spare office chair and holds the knife against my throat. "Move and I gut your daughter," and I say *okay okay okay* and he gives me a filthy look before producing a semi-flattened role of duct tape from his back pocket that he uses to secure my wrists and ankles to the chair.

"Now…what's the combination?"

The door is open and I can hear Nick panic-grunting across the hall as if Greg's knife were being held against *his* throat. Jolie appears in the threshold, then shuts the splintered door to the guest room, closing out Nick's muffled protests and my only line of sight toward Rachel.

I look up at Greg, helpless. He's panting like a caged beast, a fucking ogre, jet-black beard glistening with spit and sweat, heat shimmering from his immense body in near-visible waves.

"What's the combo?" He doesn't give me a chance to answer before striking me in the face. Pain lances out from all my previous injuries like a series of electric currents. Blood spurts from my nose into my mouth and down my chest. "Tell me!"

I take a deep choking breath with my mouth wide open and start stammering my childhood phone number out loud: "Four-two-three…" He takes everything hanging in the closet into his muscular embrace—mostly my father's Wall Street suits he no longer wears—and hurls them onto the floor. I look into the closet, at the open door with the tie-rack on the inside…

…and hanging from it like a monument to everything my life has become is my father's belt, THE BELT, thick rawhide with tarnished brass Mustang buckle. Everything rushes back to me, *closetBELTclosetBELTclosetBELT…*

Greg's fist finds the other side of my face, ripping me free of my poisoned reverie and causing a clot to explode from my nose. He goes back to the safe and calls out the numbers as he punches them in. "Four…two…three…what's the rest?"

"Seven…two…six…nine…"

The safe beeps.

Greg sings his praises, "Fucking finally," and pulls the door open.

The safe is empty.

CHAPTER 65

He's staring into the eight-square-foot void, under-the-breath grumbles rising into strings of screaming expletives, "What the fuck!?" and "You gotta be fucking kidding me!" and so on. Then, as if I were the sole one responsible for hiding the money, he turns around and punches me in the ear. My head gets hot and my vision blurs and I slump forward. A ruckus follows and I can't see what's happening, but he's destroying stuff, my mind's eye envisioning him as that luggage-tossing American Tourister gorilla. The standing lamp crashes down, gunfire-popping lightbulb making me question if I've been shot. The computer monitor explodes into dozens of pieces against the hardwood floor. He flips the desk, punching jagged holes into the sheetrock. He's a caged beast, pacing back and forth, huffing and puffing, obliterating anything he can get his tattooed mitts on. My vision creeps back and I watch as he rummages through the closet, screaming *Where is it!?*, tossing shoes and shoeboxes—*the BELT is still dangling*—and plastic Home Depot bags filled with small home improvement staples, like wood glue and sandpaper and bungee cords, duct tape and nylon rope, and isn't that just fucking convenient?

He grabs the rope, *c'mon Greg I'm not going anywhere, my ankles and wrists are fucking duct-taped to the chair*! But he's in his element and this is exactly how he's made his ends meet over the years, so he "dots his i's" by knotting the fishing rope around my chest, and "crosses his t" with another slap across my face. I start screaming for *HELP!* as loudly as the sliver of energy I have left will allow, pleading for Nick or Jolie or even a passing stranger to come to my rescue. But it's futile; the nearby ocean is loud as fuck even with the windows shut.

Greg screams, *"Shut the fuck up!"* But I don't shut the fuck up. I just keep screaming until he grabs one of Nick's socks from the floor and shoves it in my mouth. Then, for good measure I suppose, he fashions one of Nick's neckties into a gag. Now I'm grunting and thrashing and the chair is *squeaking* and this isn't going to end well for me. He says, "Stay the fuck put," and I mumble, "Where the fuck am I going?" which earns me another smack across the face—understood or not—before he exits the room.

He doesn't shut the door, and also leaves the guest room door open, possibly so I can witness what's going to happen next. I blow a clot from my nose and it pools on the rope around my chest and I twist back and forth to work the blood-sweat-spit mixture into the threads. I blow again, aiming for my wrists. The tape around them feels like it's giving, but not enough for me to make an escape. *Baby steps.*

As I attempt to free myself, I watch and listen as Greg removes the tape and rubber bone from Nick's mouth and begins harassing him again, *Where's the fucking money gramps?* and *More people are gonna start dying* and...and he just said *more people,* so in my head I check off Carmen, and Popeye, and maybe Gail. I don't think he would kill Rachel, but he might Jolie because she's a major cunt, and he definitely would me and Nick, bullet-points one and two on his shortlist. He slaps Nick across the face, once *Where's the money?* twice *Where is it gramps?* and just as slap number three touches down, Nick blurts out, "I had an armored car company pick it up. It's in the bank."

Best-worst advice I ever gave Nick.

"Fuck, pops, you must really want to die. You don't get it, do you? Me and Jolie ain't leaving here until you deliver the half mill. So where is it?"

I hear Nick repeat timidly, "In the bank."

I watch as Greg leans in toward Nick. I can't see what he's doing but he must have a hand on Nick's neck because all I hear are *ack-ack* sounds. "Where's the receipt, then? You don't just deposit a half mill and not get a receipt for it. Show it to me."

There's a gap of silence, and I'm figuring if there is a receipt, Nick will produce it. But he doesn't say anything. He just coughs and chokes in lieu of fessing up.

"Greg?" Jolie's voice, meek, hesitant.

He snaps, "Not now!" Glaring at Nick, he cocks an arm back, fist clenched, and *fuck me*—I'm going to need a miracle to step in and save my father's life.

Jolie appears in the threshold. "Seriously Greg, you're gonna want to see this…" She shows Greg the phone, then looks up at him with her pretty face all messed up by the shiner I just gave it. "She's in the house. Look…" She taps and swipes and from across the hall I can just make out the Argent Security logo on the screen of the phone. She's pulling footage from one of the cameras. "See? Here she is, going into the shed. Then she runs from the shed to the side of the house."

"What's there?"

"The door leading into the basement."

There's my miracle. Lily couldn't have picked a better time to get noticed. It buys me more time to free myself, and Nick more time breathing on the planet. But she does one better. Like an angel's call from the heavens, Brutus starts barking. It's distant, and weak, but it's *there,* and despite my pain and the life-threatening circumstances, I couldn't be more excited. Thank you Lily.

Greg screams, "That bitch!" then hollers at Jolie, "I thought you took care of the dog?" Tsk-tsk-tsk, shame on you Jolie, you didn't give Brutus enough Ambien either it seems, because *just enough to keep him down* probably doesn't apply to yellow labs, and because there still might be a modicum of goodness buried deep in that black heart of yours. It's a hopeful thought that's quashed when Greg screams at her, "Don't just fucking stand there, go find her!" He races back into the office and grabs my hair and pulls my head back and says, "When I get back, you *will* tell me where the cash is."

Jolie shuts the broken door to the guest room, then races down the hall, and I can only hope and pray that Nick has the fortitude to try to get Rachel out of there while she's gone. Greg closes the door behind him, chasing Jolie's footfalls downstairs. I struggle against my bonds while trying not to tip the chair, listening to Brutus's barking growing louder by the second. Lily must've found him in the basement, woke him up, and released him onto the main floor.

I can't see what's happening, but my photographer's-eye records the sounds present and develops the images of the events in my mental darkroom. It's like this: Jolie is squealing and Brutus is snarling and Greg is shouting and it goes on for about thirty terrifying seconds, and then...*oh no,* the knife was in Greg's hand when he left, wasn't it? And now it...it must be in Brutus, as evidenced by the horrific wail discharging from the dog's muzzle. I'm fighting the duct tape and sweating profusely and I'm blowing bloody snot-clots on the rope and tape and I can feel them slackening ever-so-slightly. Everything hurts and burns and part of me just wants to just give in and die...but then I think of Rachel, and my higher purpose takes over, superseding the devil: *if I live, she lives.* Simple as that. Brutus is whimpering and Greg is cursing up a storm...and then he screams something unintelligible before producing a series of awful thudding grunts, a dozen or more in all, until Brutus wails one last time and goes silent.

Fuck.

CHAPTER 66

Time passes. Minutes? Hours? At some point I must've passed out and in the dream I had, I was no longer HIM, I was six-seven-eight years old hiding in the closet no longer REPRESSED dusty shoes mothballs BELT my mother screamed she fled she couldn't stop it she couldn't help me…

I come to and open my eyes to the Mustang belt, hanging from the hook on the inside of the closet door. Taunting me, a reminder of everything that used to be, of what could be. I continue fighting my restraints, the chair *squeak-squeak-squeaking* as I rock back and forth. I call out to Rachel and Nick, but only muffled cries of panic emerge from my bound, acid-dry mouth. Unconsciousness threatens to whisk me back to my dream-memory world…but the will to protect my daughter keeps me present in the even-more-dreadful waking world. That, and the pain.

My ankles are still well-fettered (despite my efforts), but I've managed to stretch the tape around my wrists a bit. The once-white-now-pink rope digging into my nipples is also a bit looser, thanks to the sweat pouring down my body, and the blood gushing from my nose. As I focus on the pain, I beseech the devil and the angel, but they are gone, seemingly dead and buried.

The door bursts open. Even with the gnawed tear in his right calf, Greg lunges at me with aggression, brandishing the now bloodstained steak knife with dexterity. The lower half of his jeans leg, moments ago in Brutus's jaws, now dangles in bloody shreds. His left hand, the one *not* holding the knife, is gloved in gore-matted dog hair. He pulls the necktie and sock from my mouth—*finally!*—and keeps up with his harsh demand.

"Where's the money, asshole?"

"Where's Rachel?" My throat is like used sandpaper, the words barely escaping my inflamed lips. He beats on me a little more and my wrists slip back a little further and I almost pass out again. After threatening to kill everyone, including me, he limps out of the room and again time is lost to me as I fade in and out of consciousness. When he returns, minutes or hours later, he has Rachel in the crook of his huge arm. Using the booted foot of his injured leg, he slams the door, then holds the knife to her neck and puts forth an ultimatum: "Where's the fucking money or this will be the last time you see her."

No-no-no-no-no-no-no! My body begins to spasm, muscles screaming, adrenaline flowing, nerves igniting, I can feel the chain reaction, speeding heart rate, increased blood pressure, labored breathing…*synapses bursting, amygdala shutting down.*

I face my attacker.

I have to act now. If I don't, Rachel will die.

I lie, "I'll show you where the money is."

"Tell me!"

I'm flying by the seat of my pants when I blurt, "I have to show you. It's not in the house." I choke back my gorge in anticipation of another punch that doesn't come.

"Fuck that, pumpkin-eater…" He presses the blade against Rachel's back. Her sobs turn to screams. No, not screams. If there was ever a time to use the word *caterwauls,* it would be now.

I continue my charade, my defense-in-progress, shouting, "Okay! Okay! Okay!" I tell him that Nick's stash is buried in the dunes, beyond the backyard fence, a lie that could very well evolve into suicide-by-psychopath.

"Exactly where?"

It takes all my strength to say, "In the dunes, sixteen feet east, ten feet south, three feet down. I have to show you."

He screams, "FUCK!" then growls, "Don't you fucking move!" Using his free hand, he kneels down on his good leg and cuts my feet free. He then slices the fishing rope, nicking me a few times and not giving a shit. After he slices the tape around my wrists, he hobbles back and presses the knife against Rachel's neck. "Let's go, asshole."

Rachel's *caterwauls* have tapered down into sobs. She squirms in an attempt to get away…and then…

…and then she pees all over him. My almost-four-year-old, who doesn't have the whole potty-training routine down yet, releases her bladder at the most opportune time…and in spite of the blood and in spite of the pain and in spite of a life of crime that includes murder and kidnapping and God-knows-what else, Greg Strand literally freaks out now that he's soaked in warm toddler piss.

Thank you Rachel, it's the distraction I need…

The distraction HE needs.

(…HIM. I am no longer six-seven-eight, I am HIM now, in no pain and exploding with energy. I leap from my chair and grab the Mustang belt from the closet, wrap it around my fist with the buckle dangling, and in the face of my injuries where I've suppressed my pain, my agony, I am hyper-focused and strong, in changed mode, exactly as I was in the storage locker when six-seven-eight became witness to not-my-crime…)

Greg screams "What the fuck!" He drops Rachel. She thuds to the floor like a sack of laundry…

(...the devil isn't present, I've risen above him now, I am still HIM and I see through HIS eyes and see the BELT in my white-knuckled grasp, wrapped three times around my fist, business end dangling, and I look at Greg but he isn't Greg anymore, he is six-seven-eight and he sees the TRUE devil in my eyes and it distracts him, and before he can raise the knife, I bring the belt around in a lightning-fast arc and slam the brass buckle into his head...)

...I emerge from being HIM and shout to Rachel "Get out of here!" but she's frozen, cowering and again *caterwauling* in the corner, a terrified puppy. Greg twists around and reaches for her, favoring his chewed-up leg. Blood pours into his vacant eyes and he trips on the tilted base of the no-longer-standing lamp. He lands on one knee, right onto a jagged shard from the one-time computer screen. He howls in pain...and I go back to being HIM...

(...I can't control myself, I am HIM and I'm furious, I must protect my daughter from six-seven-eight, this threat to her life, my life, and before six-seven-eight can latch onto Rachel I swing the BELT again and it connects with his forehead and I hear something inside his massive head go CRACK! He drops to both knees, stabbing aimlessly at the floor with the knife, unfocused eyes rolling chaotically beneath their bloody death-mask. I scream, "HOW DARE YOU TAKE A PICTURE OF ME! HOW DARE YOU SHOW YOUR MOTHER! YOU HAVE DESTROYED THIS FAMILY! IT'S YOUR FAULT! YOU DID IT! YOU!" I swing the BELT and the oversized buckle connects with his head, CRACK!, and again, CRACK! and I'm gasping and there's blood on the walls and on the floor, oh yes the little shit is getting what he deserves, he took the picture, he destroyed this family, and I swing and CRACK!...and swing and CRACK!...

...until I can swing and crack no more. Winded and on the verge of joining Greg on the floor, I kick the knife away from his jittering hand. Rachel hasn't moved from the corner of the room. She's blood-spotted and trembling, hiding her face from…from me. From *HIM*. From everything her life has become.

I take one more swing, a giant wallop across the ribs, *crack!* "That's for Brutus." *Man, this feels good. Right. I get it now. I understand you, Nick…*

Squelching in a puddle of Greg's blood and leaving in my wake two gummy footprints for forensics to puzzle over, I step over to Rachel. Her cries have reduced to whimpers, little pink hands ineffectively covering her snot-coated face. I grab her by the arm, but she doesn't know it's me, her father—defeater of the boogeyman—and she kicks and screams and pisses herself again. *This day isn't going to help nurture her future development…and by the way Jolie, how the fuck do you not come in here to help your terrified daughter?*

Before exiting the room, I retrieve the knife from the floor and admire up-close-and-personal the sputtering mishmash I made of Greg Strand's face. He's still breathing, but it's raspy and wet and labored through split lips. I want him gone, gone for good, out of my life and out of Lily's life, but most of all out of Jolie's life because, like me, she's looking for love, and I don't want her to have it, not with Greg, not with anyone. A threesome? Yeah, fuck you both.

I squeeze the knife handle. One swipe. That's all it will take. But…I'm fighting the urge. I don't want to become HIM again, not now. I loosen my grip. Rachel has seen enough bloodshed for one day. I take a deep breath, then drag my baby kicking and screaming across the hall into the guest room.

Nick is just about passed out, bloodied and beaten and still fettered at the wrists. I put the belt on the dresser and, using the same weapon that killed his dog, cut him free. Rachel leaps on the bed and hides under the covers because this preschool technique *always* works against the boogeyman; I'm just not entirely sure, however, how many boogeymen there are.

Nick shivers in a panic and I tell him that the *bad guy* is incapacitated in the office. He peers over at the belt, then looks at me and gently smiles. *You did good, son.*

"You okay?"

He nods. "I'm fine." But it's a lie. He's not fine. His eyes are swollen, his face is bruised, and he's bleeding from the scalp.

I put my hand under his chin to get him to focus on me. "Listen…I need to go find Lily. Linda. She's the reason why you and I are alive right now. Jolie just went after her, and that's not a good thing. You hear me?"

He nods.

"Good. The door is broken, but if you wedge the chair under the doorknob after I leave, it should hold." He nods again, wobbly on his feet as I help him stand. He takes a few moments to gain his bearings before saying, "I'm okay." He looks at me. "Where's Brutus?"

I don't offer my highly educated guess, but my silence is telling, and he knows it. His swollen-rheumy eyes ponder me for long seconds until he mutters, "I'm sorry, Pete. For everything."

For the first time in my life I think I see sorrow in his injured eyes. *Too little, too late?* "I have to go now…"

Barely holding a hand up, he says, "Wait…" He appears to lose his focus for a moment, then captures it and speaks, his words emerging as scattered thoughts. "I-I was a…a bad father, a bad person…you'll know…soon, very soon, you'll know…I…I did to you, just as my father did to me…made me into the man I became…I tried to do the same for you…I *had* to…"

I nod, his painful and confusing statement joining forces with everything else that's already painful and confusing in my life. *I know all about it, Nick. My memories of that night are no longer REPRESSED. I can recall every detail now, my bedroom window, the camera and the photo I took of the woman. Even what you did to me for three years after that.* Despite having faced his twisted method to REPRESS for three years, I've seen through his eyes, have *felt* him, *became* him, and am now forever reminded of that fateful night's events from his point of view as clearly as a scene in an unforgettable movie. The inventive photographer's mind never completely forgets the images his eye captures in time. He did what he had to do, to preserve himself and his family…and so did I. *I understand now.*

I look down at the steak knife still in my hand, and immediately struggle with whether I should finish off Greg Strand. I peek across the hall. He's still prone, snoring loudly and sloppily as if gargling with soup. The very moment he comes to, near-death or not, he's gonna come looking for me.

Nick sits on the edge of the bed, voice clearing as his words, more comprehensible now, slip past his bloody lips. "In the shed…under the workbench…there's a floor mat. Beneath that is a padlocked compartment…" He opens the nightstand drawer, pulls out a small keyring with a single silver key on it, and hands it to me. "There's a duffle bag in there. It contains everything from the safe. Take it. I need it gone before the cops come."

The cops? I say, "Please, don't call the cops."

"I'm not planning to…but eventually they'll come…for reasons you'll soon understand." The very reason the cops might show today is an obvious one, so I don't say anything else about it. We lock gazes and he nods as if finally seeing that special something in me: the chip off his block who decided to kill in a moment's panic, him the neighbor, me Chico (and maybe the scumbag in the office). He says, "Take the Range

Rover, it's in the garage. The keys are hanging above the cookie jar in the kitchen."

More than half-a-million and a Range Rover doesn't resolve how fucked-up I am in the head, but I'll take it. And let the truth be told: I will not be paying Jolie's bills with it. I step over to Rachel—now passed out under the covers—and kiss her sweaty blonde hair. In silence, I promise to be back for her, but don't promise when; with two dead bodies in the basement of my building, and another in my apartment, I'm going to have to hightail it of here. Leave New York and flee the chaos I've left in my wake to find a new life, one I can start anew with Lily at my side. Then, maybe one day, I'll come back for her, however old she may be.

I'm sorry.

Nick stands and leans on the head of the chair, ready to wedge himself in. I swipe the belt from the dresser and in its place leave the knife behind; he may need it if Greg wakes up to continue his rampage. I hold the belt up like the trophy it is, and say, "Thanks for everything."

He nods. Smiles. *Understands.* "It's happening to you, just like it did to me." *Change.* He pauses, takes a labored breath, and adds, "You're just like me, son."

I walk out into the hall, and he closes the splintered door behind me.

Bye, Nick.

CHAPTER 67

The first thing I do is check on Greg: he's still breathing, and still spraying human fluids with each snore. Nick's sunny office has morphed into a horrific vista, one that something comparable in a movie might force me to look away from. But here in the *changed* world, it invigorates me. I admire my handiwork and take note: I did a better job fucking up Greg's face than Brutus did his ankle; on any given day the injury to his ankle would demand immediate medical attention, but his *face*...if not for the hummingbird tattoo on his neck, Greg Strand would be unrecognizable to anyone who knew him. His beard, once jet-black, is now a tacky maroon, an irregular coating of gore sourced from the well-defined dents in his hairline (BELT buckle impact points) down to his tree-trunk neck. The once defined angles of his chiseled face are now messy and indistinct.

Removing Greg from my life would be the *now me* thing to do. Would put an end to this ongoing nightmare. I grip the belt and it *yes*...it *feels,* strengthening me with its almost-alive warmth. The well-oiled rawhide digging into my palm empowers me dramatically, even with my injuries, my pain. I beseech HIM—seeing through HIS eyes is the only way I can do this...

But HE does not come.

So, still holding the belt and resigning myself to failure for not being able to end Greg Strand once and for all, I waste no time and race downstairs into the living room. As I turn into the kitchen, I nearly trip over Brutus's corpse. It's an awful sight, one I can't help but grow furious over: a dozen or more knife wounds perforating his torso and head. My photographer's eye imagines the lab's jaws locking onto Greg's ankle, teeth on bone, blood and froth spewing in snaky ribbons; it envisions the knife in Greg's tattooed hand, arcing up and down, up and down, the first blow producing the deep gash in the dog's left eye, each subsequent strike forming the jagged path down the side of its furry belly. Blood spatter in most of its forms paints the white ceramic tiles, the dishwasher, the cabinetry. And with my gift (or curse) of audio recall, I can still hear the ferocious grunts Greg made while committing the brutal act, *Umph!...Umph!...Umph!,* and the dying wails of Brutus, *Whaaaaaaarrrr!* Sometimes the innocent, our protectors, put themselves in harm's way for us, and as a result pay the ultimate price; if it weren't for Brutus, Nick and I might not be breathing right now.

I step around the dog, sneakers leaving prints again, Velcro-tacky on the smooth tiles. I locate the fob to Nick's Range Rover and race out into the sunny August morning, taking in large gulps of sea air as I catch my breath. There's not a cloud in the sky as the perfect eighty-degree day welcomes me, the Atlantic's waves crashing into the shore, inviting me to *take a series of deep breaths, in through your nose, out through your mouth, and relax,* sunbeams glimmering upon the surface of the pool, so fucking pretty. It's a sight for the world's sorest eyes.

From somewhere behind me comes a scream.

Screams.

I recognize Jolie's wretched wail, and even though screams don't distinguish accents like they do gender, the second one must be Lily's. I race around the pool toward the shed. The sound of the ocean muffles the now ongoing barrage of girl-fight *caterwauls* coming from somewhere inside the house. I look into the shed, toward the space under the workbench. About sixty seconds is all it would take to retrieve the duffle bag, get in the Range Rover, and get the fuck out of Dodge.

But Lily, my one and only true love. She saved my life.

Now, I have to save hers.

I spin away from Nick's hidden stash and stumble back inside, fighting against the beating pain in my legs, body, and face. Like a holster, I wrap the Mustang belt around my waist and tighten it, then grab a knife from the butcher block (another ongoing trend, it seems). I step over Brutus and peer upstairs. All is quiet aside from Greg's gurgling snores. I look out the front window and find nothing but calm. No neighbors, no cops.

The door to the basement is open, beckoning me to end this shitshow once and for all. I step to it and peer downstairs. The lights are on but they're dim, barely illuminating the damp, unwelcoming environment. Somewhere below, the women are shouting and grunting and likely taking swings at one another…but the sound of their skirmish is muted, as if they're not actually in the basement, but rather somewhere within the walls of the house. My entire body fucking hurts and I can only see partway through my swollen eyes, so I take each wooden step slowly, sweeping the steak knife out in front of me as if it were a flashlight. The steps creak, announcing my arrival to anyone nearby. Halfway down, the unfinished basement comes into view. Boxes, many of them Sharpie-marked as containing my mother's old things, are stacked everywhere like giant blocks. I can still hear the women grunting and exerting themselves, louder now but still not pinpoint-obvious to their location.

I'd only been down here a couple times in the past—there'd never been any reason to fight the dust other than to help my dad move some furniture—so I'm not entirely familiar with the lay of the land. I reach bottom and try to follow the still-muffled sounds of their screams and shouts. The basement is big, encircling the steps and running the entire expanse of the house. Bare lightbulbs jut from the ceiling like weird growths: dim beacons guiding the way.

I turn a corner and find a plywood door that spring-shuts behind me as I move into the boiler room. A single overhead bulb casts a pallid glow across the water heater and oil burner. The entire room, maybe ten by twenty feet, is devoid of life outside of a few leaping spider-crickets and skittering millipedes. *Where the hell are they?*

Then I hear both of the women scream, at the same time as if another threat existed apart from each other. I look in that direction and notice a dark hole in the cement foundation above the tank, leading into what must be a crawlspace. It appears to extend under the sunroom, beyond the perimeter of the house, more than likely installed as a conduit to the inner workings of the pool. A small steel ladder ascends up and over the oil tank into the crawlspace. After another set of screams from both women that appears to be coming from somewhere beyond the crawlspace, I climb up and shimmy head-first into the dark, unfamiliar area.

I clamber to my feet, and as if to add insult to injury, smash my head on the low cement ceiling. Now I'm hunched over like Quasimodo and pointing the knife forward and I wish I had a fucking flashlight but my phone is in my backpack and my backpack is somewhere in the living room, thank you Greg you super-fucking-asshole.

I hear another scream followed by a thud, and then more screaming followed by *Oh my god* and *Fuckfuckfuckfuck* and

What the fuck is that? I move toward their voices, unable to see anything until I notice a flicker of light coming from a hole similar to the one I just crawled through. Below it is a haphazard pile of bricks and crumbled cement, presumably torn away from the now visible space. I crouch in front of the hole. Their voices echo out loudly, both Lily and Jolie, two sets of breaths and grunts surfacing from what appears to be a tunnel extending beneath the back yard patio. *What is this?*

I call inside: "Hello?"

And from the looming darkness, both women cry out: "Peter! Help!"

CHAPTER 68

The tunnel is pitch-black and damp and slick with mold. The motorized hum of the pool pump resonates from somewhere nearby, gently vibrating my hands and knees as I crawl toward the wavering cell phone light. The same stench that blew me away inside my locker does so again here, hitting me like a Greg Strand slap across the face. My hands slip forward through the cold mucky surface and my head scrapes the ceiling of the tight shaft when I lean up. Things skitter and squirm all around me (and on me). I call out, "Lily!" and wriggle toward the light, moving about six feet before my left hand finds the edge. I lose my grip and my torso thumps down and my chin slams against the hard surface, bringing a jolt of pain to my already-jolted head. I lay dazed for a moment with my left arm dangling freely over the edge and my fingertips grazing wetness.

The light hits my face: a tiny blinding orb piercing my eyes like a doctor's otoscope. A slimy hand grabs my wrist and nearly pulls me into what can only be described in the darkness (and from the stench) as a sewer. My body starts sliding forward…but I'm able to scoot backward from the edge and with luck find an iron grip above me to help keep me in place. The light sways back and forth, a beacon in rough seas, sending brief glimpses of the subterranean space into my field of view. For a moment I wonder what in God's name this space could be here for, then recall the zoning issues Nick encountered when the pool was first being installed, how the original location they dug (and paved) was inspected by the town and deemed too close to the electrical source running the pump and heater. It was a fiasco that resulted in a lawsuit and the hiring of a new pool company. This is the space originally dug to house the pool's plumbing, never entirely filled in, sitting alongside the existing pool and only partially filled with mud, roots, and ground water.

Multiple hands reach for me, the female voices behind them finally clear: "Help me Peter! There's something in here with us!" and "I can't get out! Something's got me!" As the two women continue their clawing and pleading, a third body bobs up from the muck between them, this one no more alive than Carmen or Chico. The corpse is bloated beyond recognition, a swamp-thing saturated with mud and slime, and the source of the putrid stink down here. The light from the cell phone—in Jolie's hand—captures the waterlogged cadaver's face, the features distended and barely human. But the long black hair, tangled into a rat's nest, and the muddy apron that says *Oh Crepe!* immediately tells me who I'm looking at.

It's Gail, my father's former housekeeper.

She never made it to California. I immediately (and again) surmise: *Greg killed Gail and then Jolie introduced Lily to Nick and then Lily got Gail's job and then Greg got his foot in the door to the kingdom.*

But then...who dumped Gail here? Given my Occam's razor supposition, whatever happened in the time between Gail's murder and her body being dumped down here doesn't play into my theory. Greg hadn't stepped foot in the house until today. If he were in fact Gail's murderer, then he would've had to have killed her someplace else before bringing her back here, and that doesn't make sense unless...unless they were planning to frame me again? And just how would he have known about the crawlspace? Did Jolie help him? Or…Lily? There's gotta be something else, something I'm completely missing.

The devil shows up out of nowhere: *You're not seeing it because you haven't watched all of Nick's security footage. That's right, almost everything that's happened inside this house will soon be seen by the police.*

The women scream and shove Gail's bobbing corpse back and forth, as if watersporting. I shout, "Stop it!" and like obedient children, they do just that. I reach out to Lily and say, "Grab my hand."

"Why does she get to go first?"

"Really? Jolie? Do I need to answer that?" I wedge my feet against the concrete walls and pull Lily out of the future sinkhole, into the short tunnel. She turns on her side and snakes past me all the way back into the crawlspace, where I tell her to wait.

I look back at Jolie.

She reaches for me. But I don't react, not right away, and for a passing moment stare into her mud-coated face and enjoy my sudden power over her, doing nothing to mask my hatred of her. It's hard to imagine that, at one time this was face I wanted to look at while cumming.

(…REPRESS…)

"Peter…what are you doing?"

"Trying to convince myself not to leave you behind."

She reaches hard for me. "No, Peter…please don't…I'll die down here."

"Why shouldn't I? I've got every reason to leave you to rot down here, starting and not ending with how you put fucking sleeping pills in my food."

"Peter, please! Rachel needs me! She needs her mother!"

"Her mother? Are you kidding me? No, Jolie, she needs to be with someone who won't allow her to be used her as a hostage-at-fucking-knifepoint. And your boyfriend? Just watch how fucking fast he drops you when he finds out the money really is gone."

I inch backward and Jolie's voice rises an octave as her anxiety surges. "Pl-Please Peter…just get me out of here. I promise I'll get help. For me, for Rachel—"

"You murdered a bouncer in our home Jolie. Do you really think they're going to let you be Rachel's mother after that?"

She shakes her head violently, like a dog de-wetting itself. "That was an accident. The shelf fell on him and Greg lifted it so I could reach in and cut him free, but the floor was wet and I slipped and fell on him and the knife was in my hand…" She glares at me through her mask of mud, those once beautiful brown doe-eyes haggard and desperate in their plea for freedom. "Peter, I'm still the mother of your daughter. Please, don't leave me here."

I lean forward, impulsively because I'm not sure if keeping her alive does me any good, then grab both of her wrists and pull her up and out of the underground dungeon (and in the process, knock her phone into the waist-deep sludge). That earns me a familiar response, "What the fuck Peter!" and I bite my tongue as I—still holding her outstretched arms—begin inching backward. As soon as my feet reach the crawlspace opening, I let go. Lily grabs my ankles and pulls me in. I kneel (because I don't want to bang my head again) and remove the Mustang belt from around my waist.

I wrap it around my fist, business end dangling.

As soon as Jolie's head appears in the opening, I arch back and swing. The buckle whips her once-pretty face with a dull *thunk*, promising a nasty scar on her left cheek for the rest of her

God-forsaken life. Lily pulls Jolie's now twitching body out of the tunnel and lets her down onto the cement foundation.

"Grab her feet." I wrap my arms around Jolie's shoulders and together, stooped like a pair of dungeon-dwellers, we drag my lovely fucking wife out of the crawlspace. I climb back down the oil-tank ladder and help Lily as she exits the same way, crawling over Jolie's unconscious body. With Jolie draped over the top of the tank like a post-collision crash-test dummy—feet still lost inside the dark crawlspace—I use the Mustang belt to secure her neck to the top rung of the ladder. It won't keep her put, but will definitely slow her down when she comes to, long enough I hope to grant our escape.

We exit the basement holding hands, light on our feet as we take the stairs gently, one at a time. Once in the living room, I peer upstairs to the second floor and promptly find myself in a dilemma. Should I get Rachel? With Greg still snoring, there's a chance I can move her (and Nick) out of here safely. But then what? They don't fit into my plans to flee New York with Lily and the money, plus taking Rachel would only add kidnapping to my growing list of crimes. I've got no choice. I have to leave her behind with Nick, trusting he'll do right by her as long as he stays alive.

"Peter?" I look at Lily, slathered in mud and slime, jaded baby-blues in need of asylum. "We have to get out of here."

I'm struck with a wave of lightheadedness: not enough sleep and too much pain catching up to me, skewing my thoughts, my intentions. On a whim, I say, "Rachel…she's sleeping. We could…"

She head-shakes her point across, not needing to say, "Peter, if we take her, they'll never stop looking for us. She's with your father, and I've spent enough time with him to know that over his dead body will he let anything happen to her."

"Over his dead body is the problem."

From upstairs, a groan and a cough.

"Shit. That's Greg."

"He's hurt. Brutus got him good in the leg and…" I feign holding up the belt, wishing it was still in my hand and not around Jolie's neck. "…I got him good in the face. He's not as fast—or as handsome—as he once was."

"Yeah, well I've seen him kick down doors after being shot, so we really need to scram. *Like now.*"

"Okay." I take her hand. "But first, the money."

"Isn't it in the safe? Where Greg is?"

"Nick is smarter than that. C'mon." I guide her into the kitchen and only as I trip over Brutus's body do I remember he's still there. Lily stifles a scream as I fall to the floor in an agonizing heap, the noise of it stirring both Greg and Jolie from their slumbers. Both of them start yelling for each other from their prospective precarious situations, like wolves bemoaning the night. Before I climb to my feet, Lily places a hand on my back.

On my scars.

I know—I should have mentioned them earlier. But they shame me. I've got hundreds of them, maybe more, puckering my entire back into a knotted carpet of flesh: three fucking years the recipient of my father's sick justice. You can even see the F and O of the Ford logo in a couple places. I stand up with Lily gently rubbing her hands on them. With tears in her eyes, she asks, "What happened?"

"I was training for this day." Soon my dark past will be spoken about out loud for the very first time, but for now, we have to keep moving. We exit the kitchen into the backyard and hobble across the patio into the shed. Still trying to catch my breath, I say, "Keep a lookout, and stay hidden." I crouch under the workbench, remove the rubber floor mat, and use my hands to dig away the loose soil.

Missed Connection

An inch down, I unearth the lock.
I reach into my pocket for the key…

CHAPTER 69

…and it's not there. I check all my pockets. I've got the key to the Range Rover but *fuck!* The key to the compartment Nick gave me is gone. I check again, only because I'm apt to miss something in my beat-up, broken-down state, and discover that the pocket I put the key in has a small hole in it, and isn't *that* just fucking grand?

The concern on Lily's face is clear. "What is it?"

"Nick…he gave me the key, but I lost it."

In a cool panic, she kneels down alongside me. We brush away more dirt from the well-carpentered lid, clearing a path to the padlock, held in place with shiny steel brackets and soil-clogged screws. She stands up, shifts a few objects around on the workbench, then kneels back down with a crowbar in her hand and warns me to *watch out*. I observe with interest as she wedges the tapered end of the tool through the lock before planting her ass on the rest of it. The brackets holding the lock in place *crack!* She repeats the action a half-dozen times, up and down like a child on a hippity-hop ball until the screws rip free and the lock tumbles away.

"Nice move, LD."

She tosses the filer aside. "Me and tools, we have a thing."

We tear away the wooden lid…and there it is, my future in a glossy leather Hilfiger travel bag, possibly purchased for this reason alone. I remove it. There's a good amount of weight to it, what I'd imagine 550k in cash might feel like. When I peek inside, Ben Franklin's deadpan expression peeks back out at me. "We're good."

But…why did Nick relocate the cash from an impenetrable safe in the house, to here, inside an unlocked shed, in a makeshift compartment a girl with a tool fetish could get into? Perhaps after seeing Jolie plotting on the security footage, my handy-around-the-house father decided to throw this little hidey-hole together in the event that what-ended-up-happening actually happened. He *knew*. He told me, *I need it gone before the cops come*. That he wants me to have the money. That he *needs* me to *take* the money. *Away from here*. I'm guessing a bag full of cash on someone's person is a cop-magnet inside a house where people have been beaten and dogs have been murdered. Nick was right. Getting it out of the house was/is the correct move to make. But then: why take it out of the bank in the first place? Not wanting to pay medical bills that don't exist doesn't really fit into any equation. Just like Gail's murder, there's got to be another explanation.

I loop the duffle bag over my bare shoulder and it really fucking hurts. Everything fucking hurts. I'm in so much physical pain that it's starting to feel normal, like my emotional pain. I press unlock on the Range Rover fob, and like a tempting siren the truck *beeps!* from inside the garage. A hundred feet away and we beeline for it, holding hands, the strap of the duffle bag in my one free hand, a crowbar from the shed gripped in Lily's other.

Good thing she grabbed it too.

Because like a sudden burst of flames, Mount Jolie erupts from the kitchen and charges at us. Once a woman who refused to do housework because she might break a nail, here she is gunk-swathed and hair-matted, the BELT—*my* BELT—looped around her fist. She stops and whips the buckle against the patio, once, twice, three times in succession *"Yah!"* then grins like the fucking lunatic she is and raises it with a glimmer of crazy in her eyes that would send the most criminal of men packing.

Crowbar cocked and readied, Lily darts in front of me, a human stealth missile, her silence unnerving as she locks onto her target. Jolie whips the belt around and the crowbar swings out and they meet with a tuneful, reverberating *clank!* Both women are thrown off-balance. Lily falls to the patio with a thud. Jolie teeters near the edge of the pool, both arms and one leg seeking purchase.

I rush to her and grab the swinging buckle before she falls into the pool. *The BELT*. Back my hand, as if a higher power insisted it *be* right where it is, where it belongs. *Now* I can feel HIM, trying to return. Trying to take over. I demand, "Let go of it," and HE thinks, *It's mine*, and I'm immobile and so is Jolie. We stare into the other's eyes, recognizing the opposing madness within, so fucking different, two wholly incompatible illnesses destined for relationship failure and marital tragedy.

Our pause, lasting only a few seconds, is just enough time for Lily to roll in and strike Jolie's shin with the crowbar. My soon-to-be ex-wife screams and buckles to her knees. I *whip* the belt out of her loose grasp and she howls as the rawhide slices into her palm, eyes beseeching me through layers of mud and slime, a despondent someone who should be locked away in a padded room.

I say with a smile, "Fuck you, Jolie," and a shove from my right foot against her shoulder sends her splashing into the pool.

We waste no time. I help Lily to her feet and we race to the garage. The side door is locked so we continue to the front and...and that's when I realize I don't have the code to open it. I bang the keypad and shout "Fuck!" more than once, much too loudly now that Nick's neighbors might be up and about on this sunny weekday morning. Lily peeks around the side of the garage for Jolie.

Then, just as I recall the combination to Nick's safe, I punch in the last four digits to my childhood phone number, 7-2-6-9 and press enter…and if there was ever any doubt in my mind that a God exists, it is extinguished as the garage door begins churning open. "Yes!"

I toss the duffle bag and belt onto the back seat, then slide into the front with Lily. The SUV starts right up and I waste no time backing out, wheels skidding as I…

…nearly run over Greg Strand.

Nearly, but not nearly enough.

The injured goliath, who must've charged out the front door while we were in the garage, leaps onto the hood. His left hand latches onto windshield wiper and his other starts slamming the glass. Fast and hard. I can feel the vibration of each strike through the steering wheel, and that scares the fuck out of me. He's a beast, straight out of a horror flick, a six-foot-five tsunami of muscle covered in blood, snot, and bone-chips, right leg gored, calf to ankle, smearing blood on the hood, fist smearing blood on the glass with every take-no-prisoners strike. He rips the wiper away on the first try and I slam on the accelerator and reverse into the street without looking…then hit the brakes. He flops and spins on the hood like a captured crocodile, still holding onto the edge, screaming—no, *roaring*—as he yanks himself forward. With remarkable speed (in spite of his gnawed leg), he leaps to his feet and, using both elbows, smashes the weight of his entire upper body onto the windshield. It cracks, but thankfully does not shatter. I want to drive away, but can't see ahead; there's too much blood—and too much Greg—blocking my view.

So I move on to my only possible line of defense: I turn on the washers.

The blue fluid sprays into his face and makes him roar like a bear. That shit must really burn! As he claws at his injuries, a soaking wet Jolie appears from around the side of the garage—a limping, useless spectator—waving both arms, shouting *Greg! Greg!* over and over like some kind of pathetic cheerleader. By now the neighbors must be peeking out their windows, meaning calls to the police are next.

With his hands still trying to wipe the burn from his wounds (instead of holding onto the hood's edge), I slam on the accelerator. Greg's heavy-duty body somersaults over the top of the Range Rover, *thud-thud!* and slams into the street behind, *kerplunk!* I watch in my rearview as he tumbles to a dead stop in front of the white picket fence at 426 Beacon Lane.

I scream and pound the steering wheel, victorious, *I win you fucker!,* the irony of having defeated my nemesis with toddler piss and washer fluid making me giddy. Jolie's reflection in the rearview mirror shows her limping to Greg's aid, her super-grimy appearance mimicking some pathetic Halloween costume. I keep laughing and pounding as I ignore the stop sign at the end of the block and skid into the cross street. Lily flips a bird out the window, shouting in a thicker-than-usual redneck drawl, "Woo-hoo! Good riddance assholes!", and we pull away as an elderly woman walking her dog (and holding a fresh turd in a plastic grocery bag) gives us a wary look.

I waste no time. I speed out of town, through Far Rockaway and Brooklyn and onto the Verrazano Bridge, where Lily chucks her Greg-tracked burner into The Narrows below. I tell her about how I nearly beat the life out of Greg with Nick's belt, *I should've finished him off,* and she tells me how *that crazy bitch* came at her with a knife, which she dropped and couldn't find in the muddy water after being chased into the sump.

Soon Lily falls asleep, and I drive in silence, second-guessing my decision to leave Rachel behind. I keep reminding myself that by choosing not to *kidnap* her, they won't come looking for me right away, and that should give us the time we need to get lost somewhere in the country. Once the dust settles in New York, and we get settled someplace else, only then will I look into Rachel's whereabouts.

The devil wakes up: *better hope her whereabouts aren't anywhere near step-daddy Greg.*

At some point near the Pennsylvania border, Lily wakes up. She nestles her head on my shoulder, and utters the words I so desperately want—*need*—to hear.

"I love you, Peter."

"I love you, too."

It will take a lot more than Greg Strand's muscles to wipe the smile off my face.

CHAPTER 78

I drive, and Lily sleeps.

We travel non-stop, late into the afternoon, through New Jersey and deep into the bowels of Pennsylvania. In some God-forsaken nowhere part of the state, we stop at a Wal-Mart and I send Lily inside (dirty clothes and all) with $500 from Nick's stash to purchase food, clothing, burners, and whatever other must-haves she thinks we need. She looks like a red flag with her soiled appearance and hundred-dollar bills, but then I remember: this is Walmart. Red flags inbreed here.

The entire time behind the wheel I've been shirtless and filthy, so it feels good to finally baby-wipe my parts (a déjà-vu moment) and slip into some fresh clothing. Lily uses the screwdriver she bought to remove the license plate from a Dodge Ram, after which she informs me that *we will change the plates again before tomorrow, and at some point we're gonna have to ditch the fancy wheels.* I chase four Advil with a Red Bull and continue driving west, eating protein bars until we stop at a sketchy-looking motel somewhere near the Ohio border.

We shower together in a 1980s back-of-the-catalog bathroom, soaping each other's bodies and gently cleansing each other's wounds, both new and old. I allow her to examine the scars of my past, keeping the story behind the scenes for now, at least until she brings it up again during our drive to somewhere else.

Despite the head-to-toe pain dragging me down, we fuck standing up in the shower, facing each other like we did in the Artful Dodger bathroom: absorbing each other's energy, drive, *love*. Afterwards, she dresses my wounds with antibiotic ointment and gauze before settling into bed alongside me.

I sleep dreamlessly.

I am changed. I am HIM…

Morning arrives and we awake and stretch and fuck again and after thirty minutes of post-orgasmic blissing between the sheets, I go into the bathroom and attend to my wounds. The swelling in my face has gone down, but the scabs and bruises left behind are still a jarring sight, a you-should-see-the-other-guy look still in need of a week's worth of healing. Afterwards, I tell Lily that I'm going to get us some breakfast and for a brief moment second-guess my decision to leave her alone with the money.

But then I remember.

I love you, Peter.

I grab the key to the Range Rover (now sporting Pennsylvania plates), and drive to the closest restaurant—a pretend IHOP called THOP—and order enough takeout to feed four people.

When I return to the motel, I notice a public computer in the tiny lobby and give the attendant, a woman whose smoking habit has her looking less than a few days away from the grave, twenty bucks for a thirty-minute session. I sit in the torn vinyl chair (also left over from the '80s) and check the *Long Island Newsday* website, where I discover no major crimes being reported out of Long Beach—nothing about the events that took place at 426 Beacon Lane. The Long Beach Patch has a police-blotter report about a woman whose flowers were trampled by "those pesky neighborhood kids," and one about a 2001 Nissan Altima stolen from the same block on the same morning, both offenses occurring in Nick's neighborhood. It's easy to think that Jolie and Greg just got the hell out of there before any—if any—police activity woke up the neighborhood. Can't say I blame them, with Brutus's body in the kitchen, and Gail's body floating ten feet beneath the patio.

The question is: Did they take Rachel with them?

Time will tell.

Jolie's Instagram and Facebook have never been more silent, so I start checking some NYC websites and it doesn't take long before I locate an article of interest that was published this morning on page five of the New York Post:

> *Suspect Questioned in Double Murder*
> *A New York City resident was brought in for questioning today in connection with a double homicide that took place in an Upper East Side apartment building. Theodore K. Sonander, 41, was taken into custody after the discovery of two bodies in a storage unit rented by Sonander in the building's basement. A tenant doing laundry discovered blood seeping from the unit and called the building's landlord to report it. When the unit was opened, two deceased individuals were found, both of whom, according to detectives, had been brutally murdered. The identities of the victims have yet to be released as police continue with the ongoing investigation. In an interview with a Post reporter, one of the building's tenants, 89 year-old Garvin Mooney, stated, "The guy gives me the creeps. He looks just like Ted Bundy." The police are asking anyone who has any*

information to please contact them at the 19th precinct.

Below the article is a mugshot of my building mate, "Ted Bundy," who not only looks like the infamous serial killer, but also shares the same first name—he *really* must've gotten hazed in school. And by luck of the draw, it was his storage unit that Chico—poor dead Chico—was changing the lock on at the most inopportune time, super-duper lucky for me.

Most interesting, however, is that there's no mention of a third murder: the one that Jolie committed in my apartment. While on my way out of the 19th Precinct yesterday (was that only yesterday, or the day before?), Murphy and Molloy claimed to have obtained a search warrant for it, so by now they must be scratching their heads over how Popeye's murder could be connected to that of Chico's and Carmen's. Good thing I got a head start getting out of town. No doubt Ted Bundy has already tapped his finger on my photo. *This is the guy I saw in the basement. You need to check his locker.*

Then there's Nick and Rachel. When the time is right, a phone call to Nick from one of the disposable burners Jolie purchased should provide me with enough comfort knowing that Rachel is okay. *If* I can get in touch with him. Time needs to pass and dust needs to settle and more innocents need to take the fall for me before I can risk reaching out to my daughter, wherever she may be.

I close the browser and am about to head back to the room when I decide, *just for shits and giggles*, to check my Missed Connection account, which is also accessible via the web.

I pull up the Missed Connection website, and log in.

There's one new response:

Hi—a friend from New York forwarded me the ad you posted of the girl you're looking for.

> I too have been looking for her, for over ten years. Since this photo looks recent, I'm hoping you may know where she is. Her name is Lola Dawson, and she is my daughter. I am her mother, Sara Dawson. Her father Ed is here as well, beside me as I write this. Ten years ago, she left with a man named Greg Strand, and we haven't seen or heard from her since. We are terribly heartbroken! If you know where she is, please call us. 702.791.7111.

I read the message three times, then ask the smoking woman (now sequestered in the *office*) if she has a pen and paper. I jot down the number on a Post-it (Jolie's favorite means of communication), a Las Vegas exchange, as well as the names of Lily's parents, and hide it in my pocket.

I thought your parents were dead?

I'll broach the subject when we get there. Las Vegas. It's in the same direction that we're traveling, and the perfect hide-in-plain-sight kind of place we need to be.

When I return to the room, I stand outside the door, a sudden surge of nausea tearing apart my soul. What if Lily and the money are gone?

I open the door.

Okay. She's still here.

But…something's wrong.

It's like this: I walk in and she's sitting crossed-legged on the bed and the duffle bag is zipped open and I'm thinking okay, there must not be as much money in it as we thought. But that isn't the case. The bag is exploding with bricks of 100's. I put the food down on the desk and take a step toward her.

She looks up at me with tears in her eyes. She's trembling, looking nervous and scared.

"Lily…what's wrong?"

She shakes her head, then swallows what looks like a golf ball in her throat. "I…I just wanted to see what *that much money* looked like, you know? I was holding it and smelling it and I was feeling so happy, and then…"

"And then what?"

"And then I stuck my hand into the bottom of the bag and…and I felt something under the money, and…I found this black velvet bag…" She holds it up. It's empty.

Was it in a side zipper? "My mom's jewelry is supposed to be in here."

She slowly shakes her head. "There wasn't any jewelry in it. But there was something else. An old camera."

A camera…?

I didn't see it right away because it was on the bed behind the duffle bag. She brings it out and my heart pounds and my breath escapes me and…*it can't be, can it?*

It can. I haven't seen it since the day HE took it away from me, but I recognize it right away, my Polaroid, *the* Polaroid, the one I used the day my universe changed, the day HE *changed*. She hands it to me and my entire body shudders as a cold draft passes through me…but the camera remains warm in my hands, as though alive with the harsh memories it captured all those years ago. I look at Lily. Tears keep building in her eyes and it doesn't compute because I never told her about this REPRESSED part of my life: the Polaroid camera and HIM and HER, all the events that formed my scars, that planted the seeds to my *change*.

So then, why would an old camera bring so much disquiet —and what looks like fear—into her face?

I say in truth, "It used to be mine, but honestly, I have no idea why he would hold onto it for so long." *Or why he would keep it in the safe. Or why he's now giving it back to me.*

She shuts her eyes and blows out a long, deep breath, strapped in, ready to ride. I sit on the bed facing her.

"What is it, Lily?"

She opens her eyes and looks into me, and says, "Peter…"

"What?"

"I'm sorry. I really am."

I'm sorry.

She reaches behind the duffle bag and produces an envelope. "This was also in the bag, with the camera." She hands it to me.

I need it gone before the cops come…

I view the contents of the envelope…and my heart reaches into my throat and chokes me. It's a stack of Polaroid photos. The top one is the photo I took of Nick and the neighbor on that fateful night. A tidal wave of brutal memories flood back, once REPRESSED, now invading my head like an unstoppable virus. My cage has been opened, my monsters have been released.

You're just like me…

Written in black Sharpie on the white band below the image is the # sign followed by the number 1.

#1.

I look at the second photo, an image of a young brunette lying in bed. I want to believe that what I'm looking at is a photo of an unknown woman sleeping, but the zip-ties around her wrists…

…the supplies in Nick's closet, the nylon rope and the duct tape and the plastic bags…

…and the belt—the *BELT*—wrapped tightly around her neck, tells me otherwise. In the white space, written in black Sharpie, is the # sign followed by the number 2.

#2.

I look at Lily, and she says, "Keep going…"

Photo #3 shows a middle-aged blonde woman in the same helpless position as #2, only this time the BELT was used to fetter her wrists, her throat slashed deep enough to expose a glint of spine. The woman in photo #4 has a plastic bag over her head, and #8 is partially disemboweled. Victim #10 is missing all the fingers on one hand, and an arm at the elbow. The only common denominator between them all is the BELT, his weapon of choice, wrapped tightly around their necks or wrists, and in one case, over the victim's eyes.

I tremble with the knowledge of what my father is.

Trembling not out of fear, but of *exhilaration*.

Nick's final words filter back to me like a dream-memory.

I'm a bad person...

You will know...soon, very soon...

And then, as we parted ways:

You're just like me, Peter...it's happening to you now...

Change.

There's one photo without a number, where #13 should be, a single inscription noted in the white space below, *RIP*.

My mother.

It's here real tears begin pouring from my eyes, making me grateful for the blurred vision they bring. Looking at the woman who raised me, who I thought died of cancer but was in fact murdered by my father in her hospice bed, the BELT dangling "business end" from her neck, just tears me up inside.

Lily offers a comforting hand on my knee.

I wipe my tears and flip through the last few photos, seeing more of the same until I get to #18, the very last photo. The woman in the final photo is lying face-up on the crawlspace floor, the entrance to the cement tomb under the patio visible above her head: a ravenous monster waiting to digest her. Her long black hair is splayed out behind her, the *Oh Crepe!* apron she's wearing still crisp and new.

Gail, my father's housekeeper.

Lily says, "Now you know why I'm so freaked out."

"Nick. He's a fucking a serial killer."

"And I could have been his next victim."

I hear her, but don't compute, Nick's words resounding in my head instead: *You're just like me, Pete…*

My conscience questions why he would reveal this to me, but my *changed* mind already knows.

He wants me to continue his life's work.

I did to you…just like my father did to me…

Fucking Nick. He groomed me.

(…six…seven…eight…)

I put the photos back in the envelope, then put the envelope in the duffel bag.

A moment of uncomfortable silence emerges between Lily and me. I watch her wipe her tears and a tempest of hot-flashes and maddening urges strikes my brain, body, and soul. Just as they did in the storage unit with Chico. Just as they did with Popeye in my apartment, and Greg Strand in Nick's office. A temporary blindness sets in, replacing my real-world vision with remembrances of the past…

…it's all your fault. You did this to me. This never would have happened if you didn't come into my life…

I look at Lily, fighting the urge. *Trying* to fight the urge.

The BELT is draped across the chair, begging me to take hold of it. To *command* it.

I stand from the bed, step to the chair, and pick it up.

My entire body quivers with pleasure.

I'm not only hard, but I'm approaching orgasm. *This is how HE felt.*

The Mustang buckle dangles.

It feels so right, so very fucking right.

I turn and face Lily.

She wipes her eyes with the bedsheet, then picks up the camera. "There's still film in the camera. I think you should let me take a photo of *you*."

I say nothing. Just stare. At her. At the camera. *My camera,* now in *her* hands. I squeeze the belt and allow the urge and *desire* to continue Nick's life work flourish.

She peers through the viewfinder. "Smile."

I do, not because she asked me to, but due to the pleasure I'm feeling with Nick's BELT in my hands. I'm a *changed* man now, a man who all his life wanted nothing more than to love someone, and to be loved by someone, but got something completely different instead.

Something *better.*

I take a deep breath…and raise the belt over my head…

Point.

Click.

ABOUT THE AUTHOR

Michael Laimo is the author of eight novels and over 100 short stories. Twice nominated for the Bram Stoker Award, his novels *Deep in the Darkness* and *Dead Souls* have been made into feature films. He currently resides on Long Island with three women, two cats, and a parrot fish.

CROSSROAD
PRESS

Made in United States
North Haven, CT
23 May 2024

52826757R10212